Amazing Praise for Christopher Kelly and
A PUSH AND A SHOVE

"*A Push and a Shove* is an intriguing portrait of a bully and his victim, of the way hatred, when it's pushed (shoved?) far enough can start to look an awful lot like love—and vice versa. Christopher Kelly doesn't flinch: he shows us the emotional myopia inherent in all obsessions, and the damage such myopia can inflict, not just on the bully and the bullied, but on the lover and the loved one, too. He's written a complexly layered story, expertly moving between past and present to reveal how his characters—like all of us—inherit both the wounds and the crimes of their younger selves."

—Scott Smith, *New York Times* best-selling author of *The Ruins*

"Ben Reilly, the protagonist of *A Push and a Shove,* is both psycho and endearing, the perfect narrator for this compelling story of revenge and closure. Christopher Kelly's novel is a meaningful page-turner that I couldn't put down."

—Mark Jude Poirier, author of *Naked Pueblo*

"Christopher Kelly's debut novel is a tour de force examination of character and lack thereof. With a power and intensity that's reminscent of *The Talented Mr. Ripley,* Kelly explores the tortured relationship between a bullied boy and his bully—and the spellbinding consequences when this formerly defenseless victim determines to even the score."

—Sarah Bird, author of *The Yokota Officers Club*

a push

and

a shove

Christopher Kelly

© 2007 by Christopher Kelly

Manufactured in the United States of America

This trade paperback original is published by Alyson Books
245 West 17th Street, New York, NY 10011

Distribution in the United Kingdom by Turnaround Publisher Services Ltd.
Unit 3, Olympia Trading Estate, Coburg Road, Wood Green
London N22 6TZ England

First Edition: September 2007

08 09 10 11 a 10 9 8 7 6 5 4 3 2

ISBN: 1-59350-048-3
ISBN-13: 978-1-59350-048-1

Library of Congress Cataloging-in-Publication data are on file.

Cover design by Victor Mingovits
Interior design by Jane Raese

To my parents, Maxine and Edward

A Routine Procedure
(1982)

Early on the morning of Thursday, April 22, 1982, my older sister Mary stood next to the refrigerator in the cramped kitchen of our house in Staten Island, New York, waiting to be taken to her death. My father sat at the kitchen table, sipping black coffee from a Walt Disney World mug, absentmindedly turning the pages of the *New York Post*. I sat on the chair to his right, eating a bowl of dry Frosted Flakes, groggy and out of sorts from having been dragged out of bed an hour earlier than usual. My mother, who had insisted we wake up to bid my sister farewell, was still in her bedroom getting dressed. My brother Danny—never one to sit and wait patiently—was out walking our dog, a twelve-year-old Labrador retriever named Sam.

Mary, who had turned eighteen two months earlier, wore a linen and cotton, spaghetti-strap sun dress, bright yellow with inky black squiggles running across the fabric. It had been purchased for her by my mother to wear on this very day—the day she would go into the hospital. I had been with them when they bought the dress, seven days earlier, at the Macy's in the Staten Island Mall. My sister, with her oldest-child awareness of how far our family's dollar could be stretched before it snapped, resisted my mother. She said that it cost too much; that for $115 she could buy three or four dresses. But my mother insisted that my sister try the dress on, and then she trilled in delight when my sister emerged from the fitting room, her long mane of jet-black hair flowing over her bare, olive-hued shoulders, the bright yellow fabric neatly complementing her soft brown eyes.

"Just this once," my mother told Mary. "So you'll look beautiful. I want you to look beautiful when you go into the hospital."

I was barely paying attention to them. I was bored. I wanted them to finish and take me to the book store. I walked around the circular clothing racks, letting the dresses brush up against my face. I ran my fingertips over the plastic hangers, enjoying the click-click-click-ing noise that they made. I was too preoccupied to even think of making the most obvious connection: Why this urgency to make my sister look beautiful before she went into the hospital, unless whatever happened at the hospital was going to spirit her beauty away?

And now, sitting in our kitchen, with its table that wobbled and its stove burners that needed to be lit with a match and its ceramic tile floor that had begun chipping and cracking in a half dozen different places, I didn't think to make the other, just-as-obvious connections: Why had my mother insisted upon this unusual ritual, this group farewell to my sister? Why did my father—a man prone to begin shouting at my mother that they were going to be late at least ten minutes before a scheduled departure time—seem so subdued and so weary? Why did my sister—a generous, but impetuous and mulish girl who took every opportunity she could to bicker with our father—seem so relaxed? Why was she smiling in the same way that the nuns at Holy Child Roman Catholic Church smiled each Sunday during services, at once beatific and yet very far away? Why, on this morning that she was headed to Mount Sinai Hospital in Manhattan, was Mary wearing a $115 dress? Why did she look so beautiful?

This is what my parents had told me: My sister, after suffering severe headaches for a couple of months, had been referred by our family's general practitioner to a specialist at Mount Sinai, a large and very famous hospital in Manhattan, about an hour's drive from our house. The specialist there determined that my sister would need to be operated on to cure whatever was causing the headaches. She would be in the hospital for a week, possibly two, but the doctors expected a full recovery. She would be able to return to high school within a month, and her principal would allow her to graduate with the rest of her class in June, provided she made up her missed course work over the summer.

My parents assured me that there was nothing to worry about; that Mary would pull through just fine. I had no reason to think that they might be lying.

But a few other connections I failed to make:

Two weeks earlier, my uncle Tony, who lived in New Jersey and owned his own dry cleaning business, came to our house for dinner. We all sat in the dining room eating spaghetti and baked chicken, answering my uncle's questions about school and about our plans for summer vacation. After dinner, Uncle Tony gave my sister a $20 bill and told her to take his car and go to Carvel and buy Flying Saucers for everyone. My brother went along with her. I stayed behind and retreated to the living room to watch television.

"With all the technology they have today, with all these instruments they use, it's nothing for them," I heard my uncle say a few minutes later. "It's a routine procedure."

"Tony, it's not routine," my mother said to him, and I was startled by the anger in her voice. When I glanced over at her, it looked as if she was on the verge of tears.

A few days after that, my sister sat at the kitchen table, telling Danny and me about a test she had undergone that morning at Mount Sinai. She had been required to sit in a chair with her eyes wide open and remain perfectly still as the doctor touched a six-inch-long needle to her cornea. But each time the needle drew closer, she told us, she would blink and then burst out laughing. The doctor slowly but steadily lost his patience. After twenty minutes, he called in a nurse to try to hold my sister's eyelid open, and even then Mary blinked during the first half-dozen tries. When the doctor finally succeeded, Mary said she didn't even feel the needle touching against her eyeball. She told us that had she known it wouldn't hurt, she would have kept her eye open much sooner. Mary giggled as she recounted this story. She made it sound like a routine test that you submit to, just before you go into the hospital for a routine procedure.

"Where is Daniel?" my mother asked as she came into the kitchen. "He's not still sleeping, is he?" And without waiting for an answer—Danny had in fact been awake for an hour, he was the one who had awoken me—she walked out of the kitchen and up the three steps in the dining room that led to the bedrooms at the rear of the house and began shouting his name.

On any other morning, this sort of action would have set my father onto his own course of shouting, and the two of them would have gotten into a fight. But this morning he just sat there quietly turning the pages of his newspaper, waiting for my mother to figure things out on her own. She shouted Danny's name three or four times. Then, abruptly and totally, she was quiet. She came back to the kitchen and asked my sister, "Is he outside with the dog?"

My sister nodded. And then my mother—a proud, stubborn, often very frustrated woman who stalked through life in the manner of someone who has just won the lottery, only to find out that hundreds of others have also won, and that her share of the prize money will barely afford her a cup of coffee—said two words that I couldn't ever remember hearing her use before: "I'm sorry."

My mother poured herself a cup of coffee and sat down at the kitchen table. After a few minutes, Danny came in from walking the dog. He stood at the edge of the kitchen, not knowing what to do. I looked back and forth between my mother and father, waiting for their instructions. Another minute of silence passed, before my mother finally turned to me and said, "Ben, say good-bye to your sister."

I had no idea what was expected of me. We were not the kind of family that hugs and kisses each other good-bye. We barely said good-bye to one another at all—we usually just waved our hands and made it clear we were leaving. Mary, sensing my uncertainty, grabbed my elbow and lifted me up from my chair. She wrapped her arms around me and hugged me lightly—not squeezing me, just kind of holding me there in her arms, just for a few seconds. And when she was finished with me, she turned to Danny and hugged him in just the same manner, just long enough to satisfy my mother. All of this to satisfy my mother. To make her feel better that her first-born child was going into the hospital for a routine procedure.

"We need to say good-bye to your grandparents," my father announced, after the hugging had concluded. Our house was a "mother/daughter"—like a duplex, but with only one entryway, with six rooms on the top floor, where we lived, and a one-bedroom apartment on the bottom floor, where my father's parents lived. Thousands of these houses had been built in Staten Island in the early 1970s, to accommodate the thousands of newly married couples from Brooklyn—working-class children of immigrants, still a generation away from seeing their progeny go off to college and make good on the American dream. They moved to Staten Island seeking out more space and cheaper real estate, and, also, a place where they would be able to keep an eye on their aging parents. My father's parents, who had come to America from Ireland in the 1930s, were now in their late seventies. Both of them suffered from diabetes. If anybody should have been going to the hospital that morning, it was one of them. But even this obvious conclusion I did not draw until many, many years later.

My mother took Mary by the hand and led her down the steps. My grandmother was waiting at the door. My father lingered behind to repeat his instructions to Danny and me: Our Aunt Louise would arrive that night at 6:00 P.M. She would be staying with us through the weekend. The number of the hotel in Manhattan where my parents were staying was posted on the refrigerator. They would call us Friday afternoon, as soon as my sister was out of surgery.

"Your sister is going to be fine," he insisted to us.

So many details I never bothered to consider. If it was serious, I reasoned, surely they would have told me.

Why, for instance, was our aunt coming to stay with us, when every other time our parents were gone for an evening, or even an entire weekend, it was enough that our grandparents lived just one floor below?

Why, as I stood at the top of the steps watching my grandmother hold on tightly to my sister for nearly a minute, was my grandfather holding a handkerchief in his hand, surreptitiously wiping tears from his face, when I had never seen him cry before?

Why, the next afternoon, as I played wiffle ball in the street with Danny, were there tears streaming down my Aunt Louise's face as she came outside to tell us that our sister was out of surgery; that the operation had been a success? Why this sense of huge relief?

Of course the surgery was a success. It was just a routine procedure.

Or maybe I am remembering this all wrong. I was a precocious boy, probably the brightest kid in my class. I was capable of understanding. And maybe I did. Maybe I sensed the gravity of the situation, the expanding doom on the horizon, the headaches that wouldn't go away—and simply chose to ignore it all.

Three days later, my sister was dead.

part one

chapter one

What Started It
(2000)

I heard the scream, high-pitched and defiant, ripping through the quiet of the empty high school corridors, like a chainsaw cutting through butter. I heard the sound, a crack and a thud, like a bowling ball smashing into pins, sending them somersaulting through the air and then crashing to the ground.

I leaped out of my chair. I pulled open the door of my classroom on the second floor of Tottenville High School, where I had been spending the afternoon grading my students' papers. I turned to my left. There were a dozen teenagers clustered near the stairwell, about fifteen yards away, looking to the bottom of the steps.

"What happened?" I shouted at them. None of them turned to answer me.

A fight. I assumed that it must have been some kind of fight and that they just needed someone to break it up. I picked up my stride and moved closer. That's when I saw their faces, contorted into grimaces of panic and confusion. I couldn't see what they were all looking at—their bodies formed a protective wall in front of the stairwell. I barked at them, "Get out of the way" and "What happened?" I surprised myself with my own authority. I had a reputation at Tottenville as one of the "nice guy" teachers: a little reserved and serious-seeming at first, but deep down a softie; someone who was always threatening to give them zeroes when they handed in their assignments late, but who usually let them slide. I never would have thought that I could slip so easily into this role of the teacher in charge—the one who would set things right.

But then the kids moved apart and let me through, and I saw the body, tangled and immobile on the landing, a small pool of gooey, cherry-colored blood slowly dribbling out from the side of the head. I started to ask: "Whose body is that?" But then I saw his face, and I recognized him. It was Elliot Applebaum, one of my seniors. Just two hours earlier, he had been sitting in my classroom, barely paying attention.

I froze in place. I was struck silent. I heard a girl behind me, wailing and hysterical; all she could say, over and over again, was "Oh, my God. Oh, my God." I heard another student—a boy whose voice sounded familiar to me but whom I couldn't immediately identify—say, "Mario pushed him. Mario Tropiano." And then another of my students said, "I think he may be dead."

All of my authority abandoned me. I felt just as helpless as the students. Just as terrified.

I heard someone yelling, "We need to call the police." A few moments after that, two of our school's security guards—two pot-bellied men in their fifties named Jed and Gary—came barreling down the hallway. They made their way to the bottom of the steps and crouched next to Elliot's body. I watched Jed check to see if Elliot still had a pulse.

I still didn't do anything. I *couldn't* do anything. I couldn't move. I couldn't speak. I couldn't bring myself to ask what had happened.

All I could think of was Terrence.

All I could think was: *He did this. Somehow he is responsible for this.*

He is still sixteen. He is still in high school. He is in this *high school. He stepped into a time machine in the summer of 1990, a week or two after I last saw him, and landed here.*

Terrence O'Connell pushed Elliot Applebaum down these stairs.

I heard one of the students shout, "The police are coming." I heard Gary say to Jed, "He's breathing." Then Jed said to Gary, "We need to clear these kids out of here."

I stood there pathetic, useless. I knew that I should take charge. I knew that someone needed to usher the students outside and start asking them questions about what they had witnessed. I knew that someone should be trying to chase after Mario before he fled the school and was able to get too far away.

But that someone would not be me.

All I could think was: *Terrence is still here, still in the building—lurking, hiding, ready to pounce. He's coming to get me next.*

You fall into one thing. You follow it as far as it goes. You fall into another, and you follow that, too. And you allow yourself to fall—that's the key—you're *conscious* that you're falling. But you live with the bad decisions. You own them. You try not to beat up on yourself too hard as the disappointments and compromises begin stacking up all around you.

I entered Wesleyan University in Middletown, Connecticut, in the fall of 1991. My parents resisted sending me away to college. They said that, with my sister gone and Danny out of the house, they couldn't bear the thought of an empty nest. They didn't understand why I couldn't go to Hunter or Fordham or Brooklyn College—there were plenty of good schools, they argued, to which I could commute. They told me there was no way they could afford it, either, short of bankrupting themselves or eating nothing but bread and water for four years.

But I persisted. I begged and pleaded. I knew that if I had any hopes of escaping the plaguing memories of junior high school and high school, I needed to break away. Good luck intervened, in the form of a letter from the corporate headquarters of my father's company. I had won a $40,000 scholarship that could only be applied to private university tuition—so Wesleyan would end up costing the same as if I stayed at home and went to school in New York City. My parents finally relented. They said I could go, provided I returned home every Christmas, Easter, and summer break; and provided I didn't move too far away after graduation. Even though it was only May, I immediately began packing my bags.

I loved Wesleyan, from the moment my father dropped me off and drove away. During freshman fall, I studied art history, astronomy and philosophy, courses unlike anything that would have ever been offered at my factory-like public high school in Staten Island. I also took a required freshman English seminar, where the professor spent thirteen weeks on just four novels. I pored over each of those books, committing whole paragraphs to memory; I spent twice as long on my papers for that class than I did for any other. By the end of the semester, I declared myself an English major and signed up for two more literature courses in the spring.

But more than the pleasure of the schoolwork, what I relished most was the simple fact of being there. Away from the sadness and silence of the house in which I grew up. At a place where all of the students respected all of the other students, because we had all *gotten in,* we were all part of the same club. At a place where it didn't seem to matter if you were gay or straight or bisexual; Catholic or Jewish or Muslim or atheist; rich or poor or middle-class and just getting by on scholarship and financial aid. At Wesleyan, there were very few class distinctions, at least none that I was consciously aware of, and there were certainly no bullies. And for many months at a stretch, I didn't think of Terrence O'Connell at all.

I developed a small circle of friends: Jonah, a handsome, sarcastic chemistry major who lived on my floor in the dorms; Jennifer, a strikingly tall brunette who loved history, equestrian and The Smiths; and my roommate David, a surprisingly down-to-earth New York City blueblood with whom I went to see foreign films every Saturday night at the campus theater. My friends occasionally asked me about my family and about my life before college, but I was never especially forthcoming, and they never pressed me for details. That was another thing I loved about being at Wesleyan: the unspoken understanding that we were all there, in part, because we wanted a fresh start; that everyone had *something* they were trying to leave behind. By the end of freshman year, after weeks of agonizing and deliberation, I came out to Jonah, Jennifer, and David, in three separate conversations on the Saturday just prior to finals week. I felt an almost unquantifiable sense of relief when they each assured me that it wouldn't impact our friendships; that they didn't view me in the least bit differently.

During the fall of my sophomore year, I dated my first boyfriend. His name was Anthony. He had a big nose and stringy black hair, and he lived on the floor below mine in the dorms. One night in my room we were watching *Saturday Night Live,* and he asked me, apropos of nothing, whom I thought about when I masturbated. I lied and mentioned a couple of girls in our class. He lied and mentioned a few girls, too. But then, a few minutes later, Anthony said that sometimes when he masturbated he also thought about me.

We were together for two months. He forbade me to tell anyone. We weren't even supposed to be seen coming into and out of each other's dorm rooms, because technically Anthony was still with his high school girlfriend, Alicia, who went to school at Connecticut College, about an hour away. Eventually she figured things out, during a weekend visit to Wesleyan early that December. The three of us had gone to the movies. Anthony was in the lobby buying popcorn.

She turned to me and said, in a mock-serious tone of voice, "So I hear you're sleeping with my boyfriend."

I turned green and—not realizing that she was joking—responded, "He actually came out to you?"

A few days after that Anthony broke up with me. He accused me of deliberately destroying things between him and Alicia. He said I was trying to make people think he was gay.

I was desperate to try to keep him. "But you *are* gay," I pleaded. "You like having sex with me, you like"—and here I lowered my voice to a whisper, even though there was no one around who could overhear us—"you like sucking my dick."

He scowled at me and said, "No, I don't. It makes me sick." And his words filled me with such humiliation and shame— they made me think all over again of every insult and epithet that Terrence O'Connell had ever hurled in my direction— that I could barely eat for a week.

I dated another guy in the spring of sophomore year. His name was Brian. Junior year I dated two more. Their names were Scott and Brandon. None of these relationships lasted more than four or five dates, two or three fumbling sexual encounters. My boyfriends were all skittish sorts, afraid that someone would find out that they were gay. Then again—no matter how "out" I pretended myself to be at Wesleyan—so was I. Each time I returned home, I pledged that I would tell my parents. A few times I think I even came close. But I could never bring myself to do it. I feared my parents' tears. I feared their embarrassment. I guess I feared adding yet another item to the already long list of their lives' disappointments. Eventually, I just told myself that they already knew—because I had never brought home a girlfriend; because I never even talked about girls in their presence—and decided I could leave it at that.

Senior year I swore off boys. I determined, instead, that I would concentrate solely on my schoolwork. I proposed an honors thesis, and I spent hundreds of hours working on it, trying to turn it into the best thesis the department had ever seen. That winter, I applied to a handful of English literature Ph.D. programs, and I was accepted at the University of Wisconsin-Madison. I wasn't sure if I wanted to become a professor, but I was intrigued by the possibilities: the chance to keep reading, writing, thinking; mostly, the chance to continue marking distance from my family and my adolescence.

But this time my parents were much less accommodating. When I called my mother to tell her the news, there was a long, studied pause on the other end of the line.

"Am I supposed to be happy for you?" she finally asked.

She insisted that I move back to Staten Island. She said that there was no future and no money in teaching college-level English; that I would end up teaching high school anyway, and that I could do *that* without spending tens of thousands of dollars on a Ph.D.

"You've been away for four years, Ben," she said, "but, come on, enough is enough."

My father called a day after that and said, as much as he

wanted me to be happy, he had to side with my mother on this one. It wasn't so easy, he said, with my sister gone and with my brother living a three-hour drive away. He pleaded with me to defer my admission to graduate school, just for a year or two, and move back to Staten Island. "Just so your mother won't feel like she's losing you, too."

Why didn't I put up more resistance? Why couldn't I just tell them that I was moving to Wisconsin, whether they liked it or not? I don't really know. I suppose that at the time I didn't grasp the significance of the decision; that the next decade of my life would be defined by it. And I suppose that part of me worried that my four years away at college had already been enough of a betrayal of my parents—and that to move further away would be the act of rebellion that finally destroyed them.

But mainly I think I was terrified of proving their coarsest working-class suspicions right, that for all of my "book smarts," as my father often termed it, I lacked much in the way of common sense, the "street smarts" needed to survive in the real world. What if a Ph.D. really was useless? What if I ended up broke and underemployed? I imagined my parents talking to their friends about me, and I could almost hear the disgust in their voices: *All of his fancy degrees, but he'll still never make as much money as his cousin Jamie the electrician.* And, for whatever reason, I could never bear the thought of my parents being ashamed of me.

So I went back home. Two days after the Wesleyan commencement, I moved back into my old bedroom, the bedroom that once belonged to my sister. I told myself that it was only temporary; that I was just going to take a year to save up some money and sketch out a plan. My college friends had all scattered to other places: Jonah found a job in Boston; Jennifer returned home to Oregon; David entered law school at Stanford. I called them all regularly, and I occasionally took the bus to Boston to spend the weekend with Jonah. But mostly I led a solitary existence. I began commuting to Brooklyn College for my teaching certificate. I came home each night and read novels and fell asleep by 10:00 P.M. Six months into this routine, I ran into one of my old teachers from New Dorp High School, who told me to contact the principal at Tottenville. One of their English teachers was going on sabbatical, and they needed a replacement. That teacher got sick during his sabbatical and went on permanent disability. One year became two, two turned into three. Three years were now going on four.

I moved into my own apartment, a one-bedroom place, the bottom level of a small duplex, about two miles from school. Each day I taught one hundred twenty students, none of whom knew about my dead sister, or Terrence O'Connell, or the four men that I had slept with in college, or the plans that I had once had to go to a good graduate program. When the students asked me personal questions—where did I attend college? was I married or single?—I looked at them with disdain and exasperation, as if they had asked me for the answer key to the final exam. When my fellow teachers asked me the same questions, I gave them one or two word answers, usually the truth, but sometimes, necessarily, a lie: *My girlfriend is in law school in Massachusetts. It's difficult, but it's just for another year or two and then she's going to move down here and join me.*

But what of it? That's just how life goes, right? You learn to contend with the disappointments and frustrations. You do your best, when your friends call, to ignore their playful chiding: *Are you* ever *going to get out of Staten Island? It's like you're imprisoned there or something?* You try not to grind your teeth in envy when they tell you about the huge promotion they've just gotten or the expensive European vacation they'll soon be taking. And, yes, you're conscious of the fact that you're not dating anyone, that you're letting weeks and months float by in self-imposed celibacy. But you convince yourself that there will be plenty of time for boyfriends and romance in the future. And, yeah, sure, you feel stuck. You feel yourself slipping away from the adult you wish you could be. But you try to keep your sense of humor about things. Nobody's life is perfect just out of college. At the very least, you remind yourself, you get summers off and the benefits are excellent.

And on some days, when one of your students' eyes grow very wide, something you've said has penetrated his gray matter, he's made some sort of connection in his brain that he will carry with him all through the day—well, on those days, the compromises don't seem to matter so much. On those days, you feel optimistic, energized; you feel as if maybe you *have* found your niche and that everything else will fall into place. Some grand plan will reveal itself, and then—*finally*—everything will make sense. And as for right now, for the next year or two or three, for as long as *right now* lasts, it's hardly the worst thing in the world.

That's the thing I can't quite emphasize enough. Until Mario Tropiano pushed Elliot Applebaum down the stairs at Tottenville High School, it hardly seemed terrible at all.

"What started it?"

Meredith McBern—a beautiful woman with alabaster skin and long wavy black hair, the only teacher at school who was close to my age, who taught history and advised the yearbook staff and who, in her spare time, resisted the advances of a half-dozen middle-aged men in the biology, physics, and math departments—was standing next me. She was asking me the one question that no one around us could answer.

Two hours had passed. We were standing outside the school, about twenty yards from the front doors. The police had arrived very quickly, and they ushered us out of the building and told us not to leave the area because we would all need to be questioned. As we were exiting, four emergency medical technicians scurried inside. Five minutes later, they emerged with Elliot's body on a stretcher, a sheet pulled up to his neck, his face bloodied, his eyes closed. They loaded the stretcher into an ambulance and quickly raced away.

By now, the account of the fight had been passed back and forth through the crowd repeatedly. Some of the details varied, depending on whose version of the story you heard, but the essence of what had happened seemed to be this: Mario had been wandering through the hallway alone, presumably on his way to baseball practice. Elliot was coming from the opposite direction, part of a pack of a dozen kids, mostly Asian and Jewish, who hung out together and played Ultimate Frisbee every day after school. Mario called out to Elliot and said there was something he needed to talk to him about. This was a surprise to Elliot's friends, none of whom had ever seen Elliot speak to Mario, but Elliot told them that they should go on ahead without him. Mario and Elliot huddled together near a row of windows, directly opposite the stairwell, while Elliot's friends kept on walking in the opposite direction. But then, maybe fifteen or twenty seconds later, Elliot's friends heard raised voices. They halted in their tracks and turned around, trying to decide if they should reverse course and intervene. Then the argument between Mario and Elliot got louder. His friends began walking back toward Elliot, to see if he needed their help. They told the police they saw Mario poking Elliot in the chest, very sharply and repeatedly—like a kid with a stick poking at a piñata—and then they saw Elliot trying to push Mario away from him, and then Mario lowered his voice and said something no one could hear, and then Elliot shouted "No," and then Mario smacked Elliot's face with his open palm, and it must have stung, because that's when Elliot let out a scream—that was the scream I had heard in my classroom—and then Mario grabbed Elliot by the shoulders, and pushed him or shoved him or threw him (depending on whose version of the story you were listening to), and then Elliot went skirting across the floor, and right over the edge of the first step, tumbling down the stairwell, smacking his head repeatedly as his body fell forward. That was the noise I had heard. The cracking and the thudding. The sound of a defenseless boy getting the daylights knocked out of him by a bully with twice the brawn.

But as for *what* started it? Not one person among the hundred or so gathered outside Tottenville High School could even put forth a plausible theory.

"Do you think it might have been some kind of lover's spat?" Meredith was saying.

"A lover's spat?" I repeated incredulously.

"Yeah, do you think they might have been boyfriends?"

This was just the sort of thing Meredith loved saying to me, acknowledging my sexuality in public in some cryptic and teasing manner. We had known each other since my second day at Tottenville, when she tapped me on the shoulder as I was eating lunch and said, "Hey, sexy," and then sat down across from me and started telling me her life story. At first, I was a little afraid of her, but she seemed determined that we should be friends; and after a few weeks of eating together, gossiping about our students and fellow teachers, I realized I liked her. We began hanging out together socially, meeting up for a movie or drinks. It was during one of these nights out that Meredith, drunk off her signature cocktail of rum and Diet Dr. Pepper, blurted out: "So do you have a boyfriend? A cute guy like you definitely needs a boyfriend." I tried to stammer a denial, but she just shook her head at me and giggled and said, "Oh, don't worry, honey. I'm not going to tell anyone."

"You think they were boyfriends?" I said to her now, a little sourly. "That sounds a little far-fetched to me."

"What started it then?" she shot back.

Terrence started it. Terrence O'Connell.

I didn't answer her.

"I feel like it has to be something really melodramatic like that, you know?" Meredith continued. "I mean, Mario is a brat, but he's not exactly the killing type."

I still didn't answer her.

Meredith went on talking, refusing to give up on this: "Maybe they were boyfriends and Elliot was threatening to expose Mario's secret. They would have made a cute couple, too. Mario's thick and beefy, and Elliot's kind of lean, but they're both kind of tall, right? I always think gay men must feel so self-conscious, when one of them is much taller than the other."

She threw her head back and laughed very loudly. But then,

when I didn't respond, she stopped abruptly. She looked disappointed that I wasn't laughing along.

"Is something wrong, Ben? You look a little clammy."

"This whole thing," I said softly.

"Oh, come on. Kids get into fights like this all the time. Don't make it into anything bigger than it is."

I shook my head at her and shrugged my shoulders.

"They're just kids being kids," she went on. "Elliot's going to be fine." She paused and lowered her voice and added: "This isn't Columbine."

"Something like this happened to me," I said. "When I was in high school."

"Really?" she asked, suddenly tantalized.

"It's hard for me to witness this kind of stuff."

"What happened? Tell me."

For a moment, I thought of telling her everything. Other than Jonah, whom I still talked with regularly on the phone and visited in Boston for a week each summer, Meredith was probably my best friend. And she would welcome the burden of my confession; she would delight in the soap opera.

She would probably even tell me what I wanted to hear: that Terrence had secretly been in love with me; that his repressed desire for me was what had started it all.

But I couldn't. All these years, I still couldn't even speak his name aloud. I was still afraid that he was standing right behind me, poised to shove me to the ground.

"Nothing," I told Meredith. "Nothing worth remembering."

You crush on them. You fall a little bit in love with them. It's perfectly normal. Ask anyone who teaches, and they'll tell you the same thing. The sooner you realize this, the better for everyone involved.

My first year at Tottenville was pretty much a wash. I stood in front of the students each morning, anxious and halting. I was afraid they would see right through me, laugh at me and boo me out of the room. I was afraid, too, of getting too close to them; afraid that I would fall in love with every last boy in the senior class. So I kept my distance. I ran a stoic and humorless classroom. I met some of their friendlier gestures—inviting me to their basketball games, for instance, or asking my advice on where they should apply to college—with solemn indifference.

Meredith was the one who made me realize that I wasn't the only one who suffered these fears. We were sitting in her classroom late one afternoon, just killing time because neither of us wanted to go home to our empty apartments. She was just fooling around when she said it.

"So whose eighteenth birthday are you most anticipating?" she asked.

I laughed and shook my head at her. "I don't go there, Meredith," I said.

She answered, "Oh come on, Ben. It's the most interesting part of the job. Probably the most challenging, too. Managing your crushes on them."

And once she said that to me, it all seemed so much simpler. *Of course* teachers would have crushes on their students. Crushes are born out of proximity and a certain hothouse intensity: You see them day after day; you register their boredom and their delight; you come to feel as if you know them better than they know themselves. Crushes are born, too, out of envy: You hate them, just a little bit, because they stay the same age, always sixteen or seventeen, a new set of them arriving each September to replace the ones who graduated the previous June. But you stay behind. You hate them because you look into their eyes and see vast reserves of promise—and, also, a little bit of your own promise, unrealized, reflected back at you.

In which case: The crushes are more than inevitable. They're fundamental. You'd be inhuman not to have them.

And once I realized *that*, I was finally able to relax and teach.

It was a few hours later. I was sitting in front of the television in my apartment, surfing the channels, trying to find a news report about the fight between Mario and Elliot. At least a dozen reporters and cameramen had shown up outside Tottenville in the aftermath of the fight, but now all I could find were teasers for the late newscasts, and none of those made mention of the incident. I decided to get undressed and climb into bed. But I couldn't relax enough to fall asleep. Every time I closed my eyes, I just kept picturing Mario sitting in my classroom nineteen months earlier, waiting for me to impress him.

I wasn't sure if I had ever seen him before that morning, the first day of his junior year. But suddenly I couldn't not notice. He was one of those boys Meredith especially liked to gush over, the ones who bloom into something very beautiful the summer between their sophomore and junior years. He had thick, curly black hair and dark brown eyes and the kind of complexion that made it look as if he had just come in from the beach, even in the middle of December. He knew that people found him extraordinarily good-looking; that they were apt to turn their heads and stare when he passed them in the hallway. But he acted as if he didn't care. And *that,* I would soon come to realize, was Mario Tropiano's trademark: his cultivated air of indifference. He was neither smart nor stupid, neither engaged with his studies nor careless about them. He was a popular boy, a leader with a devoted circle of male and female acolytes who made his lunch table the most crowded one in the cafeteria. But even his own popularity failed to interest him, even *that* he could have taken or left. In class, it was impossible to get any kind of reaction out of him: If you called on him to answer a question, he would respond tersely and dutifully; if you chided him for not paying attention, he would quietly apologize and never attempt to mount a defense. There had to be something that could penetrate the core of this kid—something that might fill him with sadness or joy, terror or elation— but whatever it was, he steadfastly refused to let on.

When I first started teaching, I thought it would be the boys like Mario whom I wouldn't be able to get out of my head. The big and solid jocks with their incongruous muscles, their upper bodies developed to twice the size of their lower bodies; with their cheeks miraculously smoothed free of the pimples and pockmarks that plagued the rest of their classmates; with their easy manners and merciless eyes that projected self-satisfaction and relish, but never gratefulness, because they truly believed that their lives would always be like this, that they would never have to work at it. Why should they be grateful for getting exactly what was their due?

But I was wrong. By my second month of teaching, the Marios—and there were perhaps a half-dozen boys in each class just like him—started to lose my interest. After awhile, I began to wonder if maybe it was all just an act for them—or if, even worse, they were elusive simply because they had nothing inside of themselves to reveal. By my fourth month of teaching, I had trouble telling the Marios apart or even remembering their names.

As it worked out, the ones I developed crushes on were of a different genus entirely. They were the boys who first walked into class with their heads hung low and their eyes cast to the ground. The ones you had to ask to repeat their names three or four times, because they tended to mumble their words. The quiet ones; the easily overlooked ones; the ones who seemed half-asleep most of the time, except for when they abruptly startled awake, and then they would talk animatedly about Thomas Hardy or E. M. Forster or Gertrude Stein, making observations so unexpected and thoughtful that they instantly reminded you of why you liked your job.

I crushed on the Elliot Applebaums of Tottenville High School.

The boys I could pretend that I had once been just like when I was in high school, had Terrence O'Connell never entered the equation.

I had drifted off to sleep. But it wasn't really sleep. It was that semi-conscious state where you keep replaying the events of the day in your head; where you think your thoughts are lucid, but everything is rapidly beginning to blur together and turn into an elastic dream.

I was thinking: *What if Meredith was on to something about those two boys being lovers? What if she had been speaking to me some awful truth?*

I was imagining Mario and Elliot in bed together, naked, touching each other.

I was picturing Mario shoving Elliot down the stairwell, and then Elliot's head knocking against the steps, *thump-thump-thump-thwack,* until Elliot was no longer conscious.

I was picturing Mario being led away in handcuffs, imprisoned for now but probably not for long—not for so long that he wouldn't be able to get out and one day do this again.

And then suddenly I was thinking of Terrence. An image of his face expanded in my mind: those glimmering eyes; that bottomless dimple; that unforgiving smirk.

And then his words filled my head, those last two words that he ever spoke to me, I heard them over and over again, almost as if he were lying in bed beside me, whispering in my ear . . .

Don't fall, don't fall, don't fall, don't fall . . .

And then he *was* there. In bed with me. He was gripping me tightly. He wouldn't let go.

I was thinking: *He is responsible for what happened today. Somehow he possessed Mario's body, or whispered instructions into his ear, Iago-like, or brainwashed him. Terrence O'Connell pushed Elliot Applebaum down the stairs in Tottenville High School. And I'm the next person on his list . . . he's coming to get me . . . to finish what he once started . . . I'm running out of time . . . every second counts . . .*

I need to beat him to the punch . . .

I snapped awake and bolted upright. My heartbeat was racing. My entire body was shaking. It took me a couple of seconds to remember where I was and to realize that Terrence wasn't sitting there next to me. I tried taking long and deep breaths to calm myself down. I told myself to laugh; that the best and fastest way to recover from a nightmare is to look under your bed and see that there's no boogeyman there and then *laugh.*

Except the more I thought about it, it didn't seem funny at all. It had been ten years since I had last seen Terrence O'Connell. Yet no amount of time or distance ever seemed to make a difference. A few weeks might go by in peacefulness, maybe even a few months. But always he returned. A tall, sandy-haired student might be walking past me in the hallway, and I would have to stop and do a double take, just to make certain it wasn't my old nemesis. Or I would fall asleep at night and be dreaming some perfectly ordinary dream—and then all of a sudden Terrence would be there, lurking menacingly in the background, the extra in a movie who somehow manages to wrestle your attention away from the lead actors. Sometimes I feared that, for as long as I lived, I would never be able to stop thinking of him. Sometimes I feared that, when I died, his would be the first face I saw when I arrived in heaven.

I gave up trying to sleep and climbed out of bed. I sat down in front of my computer, and I did what I always did when my thoughts of Terrence became too much to bear. I typed his name into an Internet search engine, hoping to find some shred of evidence, any hint of what might have become of him. But the same results that were always returned to me were returned once again: There was a Terrence O'Connell who was a forty-five-year-old trial lawyer in Seattle; there was one who had graduated from Emerson College in 1989; there was another—quite possibly the one I was looking for—who, in 1998, had finished fourth in a half marathon in Memphis, but no other information or identifying characteristics were listed.

A reckoning. There needs to be a reckoning.

Some sort of evening of the score.

Ten years overdue. Ten years too late.

I need to make Terrence O'Connell stop bullying me, once and for all.

I stared at the computer screen for a while longer, as I tried to weigh my options. I could go to work in the morning and do my best not to think about the fight between Mario and Elliot. I could try once again to forget all about Terrence. I could go back to pretending as if everything about my life was proceeding perfectly according to plan.

Or I could go off and find him. I could force him to answer for his actions. I could do what needed to be done to make these relentless, poisonous memories finally go away.

It hardly seemed like a choice at all.

I opened the word processing program on my computer. I typed a first sentence without entirely knowing what I was going to type. I stared at that sentence for thirty minutes before deciding to type another. It took yet another hour to add a third sentence, at which point I decided I needed to rework the letter entirely. It wasn't until 4:30 A.M., after trying out a half-dozen different drafts, that I decided I was comfortable with what I had written.

I looked over the letter one last time. I spell-checked it and saved it and printed it out and then climbed back into bed. I still wasn't sure if I was about to make the worst mistake of my life. But I couldn't fathom any other solution.

I drifted off to sleep telling myself that I had just written the only possible prescription for my salvation.

"Let them talk," the psychologist told us, her raspy, high-pitched voice reminding me of Marge on *The Simpsons*. "Let them be unruly. If a few of them make inappropriate jokes, don't get upset. Just let them work their anxieties out of their system."

We had been sitting in this emergency faculty meeting for the past thirty minutes. The principal, Barry Marcus, began by telling us that Elliot had broken his arm and suffered a mild concussion, but that he would return to school the next week. Mario, meanwhile, had been arrested for aggravated assault and charged as an adult; the judge released him into the custody of his parents, but Marcus had issued an immediate suspension for the remainder of the school year. He told us that a police investigation was still ongoing and that they still didn't know what started it. Marcus then handed his microphone over to the psychologist, who talked for twenty minutes straight, drilling into our heads a speech that we should deliver before each of our classes, about how rage is a very normal part of adolescence, but violence is *never* the solution. My colleagues were now beginning to sigh and whisper their complaints. Meredith, who was sitting next to me, cracked a joke: "Where did this woman get her degree? At the Touchy-Feely Institute?"

"Does anyone have any questions?" I heard *The Simpsons* lady ask.

No one did. It was ending. I made a beeline for Barry Marcus, who was standing with the psychologist, thanking her for coming on such short notice. I touched him on the shoulder. When he turned around, I thrust my letter into his hands.

Dear Principal Marcus,

Due to a medical emergency involving my sister, I am requesting a leave of absence, effective immediately. While I deeply regret leaving the students this late in the term, my sister is seriously ill. I will be traveling to Ohio to care for her. I have no idea how long I will be away.

Sincerely,
Benjamin Reilly

I watched as he eyeballed the letter up and down. When he finally looked up at me, his face was twisted into a grimace. I couldn't tell if he was angry with me; or worried for me; or just wholly baffled. He excused himself from the psychologist and beckoned me to follow him.

A few minutes later, seated behind the desk in his office, he finally spoke up: "Benjamin, I'm at a loss here. I don't know what to say. Your sister . . . I hope she's going to be OK."

The softness of his voice and the sincerity of his words surprised me. He was a hulking man, six foot five, two hundred and sixty pounds. He was famous at our school for being extremely gruff and curt, even with the teachers he liked.

"I hate to leave you in a lurch like this," I told him. "Especially after what happened yesterday. But I don't have a choice. I need to be on an airplane tomorrow morning." I had been rehearsing all of this in my head during the faculty meeting. I was surprised, now, at how easily it all flowed out of my mouth.

"I don't want you to worry about school," he said. "You need to go and take care of your sister. Worry about that."

"I feared that it might come to this—that I might have to go on leave—but I kept hoping the situation might improve. Hoping against hope."

"Benjamin, I'm so sorry to hear this," he said.

I could have stopped there. I *should* have stopped there. Certainly the last thing in the world I should have done was begin spouting a ludicrous-sounding story that I had made up in my head while listening to a school psychologist drone on about adolescent anger management issues.

But I also felt compelled to keep talking. To keep lying.

I guess I needed to know I had it in me.

"Her name is Mary," I told him. "It's all so sad and confusing. She was diagnosed with HIV about fifteen years ago. She contracted it from an ex-boyfriend who had been sharing needles. We thought she would be dead within a year. Back then, HIV was a death sentence. But she persevered. And then, a few years later, they put her on these drug cocktails, and suddenly the doctors were changing their tune. They said she'd be able to live for decades. They told her that living with HIV would be no different from living with diabetes or high blood pressure.

"But they were wrong. The drugs aren't working for her anymore. She doesn't think she has more than a few months left."

I paused for a moment and looked at Marcus to see how this was playing. He wore that pinched, pained expression—poised somewhere between empathy and revulsion—that people make when they're hearing tragic stories about strangers they've never met. For a moment, I felt a beaming sense of pride and accomplishment. I had contrived an improbable lie and sold it to Barry Marcus wholesale. And if I could convince someone as naturally skeptical as Marcus—a man well-trained in seeing through others' tall tales, a man who probably spent half his day listening to students make stuff up—well, maybe that meant I was good at this. Maybe it meant I had many more lies within me, enough to carry me all the way to Terrence O'Connell's doorstep.

But then I caught myself. What was I doing? I was saying that my sister who had been dead for nearly twenty years was still alive, but now dying of AIDS. I was betraying the man who had hired me and mentored me. I was on the verge of walking away from a perfectly tolerable job with security and benefits and colleagues who liked me and students who looked up to me.

Stop this right now. You've ceased behaving rationally.

Stop this before you ruin everything that is going well in your life.

"My mother doesn't even know about this," I heard myself saying. "My sister is afraid to tell her that she's dying. She feels nothing but disappointment coming from my mother."

Then again, what's so rational about getting stuck? What's so rational about letting yourself stay stuck?

Maybe rationality is just really fucking overrated.

"Benjamin, I don't know what to say," Marcus ventured.

"I'm sorry. This is more than you wanted to know."

"Is there anything . . . any way we can help you?"

I didn't hesitate. This, too, I had been rehearsing: "Actually, Mr. Marcus, there's a favor I'm hoping I can ask of you. My sister dated this guy in high school. We all thought she was going to marry him, but they got into some silly fight and broke up. But she'd like to find him now and maybe reconnect before she dies. I've been trying to help her track him down. I went to high school with his younger brother, Terrence O'Connell. The family moved away junior year, but I thought that if maybe I could get Terrence's forwarding address, if one of the secretaries over at New Dorp could pull it out of his file for me. . . . I thought it might be a place to start."

I talked about the fight between Mario and Elliot at the start of each of my five classes that day. I repeated the speech that the psychologist had drilled into us, the same speech the students would hear in each of their other classes. I waited until the very last minute of each class to give them my news.

"I'm hoping to return to you before the school year is out, but I'm not very hopeful." And then, during the last period of the day, there was a knock at the door. A secretary came in and handed me two slips of paper. The first one was a note on Marcus's stationary, asking me to come to his office in order to sign the necessary exit paperwork.

The other one was a fax, with most of the information blocked out by strokes of black magic marker, like some declassified document from the Warren Commission.

Everything except for the following:

Thomas and Marta O'Connell
3250 Oak Hill Terrace
Indianapolis, IN
(317) 209 5215

Down at the bottom was a handwritten note, written in looping, feminine script, but left unsigned: "Terrence graduated from Arlington High School in Indianapolis and entered Indiana University in the fall of 1991. That's all the information we have. Good luck."

You spend enough time living in your head, trapped inside the membranes of your worst memories, trying not to think about a boy named Terrence O'Connell, but thinking about him all the same, all the time, and, well, you're apt to go a little crazy. You might just start to snap.

What started it was this.

chapter two

In Exile
(1986)

Gaywad. The speedy and precipitous decline of my junior high school reputation, from anonymous, mostly unremarked upon nerd to extant social pariah, reviled and ridiculed and name-called from every corner, can be boiled down to one word, and to the one person who first uttered it, near the end of lunch period on the second Monday in April of 1986, just seven weeks shy of the end of the seventh grade. *Gaywad*. The word that Terrence O'Connell introduced into the lexicon of Myra S. Barnes Intermediate School and that spread through the hallways and classrooms, rapidly and invisibly, like a fatal, airborne virus. *Gaywad*. He was talking about me.

"That kid is such a *gaywad*."

I was sitting two tables away, poring over my notes for that afternoon's quiz on *A Midsummer Night's Dream*. I heard him say it. I froze in place. Somehow I knew he was talking about me. I knew this right away.

I heard him repeat it again, this time with a slight variation: "He's such a total gaywad. I didn't think they even made gaywads that gay."

The others at his table all laughed. David Zimmerman, Evan Sutton, Joe DeNino, and a half-dozen more of Terrence's pack, most of whom had been sitting together since the first day of junior high school. Terrence seemed to have very little in common with these other boys. David couldn't play sports, which

Terrence could. Evan was obsessed with comic books and role-playing games, a hobby for which Terrence was always calling him a "freak." Joe was fat and pimply, the "before" picture to Terrence's "after" picture in an advertisement for exercise equipment and acne cream. But they had all signed onto this clique very early on; and they all unquestioningly accepted Terrence as their ruler.

He was lean and very tall, the tallest boy in our class. His fine, dark blonde hair was cut evenly around his head and parted halfheartedly in the middle. He had bright blue eyes, the blue of a Smurf, and a dimple on his left cheek that you only saw when he smiled wide. Or smirked wide—Terrence O'Connell's smile was almost always more of a smirk. He had a habit, in class, of raising his hand and then cracking a joke before answering the teacher's question, almost as if he imagined himself sitting in the center square on *The Hollywood Squares*. The female teachers—the young, unmarried ones, and the dowdy, middle-aged ones, and even the ones who were a hair's-breadth away from collecting Social Security—giggled at these jokes every time, whether they were funny or lame. They would have denied it, but they all had crushes on him.

He came from a working-class Irish-Catholic family. It was said that he had four or five brothers; that his father drove a truck; that his mother had abandoned them all a year or two earlier and ran off with another man. There was even a rumor that one of Terrence's older brothers had done a stint in juvenile detention. Terrence himself could neither confirm nor deny these rumors. It wasn't entirely clear he even knew these rumors existed. Like all great and legendary dictators, he lorded too much power over his sycophants for any of them to ever whisper to him what others were whispering behind his back.

He wasn't one to threaten people physically. In fact, I don't think he had ever been in a fight. He opted, instead, for name-calling—a steady pitter-patter of insults and taunts, often in the form of twisting someone's real name into a cruel and silly-sounding one. Lara Spencer became "Fat Specimen." Brian DuPont became "Brian Do-Do-Pot," and then later simply "Brian the Shitter." Dana Rogers was greeted every morning in the schoolyard by Terrence, every single day for two years, with the exact same questions: "Why did your parents give you a girl's name? Did they want you to be a girl?"

He called boys "faggot" and "cocksucker" and "pussy." He called girls "dyke" and "slut" and "ugly hippo bitch" (the latter name reserved exclusively for Valerie Kroger, who, while admittedly plain looking, could not have weighed more than eighty pounds). He sprayed epithets the way a bored soldier might shoot his weapon into the empty horizon, as diversion from the monotony, probably not intending any real damage, but still relishing the sound of the gunfire. He instilled fear in almost all of the seventh graders; everyone behaved around him exactly the same way: They hung on his words; they laughed at his jokes; they handed him their homework to copy without his even asking. And if by some mysterious turn of events they were lucky enough to be invited into his inner circle—if they were given permission to sit at his lunch table, for instance, or to play handball with him after school—well, then they walked on eggshells. They did or said nothing that might contradict their leader. They hoped that he would allow them to be a part of his inner circle for life, all the way up the ladder he would no doubt decisively climb.

Everyone except me. Because for all of sixth grade and half of seventh, I occupied an unlikely, postage stamp-sized terrain: I had managed to avoid Terrence entirely, while he had always seemed just as intent on avoiding me. Despite the fact that we were both members of "The SP," our school's gifted and talented program, our paths rarely crossed. He took Spanish, and I took French; we had different homerooms; different history classes; different math classes. His house was due east of the school, and mine was due west, which placed us on different buses going home. Even in the schoolyard before classes started each morning, he tended to keep a certain wary distance, almost like a dog crossing paths with a skunk, knowing he should attack, but somehow unable to make a move.

And I might have been spared for even longer. I might have made it all through junior high school without once having a run-in with him. But fate, or God, or something much too banal for words, intervened. One day in early February our English teacher Mrs. Burns, in an effort to help another boy with bad eyes who complained that he had to strain to see the blackboard, rearranged our seats, placing me right next to Terrence. I girded myself for the inevitable, and even then it took much longer than I expected. But it came. One day in the middle of March, as I was trying to copy down Mrs. Burns' instructions for an essay that would soon be due, he began scribbling on my notebook, running his pen up and down, making aimless doodles and cross marks all over the page. I glared at him. He smirked at me. And then, after a long, tense moment, he slowly withdrew his pen.

A week after that, as Mrs. Burns was talking about the first act of *A Midsummer Night's Dream*, he leaned into me and whispered, "Why are you such a pussy?"

I stared straight ahead and kept taking notes. Maybe if I ignored him, I thought, he would let it drop. If only I could make it through just a few more weeks, just to the end of the seventh grade, then maybe he would forget about me entirely over the summer. And then, maybe next year, when we weren't sitting next to one another any longer, things would return to normal.

But ten days after that, he leaned over and wrote in my notebook, in big block letters straight across the top of the page: "I THINK YOU'RE A FAGGOT."

"Don't you think he's a gaywad?"

He said it loudly, so that all of the seventh graders, who tended to cluster together at the tables in the middle of the lunchroom, would hear him. I forced myself not to look up. I trained my eyes on the words of *A Midsummer Night's Dream*, Act IV, Scene 1, reading them over and over, certain Mrs. Burns would ask about them on that afternoon's quiz: *How came these things to pass? / O, how mine eyes do loathe his visage now!*

"I always catch him staring at me, looking over at me in English, like he's trying to check me out," I heard him say. "I think he wants to suck my dick."

I told myself to ignore him. It's a simple rule of junior high school, you learn it very early on: If you never let a bully know he's gotten to you, he will be forced to let it drop.

"He totally is. Last year when I sat next to him in math, he was always trying to play footsie with me. He would always try to rub his leg against mine." Now it was Joe DeNino's turn. He talked even louder than Terrence. A couple of the girls sitting near Terrence heard this and squealed in unison, "That's so grooooosssss . . ."

I was incredulous that they should believe Joe DeNino—that even the pimpliest, fattest boy in the seventh grade could convince these people that I was in lust with him. But the character assassination was formally underway, and I had no hopes of stopping it. Until now, I hadn't even realized that any of Terrence's cronies knew my name. But they did. And apparently they had been waiting for this opportunity—the moment they could collectively unleash their venom upon me.

Terrence repeated his story. He said that I had been checking him out that very morning during gym class. He suspected that I had a boner the whole time. A few other kids murmured the words "faggot" and "cocksucker." I heard another say, "He has a poster of Rob Lowe without his shirt, from that gay hockey movie, hanging above his bed. I've always thought he was a gaywad." And the word "gaywad" just rolled off this boy's tongue, even though—until Terrence introduced it just a minute ago—he had never heard it uttered before, much less used in a sentence. *Gaywad. Gaywad. Gaywad.* Oh how they loved this new word *gaywad!*

Terrence's entire table erupted in another wave of laughter. There were pockets of giggles at the surrounding tables. One of the girls sitting at the opposite end of my own table, Alice White, laughed along with them. A year earlier, after I had helped her with her math homework, she had told me that I was the nicest boy in our class. Now, out of the corner of my eye, I could see her looking at me and then looking at Terrence, laughing to impress him.

Sitting across from Alice was Paul Logan, who lived on my street, only six houses down the block, and who had been my best friend all through elementary school. He was the only other boy I knew who shared my exact same interests: Monopoly; Stephen King books; reruns of *Three's Company* and *What's Happening*. And he was the only other boy I knew who didn't care about any of the things our male classmates most cherished, like sports and cars and running toy trucks through large mounds of dirt. We had drifted apart since starting junior high school, but I still counted him as a friend. And I had assumed the feeling was mutual.

Except now Paul Logan had his head in his hands, *almost* as if he didn't want me to see him laughing. But he was snorting so loudly that I couldn't not hear him. He wanted me and everyone around us to understand his message clearly: He was embarrassed that he had let our friendship carry on for so long, but he would never again have anything to do with me.

I tried to focus on *A Midsummer Night's Dream*. I tried to ignore their laughter.

The bell will ring. This will pass. Terrence will forget about you entirely.

But I slipped. Thinking I could cast a quick glance in Terrence's direction without him seeing me, I looked up. He was staring right back at me.

"Yes, gaywad," he said. "We're talking about you."

And then, in the same contrived tone of voice with which he would terrorize Dana Rogers each morning, sounding almost like a guileless little boy asking his parents where babies come from, he asked me: "Why are you always checking me out?"

I stared at him blankly. I turned away and buried my head in my book. I sat there, listening to the peals of laughter surrounding me, my ears and face burning red.

I tried to think of a comeback. Something fierce and authoritative; something worthy of Terrence O'Connell; something
that would shut him up in an instant.

But I couldn't think of anything. I was struck dumb.

I couldn't think of anything to say but this: *Who told you? How
did you know?*

How did you find out that I am in love with you?

The house was empty when I arrived home from school that
day, as was usually the case on weekdays. My father, who delivered Michelob beer to restaurants and liquor stores all
throughout Staten Island and Brooklyn, didn't get off work until 5:30 P.M. My mother, who did not drive and depended on
the city bus to get to and from her job at a jewelry store, usually
didn't get home until an hour after that. My brother, over the
last year or so, seemed to arrive home later and later each
night, often missing dinner altogether, never bothering to explain where he had been.

As I did every weekday, I double-checked to make certain no
one was around. Then I immediately retreated to my bedroom,
the room that used to belong to my sister. Then, after closing
the door and slipping the hook lock into the tiny metal eyelet,
I began my daily ritual, the same ritual I had repeated every afternoon for the past eight months, ever since the first day of
the seventh grade.

It went like this: I took off all my clothes. I retrieved the jar
of Vaseline that I kept hidden at the back of my dresser drawer,
and I swirled a small dollop of the jelly inside the palm of my
hand. I lay down on my bed, and I took my penis in my hand. I
closed my eyes, and I cycled through my mind the faces of a
half-dozen boys in my class. I imagined these boys on top of
me, kissing me, pressing their erect penises against mine. Seth
Kern, Evan Sutton, James Lester. And Terrence O'Connell. Especially Terrence O'Connell.

I tried not to go too fast. I tried not to squeeze too hard.

Anything to slow things down. Even still, I rarely lasted very long, three or four minutes at the most. Today, with Terrence weighing so heavily on my mind, I barely lasted ninety seconds.

On most school days, I masturbated at 3:30 P.M. and again at 5:00 P.M.—I didn't consider the day a success unless I could work in two sessions before dinner. But on this afternoon my parents didn't arrive home at their regular time. Danny was nowhere to be seen, either. 5:30 P.M. passed, and then 6:00 P.M. and then 6:30 P.M.—and still no one. I decided to take advantage of the solitude. I masturbated again at 7:00 P.M., in the bathroom, with my pants around my ankles, keeping one ear close to the door, in case someone arrived home and I would have to abort mid-session. An hour later, with still no one home, still unable to get Terrence out of my head, I masturbated for the fourth time, tying my previous weekday record. Where was everyone? Had my parents told me they were going to be late? Had they left a note that I had failed to encounter? I didn't think so, but I couldn't be certain. Terrence had clouded all of my thoughts that day. He was the only thing I seemed capable of concentrating on.

It wasn't until 9:00 P.M., just as I was finishing my homework, just as I was thinking I would reward myself by masturbating for a fifth time, that I heard a car door slam shut. I looked out the living room windows, down onto the driveway below, where my father's car was now idling. I could see my mother in the passenger seat. I watched as my father got out of the car and entered the house. I assumed Danny was in the back seat; that they had just retrieved him from some sort of school function, and now we were all going to go out to dinner.

My father appeared at the top of the steps. "Get your jacket, Ben, we're sorry we're late," he said, on his way to the bathroom. He was back in the living room, his hands still wet from washing, before I had even moved from my spot at the window. "Come on, Ben, we're starving."

When I got into the car, I saw that Danny wasn't there. I waited for an explanation: Was he still at school for some reason? Were we on our way to pick him up before we went to the restaurant? We drove for a mile. No explanation was forthcoming. We pulled into the parking lot of the restaurant. Still nothing. We entered the Golden Dove diner and requested a table for three. I realized they weren't going to tell me.

"Where's Danny?" I finally asked, once the waitress had taken our order.

No one said a thing.

I had grown accustomed to this brand of silence in our house—over the last few years, it had become our primary means of communication. Three months after my sister's death, my mother returned to work, selling cheap jewelry to the Irish-American boys in Staten Island trying to impress their Italian-American girlfriends, just as my father had once tried to impress her. She came home each night and barked at the first person she saw, complaining that the house was a mess. Then she would silently endure whatever dinner my father had managed to cobble together and later retreat to the living room couch, where she fell asleep each night, after a couple of hours spent flipping through catalogues that advertised clothing and furniture we could never have afforded. My father, meanwhile, had taken to the television—reruns of *Hawaii Five-O* or *Quincy*, or whatever sporting event was being broadcast on Channel 9. Prior to my sister's death, he would sit at the dinner table and recount to us the mundane tales of his workday: *Gene said such-and-such to Larry, who got mad at Tony, who is planning a vacation to Florida,* hardly concerned that the rest of us weren't actually listening, or that, at least twice a week, my sister would interrupt him mid-sentence and tell him, "Dad, your work stories are boring." But lately he didn't say anything at dinner, unless he was answering one of my mother's terse, disapproving questions: Had he paid the credit card bill? Had he picked up the dry cleaning? When was he going to get to the store and buy the roast beef, it wasn't going to be on sale forever? He gave one or two word answers, almost always in the tone of an apology: *Yes. No. I'll do it first thing in the morning.*

"Where's Danny?" I repeated, louder this time. "Is everything OK?"

My mother took a deep breath and slowly exhaled. This was the sound she made when she discovered a baseball cap on the couch or a set of schoolbooks left sprawled out on the dining room table. I girded myself for one of her tirades.

But when she spoke she didn't sound angry. She sounded resigned to her very core—as if she had grown so tired of picking up my stray baseball caps or cleaning up messes of school books that she couldn't bear to raise her voice to me even once more. I felt a sudden surge of guilt. Was I responsible for this? Had something I said or done dampened the sparks of rage still burning inside of her? Had I taken from her the only emotions she was still capable of expressing?

"Your brother ran away today," she said finally. "I got a call at work from his school telling me that he didn't show up. When I went home on my lunch break, I found a note from him saying that he ran away."

This didn't make much sense to me. He had *run away*—and yet we were just sitting here in a diner, waiting for our food? Besides, since when did Danny's school call my mother at work when he didn't show up? There were three thousand kids in that school. They could never keep such close tabs on them all.

"Shouldn't we be out looking for him?" I asked.

My mother turned her head and stared out the window. She shook her head, making it clear that she had said all she was going to say on this subject.

"We know where he is, he didn't get very far," my father answered, speaking very softly and haltingly. "He was having some trouble at school. We didn't realize how serious it was."

"Is he on Staten Island? Where is he? I can't believe he ran away. That's nuts."

"We don't think he meant to do it," my father said. "He was just looking for attention."

"He got it," my mother added coolly, still looking out the window.

"Why did he run away?" I asked. "What did the note say?"

"Ben, it's been a long day for us," my father said. "Please, let's talk about something else."

But aside from thanking the waitress when she brought our food, and my father asking her for the check, the rest of the dinner passed in silence. We drove home in more silence. My parents retreated to their bedroom, and I retreated to mine, in still more silence. For the next hour, I lay on my bed, staring at the ceiling, wondering where my brother had run off to, and feeling fiercely jealous of him—part of me wished that I could have had the courage to do the same. Finally, after watching the 11:00 P.M. news and reruns of *Barney Miller* and *Good Times,* still too restless for sleep, I got up and locked the door and masturbated once again, my fifth time today, a new record for me, weekday or otherwise. I masturbated thinking about Seth Kern and Evan Sutton and James Lester. And Terrence O'Connell. Especially Terrence O'Connell.

On the second day of my brother's exile, my parents arrived home a little after 8:00 P.M., my father carrying a pizza box. Before I could even ask, he said to me: "Danny is doing fine. He'll be back home at the end of the week."

My mother took a slice of pizza and retreated to the living room. I sat down at the kitchen table. My father, who looked as if he wanted to escape to his bedroom, hesitantly sat down across from me. I knew they were lying to me; that this story couldn't possibly be the whole truth. Inevitably, I wondered if Danny's exile would be like my sister's; if I would be told that everything was fine, and that he was coming home soon, until one day I was told otherwise—that there had been an unforeseen complication, and he would never be coming home again.

"Did you go to work or were you with Danny all day?" I asked.

He shook his head and knitted his brow, as if I had just spoken to him in a foreign tongue he did not recognize. "What did you do in school today?" he replied.

I sat there quietly for a minute, feeling the resentment start-ing to bubble up inside of me. I thought of startling my father with something cruel and mocking, maybe something like: *Is Danny actually still alive, or did you kill him, and now you're spend-ing your days covering up his murder?* But then I stopped myself. I decided, instead, that I would play along—that my only real choice here was to play along. Because they were never going to tell me, no matter how many different ways I posed the same question.

So I answered my father's question. I told him what had hap-pened in school that day.

I told him about the two tests that I had scored in the upper 90s on, in math and in French. I told him about the trip to the Metropolitan Museum of Art that our teacher was planning for mid-May, and for which I would need ten dollars by the follow-ing Wednesday. I told him about the John Steinbeck novel we were going to be reading after we finished *A Midsummer Night's Dream,* even though I wasn't sure my father even knew who John Steinbeck was. I talked through mouthfuls of half-masti-cated cheese and pepperoni, telling him everything that had happened in school that I could remember. I kept on talking, even though I couldn't tell if he was paying attention. I kept on talking because, with Danny now out of the picture, there was no one to fill up this silence but me.

Of course, I left a few relevant details out of the narrative of my day.

For instance, I didn't tell him that I had been called "gay-wad" by five different people, including Terrence O'Connell. Or that I had been called "faggot" by four different people, in-cluding Terrence O'Connell.

And I didn't tell him about what happened in Ms. Buckley's home economics class, sixth period that day. How I was sitting there quietly, minding my own business; and how she was talk-ing to us about the upcoming Career Day, just five weeks away, and telling us that we should think about what jobs we might like to learn more about, because then she could try to find people who actually had those jobs and get them to come to school and speak to us.

And how Seth Kern—a popular boy who was friendly with Terrence, though not part of his immediate circle—waited for Ms. Buckley to finish talking, and then calmly and politely raised his hand and asked, "Do you know any gay rights leaders who can come? Because that's what Ben Reilly wants to be."

And how the entire class—twenty-six boys and girls—broke out in laughter, as I stared down at my notebook, tiny beads of sweat forming on my forehead, while I waited for what seemed like hours for Ms. Buckley to get the class back under her control.

And how Ms. Buckley never punished Seth Kern, never chided him for his disruption, didn't even force him to apologize. How she went on with her lesson as if Seth Kern had done nothing objectionable at all.

These relevant details I left out of the narrative of my day.

On the third day of my brother's exile, I went snooping.

This was hardly the first time. The snooping, in fact, had been going on for many years, probably since around the time of Mary's death. Whenever I found myself home alone, if only for ten or fifteen minutes, I would retreat into my mother's long and narrow walk-in closet, with its heavy air that smelled of mothballs and cardboard and Estée Lauder perfume. I would tread very slowly and carefully, making my way to the farthest end of the closet, running my fingers across the dresses and blouses as I went along. I would stand on my toes and, with both arms held high above my head, bring down the boxes that rested on the upper shelves—hat boxes, shoe boxes, department store gift boxes—dozens upon dozens of boxes seemed to be stacked on those shelves. Then I would sit down on the purple-carpeted floor, and I would open those boxes, one after another. Some of them were Christmas presents that had been unwrapped but never used. Some of them were filled with nothing other than crumpled-up tissue paper or Styrofoam packing peanuts. The majority of them were empty entirely, waiting to be recycled come the next Christmas or birthday. I would only stay inside the closet for a few minutes. I would open up a half-dozen boxes, before I would start to panic that someone was going to catch me. But I always returned, usually a week or two later. I had no expectations of what I might find—there certainly wasn't anything I was consciously looking for. I never even considered the possibility that I *shouldn't* be doing it, that the snooping might lead to darker places, into an adulthood where I lurked in shadowy corners and fetishized my own secrets. For me, the snooping was more like any casually abused drug: I did it because I could; the more I took in, the more I thought I could take. After a while, I had no idea why I had gotten hooked in the first place.

As I got older, ten minutes inside my parents' bedroom became twenty, and then thirty, and then an hour or maybe two—snatched away while they were at a neighbor's house or still at work; at an open-school night or at the home improvement store picking out wallpaper for the bathroom remodeling. By age eleven—the pangs of desire for other boys becoming increasingly impossible to ignore, the shame insistent and all-consuming—I started searching for evidence of my parents' sexual lives. It wasn't very hard to find. Tucked away in the farthest reaches of the top drawer of my mother's bureau, tangled inside a mass of cream-colored bras and panties, were a vibrator and a dildo. In my father's sock drawer were two boxes of condoms, with each condom individually packaged inside a tiny blue plastic capsule. And, in a shoe box in the bottom compartment of my father's night table, hidden beneath two thick binders of employee benefits information from his job, was a collection of porn magazines.

At first I didn't disturb what I found. I only observed. I was an anthropologist, I told myself, and I would not upset this ecosystem. That changed too. The previous August, a few weeks before the start of the seventh grade, a few weeks after I

first figured out how to masturbate, I took two of the magazines in my father's shoe box and spirited them into my bedroom. The pictures of the naked girls didn't interest me. But in
some of the magazines there were layouts featuring a man and
a woman—usually a woman on her knees, gripping the man's
balls in one hand, holding his erect penis to her mouth with
the other. There were also short stories about handsome and
athletic men who have anonymous encounters with busty,
beautiful women. I would read these stories three or four
times, savoring the most phallocentric passages: the narrator
getting his cock sucked, or his balls licked, or shooting a load
of his semen into his girlfriend's twin sister's mouth. I would
come reading the words of these stories, imagining myself in
between the narrator's legs, his hands on my head, my mouth
on his penis, sucking.

As the weeks passed, I got bolder. I decided I wanted to
know what it would feel like to ejaculate inside of a condom—
so, after three weeks of almost daily snooping, carefully in-
specting my father's sock drawer, waiting for him to replenish
his dwindling supply, I stole one of his condoms, took it out of
its blue plastic capsule, and struggled to slide it down onto my
penis. It tore after a minute of masturbating. My hand smelled
of rubber for the next two days.

The following week, I took my mother's dildo and washed it
in hot water, and then I took off my clothes and held the dildo
in my left hand and pressed it up against my anus while I
jerked off. I came within fifteen seconds, faster and harder
than I had ever come before.

But mostly it was the magazines that compelled me. There
were more than a dozen of them in my father's collection,
some of which dated back to the mid-1970s. In one of the magazines, there were pictures of two women peeing into a giant
bronze urn and then pouring the urine onto each other's bodies. Another magazine had a layout of a skinny Asian woman
methodically demonstrating how she shaved her pubic hair.
Still another had a naked woman splattered in enormous

quantities of spaghetti and meat balls, the bright red pasta sauce covering almost every inch of naked flesh, making it look like a scene out of a slasher movie. I revisited these magazines once or twice a week. I committed dozens of these pictorials to memory. I reasoned that, since I had discovered them through my own ingenuity, searching every last corner of my parents' bedroom to find them, that I had earned the right to look at them as often as I pleased.

As I opened up the shoe box that day, the third day of my brother's exile, I saw that the magazines were stacked differently from the last time I had looked at them. There was an issue of *Club* at the top, a new one that I had never seen before. A blonde-haired girl with enormous breasts beckoned from the cover. She was holding a giant red-and-white candy cane in one hand. In bright green type, just above her right shoulder, were the words: "Sweet and Sticky."

I grabbed the issue of *Club* and a few of the other magazines stacked beneath it. I fanned them all out on my parents' bed, and I crouched down next to the bed on my knees. Usually I didn't take such care in choosing the right magazines to bring back to my bedroom—I would just grab the two or three magazines that were atop the stack and make a run for it. But today I had no worries of my parents catching me. They had told me that morning that they wouldn't be home until after 9:00 P.M.

On any other day, I wouldn't have even noticed. I wouldn't have seen that, tucked inside one of the magazines, was a set of pages torn from another magazine.

On any other day, I wouldn't have paid any attention to this particular magazine, which I had flipped through a number of times before. It was called *Swank,* and none of the layouts included any pictures of men. It was also the oldest magazine in my father's collection, and I was always afraid that I would tear its brittle, yellowing pages and leave behind evidence of my trespassing.

On any other day, I would have left this magazine behind.

But today, because I could take my time, because I could

take as long as I pleased, I noticed. I was carefully studying the covers of each of the magazines in my father's collection, trying to pick just the right ones to suit my mood that day. And I saw that tucked inside this issue of *Swank* were pages from a completely different magazine—tucked inside the way you would slip a bookmark inside a book, or the way a teenage girl might place dried flowers inside her diary to commemorate the day of her first kiss.

I felt a rush of enthusiasm. What extraordinary good luck! Not only was there a new issue of *Club,* but there was also some sort of supplemental pornography hidden inside of *Swank,* a bonus. I withdrew the pages carefully, taking care to note exactly the place inside of *Swank* where my father had inserted them. I looked closely at these pages, a four-page layout that looked as if it had been pulled from the very center of another magazine. That's when my pulse began racing.

Who put these here? This can't possibly be for real.

On each of the four pages was a simple black-and-white portrait. The photographs seemed to have been taken in the same room, or at least two different rooms with the same drab off-white carpeting and dreary gray walls. At first glance, the model in all four of the portraits appeared to be the same person. But as I looked closer, I realized that there were two different models who happened to look very much alike: two sandy-haired, clean-cut, well-built young men, no older than twenty, naked but for their white tube socks.

My first thought was to slide these pictures back inside the copy of *Swank* and return the magazine to the shoe box and then never think about them again.

Put them away before the worst thing in the world happens. Put them away before someone comes home and catches you staring at these pictures with a hard-on.

But it was already too late for that. The moment I registered what I was looking at, it was too late to go back. The pictures had cast an immediate spell on me. I couldn't move from my crouched position beside the bed.

I tried to imagine a few possible scenarios to explain where these pictures might have come from. Maybe my father had stumbled upon them in another magazine, and he had brought them home to show my mother, perhaps as a gesture of good will, something to add seasoning to their increasingly flavorless marriage. Or maybe someone had given these photos to my mother, a single girlfriend from her job who subscribed to *Playgirl* or one of the magazines like it; maybe this woman had passed along these pictures to my mother because she thought she would get a laugh out of them, and maybe my mother had given them to my father, and then told him to file them away. Maybe it was as simple as that.

Except these explanations didn't make any sense, and I knew it. Husbands didn't entice their wives back into the bedroom with pictures of naked young men. Coworkers at jewelry stores didn't pass along pornography to one another during their lunch breaks. These pictures had to belong to my father. They were in *his* shoebox, in *his* night table, in *his* collection of pornography.

But once I answered that question, I was left with many more: Where had he found them? From what other magazine had the pictures come, and why was my father reading *that* magazine? Did my father get turned on by looking at naked young men? Had he ever been with a man? And what about my mother? I assumed that she knew about my father's pornography, but did she know that these pictures were also a part of his collection? Or would she be horrified to find out about them? Would she be so sickened that she would immediately file for divorce?

Question after question after question. Until I realized, after a couple of minutes of staring at these pictures, an erection burning and throbbing inside my underwear, that none of these questions mattered. Much like the questions surrounding my brother's disappearance, none of these questions would ever be answered. There was no use even wondering. Much more important was the fact that these pictures existed—that they were here, buried inside my father's night table, waiting for me to discover them. Waiting for *me*. I had certainly seen pictures of naked men before, in the layouts in my father's magazines. But these were the first pictures I had ever seen where it was *just* a naked man—where the man's private parts were the center of the camera's attention. These were the first naked pictures I had encountered that were intended expressly for my consumption; the first pictures that made me realize that I wasn't the only boy in the world who liked other boys.

My father could not have known that he had left behind for me to discover the greatest gift of my adolescence.

I returned all of the other magazines to the shoe box, and I put the shoe box back in its place in my father's night table. I tucked the loose pages into the copy of *Swank,* and then I took the copy of *Swank* to my bedroom. For the next two and a half hours, I stared at those four pictures, absorbing every last detail of the models' bodies: their muscular, hairless chests; their skinny, flat stomachs; their shadowy, smooth inner thighs; the arch of their erect penises. I came four times in three hours before returning the pictures to their hiding place. But I knew that I would be borrowing them again. I knew that, in the days and weeks and months and years to come, they would never be out of my possession for very long. My father had given me this gift.

On the fourth day of my brother's exile, I was called "gaywad" ten times, "cocksucker" four times, and "faggot" seven times. In English class, Terrence interrupted my note-taking to write on my notebook, in huge block letters with a red Sharpie, the word "HOMO." Just before class ended, he leaned over and whispered to me: "I hate you, you fucking faggot, you are going to get AIDS and die."

That evening, after I borrowed my father's pictures and jerked off to them three more times, my brother returned home, trailing just behind my parents as they came up the stairs a little after 7:00 P.M. We went to the Golden Dove diner, for the second time in a week. My father talked for a few minutes about the start of the baseball season, and how he thought the Mets might have a shot at the World Series this year. He made a promise that we all knew he would not keep, to take us to see a baseball game as soon as school let out for the summer. And then the table went silent. For the next forty-five minutes, until the waitress brought the check, the only sounds were the sounds of silverware scraping against plates and the four of us chewing. No one made mention of the word *gaywad;* of the name Terrence O'Connell; of the pictures of naked men hidden away in a shoe box in my father's night table.

Or of the fact that my brother had run away to some undisclosed location, and, for the last four days, stayed there.

chapter three

Indiana
(2000)

"I have something to tell everyone." It was Sunday afternoon, five days after Mario had shoved Elliot down the stairs at school. I was sitting at my parents' dining room table, with my father and mother, and Danny and his wife, Megan. Everyone looked up from their now-empty plates with the same beleaguered, tinged-green expressions on their faces. I wondered if they all thought that I was about to come out of the closet to them.

"I've left my job," I hastened to add.

"What do you mean you *left?*" my mother asked.

"I asked for a leave of absence," I said.

"What are you going do to for money?" she asked, sounding like the prosecutor on a television legal drama, quietly out-raged, barely able to contain her disdain.

"Aren't you even going to ask me *why* I left?"

My mother stared at me across the table and then shook her head to dismiss me. She stood up and started clearing the plates from the table, carrying them into the kitchen.

"I'll play along," Danny chimed in. "Why did you quit your job?"

My brother Danny: In the fourteen years since his exile, he had steadily emerged as the glue holding all of our family's broken pieces together. He would regularly run errands for my mother, even though she never asked for his help. Almost every night, he would call my father and pepper him with questions about baseball trades or the football playoffs or whatever other professional sport happened to be in season. Around the dinner table, he was our clown, eager to entertain us with stories about his ongoing battles with his next-door neighbor and the neighbor's noisy dog. Even these Sunday dinners were usually at his insistence. He would invite himself over, and then call me up and insist that I tag along.

"I decided that I needed to take some time off," I told him now, grateful for at least his audience of one. "I was afraid that I was getting stuck on a teaching track, and that soon it would be too late to make a change."

"And this couldn't wait until June? You just walk out on the kids?" my mother asked, back from the kitchen, gathering in her arms a new set of dirty dishes.

"I just couldn't keep going there," I said. "That fight between those two boys, it shook me up. These kids today have all of this rage, and I feel like I don't know how to help them." I was being honest with them. Or at least as honest as I could be without also mentioning the name Terrence O'Connell.

"You aren't supposed to be their psychologist," my sister-in-law offered, in her trying-to-be-helpful voice. "There are people at the school for that, aren't there?"

"But if you can't understand what they're going through, how can you teach them anything?" I answered.

My father looked down at his hands, tapped his fingers against the table, and said nothing.

My mother, from the kitchen: "Just don't let me hear you crying in six months that you can't find a new job."

My brother drove me home a few hours later, going out of his way to drop Megan off first, telling me an implausible-sounding story about how she had to get home in order to make an important phone call for her job. I thought of making up my own story, telling him to drop me off at a movie theater where I was scheduled to meet Meredith—anything to avoid being alone with him and having him interrogate me on my mother's behalf. But I decided that I should just listen to what he had to say. He had been decent enough, during dinner, to hear me out. I figured I owed him at least that much in return.

"I think it's good that you're taking a break," he said, as soon as Megan got out of the car. "You shouldn't have to suffer at a job that makes you miserable. And, honestly, you've just seemed miserable for the last two years."

"I don't know if I'd say that," I answered sharply.

He said, "Well, I don't know, Ben. It's just that sometimes you just don't seem as *engaged* as you used to. Is that the right word? You don't seem all there. Not that I'm saying you've been abducted by aliens or anything"—he paused here and let out a nervous chuckle—"but you always seem so bored. Like you're just going through the motions."

I wasn't accustomed to Danny speaking to me so directly, without any of his usual glib defenses. I was surprised, too, that this was the way he viewed me. Had it been so obvious to everyone? Was I the last person on the planet to realize that I had fallen into an awful rut?

"Going through the motions," I parroted back, not knowing what else to say.

We drove a few blocks in silence. I assumed that was the end of it. We had never been especially close, even before my sister died; and we had certainly never had conversations like this one, where we openly discussed our feelings.

But just as I allowed myself to relax, he started up again: "Are you depressed, Ben? Do you think maybe seeing a therapist might help?"

"Depression is a big word," I said. *Enough of this, Danny. Just let it drop now.*

"It's nothing to be ashamed about," he answered. "Therapists can help you sort through things, figure stuff out. No shame, man."

Stop. Please stop this. Just let me go and find Terrence O'Connell, and then, in a couple of month's time, I'll be normal again.

"Or maybe you should do some traveling," he continued. "Clear your head a bit."

"Actually, I've been thinking about going to Indianapolis," I said, eager to change the topic.

"What's in Indianapolis?"

"Someone I know. A person I used to go to school with. An old—" I hesitated for a second before I said—"an old friend."

He didn't respond for at least thirty seconds. I looked toward him. His eyes were narrowed; his brow was furrowed; his mouth was twisted into a crooked grimace. He looked like a contestant on *Jeopardy* trying to puzzle out an impossible final clue.

And—who knows—maybe if he had come up with a perfectly formulated next question, then it might have ended right there.

Maybe if he had just said, *Is this a boyfriend?*, or perhaps just, *Is there something you want to tell me, Ben?*—well, then maybe I would have cancelled my plane ticket and forgotten about Terrence and gone and begged Barry Marcus for my job back. Maybe I would have figured out a much less self-destructive way to get on with my life.

But he didn't. We had drawn too close. This time he really did let it drop.

"Wasn't Indianapolis where they filmed that show *One Day at a Time?*" he asked, cheerful and clownish all over again. "Maybe you'll run into the guy who played Schneider."

The following Thursday afternoon, I stepped onto a Continental Airlines 757 at the Newark International Airport, bound for Indianapolis. The airplane was barely half-full. The flight lasted just ninety minutes. We landed a little after 4:00 P.M. I made my way to the Avis counter, where I rented a car and asked for directions to the O'Connells' house. The rental agent handed me a map and a set of directions printed from a Web site. He told me that it wouldn't take more than twenty minutes to get there, even in rush hour traffic.

The O'Connells' neighborhood was just a few miles west of downtown—the sort of old neighborhood in a mid-sized city that probably had gone derelict decades earlier, after its original occupants moved farther and farther into the outlying suburbs, until new money brought things back to life, probably sometime in the early 1980s. *Lots* of new money. The houses were set up on low hills, far off the street. The expansive, neatly mowed front lawns were dotted with ancient-looking trees that reached far into the sky. The driveways seemed to have a disproportionate number of Audis, BMWs, and Mercedes parked in them. I immediately started to worry that I had made a spectacular error. There was no way a truck driver could possibly afford to live in such a neighborhood.

After driving past it on my first try, I circled back and found the O'Connells' house. It was a brown-brick, two-story saltbox, with a long driveway that came up off the street, extended across the front of the house, and then continued around the side to the garage and the backyard. The lawn was bright green and freshly watered. Beds of newly planted petunias, in shades of pink and violet, lined the driveway. I considered the possibility that I had the wrong address, or the wrong O'Connells, or that I was in the wrong state altogether (for some reason, I had always thought that Terrence had moved to Ohio after junior year of high school). But I brushed these fears aside. There had to be a simple explanation for all of this. Perhaps Thomas had gotten lucky and remarried into money. Or maybe he had hit the lottery; maybe that was the reason he had moved to Indiana in the first place. After squeezing the entire O'Connell brood into a too-small house in Staten Island, with at least two boys to each bedroom, he wanted a house and a city where they could all spread out.

There were no cars in the driveway and no lights on in the front rooms. I decided to keep on driving. I found a Radisson and checked myself in. I ate dinner at a Chili's across the street from the hotel. At every turn, I was acutely conscious of the fact that Terrence O'Connell could suddenly appear: in the car next to mine, stopped at the streetlight; in the lobby of the hotel, waiting for an early-evening business meeting to commence; at a table across the room in the restaurant, ordering a hamburger and cheese fries. When I thought about finding Terrence, I imagined it taking much more time: a week or two at least, maybe many months. I thought of it as an epic odyssey, a story that could be told and retold to future generations. A *quest*.

But what if this all turned out to be very simple? What if his father handed me the address of an apartment building located just a few miles from here? What if, by tomorrow at lunchtime, I was standing outside his office building, waiting for him to meet with me? I had let momentum carry me this far, all the way onto an airplane and to Indiana, just moving forward, never second-guessing my decisions. But did I even know what I would say to him? Did I have any idea what I wanted from him?

When I got back to the O'Connells' house, I saw two sedans in the driveway, a Volkswagen and a Volvo, both of which couldn't have been more than two years old. I parked on the street and walked up the long driveway. A dog immediately started barking from inside. I saw a silhouetted figure moving around, standing up and suspiciously peering out the window to see what the dog was barking at.

I hesitated for a moment. What if, instead of going very smoothly, it all went terribly awry? What if Mr. O'Connell ended up involving the police?

But before I could even consider turning around, a porch light came on, and the front door opened a crack.

"Can we help you tonight?" a large man with a full head of white hair asked me.

"Hi, Mr. O'Connell," I said, stopping far enough away from the door so that he wouldn't think I was trying to bust in. "I hope you're Mr. O'Connell. I know your son Terrence. We went to high school together in Staten Island. Junior high school, too. My name is Ben. Benjamin Reilly." I took two awkward baby steps forward.

The door opened a little wider, enough so that I could see his face and maybe a third of his body. He had the brawn of an aging cornerback, a barrel chest, and a substantial but solid gut. He was exceptionally tall, at least a half-foot taller than me. He was still wearing his work clothes, pale blue shirtsleeves and navy suit pants. His rigid posture and nonplused expression suggested a man who was hard to please; a man used to being in charge of things; a man who probably had a cadre of assistants and secretaries to make certain that this very thing didn't happen, that visitors didn't just show up on his doorstep unannounced. Whatever he did for a living, this man most certainly did not drive a truck.

"Is everything OK with Terrence?" he asked, his voice cool and indifferent. He knew perfectly well that everything was OK with Terrence. He had probably just spoken to Terrence on the telephone a few hours earlier.

"I actually haven't talked to Terrence since high school," I told him. "Since he moved away. That's why I'm here. I'm working on a project—a documentary film project—tracking down my former classmates, finding out what's become of them." I had practiced this speech for days, intending to deliver it to a truck driver, hoping to awe him with something so intellectual-sounding. But it worked just as well, even better I decided, with a businessman in a suit—a hardworking executive who would surely appreciate the efforts of an ambitious self-starter.

He went on eyeballing me, waiting for more information. "I'm a student," I offered. "This is my dissertation project. I'm a film student at NYU." This part, too, I had scripted. I thought it would give my story more legitimacy to put a fancy university name on it.

He raised his eyebrows and nodded. He opened the door wider. I saw his wife hovering in the background, near an enormous, floor-to-ceiling mirror that hung just inside the door. She was holding a golden retriever by its collar.

"Marta," Mr. O'Connell said, turning around to her, "this is

Benjamin, an old classmate of Terrence's, from Staten Island."
And just like that he welcomed me inside their house.

I stepped into the small, shallow foyer. To the immediate left
was a staircase; to the far left was the living room; and to the
right was a corridor into which Marta disappeared with the
dog. I quickly looked around, taking in as much as I could
from my limited vantage point. The decor suggested the brand
of understatement which only vast sums of money can buy:
large and solid wood furniture; two small Tiffany table lamps
resting on an end table just inside the door; oak floors, pol-
ished and shining like the teeth on a toothpaste commercial,
covered by what I thought looked like authentic Persian rugs.
Definitely, definitely, *definitely* not the house of a truck driver.

Mr. O'Connell gestured for me to follow him into the living
room. The first thing I noticed was a painting hanging on the
far wall, a huge abstract, perhaps eight feet by six, some sort of
cross pollination of Pollock and Rothko, with streams of candy-
colored squiggles that flowed together and formed square
blocks of nearly blinding brightness. Mr. O'Connell saw me
looking at it, and he immediately began beaming.

"It's certainly something, isn't it?" he said, leading me closer
to the painting. "Terrence's older brother Jay painted it. Do
you like it? It's a little too bright for me." He laughed and
tapped his fingers against his chest, ready to tell me a story he
had no doubt told dozens of times before.

"When he was still at art school, he'd bring all these paintings back home. And we'd hang them on the wall and cringe
whenever we walked past them. It became a running joke between me and my wife and Terrence: Which room was Jay going to ruin next with one of his paintings. Shows you how
much we know. This one has been on 'consignment'"—he
made quote marks in the air with his fingers—"to us. He just
asked for it back, because he says someone is willing to pay him
$20,000 for it."

He paused and added: "Marta refuses to part with it." And
just then, like the star of the play making her entrance from

stage right, Marta appeared in the living room, carrying a tray with a bottle of red wine and three empty glasses.

"I'm trying to get him to just buy it from Jay, but he doesn't think we should have to pay for something we used to get for free," Marta said, her voice cold and brittle. "Sort of like how he forbids me to stock the refrigerator with bottled water." She did not laugh at her own joke.

I took a closer look at Marta, who was clearly not a second wife. She was only a few years younger than Mr. O'Connell; and her features—the dark blonde hair, the hint of a dimple in her left cheek—made it clear that she had given birth to Terrence. Nor was this woman—with her fierce set jaw, and her dry wit that, in an instant, could curdle into toxicity—the sort of woman who would have ever abandoned her family and run off with another man. This was the sort of woman who had made her bed, with its goose down pillows and its 400 thread count Egyptian cotton sheets, and now lay in it, if not contentedly, at least with her eyes wide open.

"Were you and Terrence friends in Staten Island?" she asked me, after she had poured the wine, and we had all sat down, Mr. O'Connell on the couch, Marta and I on matching dark red velvet armchairs across from him. "You have to forgive me if I'm wrong, but I don't remember you ever coming over to our house there."

"We weren't friends then," I told her. "That's the point of my project. I'm trying to track down five people I didn't know very well, but who I thought might do something interesting as adults. And I'm trying to see if my predictions match up to the reality. So far I've been totally wrong. One person I interviewed turned out to be a human resources manager in New Jersey. In high school, I thought he was going to be a rock star."

Marta nodded and looked impressed. "That sounds like an excellent idea for a documentary," she said.

"I'd like to think it's especially relevant now," I told them. "There's so much pressure on high school kids to succeed now. I think that pressure translates into a lot of frustration and violence." This part I had not rehearsed. This part I was making up as I went along.

"Terrence would probably be interested in a project like that," Mr. O'Connell said.

Marta added: "He mentioned a few weeks ago that he might try to go out to Colorado, and do some kind of one-year-later story on the Columbine shootings. I'm not sure if that's still happening, but I know it's been on his mind."

I stared at them, looking back and forth, very confused.

Marta, reading my mind, said: "He's a writer. You knew that, didn't you? He writes for a magazine in New York."

I tried to imagine what casual and indifferent curiosity looks like on one's face—when you have no emotional stake in the outcome; when you just want the other person to tell you more. I tried to make that expression. I'm sure Marta saw straight through me. She saw that inside of my chest a grenade of envy had just exploded, sending green shrapnel in every direction, tearing my guts to shreds.

"I don't know anything about what he's doing now," I answered. "All they told me at our old high school was that he went to Indiana University."

Marta looked at me, her expression severe but amused—her bright red lips pressed tightly together and curling upward at the edges, like the witch in a children's fairy tale still pretending to be gentle, just seconds before she will unleash her wickedness. She said, "He didn't go to Indiana University."

"Actually, Terrence went to Yale," Mr. O'Connell chimed in. "Both of my boys did. What made you think that he went to IU?"

Yale? *Terrence went to Yale.* Were we talking about the same Yale? The one to which I had applied, and from which I had been rejected? (And, wait a minute, weren't there supposed to be *six* O'Connell boys. What had happened to the rest of them?) Were we even talking about the same Terrence: the one who had been ranked eight slots lower than me on the honor roll? the one who turned in copied versions of everyone else's homework? the one who—after I once refused to let him copy off a math test—shouted at me, two periods later, across two lunch tables, "How many assholes did you lick over the weekend, gaywad?"

That Terrence O'Connell had leapfrogged right past me, straight into Yale?

"A secretary . . . at our old school . . . that was the information she had . . . from his file . . ." I was sputtering. I couldn't speak clearly.

"Well, he did that program with Indiana University his senior year," Marta said, standing up to pour more wine, quietly relishing this moment, the side-by-side comparison of her successful writer son and his old schoolmate, who just couldn't measure up. "They had a program that took a bunch of advanced placement kids up there for college prep."

"What does he write?" I asked. *Please, please, let it be for* Tiger Beat *or* YM *or the* Weekly Reader, *or some other magazine not read by anyone over the age of fourteen.*

"A little bit of everything at this point," Marta said. "After college, he moved to New York and started at the *Village Voice,* freelancing for them. Then they made him their television critic, which was something Thomas found especially galling. He wouldn't tell our friends. He thought it was trivial that our son should make a living watching television."

Mr. O'Connell laughed boisterously and nodded with pride. He had that captain-of-industry trait, where you own your misjudgments with arrogance and do not apologize for them. Terrence was very much a chip off this old block. *And this old block has never driven a truck. He's probably never even seen the inside of a truck.*

Marta continued: "And then he started freelancing for the *New York Times* and *Rolling Stone.* They would pay him absurd amounts of money to go and eat meals with movie stars and write about them. You might have read some of his work and not realized. He writes under the name T. R. O'Connell."

"He thinks it makes him sound more *literary,*" Mr. O'Connell jumped in, saying the word "literary" with an affected British accent. He was pretending to poke fun at Terrence, but I could tell he didn't really mean it. This was a man who boasted all the time, to anyone who would listen, about his two successful sons, the painter and the writer.

"He writes for *GQ* now," Marta went on. "They put him on staff two years ago. Though depending on how the novel turns out—his first novel is being published in November—he may give that up. He told me the proofs are circulating in Hollywood, and there are a couple of producers interested in optioning it. I'm not even sure I know what that means, but I think it's something good."

I nodded at her and tried to smile. *It's a crock,* I told myself. No one's life flowers so quickly after college. I was simply getting a highly subjective version of the truth. He had probably interned at the *Village Voice* and persuaded an editor to let him write a couple of short pieces. He had probably written for a section of the *New York Times* that no one reads, a story that got buried in the bowels of the real estate pages. At *GQ,* he was probably just an expendable cog in a vast editorial machine— the assistant to an associate to an assistant to the editor's third cousin. And the novel? Whatever. So what? *Anyone* can write a novel. But did he have a major publisher? A national advertising campaign behind him? As for this business about it "circulating in Hollywood"—well, isn't that what all first time novelists tell themselves, that a top producer is interested in optioning it? That Ridley Scott or Stephen Frears wants to direct and that Matt Damon or Tom Hanks is going to star?

A crock. Every word of it. The bluster of too-proud parents. *Don't let it get to you.*

I concentrated on my game face: a Cheshire cat grin; a polite forward nod; my eyes open in enthusiasm. "He lives in New York?" I asked.

"In the city, yes," Marta said. "We're very proud of him, as you can probably tell."

"You should be," I said, slipping up, sounding more petulant than I intended. I felt my cheeks go flush—from the wine, the envy, the embarrassment. So much for a game face.

"I know people had high expectations for him in high school, but it sounds as if he's gone above and beyond," I added, slipping up even more, this time sounding like a Stepford Wife. "Do you think he'd be willing to be interviewed for my documentary?"

"Oh, I think Terrence is sympathetic to fellow artists," Marta said, turning to her husband, smiling cryptically.

Mr. O'Connell grunted in response. Over the last minute or so, as Marta was gushing about Terrence, his expression had begun to sour. His face conveyed the dismay of an accountant used to his ledgers balancing—but now, here, as he counted over and over again, he was coming up a few pennies short. He couldn't figure out if this stranger whom he had invited into his house was a charlatan.

"Is there any way for you to put me in touch with him?" I ventured hesitantly.

"Oh, I don't think that would be a problem," Marta began.

Mr. O'Connell cut her off. "Well, I don't think it would be appropriate to give you Terrence's number, not before checking—"

"You can always just contact him at the magazine," Marta interrupted, standing up to collect the half-empty wine bottle and take it back to the kitchen. "Just call the main number at *GQ* and they'll connect you."

"Marta, I think it's better if we talk to Terrence first, and let him know that Benjamin wants to speak to him." Marta had disappeared from the room before he could even finish his sentence. He turned to me and said: "Why don't you let us know where Terrence can reach you? We'll call him tomorrow and pass along your information."

"That would be great," I said. "I'm going to be at the Radisson hotel downtown until Sunday."

I stood up and shook his hand and then I followed him to the front hall. "One last question, Mr. O'Connell," I said, as he opened the door for me to leave. "Were you ever a truck driver?"

He furrowed his brow and squinted at me. "No, I'm an attorney," he said. "Corporate counsel for an office supply company."

"That's so weird," I said. "The kids in school used to say that Terrence's father was a truck driver and that his mother had abandoned the family."

Mr. O'Connell frowned at me. He was opening his mouth to say something when Marta suddenly reappeared. She reached for my hand and shook it.

"It was really lovely meeting you, Benjamin," she said. "We'll call Terrence tomorrow—or maybe tonight, it's still early—and let him know that you're looking for him."

If Mr. O'Connell saw the slip of paper being passed into the palm of my hand, he said nothing. Propriety dictated that he would wait until I left before he tore into Marta. Or maybe he didn't notice at all. He seemed too flummoxed by the thought of his life as a truck driver to be paying careful attention to anything.

I thanked them both again. They watched from the door as I made my way down the driveway and got into the rental car and drove away. I was halfway back to the hotel before I turned on the interior light in the car and opened up the scrap of paper Marta had given to me.

There were two phone numbers, printed very neatly in green ink, one marked "home" and the other "work." Below the numbers were two words: "Good luck."

From the outside, it looked like a concrete mausoleum—a windowless, square-shaped box, dropped onto an underlit street corner, in an otherwise decaying neighborhood of boarded-up buildings and crumbling one-family houses. I drove past it three times, around the block and back again, peering out the car window, trying to do the math: Were there enough cars in the parking lot so that there would be enough bodies inside?

So that I could disappear in the crowd and wander around un-remarked upon? So that I wouldn't be trapped at an empty bar, forced to make conservation with a pockmarked old man with a scraggly mustache and a gut that billowed over the waist of his too-tight jeans?

It was Friday night, nearly midnight, but was that late enough? Was it safe to go inside?

This was all very alien to me, this world of gay bars. It's not that I had ever consciously given up on going to them or think-ing of them as a place where I might meet other guys. It's more that I had never really tried. At Wesleyan, there was only one gay bar within twenty miles of the university, and it was ru-mored to be a dank, crumbling place, where sixty-year-old weirdos preyed on college boys foolish enough to walk in there alone. And in the months after graduation, when I was still liv-ing at home, going to a gay club in Manhattan just seemed out-side the realm of possibility: Was I supposed to ask a guy back to my parents' house in Staten Island? Stay out all night and then invent a story the next morning about where I had been? Even after I moved into my apartment, well, it just seemed so much of a chore; so much more effort than it was worth. I went out a few times during my first year of teaching. I would shower and shave and carefully style my hair and get dressed up. I would make the long commute into Manhattan. And then . . . I would cower in a corner, too shy to strike up a conversation with anyone. I was always so anxious that I might run into someone I knew; or that—God forbid—I might run into one of my students. So I would drink to try to calm myself down, three or four beers in rapid succession. But that didn't work, either. My brain would be working overtime, carrying on an endless, rapid-fire monologue—*what am I doing here? why would anyone want to sleep with me, I'm not rich and I don't have big muscles and a bald spot is beginning to expand around my scalp*—making it almost impossible for me to get drunk. And after a couple of hours of this, feeling exhausted and bored and frustrated, the only thing I could think to do was go home.

But here, in Indiana, I decided I needed to experiment. I had nothing to do until Sunday, when I would fly back to New York and continue my hunt for Terrence. I had already pin-pointed Terrence's whereabouts; I had accomplished what I had come to Indiana to accomplish. In which case, I could consider the rest of my weekend like a vacation.

And what are vacations for, if not to indulge in the things that you can't indulge in at home?

After driving around the block a few more times, I finally pulled into the parking lot. It was an expanse of errant gravel and cavernous potholes. There were no painted lines on the asphalt, just crooked, makeshift parking spaces made by the other drivers' cars. I watched another car parking, a dented Honda hatchback, out of which four thirtysomething men climbed. I parked my car next to theirs, and I followed them into the bar. There was a lumpy old man sitting in the dark, just inside the heavy industrial door. I handed him the three-dollar cover charge. He looked me up and down as he took my crumpled bills and pressed a stamp against the inside of my wrist.

"Have fun," he said, sounding like a warden welcoming a new inmate to the prison.

I stepped past him and into a long, narrow corridor. Tiny, purple-shaded track lights illuminated a series of posters on the walls, advertising gay cruises, the Indianapolis gay and lesbian film festival, and an upcoming "Student Body Amateur Strip Contest." At the end of this corridor was a small, brightly lit bar area, with four or five tables, a jukebox, and a foosball machine. For a moment, I panicked. There were only a dozen men here, scattered on stools at the bar, or leaning against the wood-paneled walls. *This* was the bar that the alternative weekly newspaper which I had read that afternoon termed "the city's best gay scene"?

But then I saw the four men in front of me continue walking past the bar and down a stairwell at the far end of the room. I followed close behind. Halfway down the stairs, I began to hear loud, throbbing dance music. A few moments later, I came upon the club area, and I breathed a sigh of relief. It was a large, square space, probably fifty feet on each side. Bars lined the near and far sides of the square. The deejay booth was on the right side, and the bathrooms were on the left. In the middle was the dance floor, packed with bodies, big and small, clothed and shirtless, mostly men and a few women, many more bodies than there had been cars in the parking lot. So many bodies that I wondered if they had been bussed in.

I bought a beer, and I slowly made my way around the perimeter of the dance floor. I stared into the eyes of some of the men I passed, and some of them stared back. But when our gazes held for more than two or three seconds, my heart would skip a beat, and—without even meaning to—I would look down at the floor. In college it had been so much easier, simple happenstance, two horny young boys, right place, right time. But here, now: This required skill, courage, persistence; it required the ability to not look the other way when you lock eyes with a cute guy. I drank another beer, and then another. I went upstairs and wandered around there. At one point, an older guy, maybe in his early forties, soft through the middle, but with a cute-enough face that suggested a sort of down-market Dennis Quaid, approached me and started a conversation. His name was Eric. He said that he managed a Target store. And for a minute or two, I entertained the possibility . . .

Easier to do it with someone who will be grateful to have scored you, someone who won't be disappointed if you've forgotten how things work . . .

But when he asked me if he could buy me a drink, I said no, because I already had one, and it must have sounded more vituperative than I intended, because he wandered off to the bathroom, and he never wandered back.

I returned to the lower level. I asked for a fifth beer. I couldn't leave. I told myself that I would stay there until this club closed, or until I found someone to take back to my hotel, whichever came first.

I moved on to my sixth beer. That's when I saw him, as I was waiting for the bartender to make change, after I had handed over my last twenty. He was leaning against the bar, facing the dance floor, ten or fifteen feet away from me. He saw me staring at him, and he stared back. And this time I did it; I forced myself to hold my head up. I held my gaze, and he held his, and I held mine still longer. And then, finally, he smiled.

He was small: 5 feet 6 inches, maybe 140 pounds. Hispanic. He had very dark, almond-shaped eyes and flowing eyelashes and thick but not bushy eyebrows. He was wearing pressed blue jeans, a white button-down shirt, and a red Indiana University baseball cap. I smiled back at him. He kept on smiling at me.

I felt the six beers sloshing through my bloodstream, the throbbing techno music reverberating in my jaw. I looked down at my shoes. I tried to will this stranger closer. *Just take a step toward me, please, just one little step. . . .* But when I looked back up at him, he was staring in the other direction. (At another guy? Had I lost him so quickly to another guy?) I saw him push off the bar. He was moving away, headed toward the dance floor. I had only a fraction of a second to act.

Just stop thinking. Thinking is overrated. Being intelligent is a curse. No great man ever accomplished anything by standing around and thinking. *You must act right now or forever accept your defeat . . .*

And then I did it. Somehow I forced myself to do it. I twisted my body and took three backwards steps, so that I was suddenly standing in front of him, blocking his path.

"Hey." It was all I could think to say.

"Hello," he said. He had a Spanish accent. He smiled again. Up close, I could see that he had a mouthful of slightly crooked teeth. He told me that his name was Alex.

We talked for the next fifteen minutes. He said that he was from Colombia and that he had come to Indiana when he was twenty-five. He worked construction jobs and sent home money each month to his family. His sister and her baby daughter had moved to Indiana six months earlier, and they were living with him in his one-bedroom apartment. He said he liked to come to the clubs to dance and to get away from the baby's incessant crying.

"Would you like to dance?" he asked me, when our conversation hit a lull.

"I don't really dance," I told him.

He smirked at me, a bona fide Terrence O'Connell-ian smirk, taking substantial pleasure in another's unease. "What do you do?" he asked.

I couldn't tell if he meant, "What do you do *instead* of dancing when you are at a gay club?" or if he was asking me what I did for a living. So I said nothing. I just shrugged at him.

A few moments later, the lights came up halfway, turning the entire room a sickly shade of amber. All of the bartenders began shouting in unison: "Last call, last call." Without any warning, Alex leaned into me and kissed me, his lips slightly open, his tongue pressing against the tip of mine, his right index finger and thumb resting on my cheek.

"What would you like to do?" he asked me when he pulled away.

I stared at him blankly, confused and drunk. Faced with the prospect of getting what you set out to get, there comes that moment of doubt, which expands quickly into certainty—that you didn't really want it anyway; that the pursuit was just a means of killing time; that the risks are too burdensome. There comes that moment when you think: *It would be so much easier to back off; to concede defeat to all of the others competing alongside you.*

The world divides evenly: between those who brush the uncertainty aside and get laid; and those who think, and think, and think, and then, finally, shrink away.

"Do you have a roommate?" he asked me.

"I'm staying at a hotel."

"Alone?" he asked, and before I could answer, he leaned in again and kissed me, slipping his tongue deep inside my mouth, swirling it around inside there.

"We can go there now?" he asked when he pulled away.

The beer seemed to reach into the farthest corners of my body, into my chest, my fingers, my feet, my eyes, my ears. And my rapidly hardening penis. That's when I realized that there could be a third category of person: those who let the alcohol make all the decisions for them.

"You can follow me in your car," I said to him.

We made out in the elevator, our mouths running across each other's faces, our hands running over each other's chests. His body was solid from the construction work, heavier and thicker than it had seemed in the bar. His breath smelled of whiskey and cigarettes. In between the kisses, he whispered into my ear, breathy moans or imperceptible words in Spanish.

Inside the room, he saw the two queen-sized beds, one neatly made up, the other one a sprawl of clothing and toiletries spilled out from my weekend bag.

"Who else here?" he asked. "Is someone else here?"

"No," I said. "I'm here alone."

"Why you have two beds?" he asked. He was talking fast, dropping words from his sentences. I leaned in to kiss him, but instead he grabbed my shoulders with his hands and held me at arm's distance. I tried to pull away from him, but I couldn't. His grip was tight. His fingers sunk deep into my flesh. My shoulders immediately started to ache. Despite a five-inch, fifty-pound difference, he was much stronger than me.

"It's a hotel room," I said, incredulous and befuddled. Surely he had seen the inside of an American hotel room before.

"You are certain? No one else?" His eyes were darting around the room. He still wasn't letting go of my shoulder.

"Just me, I promise. I'm the only one staying here."

He eyed me warily, the way a drug dealer might stare down a new client, trying to determine if he's a narc. I realized, in that moment, that he had probably seen plenty of American hotel rooms in his day; that his paranoia was likely born out of past experience. Someone must have brought him back to a hotel, and then sprung a third player on him, and then perhaps forced him to do things he didn't want to do.

How many threesomes has he been tricked into? How many dozens, or perhaps hundreds, have there been before me, strangers whom he has met at that bar and gone home with, without even remembering their first names?

But then I stopped myself. Opportunities like this did not come along very often for me. I couldn't keep thinking. I just had to go ahead and *do it*. I tried to kiss him again. And this time, when I leaned in, he let his arms go limp and brought his mouth to mine. We made out for a minute or two more. Then I told him to get into bed and said I would join him there in a minute.

In the bathroom, I scrubbed my hands and face. I stared at my reflection in the mirror. I tried to give myself a pep talk.

Erase from your memory the last six years of your life.

Pretend that you are still in college. Pretend that you are still a kid.

Pretend as if you have taken complete strangers back to your hotel room dozens of times before. Pretend as if this is old hat for you.

This is not rocket science. A good-looking Colombian man is in your hotel room. He is willing to have sex with you.

It is the next necessary step. It will carry you closer to Terrence.

When I returned from the bathroom, he was lying on top of the bedspread, completely naked. Without his baseball cap, he looked older: His hair starting thinning on top; worry lines ran across his forehead. He was rubbing his hand over his belly and his chest, smiling at me. I hurried to get undressed, keeping my eyes focused on his body the entire time. The curly black hair on his shins that tapered and finally disappeared further up on his thighs. The slight rightward curve of his erect penis. The tautness of his stomach muscles. The purple, obelisk-shaped nipples. The ears that jutted out too far from his head. How long had it been since I could take in the details of another man's body like this and memorize them? Much too long. Years and years too long.

"You look very sexy," I told him.

He smiled at me and patted the empty space next to him on the bed.

"Come here and fuck me," he said.

We fooled around for fifteen or twenty minutes, trying out all sorts of positions and permutations with our mouths and penises. Periodically I would giggle, and he would back off and look at me quizzically, until I assured him that I was having a good time; that it was just that I hadn't had sex in a while, and I had forgotten how much fun it could be.

And then, without warning, he pushed off the bed and walked into the bathroom.

"Do you have lotion?" I heard him shout.

Fifteen seconds later, he emerged from the bathroom, a tiny bottle of hotel hand cream in his hands. I watched as he squeezed some of the cream onto his fingers and then began rubbing his fingers into the crack of his ass.

"No, I don't do that," I said, seeing where this was heading, not wanting it to go there so quickly. "I don't have any condoms."

"I want that you put your dick in me," he said, squeezing still more lotion onto his fingers, returning his fingers to his ass.

"I don't do that without condoms," I said. The truth was that I had never done it at all.

He rested the bottle of cream on the night table and climbed on top of me, straddling my chest. "I want that you fuck me," he said.

I began to squirm beneath him, trying to lift him off me.

"No," I said, more sharply this time. "I don't fuck without condoms."

"I not sick. Are you sick?"

"No, but I don't want to get sick," I said. "It's not safe."

"I not sick," he repeated, bearing his weight down onto my groin, trying to guide his ass onto my penis.

I buckled my waist upward, trying to knock him off balance and throw him off me. "No," I said, almost shouting now.

He leaned forward and grabbed my wrists, pinning my arms

against the bed on either side of me. Then he leaned down and kissed me on the mouth, pushing his tongue all the way inside, as far down my throat as he could get it. When he pulled away, he whispered into my ear, "I not sick. Now I want that you fuck my ass."

I tried to free my arms and push him off me. But his grip tightened. I felt the full force of his weight upon me, and it hurt. Who knew 140 pounds could weigh so much?

"I don't want to."

His stare was penetrating, venomous—like a hunter in the woods just as the morning fog has lifted and revealed, directly in the line of fire, a helpless object of prey. "What you want?" he said. "Why you bring me here?"

"I want to fool around," I pleaded. "I just don't want to fuck you."

His right hand released its grip on my wrist, and his open palm tore across my face. It was sudden, unexpected, and very quick—the sting burrowing deep into my skin before I even had time to register what had happened. He slapped me hard enough so that it hurt; hard enough so that it might leave a mark on my cheek.

But not so hard that that the message wasn't clear: *I can hit you even harder if I choose; I can make it hurt much more.*

"Put your dick in me," he said.

I ran through my options. I could push him away and hope that this did not escalate into a fight that would wake the other hotel guests and require the police to be summoned. Or I could plead with him, gently and earnestly, and hope that his temper would cool.

Or I could submit. He didn't look sick. He looked young and healthy and robust. And it was virtually impossible, I thought I had once read, for the insertive partner to catch HIV from putting his penis into another guy's ass.

It made the most sense to submit; to get things back to where they had been just five minutes earlier.

Besides, what is sex without risk?

And what is risk if it cannot be elided, and vanquished?

I pretended he had never slapped me. I told myself that it had all been foreplay. This time, as he pushed his ass down onto my dick, I let it slowly slide in.

And, all at once, a dozen sensations overwhelmed me: Pleasure, of course—an echo that started in my groin and reverberated up from there; and then shame—a memory, from age thirteen or fourteen, of masturbating four, five, six, seven times a day, to the pictures I found in my father's night table, telling myself over and over again that it was OK to like other guys, provided you never, ever put your penis into another man's ass and provided you never allowed another's penis into yours. Then elation, giddiness, a flood of confidence—I was still young and good-looking; I could get any boy I wanted.

And then: nothing but fear; a vision expanding in size and clarity in my mind, like a distant, fuzzy cluster of stars slowly coming into focus in a telescope to form a constellation, of my penis sliding into and out of his rectum, bursting dozens of tiny blood cells and papules with every thrust, through which disease would seep out and find its way inside of me—through my urethra, or though a microscopic cut on my shaft—and infect me. This was the way gay men contracted AIDS from one another and died.

He pulled off me and shifted around on the bed, positioning himself on all fours. "Fuck me," he said. Too late to stop now. This time I didn't even pause. I placed myself behind him and entered him. He thrust backwards as I thrust forward. His sighing grew heavier and louder with each passing second. I told myself that provided no semen was exchanged, as long as I didn't ejaculate inside of him, I would be safe.

Less than a minute later, he came: a high-pitched squeal; a spasm; and then his body suddenly limp and rubbery beneath mine. I pulled out of him and surreptitiously inspected my penis, looking for specks of blood or shit or anything that might have gotten into my bloodstream and was now coursing through my veins, poisoning me. I spit into my hand and started masturbating; and then, maybe twenty seconds later, I came all over his lower back. It hardly felt momentous at all.

After a couple of minutes of lying next to each other in silence, Alex got up and took a shower. I watched him as he toweled off, and dressed, and scribbled his number on a piece of hotel stationary. He kissed me and told me I should call him sometime. He left without mentioning the slap, or the fact that we had fucked without condoms, or even my name.

When I got back to my apartment in Staten Island two nights later, there were two messages on my answering machine.

From Meredith, sounding playful and typically high-spirited: "What the *hell,* honey? You just up and leave and you don't tell me? Well, don't sweat it. I'm not mad. I'm thinking you met the man of your dreams and you quit so you could have sex all day. Let's go to Bistro on Saturday night and you can tell me all the juicy details. It will be my treat, since I guess I'm the only one who still has a job."

And from my mother, sounding thoroughly wronged and hellbent on justice: "Ben, I know you're away, but when you get back, I need you to call me. I heard something today—I hope it's not true—but I heard something today from one of the teachers at your school. And if it's true, then I need you to call me and explain. I think you know what I'm talking about. I want you to call me and explain why you're telling people lies about your sister."

chapter four

Junior Year
(1990)

The blue and white paint on the door had faded and chipped over the years, so that the word "BOYS" was no longer discernible. Only half of the overhead fluorescent bulbs burned to their full wattage, casting the entire space in flat, shadowy brown light. The skinny, hospital-green metal lockers, splotched with oval-shaped pools of rust, had been banged and punched and dented so many times that you had to use the full weight of your body to get them to close. The showers did not function, water no longer flowed through the exposed gray pipes—the space, instead, had been given over to storage, cardboard boxes of basketballs and jump ropes and the red felt dickeys that we used when we wanted to approximate skins versus shirts, without anyone having to take off his shirt. This was the locker room of New Dorp High School, tucked away behind the bleachers at the far end of the gymnasium, where each day I spent five minutes before class, and five minutes after, in terror and in ecstasy, changing into and out of my gym clothes, sneaking glances at the other boys changing into and out of theirs, just two or three glances each day, afraid that I would be caught, knowing full well that getting caught might lead to all kinds of wretched trouble, but still unable to stop myself. Never able to stop myself. I couldn't not try.

Gym took place during third period, four days a week (the fifth day was given over to "health class," our school's euphemism for sex education). One hundred and twenty boys (gym

class was divided by gender in our coed school), freshmen
through seniors, all gathered under the tutelage of Jay Lavner,
a balding man in his late twenties who insisted, with a fierce-
ness and single-mindedness that approached religious scrupu-
losity, that we *change* into and out of our gym clothes, that we
couldn't just wear them under our regular clothes. "I'm not going to let you people sweat up the hallways," he would bark it at
us at least once a week, as if we were skunks apt to leave his gym
and spray the school walls as we scurried off to our next class.
But if some of the other boys grumbled and complained, and
others undressed each day with a certain amount of dread and
shame, I was grateful for Mr. Lavner's zealotry. I took his direc-
tive as an invitation open expressly to me. Because much more
so than "Lavner Ball," the anarchic version of dodgeball that
Mr. Lavner forced us to play almost every morning, the locker
room was my real daily workout—a high-velocity, fast-moving,
potentially fatal form of aerobic exercise, conducted in two
separate, five-minute sessions, stealing glances of teenage boys
climbing into and out of their gym shorts, and, once stolen,
burning those glances into my brain, storing up images that
could be called up later that day and jerked off to, over and
over again. All the while hoping and praying that I wouldn't be
caught. All the while rehearsing innocent-sounding defenses
just in case I was.

I studied the layout of the locker room the way I might a
map of Hapsburg-era Prussia for a global history test, memoriz-
ing where all my targets were located, and where they stood in
relation to one another: Vincent Grasso in the second row;
Jimmy Losciavo and Dave Leferink in the fourth row; Thomas
Agnello in the sixth. Each day I worked on perfecting my tech-
nique, on maximizing my few minutes' opportunity. My row of
lockers was one of the farthest from the entrance—one of
those turns of good fortune that only strengthens a gay teenager's belief in God. It meant that I had to walk past seven rows
of undressing boys just to get to my own locker. The erratic
placement of the lockers abetted me further: They fanned off
the center aisle at a slight angle, so that when I was walking in

I could see the other boys at least a second or two before they could see me looking at them. If I timed it right—forty-five seconds or a minute after the first bell rang—I was golden. I could make my way down the center corridor, casting leftward and rightward glances at ten, maybe twenty of my classmates, already in their underwear. I was like a sniper picking off targets in an open, unobstructed field.

I tried to be surreptitious. I tried to keep my head to the ground and only look up when I knew the other boys wouldn't be looking in my direction. I tried to limit myself to two or three stolen glances a day, four or five at the most. I tried to make every one of those glances count.

But there were also days when, despite my best efforts, I couldn't stop myself. Days when I stared in open view and hoped no one called me on it. Days when I looked and looked and kept on looking, because I couldn't force my head to turn away. Days when a sixteen-year-old boy's erection that never seems to go away makes all the decisions for him.

Today—a warm and golden day in early May, a Tuesday morning five weeks before the end of junior year—was one of those days. Today it had to be Terrence.

In the years since the seventh grade, Terrence O'Connell's taunting came and went, flared up violently and then faded away suddenly, only to come back a few days or a few weeks later. And, for just as long, I crushed on him. I couldn't help myself. I couldn't even begin to explain it. All I knew was that I fantasized about seeing him in his underwear more than any other boy in our class.

Except it never seemed to work out that way. It wasn't until junior year that we even shared the same gym period—and, even then, he seemed to have some sort of sixth sense for eluding my gaze. He would always take his time getting dressed. I could arrive a full two minutes after the bell, but it usually earned me no more than a peek at him unlacing his shoes. And if the placement of the lockers aided a peeper upon entering the room, it hindered things considerably upon exit: Short of stopping and turning my body around by forty-five degrees—short of announcing to everyone in the immediate radius, "I am checking this guy out"—it was near-impossible to get a full-on view of someone.

But if at first you don't succeed . . .

I took longer than usual that morning, nearly the full five minutes allotted us to change. I thought if I waited long enough, and if I was careful enough on my way out the door, I might have a chance of seeing him. I slowly tied my sneaker laces, double-knotting each bow. Then I lifted myself off the changing bench and began making my way to the exit. By now the locker room had thinned out—only a dozen or so stragglers remained. I steadily made my way up the central corridor, past the third row of lockers, and then past the second row. And as I made my way past the very first row—the row where Terrence O'Connell had his locker—I craned my head slightly. It was a perfectly unremarkable and not-so-out-of-the-ordinary gesture, almost as if I were stretching out the sore muscles in my neck. I twisted just enough to discern that, at that exact instant, Terrence was entirely undressed. He was standing there in only his underwear.

Keep moving, at all costs, do not break your stride, you've seen enough already . . .

I knew that it would be crazy to stop. I knew the above-all-else value of self-preservation. I wasn't *that* stupid.

But how could I possibly keep walking? There were only five weeks left until summer break; this might have been my last chance to see him for the year. (And who knew if we would even be placed in the same gym class next year? This might very well have been my last chance *ever.*)

I took a few more steps forward, out of Terrence's sight line, a few feet closer to the door. And then I halted in my tracks and sighed loudly—hoping to approximate something like exasperation, hoping to suggest to anyone who might be standing nearby, *I have left something behind, and now I must walk back to my locker and retrieve it.* It was the hoariest trick imaginable.

Anyone paying even the slightest attention would have seen right through me. But cheesy tactics take on new meaning when you're sixteen and horny and one turn away from getting to see the most beautiful boy in your class in his underwear. The cheesy tactics come to seem like matters of life and death. Your only real option.

I spun around and began walking back to my locker, turning my head and pausing as I passed Terrence's row. My timing was exquisite. He was standing squarely in front of his locker, hanging his shirt on a hook. He wasn't wearing anything except his underwear, a pair of baby blue-colored briefs with a white waistband (even when it came to his underwear, Terrence had to be cooler and more enviable than the rest of us). My eyes locked in on his butt, perfectly round and high, the excess cotton bunching up at the crack. I looked down at his legs, smooth but for the just discernible sprouting of hair on his shins. I looked up at his torso: The muscles in his shoulders and chest had broadened through the winter; the last traces of baby fat had evaporated from his midsection.

One or two furtive glances up and down his body. No more than two or three seconds could have passed. I felt like a fat lady slipping off her diet, unabashed as she shovels second and third helpings of food onto her plate, no amount could ever be enough. I felt like a young prince being handed the keys to the kingdom, exultant and power mad. It was all mine for the taking.

My eyes traveled up from his chest to his shoulders, and then to his face, and then, finally, to his eyes. He was staring right back at me. He had caught me. And I knew, in that instant, that the consequences would be brutal. Ugly. Relentless. But I didn't care. The consequences, whatever they were, would be worth it. The taunting, the name-calling, the chronic character assassination—all of it might very well hurt me. But this image, his mostly naked form tattooed permanently onto my cerebrum, would be my shield. For as long as we both lived, this would be my one triumph over him.

I picked up my stride and made my way back to my locker. Within seconds, I heard Terrence laugh loudly and incredulously. He announced, to no one in particular, "What the fuck was *that?*"

I was terrified. I thought he might follow me to my locker and smash my head against it. I thought he might punch me and make me bleed all over the linoleum floor. But he didn't. Ten seconds passed, and then twenty. The locker room was silent. I heard Mr. Lavner blow his whistle. I assumed that Terrence had finished dressing and made his way into the gymnasium.

I stood there and waited, my heart thumping wildly. An erection had expanded in my shorts—a problem considering that, by now, I was supposed to be in my spot on the gym floor. I couldn't hide here. Once Mr. Lavner started taking roll and arrived at my name, someone would certainly say that they had seen me in the locker room and a search party would be sent in. My other option was to fake illness, to say that I needed to be excused to the nurse's office. But that wouldn't work, either. The result would be spectacle, all eyes in the gymnasium focused on me. I would be handing Terrence O'Connell the opportunity to humiliate me in front of the entire class.

I waited another thirty seconds before deciding I had no other choice. I dashed into the gymnasium, doing my best to look like an overeager student who had stayed too late after biology class peppering the teacher with additional questions and then had to race all the way across the school to make it to his next class on time. I prayed that my erection wasn't noticeable.

Lavner was calling out the Ls as I found my seat on the floor. "Come on, Reilly," he barked. "What's taking so long? Get in your spot."

Terrence didn't miss a beat. From his space, one row over and two spots in front of mine, he piped up, "He was too busy in the locker room watching all the guys undress."

Everyone laughed—one hundred and twenty boys, all at once, all started laughing at me. Except for Terrence himself. Humiliation in front of a large group of people had long been his specialty, and he usually laughed the loudest. But this time, when I looked over at him, he was staring down at his hands, scowling and slowly shaking his head.

"Ha, ha, you're hilarious, O'Connell," Mr. Lavner shouted at him. "Now shut your trap." Lavner, an equal opportunist for whom nothing mattered but the Lavner Ball, never tolerated name-calling in his class, or fighting, or even the belittling of the less athletically inclined among us. The laughter in the gym faded away in an instant.

"Reilly, I'm marking you late," he said. "It happens again, you lose five points from your grade." And then he went on calling out last names, the Ms, the Ns, the Os, saying "O'Connell's here, unfortunately," when he got to Terrence's, skipping over my name entirely.

For now, there was order, calm, nothing but the syncopated sounds of Jay Lavner rattling off last names, winding his way to the Ws, Ys, and the single Z, Aaron Zilberman. But revenge, almost certainly, was forthcoming. I knew that Terrence would not let this rest; that his silence upon delivering his joke was the mark of a rage that could not be elided. I trudged through another round of Lavner Ball, worried that he would go on the attack and pitch the ball squarely at my head. Nothing happened. Back in the locker room, I changed into my school clothes quickly, hoping to race past him and avoid him entirely. I needn't have worried. He had dressed even quicker and was gone by the time I passed his row. He wasn't in the lunchroom two periods later. We shared only one other class that afternoon, math with Mrs. Dafoe. He sat in his seat just next to mine, quietly taking notes and keeping his head down low, almost as if I was the bully and he was the nerdy, defenseless boy desperately trying to stay out of my way.

"Ben, hold up."

I was on my way to the bus stop on Hylan Boulevard, three blocks from our school. Class had let out forty minutes earlier, but I had stayed late, as I did every Tuesday and Thursday afternoon, for an academic olympics practice.

"Ben, wait a sec." It was Terrence, calling out from behind me, speaking to me in a way he had never spoken to me before. He sounded polite, earnest, maybe a little flirty. This was the voice he used in class with the teachers he wanted to charm and seduce.

I stopped and turned around. But I couldn't bring myself to say anything or to even look him in the eye. I was too terrified that, after remaining quiet all afternoon, *this* was going to be his revenge; that, any second now, he was going to punch me in the face.

"What the fuck was that this morning?" he asked. But again the tone of his voice surprised me. He sounded genuinely curious, not at all angry. He sounded like he was going to let me off the hook. I looked up and into his face. His expression, too, seemed sincere, purposeful; it certainly didn't look as if he was on the verge of attacking me.

But who could trust him? I was convinced that this had to be some sort of trick.

"I don't know what you're talking about, Terrence."

"You don't know you were checking me out?"

"Fuck you, Terrence," I answered, trying my best to sound defiant.

"Whatever, Ben."

I told myself to turn around and keep walking; to get as far away from him as possible before he finally decided to drop the nice guy routine and do some real damage. But I also felt compelled to post some kind of defense. And, I suppose, to keep on talking with him. I was curious to see where all of this might lead.

"I wasn't checking you out," I said. "I went to put my keys in my locker. I didn't even know you were there."

I knew it sounded too studied, that only a guilty man could come up with a story so refined. I knew, as the words were coming out of my mouth, that he wasn't buying any of it.

"Ben, I'm not stupid," he said, very calmly and evenly. "I know when I'm getting checked out."

"You think the whole school checks you out," I shot back.

For a couple of seconds, he didn't say anything. I assumed that it was over: that he would head off in the opposite direction; that he would return the next morning with fresh ammunition; that he would tell everyone who would listen that I had been checking him out in the locker room. By lunchtime, the whispering and the giggling would be impossible to ignore. There would be at least a half-dozen other boys, probably the fattest and ugliest ones in the class, loudly proclaiming that I had tried to check them out, too. It would take at least a week for the ridicule to die down, for the junior class to move on and find their next target. And, with Terrence involved, there was always the possibility that the next target would again be me, that a new wave of torments and slanders would be invented to replace the withering first set. The next week, perhaps the entire remainder of junior year, would be dreadful.

"I'm not going to tell anyone," he said. "If that's what you're worried about." And the way he said it—with a hint of exasperation in his voice, with a soft emphasis on the word "not"—made it sound like an unassailable truth.

"*What*, Terrence? What do you want?"

"Nothing," he said.

"Then leave me alone," I told him, and I started to walk away.

Terrence followed right behind me. I kept on walking, a step or two ahead of him, right past the bus stop, heading toward my house.

Another minute passed in silence before he started up again. "Hey, there's a surprise quiz in English tomorrow," he said. "I saw it written down in Mrs. Pence's grade book."

I didn't answer him.

"I thought you'd want to know. In case you didn't read the chapter she assigned us on Friday."

"I've already read the whole book," I said.

The thought occurred to me that I should make a few wrong turns, that I should lead us *away* from my house—the last thing I needed was for him to know where I lived. But I didn't. I kept on walking. After a few more minutes, I slowed down and let him catch up to me, so that we were walking side by side.

"I don't get this, Terrence," I said finally. "What, are we friends now?"

"No, we're not friends now," he said petulantly, almost like he was mimicking me.

"So *what?*"

"Nothing," he said. "I just . . ." But then his voice trailed off. He had no idea why he was following me home.

"Is this some joke you're trying to pull off?" I said, yelling a little bit, trying to go on the offensive. "Are you going to invite me to the prom and dump pig's blood on me?"

He furrowed his brow and grimaced at me. "I don't know what you're talking about."

"It's a movie, it's called *Carrie*," I told him. "They invite the ugly girl to the prom and elect her homecoming queen. But it's a big joke. The cool kids dump pig's blood on her in front of the whole school."

He wasn't sure if he should laugh or not. He made some kind of snorting noise as a compromise. We walked some more. We were drawing nearer to my house; we would be there in two or three more minutes. I decided the only thing I could do was pull the trigger.

"There's nobody home, if you want to hang out at my house for awhile."

I said it as plainly as I could, as if his answer didn't matter to me one way or the other.

I was surprised by how quickly he said: "OK."

In the eight years since my sister's death, our house had come to seem more and more like the sort of withering eyesore where elderly people waited to expire—a place still kept up with, but just barely. An outdoor shutter on one of the upstairs windows had come loose from its hinges and hung crooked, going on two years now. The front storm door wouldn't shut on its own accord and had to be pulled open and forced closed. The above-ground swimming pool in our backyard had remained covered for the last three summers, as puddles of rain water and algae collected on top of the dark brown tarp. These were mostly easy fixes, problems that needed only a wrench and a screwdriver and a few spare hours on a Saturday afternoon. But it was enough for my mother to keep the place tidy, and enough for my father to try to cook dinner for us two or three times a week. Everything else they could let go, as they retreated further and further into their private, silent spaces: my father in front of the television in his bedroom, drinking beer and watching hockey games; my mother in front of the television in the living room, staring at the same four or five movies on HBO over and over again.

As I led Terrence inside and up the stairs, it occurred to me that I should have felt some kind of embarrassment about the state of our house: the increasingly outdated furniture, with coffee and soda stains on the upholstery; the ceramic tiles in the kitchen that had started cracking years ago; the long-broken air conditioner that rested in the dining room window, collecting the dust and weariness that floated through the stale air.

And the shrine! That was the most embarrassing thing of all. The awful shrine that my parents didn't even realize was a shrine: a framed 8x10 photograph of my sister, posed in the high school graduation gown she never got to wear for real, resting on the middle shelf in the living room wall unit, surrounded on both sides by tall, fat white candles that had never been lit. How tacky was that picture; those never-used candles; the sheer volume of space given over to these objects. How could I not be horrified to let Terrence see *that*?

But I wasn't. For some reason I felt no embarrassment on this afternoon. Maybe it was because with Terrence embarrassment seemed very much beside the point. His father was a truck driver, which meant his own house couldn't be any great shakes; and his mother had abandoned him and his brothers years earlier. Surely he understood the chill that seeps into a home when a longtime occupant just up and disappears. For all his awfulness, he would know that you can't pass judgment on the way wounded families struggle to go on living.

"Do you want a soda or something?" I asked, once we were upstairs.

"A Coke maybe," he said. "Or a Sprite. Whatever you have."

When I returned from the kitchen with our drinks, he was poised at the very edge of the couch, looking toward the television. I handed him his glass and sat down next to him. And there we sat, for the next three minutes, sipping our sodas, saying nothing.

"Dude, I don't know what I'm doing here," Terrence said finally.

I knew he would say something like this. I had my response already prepared.

"Well, you're here," I told him. "Maybe you *do* want to try to be friends. I know you said you didn't, but maybe you're changing your mind."

"Maybe I'm changing my mind," he repeated back to me, trying the words on for size, sounding none too convinced.

"It's probably not even possible," I said. "We couldn't just show up at school tomorrow as friends, pretending like nothing ever happened. People would think it was a put-on. But maybe we could be friends outside of school. Maybe we could just be friends here."

He said nothing for a bit. He leaned forward on the couch, sipping his Coke, looking around the room and then back at the television expectantly.

"Can I see the rest of the house?" Terrence asked, when it became clear to him that the TV wasn't going to turn itself on.

"Yeah, sure," I said, jumping up from the couch a bit too eagerly. "There's not all that much to see. You've already seen the kitchen and the living room, and there's the dining room." I pointed to the room just beyond where we were sitting, where an oblong wood table handed down from my mother's mother occupied most of the space.

"Who lives downstairs?" he asked.

"No one anymore. My grandparents used to live there. But my grandmother died about three years ago, and then my grandfather went to Arizona to live with his brother. We haven't seen him in two years. My parents keep saying we're going to visit, but we haven't." And then, because I had already started telling Terrence the story of my family, and because I felt a sudden need to tell him even more, I pointed to the wall unit, and to the picture on the center shelf, and I told him, "That's my sister. Her name was Mary. She died eight years ago. She had just turned eighteen when it happened."

"A car accident?"

"She got sick. She had to go to the hospital one day, and she never came back. I guess they didn't realize it was as serious as it was."

"I'm sorry," Terrence said, very softly, sounding like he meant it.

I started leading him through the dining room, and up the three stairs that led to the bedrooms in the rear of the house. "I still think about her a lot," I told him. "I was thinking the other day how I don't really remember anything that happened to me before I was, like, four. So that means I remember about four years of her being alive. Which I guess means that I now remember twice as many years of her being dead than I do of her being alive. That's the bathroom"—I pointed to the bathroom, which was just at the top of the steps and to the left, and kept on walking—"Does that make any sense?"

"Yeah, I think so."

I brought him to the back of the house, where the three bedrooms were laid out side by side, in cul-de-sac formation. "That's my parents' room, and that was my older brother's room, before he moved out, and that's mine," I said, turning to the door on the right, pointing inside. "It used to be my sister's room. It was empty for the first two years after she died. I don't think my parents wanted to change anything in there, but Danny wanted his own room, and they finally gave in. So we moved me out of that one and into this one."

And the more I told Terrence, the more I couldn't stop myself. The more I wanted to keep telling. "I think Danny took her death harder than anyone," I said. "When I was in the seventh grade, he just kind of disappeared for a week. I guess he ran away. He lives in his own apartment now in New Jersey. But he doesn't come over very often."

"I can see how that might happen," Terrence said.

This sympathy from Terrence was new. He was listening to me babble, pretending not to be bored, straining to act like a friend. I thought to myself that if he was capable of these kinds of responses, then maybe he hadn't been lying to me. Maybe he wasn't going to tell anyone about what had happened in the locker room. Maybe water could be put under the bridge.

Maybe something even better than that could happen between us.

Is that the reason he followed me here? Is he curious? Did my staring at him today set off some strange feelings inside him? Does he want to explore those feelings?

I pointed into my bedroom. "You can go in and look around," I told him. "I have to go to the bathroom."

Again he didn't hesitate: "OK."

I didn't have to use the bathroom. I just needed a minute or two alone to regroup, to hatch out a game plan. Was I just imagining things—writing myself a story inspired by the stories in my father's magazines, a boy-on-boy fantasy come to life inside my very own bedroom?

Or might this be real? Might he be open to the myriad possibilities, of two horny teenage boys alone in a bedroom, with no chance of an adult arriving home and interrupting them?

I stared into the mirror, and I struck myself a deal. I told myself that I wouldn't force the issue, and I wouldn't put myself in danger. I would let him make the first move. If he wanted something to happen, then I would let something happen.

But if it looked as if he was uncertain—if there was enough hesitancy and awkwardness hanging in the air—well, then perhaps I would try to make it happen myself. I owed myself at least that much, right? Not every day is the boy you have harbored a secret crush on since the seventh grade sitting on your bed. I couldn't not try.

I washed my hands and face, and I pulled open the bathroom door as hard as I could, so that it banged against the wall inside the bathroom. I wanted to make enough noise to let him know that I was returning to the bedroom; that his time alone was running out; that he was going to have to make some big decisions very soon . . .

Yes or no, Terrence, are you willing to hook up with me or not?

"You can put on some music if you want," I called out, still a few feet from my bedroom door. "The CDs are on the shelf above my dresser."

He didn't answer.

"Do you like Depeche Mode? Or R.E.M.? *Green* is a great CD, if you've never—"

I arrived at the bedroom door. I turned into my room. Terrence was sitting on the edge of my bed, an open shoe box resting next to his feet. He was holding in his hand the magazine centerfold, the four pictures of the two naked young men that once belonged to my father. I had taken over ownership of these photographs a couple of years earlier. After borrowing them and borrowing them, for longer and longer periods of time, I decided that they might as well belong to me; that my father would never miss them (and that, if he did, he would never make mention of it to me). I placed them in a shoe box, not unlike the shoe box in which I had first found them, beneath a stack of old report cards, and I stored the shoe box far under my bed. I still took the pictures out from their hiding place at least two or three times a week.

But now the shoe box was at Terrence's feet, and the pictures were in his lap. He had gotten down onto the floor, reached far under my bed and found the box, and then dug through it. All in the fewer-than-two minutes I had been in the bathroom.

He looked up at me and smiled—a clever, calculating, sinister smile. The guile in his eyes had returned. Terrence the Empathizer was no more.

"What the fuck are *these?*" he asked, outraged and loving it.

"That box was under my bed," I shouted, so much more shrill than I wanted to sound, just like a little sissy. "Why were you looking under my bed?"

"I kicked it when I went to sit down," he said. "I looked to see what I had kicked." He wasn't even trying to sound convincing. He knew that the burden of proof was not upon him. In our current scenario, I was the one who had to do all the explaining.

"It was *under* the bed, you couldn't have kicked it," I said, my voice rising even higher.

Terrence ignored me. "You *are* gay. You really are a faggot. I was never really sure. And after talking to you this afternoon, I *really* wasn't sure. I was starting to think maybe you were straight. But you are. I was right all along."

I gave up trying to shame him. He clearly wasn't going to start apologizing for snooping under my bed. I tried a different tack altogether. "Those aren't even my pictures," I said.

"Who do they belong to?" he answered back. "Your dead sister?" A glimmer of regret flashed in his eyes, and then, just as quickly, disappeared. He knew he shouldn't have said it, but he had, and now he was going to own it. This was the Terrence O'Connell I knew best—the one who was righteous and relentless.

"That wasn't very nice," I said.

"Well if they don't belong to you, then who do they belong to?"

I didn't have an answer. Telling him the photos actually belonged to my father obviously wasn't an option. And claiming ownership would spell my doom in the New Dorp High School lunchroom for the rest of this school year and all of the next, all the way until graduation day, fourteen months hence. All I could do was deny, deny, deny . . .

"Look," I said, starting to walk toward him. "I found them when I was a little kid, and I was confused, and I kept them. I just stuck them in that box. I don't even think I've opened that box up in five years."

"I don't believe you," he said. "And I'd rather you didn't try to sit next to me right now."

"I'm not going to try to make out with you or anything," I said. "If that's what you're afraid of."

"I'm not afraid of you. I'm just not a *faggot* like you." He relished saying that word so much. He spoke it as if it was his favorite word in the world. *Faggot, faggot, faggot, faggot!*

"I'm not gay, Terrence," I said. I was trying to remain calm, trying to force my voice down from its high-pitched perch. I told myself not to give in to the tears that were welling up in my eyes. Whatever I did, I couldn't allow myself to cry in front of Terrence.

"Evidence to the contrary right here," he said, holding out the pages to me, teasing me with them. I thought of trying to snatch them from his hands. But before I could react, he pulled the pages back and suddenly tore them in two.

I was too stunned to react. He tore the pages again. He kept on tearing. Two pieces became four, four pieces became eight, eight pieces became sixteen, sixteen pieces became thirty-two, and on and on and on, until the pieces became too small to tear, and a stream of paper began to fall through his fingers to the floor. Suddenly the pages looked like nothing, only tiny scraps of glossy black and white confetti. And that confetti spoke to none of the history of those pictures: of the mystery of my discovery of them; of the years of my adolescence spent, and the hundreds of orgasms reached, in their thrall. This was not fair. This was so fucking *not fair.*

I stood there pondering the final fourteen months of high

school ahead of me and what might happen if Terrence decided to tell people about this. How I would slip from the lowest rung on our school's social ladder to some heretofore unrecorded depth of misery, the eleventh circle of high school hell.

I could only think to plead with him.

"Terrence, please don't tell anyone—"

"You're not really in a position to be making requests." He stood up from the bed, kicking the scraps of confetti scattered at his feet, sending them flurrying through the air—a miniature ticker-tape parade in elegy of my secret that was no more. "You're lucky," he said. "If I told anyone about this shit, I'd have to come up with an explanation for what I was doing here. I could probably make something up. I could tell people that our parents are friends and that I got dragged here and that you had this faggot porno lying around."

He stared at me defiantly, listening to the echo of his made-up story fill the air, trying to decide if it sounded plausible enough to be repeated in the New Dorp High School lunchroom.

Then he said: "That seems more trouble than it's worth, though. This one will be our secret. This way you'll always owe me one."

I hung my head down. I wanted to crawl beneath the bed, where the shoe box had been just a few minutes ago, and cry myself to sleep.

"Why did you follow me here?" I asked him, so soft that I wasn't sure he would hear me, not really sure why I was asking.

He looked at me blankly. He couldn't answer. He didn't know. Perhaps when I stared at him during gym class that morning I had put him in a trance. Perhaps I had hypnotized him into being, just for an afternoon, the Terrence I wanted him to be.

But then he saw my gay pictures and snapped out of it.

"I'm getting the fuck out of here," he said finally.

He navigated past me, taking exaggerated pains to make certain our bodies didn't touch. But before he was through the door, he halted.

"No, you go first," he barked at me. "I don't want you walking behind me and checking out my ass."

The irony didn't escape me. He was right, of course. Truer words had probably never been spoken. Were I to follow him, I would be checking out his ass. Despite all of this—despite four years of taunting; despite two hours of raising my hopes high; despite his trolling around under my bed and dragging out the most private and precious thing I possessed and destroying it—there was no question. He remained the most beautiful and elusive person I knew. The one I wanted to kiss and touch and tear at more than any other. The one whose ass I would never cease checking out.

I slowly moved past him, walking toward the front of the house. The distance from my bedroom door to the three steps that led down into the dining room was only fifteen feet. What happened couldn't have taken more than ten seconds. I was walking toward the dining room, replaying the events of the afternoon through my brain. I was passing the bathroom, just a few feet from those three steps, thinking to myself, *If only I could go back in time, I never would have left him alone in my room, we could be sitting on my bed right now making out . . .*

"Hey, Ben," I heard Terrence say.

I didn't have time to answer. I felt a tremendous, concentrated force smash into my hamstring, just above my right knee. I felt both of my legs give way. For a fraction of a second, my entire body seemed to be floating in the air, sailing over the three steps entirely.

"Don't fall," I heard Terrence say, as my head smacked against the wood floor.

I scrambled frantically to get back up. But the moment I was on my feet, I felt a rush of pain behind my left ear. The entire room suddenly seemed to be rocking back and forth around me. I grabbed the dining room table to steady myself. Terrence didn't wait to survey the effect of his push. He strutted past me, through the dining room and the living room, and then down the stairs.

I reached for one of the dining room chairs and sat down. I put my hand behind my ear. It felt hot and moist. When I brought my hand in front of my face, I saw that it was smeared red and orange with blood.

A few seconds after that, I heard the front door open and then slam shut.

The next few minutes might as well have been hours, and the hours after that might as well have been minutes—it all felt as if there were a video editor inside my head, speeding some things up, slowing other things down, scrambling everything forward and backward. I made my way back up the steps and into the bathroom, where I tried to clean out the cut, even though I couldn't see it (were I to turn my head and try to look into the mirror, the dizziness would have overcome me). I put two Band-Aids at the spot I thought was bleeding, and then I slowly made my way to the living room couch.

And more than the sting of the cut, more than the swooning, liquid buzzing in my head, more than the profound drowsiness starting to overcome me, more than the humiliation of having been knocked to the floor, more than the shame of having been so foolish and thinking that I could bring Terrence here and that something might happen between us, the thing I felt the most as I sat there was disappointment. My one chance with Terrence had been squandered. He was never going to be inside this house again.

When my father arrived home, an hour or two later, he immediately knew something was wrong.

"I fell down the steps in the dining room," I told him. "I knocked my head on the floor." I thought I was speaking clearly. I learned later that I was slurring all my words.

He drove me to the emergency room at Staten Island University Hospital. We waited ninety minutes for a resident to see me. The resident sewed six uneven stitches behind my ear and diagnosed me with a mild concussion. He told me that I should try to stay awake for at least another four hours.

My mother had dinner waiting for us when we got back home. I repeated my story to her: I was coming out of the bathroom; I lost my footing; the next thing I knew my head was smacking against the floor. I suggested to her that maybe I needed a new pair of sneakers.

My mother listened and nodded and told me that I needed to be more careful.

She made no mention of the *two* glasses of soda that had been left on my dresser, which were now in the kitchen sink. She made no mention of the open shoe box, which had been closed shut and placed back under my bed by the time I arrived home. She made no mention of the confetti made from my father's pictures of naked men, which had been cleaned up and thrown away, every last scrap.

And I knew she would make no mention of these holes in my story to my father, either. As I drifted off to sleep, a little after one in the morning, I realized that this would be a secret she and I shared. For this, I would always owe her one.

I stayed out of school for the rest of the week. When I returned the following Monday, I girded myself for more of Terrence's wrath. It was not forthcoming. He ignored me on that day, and he ignored me every day thereafter, for the remaining five weeks of junior year.

And when I went back to school in September, Terrence was gone. I heard that he moved to Ohio or somewhere in the Midwest. And along with Terrence went the taunts, the name-calling, the snickering as I walked through the hallway—all of it dissipated in an instant, like a paragraph highlighted and then deleted whole on a word processor. Senior year passed in relative bliss.

part two

chapter five

The Subject of Revenge
(2000)

The room is dark and square-shaped. I'm trapped inside its confines. I'm running to and fro, crashing into the walls, pressing against them. But they won't budge. I leap into the air, bouncing off my toes, looking, searching. There must be a key hidden here, or a clue, or a secret doorway—something invisible to me, which I must stumble upon, and that will carry to the next level of my quest. I have never played this game before, but I understand the rules. I have already traveled through dark passageways and winding corridors, vanquishing mystical creatures as they leap out in front of me. With each step forward, I feel in greater control of my powers. And now, at last, I am near the end, I can hear him in the very next room, waiting to engage me in the ultimate duel to the death, the final round. But the clock is running out. I only have one life remaining. My strength is rapidly in decline. I race through the room, becoming frantic. To have traveled this far, to have come so close . . . to lose now would mean that I would have to start over at the beginning. But just then I make two successive jumps into the air, and punch the ceiling with all my might, and then a bronze key falls from the sky, and a door appears in the floor, and I place the key inside the lock, and the door springs open with a musical flourish, and I climb through it, into an entirely new room, unlike any I've seen before, the colors are blinding—bright magenta and green and pink—and then I see him, looming increasingly larger with each second I hesitate, growing to three, four, five times my size. . . .

He has been waiting for me here the entire time, licking his lips in anticipation of my arrival.

Terrence O'Connell.
Now I must slay him.

The answering machine clicked on just as I came into consciousness, as I was struggling to reconstruct my dreams. It was
Thursday morning, a week and a half after I had returned from
Indiana. I had been dreaming about Terrence, something
about Terrence. Since returning from Indiana, it seemed as if
every one of my dreams had been about Terrence.

I looked at the alarm clock on my night table. It was nearly
11:00 A.M. I heard the beep of the answering machine. And
then I heard my brother's voice, halting and uncertain.

"Ben, hi, it's me." He paused so long that I thought he had
hung up.

But then he started up again, speaking in a long, quick
burst: "Listen, Ben, Mom keeps calling me, saying you won't return her calls. She says she heard some weird story from some-
body at your school. A story about Mary. I told her it sounded
made up, but she's upset. Can you at least call me, and tell me
what's going on?"

I climbed out of bed and over to the answering machine and
pressed the delete button. No time to return this call, not today. Danny would have to wait.

Today I had to call Terrence, to see if he would take me on a
date.

How to do this? How to settle this long-standing score?

How do you plan for revenge when you are not physically
imposing; when you own no weapons and don't know how or
where to purchase them; when you are very readily stricken
with guilt, perhaps because you were raised Catholic; when the
sight of human viscera makes you so squeamish that you passed
out the last time you donated blood?

And how do you get revenge when you're not even certain
what kind of revenge you're after—or if it's even revenge that

you actually want? Would you prefer just to meet with him and talk to him and perhaps eke out of him some kind of apology? Or do you want something more substantive: a bowing down at your feet; a bit of begging and pleading for your mercy? Or do you want to get *really* serious about it, and give him back some of the humiliation he once delivered unto you, and in just the same manner, so that he will never be able to wash that humiliation away, so that it will seep into his pores like water into arid dirt?

Where do you even begin?

For the first week after my trip to Indiana, I holed up in my apartment, ignoring the daily phone messages from my mother, playing out in my mind dozens of possible scenarios for a first encounter with Terrence. My first thought was that I needed to gather as much information on him as I could. At the newsstand near my apartment, I found the latest issue of *GQ;* sure enough, there was his byline—T. R. O'Connell—on a long article about a cocaine-dealing ring at a prep school in Rhode Island. At the library I looked up more of his work, from *Rolling Stone* and the *Village Voice* and the *New York Times,* profiles of actors, reviews of television shows, stories about the mating rituals of moneyed Manhattan twentysomethings. I re-read all of these articles four, five, six times, searching the sentences for insights into the author's psychology. But there were no clues to find. Other than his rabid enthusiasm for the MTV show *Jackass* and his tendency to overuse the word "rigorous," his writing told me nothing about the kind of adult that Terrence had become.

Next I decided to find him and watch him. I needed to try to get some sense of his daily routine: what time he arrived at the office and what time he left; where he liked to eat lunch; if he preferred to take the subway home or to treat himself to a taxi. For two consecutive mornings, I woke up early, rode the ferry into Manhattan, and then took the subway to Times Square, where I stood across the street from the Condé Nast building, keeping my eyes raptly focused on the front doors. But the men who walked into the building all looked exactly the same to me—it was a building stacked high with tall, sandy-haired and attractive young men. (And who even knew if he was still attractive? Perhaps as part of his deal with the devil, he had relinquished his good looks on midnight of his twenty-fifth birthday and turned fat and bald, with hair growing out of his ears and an unfortunate tendency to sweat through his clothes—and I would have my revenge right there.)

Besides, the longer I stood across the street, waiting, watching stock ticker symbols dance across the front of the building, hoping that I wouldn't be noticed by a police officer and given a ticket for loitering, the more I realized that I was procrastinating. The longer I waited, the more likely I was to lose my nerve altogether and never do anything with the information Mrs. O'Connell had given me.

But still, still . . . I couldn't do it. I didn't know where to begin.

I thought of phoning his apartment in the middle of the workday and leaving a message. Why not shift the ball into his court and force him to make the first real move?

But that approach seemed all wrong. His parents had no doubt warned him that I would be calling; he had already had ten days to formulate *his* plan for dealing with me. In which case, what if he had already determined not to let me back into his life? What if he just pressed the delete button on his answering machine and eliminated my message entirely?

Then I thought of writing him a letter. I could put it all down on paper, explain to him how he had wronged me and precisely what I wanted him to do to ameliorate the situation. I could spend a few days laboring over this letter, so that it expressed exactly what I needed it to express, and then I could mail it to his office and give him a couple of weeks to think about it—and *then* I would call. At which point, he wouldn't be able to ignore me, not if he had any manners at all. He'd have to come up with some kind of response.

Except I knew that wouldn't work, either. A letter would give him too much time to prepare and too much information to use against me—it would be the equivalent of a football coach handing over his playbook to the opposing team's captain a week before the playoffs. Terrence would have me sacked before I even got my hands on the ball.

The obvious fact of the matter was this: I needed to call him at the office, where he wouldn't be able to screen outside calls; in the middle of the workday, when he would have to pick up the phone (just in case it was an important source on the line, or an editor from the *New Yorker* offering him an even more high-profile job than the one he had); where he would be surrounded by colleagues and minions, so he wouldn't be able to raise his voice or scream at me, "Leave me and my family alone."

At his office, in the middle of the workday, if only for thirty seconds or a minute, Terrence O'Connell would have to give his bullied an audience.

I puttered around my apartment until 11:30 A.M., figuring I didn't want to call too early, just in case he was a late riser. Then I stood in the living room with my cordless phone, pushing the TALK button and then pushing the END button a few seconds later, starting to dial his number and then stopping and hanging up again. It took a full twenty minutes before I finally allowed the phone to ring—and even then I wasn't sure if I would go through with it or if I would just hang up the moment he answered.

He picked up almost immediately.

"This is Terrence," he said. His voice sounded exactly as it had when he was younger, mellifluous and a little icy. He might as well have answered with the words "Don't fall."

"Hi Terrence, um, this is Ben Reilly. I don't know if you—"

"Hey, Ben," he said, holding out the "hey," sounding excited to hear from me. "I was wondering when you were going to call. How are you doing, man?"

I didn't answer him at first. I pictured him leaning back in his high-backed, leather desk chair in his expansive Condé

Nast office, his feet up on his desk, the fast-rising wunderkind writer looking out on Times Square and smiling broadly, like a spider who spies his insect prey at the very edge of an elaborately weaved web, drawing closer to the center, it would only be a moment or two more before he could feast upon me . . .

I took a deep breath and girded myself for battle. I had to beat him to the punch.

"Your parents told you—"

"My mom said she gave you my number," he said. "But then I didn't hear anything. I was waiting."

"Well, I just got back to New York the day before yesterday," I lied. "The project has been eating up all of my time."

"Yeah, my mom mentioned that. A documentary, right?"

"It's my project for . . . it's my thesis project . . . I'm getting an MFA at NYU . . ." I was stumbling, trying to remember all the lies that I had told his parents and line them up in my head. I silently cursed myself for not having been better prepared for this conversation. I had spent two weeks obsessing about *when* I was going to call, but I had never actually bothered to rehearse what I was going to say to him once I got him on the line.

"You should tell me more about it over dinner," he said. "Maybe tomorrow night? I have to stay at the office tonight. They're finishing up the fact-check on one of my stories so I need to hang around to answer any questions that come up. But tomorrow night, are you free?"

I didn't think he was telling the truth. It came out of his mouth too smoothly, too canned. *He* was the one who had been doing all the rehearsing for this conversation.

"I'm free," I told him.

"Have you ever been to a place called Patria? It's on 19th and Park."

"No, but I'm sure I can find it," I said. "Listen, Terrence—"

"Eight-thirty?" he asked, cutting me off. I could hear him scribbling something down on a pad, a reminder to make a reservation, or perhaps some carefully observed nugget of wisdom about this conversation, the timbre of my voice or the rhythm of our dialogue, a detail that he would later work into one of his magazine stories, or maybe even his second novel. Already he was taking notes on us.

"Yeah, that's fine," I told him, "but, listen, I know this probably seems really weird to you, I just wanted to—"

He cut me off again. "Not weird. If anything, intriguing. But not weird." He sounded sly, mischievous, a little bit of the flirt. Just as he had when he first approached me after school that day, hinting to me that maybe we could be friends.

"Intriguing." I didn't know how to respond, other than to repeat the word back to him.

"Eight-thirty, then," he said. "It's at 19th and Park. If there's any problem, just call me here. Take care, Ben."

Don't fall.

A moment later I heard a click.

The young men and women sat elbow-to-elbow at the bar, or they hovered behind those who were seated, in densely packed clusters of four and five, making loud conversation, laughing too hard at each other's jokes, straining to be heard and noticed above the din of everyone talking and laughing around them. The men wore dark business suits with pastel-colored shirts, the top two buttons undone, their ties left behind at the office. The women wore charcoal-colored suits or, if they had had enough time to go home after work and change, slinky black dresses that fell just above the knee but did not reveal any cleavage. The men gulped from bottles of Heineken and Dos Equis. The women sipped cocktails in hues of pink and lime green and violet, giggling, pretending to be more drunk than they were. They were all young, three or four years out of their high-priced colleges, places like Wesleyan and Yale. With the exception of a group of Asian men, techie types with too-short haircuts and square-framed glasses, they were all white. They were the ones who had majored in economics or computer science, who had come to New York City after graduation with jobs already lined up—the companies would have recruited them on campus—working for an investment bank or a dotcom startup on the verge of its initial public offering. Their signing bonuses would have been more money than I made in a year. They worked fourteen-hour days, skipping lunch so that they could squeeze in a forty-five minute workout at the gym. They spent most of their money on L-shaped studio apartments in desirable Upper West Side doormen buildings, and they spent the rest of their money in concentrated bursts, on Friday and Saturday night, knocking back $12 cocktails, not blinking twice at paying $38 for a plate of white truffle risotto, saying yes when the sommelier suggested to them a $97 bottle of wine, because it's an especially good bargain for a vintage so strong. These were not native-born New York City kids; it wasn't as if the town was in their blood. Most of them would end up in the suburbs, in Larchmont or Hastings-on-Hudson or Darien, commuting into and out of the city via Metro North. But for now, for their twenties, at least until they turned thirty, while they were still unattached, still seeking out a member of the opposite sex who had gone to just as competitive a university, they were here, killing their non-billable hours at this overpriced hot spot, spending money to convince themselves that they belonged, in this bar, in this restaurant, in this city, in these jobs, in these clothes, in this life. You don't run up a $140 bar tab in two hours flat without telling yourself that you belong.

I had decided it would be wise to get to Patria early, just to get my bearings and maybe get a drink in me before he walked through the door. I arrived at 7:30 P.M., and I found an empty stool at the end of the bar. I ordered a beer and hoped the bartender might strike up a conversation with me—anything to distract me from constantly thinking about Terrence. He never did. There were too many other patrons clamoring for his attention. It was a Friday night, a warm, early spring evening, and people were eager to get out of their cramped offices and apartments and be seen. All I was left to do was watch these

people—these bankers and lawyers ar
tractive and successful—multiplying a

And to marvel to myself: How ea
one of them. Before deciding to a
had considered the possibility of la
LSATs, and read the brochures fro
started asking my professors for th
tions, and they assured me that I would have no t
in. But now, just five years later, all I knew of this world was
gleaned from reading the restaurant reviews in the *New York
Times* or from watching episodes of *Sex and the City* on HBO.
Teaching high school in Staten Island, just fifteen miles due
south of this very bar stool, I had let myself become completely
disconnected from any sort of peer group. To these people I
might as well have been living in Kansas. I may have once been
every bit as smart and promising as them, but now it was as if a
terminal illness had come along and obliterated me. Classmates who once knew me might ask: *Whatever happened to that
guy?* And no one would know the answer. And someone, inevitably, would say: *I wonder if he's even still alive.*

He arrived a few minutes after 8:30 P.M., just as I was finishing
my second beer. There were two women sitting at the opposite
end of the bar, two attractive, long-haired blondes wearing
shorter-than-average dresses and expensive-looking glittery
jewelry in their ears. I watched these two women turn their
heads, and then shift their entire bodies, to take note of whoever had just walked through the front door. That was my signal—my sign from Satan—that Terrence O'Connell had
entered the building.

He was standing in front of the restaurant manager, nodding and laughing as the manager gripped him by the shoulder and vigorously shook his hand. His sandy hair had
darkened to light brown, and it was cut shorter than it had
been in high school and slicked back, almost in the manner of

...s in *The Matrix*. His blue eyes were still the same ...ue, still deep and bright and sparkling with determi-...His smile still revealed the same dimple in his left ..., the dimple all of our female teachers once imagined ...nselves sinking into. He wore a dark red button-down shirt ...nd a pair of gray, lightweight wool trousers that look custom-tailored—though, as I gave up my seat at the bar and started walking toward him, I realized that they were probably off-the-rack from Banana Republic; it was just that his body had developed into the sort of perfectly proportioned object that mass-produced clothing is designed to fit, broad through the shoulders and narrow through the waist. He looked twice as fortified as when I had known him, as if each morning the hand of God descended through his bathroom ceiling and held out to him heaven's specially formulated vitamins. He looked to be about 6 feet 2 inches, 190 pounds, solid to the touch.

Terrence O'Connell: mannequin-come-to-life; man-about-town; my bully all grown up.

"Terrence," I called out. He didn't hear me. The manager began leading him to our table, smack in the middle of the dining room, the best spot in the house. I trailed behind them, working my way through the tightly clustered tables of still more lawyers and bankers. The manager was pulling out Terrence's chair for him when I finally caught up with them.

"Terrence, hey, I was sitting at the bar."

He hesitated for a moment. His brow knitted, and a mixture of fear and uncertainty took up residence on his forehead. The manager stood awkwardly between us, waiting for Terrence to tell him what to do. For a few seconds, I feared that I might be ejected from the restaurant; that two black-suited goons would emerge from a back room and toss me onto the street. I started to wonder if this had been Terrence's plan—to bring me here and humiliate me all over again.

Until, finally, Terrence took a step forward and said, very quietly, "Ben, wow. It's good to see you."

"How are you Terrence?" I said, holding out my hand for him to shake. That seemed to snap him back into action. He grabbed my hand and shook it firmly. The manager drifted away, telling Terrence, "If there's anything you need, Mr. O'Connell . . ." We took our seats across from one another. Terrence told me that I looked great, and that I hadn't changed in ten years. He said that we had so much to catch up on.

"But first," he said, "let's order some wine." He gestured for the sommelier and selected a $92 bottle of Oregon Pinot Noir.

"It's so good to see you," he repeated to me, after the sommelier had disappeared.

"It's good to see you Terrence," I said. "It's been awhile."

"I hope this place is still good," he said, looking around the room for a few seconds longer than normal, almost as if he were searching for a better table to sit at, more sophisticated company to join. "The *Times* gave it three stars in 1997. I came here a lot back then, but I haven't been in a while."

"The bar was packed," I told him. "They must be doing something right."

"I don't know if I'd characterize attracting the investment banking crowd as doing something right." He said it matter-of-factly, but I couldn't help but feel put down. Only one of us knew New York City well enough to know when a trendy place had crossed over into has-been status.

Two minutes in, and already it's high school all over again.

"So, Ben, what's going on?" he said, looking past me, having a hard time making eye contact. "There's no documentary, is there? Unless you know something the NYU computer system doesn't. You're not registered there as a student."

He wasn't hectoring or accusing, just stating the facts as he knew them. I didn't have an answer. I had assumed my documentary charade would carry on for a little while; that, even if Terrence knew it was lie, he would play along.

"A friend of mine works at the NYU admissions office," he said, when I didn't answer. "I called and asked her to check on you. For a while I thought you might be making a documentary on your own and that you just name-dropped NYU to impress my parents—which worked, by the way—but, I don't know, the whole thing sounds a little made-up to me. You've never really struck me as the documentary filmmaker type. You're a little too respectable to be walking around in ratty jeans with a big camera on your shoulder."

"No," I told him, laughing a little nervously. "There's no documentary."

"It's no big deal," he added quickly. "I tell my parents lies all the time to get stuff out of them." He paused and smiled, just for a second, before he turned serious again. "But, if there's no documentary, then you probably have some explaining to do. Maybe you can start from the beginning. Why did you track down my parents? Or *how* did you track them down? Start there."

There wasn't a hint of approbation in his tone, only genuine curiosity and sincerity, a determination to make me feel comfortable. I wondered if this was how he wrote his magazine articles—by taking his sources to expensive restaurants; dazzling them with his authority and presence; telling them to start at the beginning. I could see how he would be successful at it, too. He had the sort of gentle and encouraging manner that made you want to confess your secrets to him. He made you feel like, no matter what you told him, he was never going to judge you.

He doesn't seem threatening anymore—that's the thing that seems most different. Actually, he seems kind of nice. And I'm not scared. For the first time I can remember, I don't feel terrified in his presence.

Before I could say anything, our waiter appeared with the wine and wanted to know if we were ready to order. Terrence asked him a series of arcane-seeming questions—*Is the drum pan seared or grilled? How does the cranberry relish pair with the quail?*—all of which the waiter dutifully answered. He finally settled on the pork tenderloin, which cost $32. He urged me to try the tuna, the restaurant's signature dish, which cost $35. He told the waiter to start us both off with salads, which cost $9 each. And then, after the waiter committed all of this to memory and shuffled away, just as I was beginning to wonder if the $200 I had in my wallet would be enough to cover my share of the bill, Terrence looked to me expectantly. He was ready for my story.

This is what I told him, some of it prepared, some of it made up on the spot, most of it true, some of it, necessarily, a lie: I told him that after Wesleyan I had drifted into teaching high school; that I had enjoyed it for awhile, but I had started to realize I wasn't going to be able to do it forever—it felt too repetitive and regressive, year to year, watching the students advance while I stayed behind. I told him that I had decided to make a radical break; that I actually left my job in January and began traveling around the country, visiting old friends from college. I told him that one of those old friends attended graduate school at Indiana University, and that I was living with this friend for a few weeks—just killing time, plowing through Russian classics by Gogol and Tolstoy that I had never gotten around to reading in college, hoping the answer to my future would soon make itself apparent. I told him that one afternoon, just a few weeks earlier, I had experienced a minor epiphany. I realized that the only way to move forward would be to lay to rest some of the things still hanging over my head from the past—and that *he* was one of those things. I told him that I started with an Indianapolis phone book, remembering from junior year of high school that his family had moved to Indiana, and then I went to visit them and made up a story about making a documentary film, so that they would put me in touch with their son. I talked for nearly an hour straight, Terrence nodding and encouraging me along. And the more I told him, the more I realized that—save for a few details and embellishments—I was telling him the truth. Or as close to truth as I could invent for him, without also telling him about Elliot and Mario and without bringing up the subject of revenge.

"And here I am now, having dinner with you," I said.

"I can see you not wanting to tell that story to my parents," he said, finishing off the last of the wine in his glass, looking around for our waiter. "They don't really cotton to people with doubt in their lives. The idea of quitting a job that doesn't satisfy you is totally alien to them. In their world, you take whatever job you get and you work really hard until you've climbed to the top." The waiter was suddenly hovering over us. "Hey, do you want another bottle of wine?" he said to me. "Let's get another bottle of wine. I want to hear more of your story." And just like that he ordered us a second bottle of $92 wine.

"That's most of it," I said. "I hope I didn't frighten your parents by showing up out of the blue. Your father seemed suspicious of me."

"Actually it was the other way around. My dad loved your documentary idea. He wants you to send him a copy when you've finished editing it." Terrence laughed at this, and I laughed along with him. How quickly this was all seeming so normal—two old friends meeting up for dinner after a decade-long estrangement, falling effortlessly back into their old ways.

"My mother was the one who was suspicious," Terrence said.

"But she gave me your number."

Terrence shrugged. "I've long since given up trying to understand my mother."

"Did you tell them about me?" I asked. "About what happened between us in high school?"

"I just said I remembered you but not very well. I don't really tell my parents very much about my personal life."

The waiter brought over our second bottle of wine and uncorked it and started pouring. Terrence took a big swallow and then, unprompted, he began telling me his story, the last ten years of his life. He said that he was furious, at the end of junior year of high school, when his parents told him they were moving to Indiana. He feared that a move might jeopardize his chances of getting into a good college. He barely talked to them while he was living there. And even after getting into

Yale, he was still angry with them, still seeking out some sort of rebellion. He spent his first year there drinking too much and doing too many drugs, nearly flunking out, ignoring his father's repeated demands that he pull his life together or risk being cut off from the family entirely. It wasn't until September of his sophomore year—when, with no drugs or alcohol at his immediate disposal, he stayed up all night reading *The Awakening* in one sitting, and then, the next morning, sat listening to his famous English professor's brilliant lecture on the book— that he realized he was squandering too vast an opportunity. He was too smart and too promising to be drinking and doping away a Yale education. Within weeks, he turned everything around. He began taking more English courses. He decided to major in creative writing—that would be his way of getting back at his parents without spiting himself, by majoring in something they found so trivial and financially unpromising. He started writing for the *Yale Daily News,* poems and essays and movie reviews. During his senior year, he wrote a short story that was accepted for publication in the *Antioch Review.* (When he told his father this news, all his father could think to say was, "How much are they paying you for it?") After graduation, he moved to New York City. And everything clicked, so quickly and so readily that it still amazed him. Everything his parents had told me was true, right down to the fact that the novel was presently circulating in Hollywood, and that some top-shelf producers were thinking of paying him a small fortune to option it. He talked slowly, but without pauses, stopping only to swallow some food or drink more wine. He spoke to me as if this were his first visit to a therapist, and he needed to get it all out there, into the air and open for diagnosis, before his fifty minutes were up.

"Sometimes I get mad at myself, for becoming exactly the kind of person my parents want me to be," he said. "Successful. Stable. Overpaid. All that crap. The rest of the time I just keep waiting for the other shoe to drop. I know that's such a terrible way of looking at things. And I know it sounds so spoiled and pretentious. *Woe is me for my life that is going so well.* But, I don't know Ben, sometimes it's hard for me to enjoy anything. I can't get past this idea that if good things are happening now, then something bad is on the horizon. That there's going to be some kind of retribution."

He leaned back in his chair and clasped his hands over his stomach. Maybe it was just the alcohol that was encouraging him to tell me more than he would have otherwise; or maybe it was the unusual nature of this strange reunion—the fear of having nothing to say compelling him to say way too much.

Or maybe my first instincts, dating all the way back to that day junior year of high school, had been correct: Maybe he was just trying to make a connection with me.

"I thought you might be the retribution," he said, smiling at me. "When my mother first called and told me about you, I thought, 'This must be the other shoe dropping.'"

I laughed too loudly. It sounded too hollow. I worried that he would see right through me and decide I was a fraud.

But I didn't know how else to react. Because isn't that *exactly* what I wanted? To knock him off his feet? To fuck things up for him a little bit?

Wasn't that how I would finally settle the score between us?

Or maybe not. Because when I looked into his eyes and saw him smiling at me—a smile of regret and wistfulness and faint self-disgust—well, suddenly I wasn't sure what I wanted from him. All I could say for certain was that I wanted to keep on talking to him. I wanted this dinner to go on all night long.

"Honestly, when my mother told me about you, I was a little scared," he said. "A part of me was hoping that you'd never call."

"But you're here now," I said.

"I'm here," he answered slowly. "It felt like something I had to make myself do."

I didn't say anything. I watched him as he lifted his glass and drank another long gulp of wine.

"Listen, Ben," he started up again. "There are probably

about seven thousand different apologies that I owe you. But pushing you down the steps that day—that was beneath contempt. I'll start with that apology. I'm sorry that happened. I wish I could take that back."

"I still have the scar behind my ear," I said. "Six stitches."

"I couldn't even look at you after that day. I couldn't believe I did something that petty. I decided I would just never talk to you again. That was my way of dealing with it."

He sounded so sincere, so intent upon mending fences—I felt my desire for revenge dissolving right there at the table. Who was I kidding? Revenge! What was I going to do: push him down the steps of a subway station? Shove him into oncoming traffic on Park Avenue?

I didn't want any of those things. I don't think I wanted revenge at all.

I probably never did.

"We were both different people then, Terrence," I told him.

"What bothers me, Ben," he said, "is that I tend to think that I was exactly the same person then as I am now. Only back then I did a lot of mean-spirited crap. I don't do bad things anymore, and I don't hurt people's feelings just because I can. But how does that make up for all the crap that I did do? I've turned it over and over in my head, and I always come to the same conclusion. If I did it once, I can do it again. I'm still the same person. I just put a better face forward now."

He sounded so sad and so anxious—he sounded like such a little boy. And I was tantalized by the fact that he had been over this in his head many times; that he had been thinking about me as much as I had been thinking about him. For the first time ever, I felt a rush of sympathy for Terrence O'Connell. And I suddenly found myself saying the words I never thought I could say.

"I accept your apology, Terrence. I appreciate it. It means a lot to me."

"You don't have to, you know," he said. "I'm not sure I would forgive me if I were in your place."

"No, it's time we both cleaned the slate," I said.

He smiled broadly, his bright, perfectly even teeth exposed, his dimple in full flush. For a moment, it felt as if I was staring into the face of my sixteen-year-old arch-nemesis all over again. And, for a moment after that, I feared that his contrition was false; that this was all part of a nefarious and carefully calculated scheme; that sitting at the tables all around us and standing at the still-packed bar were all of our old classmates, Jimmy Losciavo and Joe DeNino and Seth Kern and Dave Leferink, all grown up and all dressed up, but poised, at Terrence's signal, to launch us fifteen years back in time and start chanting in unison: *Gaywad. Gaywad. Gaywad. That kid is such a GAYWAD.* Terrence O'Connell had tricked me into rewarding him absolution. He had played me for his stooge.

But then, just as quickly, the new Terrence returned. He told me that he really appreciated my efforts in reaching out to him. He implored me to order dessert and cappuccino. And then we kept on talking, for another hour longer. He asked me to tell him more about Wesleyan, and then he told me more about Yale—and we mused over the fact that we should end up at schools located only thirty miles apart, that we might very well have crossed one another's paths without ever realizing it. I asked him about the process of writing his novel, and he said that almost the entire thing had been written in longhand, two hours a day, every day for a year, sitting in the Starbucks at 68th Street and Broadway, embarrassed the entire time that he had become one of those people who pretends to write novels in a coffee shop. He asked me what career path I might like to pursue now that I was no longer teaching. I confessed that I didn't have too many ideas, but that maybe I could finally go to graduate school, or perhaps I could try writing myself. He offered his help if I chose the latter route—he said there were good people to whom he could introduce me.

It was nearly midnight when we finally got up to leave. He paid the bill with his credit card, waving off my repeated attempts to give him cash. Then he walked with me to the subway, which I would take to the southernmost tip of Manhattan, where I would board the ferry to Staten Island.

"Ben, the next time we get together, I'd love to hear more about your teaching," he said, as we neared the station. "I could use your help with a project that I might be tackling."

The next time we get together. I barely registered his request for help. I was too excited by the certainty of his words, this assurance of a future together. Terrence was already looking ahead to another meeting.

"I've been thinking of writing something about high school violence," he said. "Maybe a one-year-later type of story about Columbine. I talked to my editor about it, but he's not sure if people still care. But I keep thinking about it. I can't quite get it out of my head. And it seems like every day there's a new report of kids killing each other."

I started to tell him about the most recent instance of high school violence, the one between Mario Tropiano and Elliot Applebaum. I was about to say, *Did you read about those two kids in Staten Island? That happened at my school. I was there that afternoon.* But I caught myself. I remembered that I had told him that I had stopped teaching in January. I had to be careful, from here on out, to keep the lies that I had told Terrence in order.

"I know you're not teaching anymore," he continued, "but I'd love to hear more about your experiences. It seems to me that high school is so different now from when we were there."

"I think high school *is* a lot different now," I said, a little too quickly. I didn't really believe this. If anything, high school struck me as exactly the same now as it had always been: a place where teachers had no idea how much resentment and hatred festered just beneath their noses; a place where half of the students wanted to destroy the other half of the students, usually for no good reason at all.

But it was a necessary lie. So that Terrence would want *the next time we get together* to happen sooner rather than later.

"I'll give you a call and we'll figure something out," he said.

On the subway and ferry rides home, I replayed every single event of the evening in my head, from the moment he walked into the restaurant to our handshake good-bye. It had all clicked so perfectly. I tried to remember the tastes of the food, the wine, the dessert, the cappuccino. I tried to reconstruct every word of every sentence that he had spoken to me. I wanted to keep these memories forever. I didn't want to forget a second of it.

I didn't have a very broad base for comparison, but it had felt like the greatest first date of my life.

chapter six

A Second Date
(2000)

Messages, messages, messages, he won't stop calling, every few days he leaves another message.

On Monday: "Listen, Ben, I didn't want to have to say this to you, and I'm not trying to make you feel bad. But you've been acting really weird. Even before you quit your job, you seemed kind of weird—and lately it's just gone off the charts. No one's trying to attack you. We just want to know what's going on. Can you please call me? I'm not going to judge you, if that's what you're worried about."

And then on Thursday: "Everybody is upset, Ben, you've got everybody worried. Mom and Dad think that you may have AIDS, and that this is your way of dealing with it. I told them they're overreacting. But it's hard to defend you when you won't call me back."

And one more the Tuesday after that: "Ben, I'm getting fed up. Just call me back already. You don't have the right to make Mom and Dad feel miserable about all of this. Or to be making a mockery of Mary. You're hurting people. And it's not very nice. For once in your life, try having some fucking empathy."

But Danny doesn't understand. I can't return his messages. I don't dare pick up the phone. Terrence is due to call me any day now, any minute, any second, to set up our next meeting, to talk about high school violence.

I can't run the risk of him getting a busy signal.

For the first week after my dinner with Terrence, I refused to call him. I still wasn't sure if any sort of adult friendship was even possible between us, but I knew that I needed to maximize that possibility. And the only way to do *that,* I reasoned, was to give him some breathing room and to let him make the next move. I couldn't fall into the trap of the overeager suitor, who calls and then lets himself talk on the answering machine, minutes and minutes of idiotic blabbering that makes the other person think: *Uh-oh, what kind of freak have I attracted here?* The last thing I wanted to do was to scare him away.

So I waited. For seven days, I waited for the phone to ring. It was not like they show it in the movies—the romantic comedies with the slickly edited montages set to some chirpy pop music hit, the heroine staring at the telephone, painting her toenails, scrubbing the kitchen floor, staring back at the telephone, cooking a gourmet meal, staring some more at the telephone, *waiting for the boy to call.* The movies never showed what *really* happens: the obsessive playing and replaying of your answering machine messages, pushing the play button again and again, because maybe the machine made an error when he called and stored his message on some hidden part of the audio tape; or the checking and rechecking of the machine when you were out of the house, checking in from a pay phone at least once every ten minutes, because all it takes is a few seconds for him to place a call, it could happen at any moment, and you wouldn't want to leave his message unanswered for too long. The movies never conveyed the *time,* its resistance to going faster—interminable seconds and minutes and hours piling up as you sit there, as you just keep sitting there. The movies never showed what happens when you finally do get a call, the cresting jubilation and then the debilitating, paralyzing disappointment, when you race to the phone and reach for the receiver, and you're praying the whole time, *please, God, please just let it be him,* and then you look at the caller ID . . . and it's just a telemarketer trying to get you to consolidate debt, or, even worse, your brother calling to chide you for not returning *his* messages. In the movies, the boy always calls.

And worst of all is your *consciousness*—the movies never got at that either—your awareness that you're acting like a fool; like a lovesick and helpless teenager. For seven days, I thought about Terrence almost every waking moment. Whenever I tried to concentrate on something else—a book, or TV show, or the increasingly pressing question of what I was going to do for money now that I didn't have a job—my mind quickly wandered back to an image of him sitting across from me in the restaurant, tentatively seeking out my forgiveness.

I knew I was being silly; and I also knew I had no control over whether or not he called me; and I knew, too, that my life would carry on even if I never heard from him again. I knew all of this. But that didn't stop me.

I told myself that he had gotten called away on business—that his editor had assigned him a late-breaking story that required him to fly to Estonia or Nova Scotia or some such far-flung place where it's a pain in the ass to make an international phone call.

I told myself that he *had* called, but that I had been in the shower, and I didn't hear it ring, and he didn't leave a message.

I told myself that he had been run over by a taxicab and left for dead; that his very last thought as he was being carted off to the morgue was: *I was planning to call Ben today, just as soon as I got home.*

I told myself a million different things, a million different ways, none of them remotely approaching the truth of the matter: Namely, that I would tell myself anything, so long as it allowed me to go on believing in the myth of Terrence's reform.

Ten years later, and you're still making excuses for him. You're still trying to convince yourself that he's not so bad.

On the ninth day of his silence, I decided I couldn't sit around any longer. I called his office. It rang five times before his voice mail picked up.

"Hey, Terrence, this is Ben Reilly," I said into the machine—trying to sound casual and indifferent, as if it had only *just* occurred to me that I hadn't heard from him in awhile—"and I just wanted to thank you again for dinner. And give you my number again in case you misplaced it." I finished by saying, "Give me a call some time." *Casual and indifferent.* As if it didn't matter one way or the other if he ever called me back.

But still nothing. Three more days passed. It was a Thursday, coming up on the two week anniversary of our first date. I was incredulous that I should be ignored. If he was going to break this off, he could at least do it with a bit of civility. I left my apartment at 10:30 A.M. I arrived in Times Square a few minutes before noon. And I once again found myself standing across from the Condé Nast building, sorely without a plan.

So I wandered. I walked to Eighth Avenue, and then up to 50th Street, and then over to Broadway, and then I walked back down to Times Square, repeating this same route for nearly two hours, always pausing and lingering each time I passed the front doors of his building. I fantasized that I might bump into him. He would be surprised and contrite: *Oh, Ben, I'm so sorry I haven't called, I was whisked out of town, but now I'm back and we can become great friends.* And I would act casual and indifferent: *Terrence, how are you? I just came into the city to see this foreign film I've been hearing about, but now I have to get home. I'll give you a call soon.* I would make it seem as if *I* was the one who had been ignoring *him*.

But who was I fooling? That was never going to happen. He was probably nowhere near here. He was probably in Starbucks, poring over the final proofs of his first novel. Or in the library doing research for his *GQ* article on high school violence (it had turned out he hadn't needed my help after all). Or maybe he was at the Prada store in Soho, getting fitted for a new suit that he would wear to some fabulous event or another to which he had been invited, and for which I—most certainly—would not be his plus one. Wherever he was, he was not sitting around and waiting, not counting each second until I called. Terrence O'Connell had already moved on.

At 3:30 P.M., I decided to head back to Staten Island. I rode the subway and the ferry, sullen and impatient. In the car, driving from the ferry terminal back to my apartment, my eyes started to sting. I had to take deep breaths and then slowly exhale just to prevent myself from crying. I kept thinking the same thoughts over and over again: *How could he do this to me? How could he raise my expectations so high and then dash them?*

And also these thoughts: *How could I let him trick me, just like he tricked me that day in high school? How could I fall for his charming-little-boy routine all over again?*

I knew I was overreacting. I knew, too, that the only way I would ever be able to get on with my life was to just forget about him; to push him out of my head once and for all.

But I couldn't help myself. All this effort . . . to have come this far . . . so that you can even begin to imagine it . . . *forgiveness and reconciliation . . . the bad memories erased . . . a fresh start . . . a long and fruitful friendship ahead . . .*

Then all of that hopefulness gets sabotaged, just because he refuses to pick up the fucking phone.

I hate you Terrence. I hate you so much for making me like you.

But then another thought occurred to me, just as I pulled up to the curb in front of my apartment. It had been nearly seven hours since I left my apartment, the longest period of time I had gone in the last two weeks without checking my messages. I felt a surge of hopefulness. All day in the city it simply hadn't occurred to me that I should constantly be calling in to the machine. Surely this was one of life's most simple ironies working itself out on my behalf: The calls you anticipate the most only come when the anticipation briefly slips your mind, when God finally stops snickering at you from above and says, *You have learned the lesson I intended to teach, so now I will answer your prayers.*

I bounded through my front door, taking giant steps toward my bedroom and to the answering machine on top of my bureau. The light was blinking. *Yes!* A message had been recorded. *Yes, yes, yes!* It had to be Terrence. I bet my entire life that it was Terrence's voice on the machine.

And it was. He had left a message at 2:00 P.M. that afternoon. And just like that everything was restored. All at once I felt saved.

"Ben, hi, I'm sorry I haven't gotten back to you. I hope you didn't think I was trying to blow you off. Listen, this is short notice, but I have this movie screening tonight, and I wanted to see if you were free. It's at seven. Give me a call at the office if you can make it."

I looked to the alarm clock next to my bed, which read 5:16 P.M. My excitement instantly collapsed into disappointment. There was almost no chance of making it back into the city by 7:00 P.M., not unless I left this very second.

But then I played the message again. And then I played it two more times after that, relishing the sound of his voice, the measure of calm and balance his words restored to our burgeoning relationship. How could I possibly allow myself to feel disappointment? How could I feel anything other than elation? My fears had been mislaid. He still wanted to try to be friends.

I dialed his office number, assuming that he had already left for the day and that I would get his voice mail. I would thank him for the invitation and explain that I didn't hear his message until too late. Then I would propose dinner on Saturday night, a second date for the day after tomorrow. Perhaps I would even tell him that it would be my treat.

He picked up on the first ring.

"Hey, it's Ben," I said. "I just got your message."

"The offer still stands," he said. "Can you get to 49th Street and Broadway by seven?"

"Yeah, I think so," I said, looking again at the clock, which now read 5:22 P.M. I would need to speed back to the ferry terminal and get onto the 6:00 P.M. departing ferry—a thirty-minute drive that, at the height of rush hour, could easily take twice as long.

"Are you sure?" he asked.

Just tell him you can't. For once in your life try playing hard to get.

"I can make it," I said. "Tell me where I should meet you."

The screening room was very small, with only twenty-four seats, big, plush, purple-upholstered armchairs, six to a row. When I arrived a few minutes before 7:00 P.M., people were still standing and talking in small clusters. They were mostly men. Many of them were wearing dark-colored business suits. I spotted Terrence in the far corner, and he saw me and waved me over. He was talking to two other men. I was relieved to see they were the most casually dressed people in the room.

"Ben, I'm glad you could make it," Terrence said. The two men turned and fanned out, letting me into their circle. One of them, I realized, was an actor, a handsome man with thick black hair and pronounced cheekbones, someone I had seen in a bunch of movies, but whose name I couldn't immediately place. The other man had a cheerful, weather-beaten face and a somewhat disheveled manner. They both looked toward me expectantly.

"Ben, this is Cameron Crowe and this is Billy Crudup," Terrence said. "Cameron directed the movie, and Billy is one of the stars. I'm going to London next month to interview him for the magazine. He's going to be acting in a play there."

I shook both of their hands and smiled. I mumbled something to Cameron Crowe about having liked his other movies. I looked at Billy Crudup and didn't know what to say.

I knew Terrence had probably done this to impress me: To illustrate to me that people regarded him as important; that he was invited to private screenings of movies with the director and star in attendance; that he was flying to London—almost certainly first class—to interview a rising young actor. And the thing was—it worked. I *was* impressed. And more than that: besotted; dazzled; dizzy with awe. I was the romance-starved secretary out on a date with the dashing brain surgeon, putting out of my mind the question of *why* someone so perfect would want to spend time with someone like me and reveling in the moment, the fantasy of long-term bliss, the possibility of having landed a real catch, someone I could bring home to family and show off to friends . . . *you're not going to believe it . . . this guy is so perfect . . . he's my very own Prince Charming . . .*

"Ben and I go all the way back to junior high school," Terrence said to Cameron Crowe, who didn't seem to hear him or didn't particularly care, I couldn't tell which. We were saved from having to make any more conversation by one of the men in suits, who announced from the front of the room that the movie was starting.

"I'm sorry, I probably should have warned you," Terrence said, leading me to two seats near the back. "These things usually aren't so formal."

"I like it," I said. "It makes it seem like we're about to witness history being made, you know? It feels as if we're at the premiere of *Citizen Kane*."

Terrence laughed at this. I laughed too. He appreciated my wit! He got me! I felt so happy and relaxed now. The drama of the last ten days, waiting and waiting for his call, was already a distant memory. How could I have ever doubted that things would work out between us?

"How have you been?" I asked.

"I'm good," he said. "Just really busy." It seemed as if he was about to say more; perhaps that he wanted to ask my forgiveness for not having called me sooner. But just then the lights began dimming, and the mumbling all around us got quiet.

I didn't think I would be able to concentrate. I expected to sit there for two hours sneaking glances at my watch, counting the remaining minutes until we could leave and go to dinner. But my body settled into the plush chair, and the movie quickly grabbed my attention. I got so wrapped up in the story that, nearly two hours later, when Terrence cocked his head into mine in order to ask me a question, his hair briefly brushing against mine, I startled in my seat and my pulse went racing.

"Is this as good as I think it is?" he whispered to me.

It was just a casual question; a few tossed off words; the kind of commonplace thing one friend says to another without thinking twice about it.

But it felt momentous to me. A clear sign of our rapid and steady progress. He was seeking out my opinion in order to validate his own. He was letting me know that he valued and trusted my analysis of things.

"It's really terrific," I whispered back to him, a sense of satisfaction and hopefulness filling me up.

It was 9:45 P.M. when the movie ended. Terrence looked at his watch and said to me, "We're running late. We have to get out of here."

I followed him to the door. But first he had to say his goodbyes and thanks, to Billy Crudup and to Cameron Crowe, and to a half-dozen of the men in suits, one of whom insisted that we join them all for a celebratory dinner.

"Wasn't the movie great, didn't you think it was just great? So, *so* great. Cameron still has some cutting to do, but we think he's going to get the Oscar," the suit said to us, all in one breath. "Please come with us and eat. You've been to the Gramercy Tavern before, right? We'll call ahead and have them set two more places at the table."

"Oh, I wish we could," Terrence said. "But my girlfriend is waiting for us uptown. She's probably there already, fuming at me. Our reservations were for nine-thirty."

I stood next to Terrence, suddenly puzzled. *Girlfriend?* Since when did he have a girlfriend?

"Call her and have her join us," the suit said.

"I wish we could. But she's probably there already. She's all the way uptown."

A girlfriend? I told myself that he had made up a story just to get us out of there, so that we wouldn't have to join a large and noisy crowd for dinner. Surely if he had a girlfriend he would have mentioned her to me by now.

In the elevator, I waited for his explanation. Nothing. Out

on Broadway, he scanned the street, anxiously holding his arm up in the air even when there were no taxis driving by. He mumbled, "I didn't realize the movie would be so long."

The girlfriend, Terrence. Get back to the girlfriend. You can't just yell fire in a crowded screening room and then not produce a few sparks of evidence.

A taxi finally pulled up and we climbed inside. "84th Street and Columbus," he said. I saw him anxiously looking at his watch. Were we really headed uptown to meet a girlfriend? Was I supposed to bring her up? Was he waiting for me to be polite and ask?

Nine minutes later, twenty blocks traversed in silence, he looked at his watch again. And then, finally, almost under his breath, he said: "She's going to kill me. I told her we'd be there by nine forty-five at the latest."

"What's your girlfriend's name?" I asked, trying to sound curious, *not* disappointed. Not as if every last bone in my body and every last fiber of my soul had just been crushed into tiny bits of dust and ephemera.

"Lisa" he said. "Lisa Turiel. Oh, God, Ben, did I not even mention that we were eating with her? I'm sorry. I've been so scatterbrained lately. I got the galleys on the book last week, and I've been going over it, deciding I hate every word I wrote."

"How long have you—"

"She's a graduate student at Columbia," he said, cutting me off. "She's getting her Ph.D. in comparative literature. You'll like her. She's great. She's so much smarter than me."

I shouldn't have believed a word of it. I should have understood it for what it was: false modesty; feigned self-deprecation; a bid for martyrdom. *I'm the dumb one, I've just been lucky, to have gone to Yale, to have written a novel, to travel to London to interview famous movie stars, it's all been my good fortune, not hard work or God-given intelligence, just a bonehead's luck that might dissipate in an instant. But my girlfriend, she's the brilliant one. I'm just fortunate she's willing to have me along for the ride.*

It was the egoist's cheapest ploy.

But something about the way he said it—as earnest as a boy scout, as matter-of-fact as a historian, as calmly authoritative as a Supreme Court justice—something about the way he said it only made me want to sleep with him even more.

The restaurant was tiny, with a narrow, smoky bar on the right just as you walked through the door, and a dining room to the left, where a dozen tables were packed tightly together. The lighting was dim and purplish. Rock music was being pumped through the speakers. Terrence spotted his girlfriend right away, sitting alone at a table near the back. I trailed behind him. From halfway across the room, he began smiling sheepishly at her, shrugging his shoulders, opening his eyes wide and imploring—his innocent-puppy-dog, please-don't-be-mad-at-me routine.

"You're lucky I was running late too," she said, when we were a few feet away. Her tone was playful but cool—just cool enough so that I couldn't tell if she was really angry.

"The movie was nearly three hours long," he said. "No one told me it was going to be three hours long."

"I was the one who said to make the reservation for later," she said.

"And then we had to chit-chat. I couldn't escape—"

"—I said make it for ten—"

"—They wanted us to have dinner with them—"

"I hate having to sit around and wait for you, Terrence. You know that." This time her voice sounded sharp and curt—she really was angry. I was a little surprised that she would so quickly go on the attack against him, especially in front of me. Was this relationship not quite as harmonious as Terrence had portrayed it to me in the cab? Was I about to witness a fight between the two of them?

For a couple of awkward seconds, Terrence didn't say anything. I looked into his eyes, and I thought I detected a flicker of frustration, maybe even disdain. But whatever ill will he was feeling toward her, he decided to brush it away. Instead, he took a step backward and turned his body toward me and made an elaborate gesture with his left arm, opening it out toward Lisa like a circus ringmaster introducing the trapeze act. "Ben, I present to you Lisa Turiel." Then he turned back toward Lisa and bowed slightly. "And Lisa, I'm sorry, but please be kind to me in front of my friend Benjamin Reilly."

Lisa giggled at this, his goofy attempt at a chivalrous and old-fashioned introduction. The tension between them immediately seemed to dissipate. "Sit down and stop embarrassing us," she said, though I could tell she didn't really mean it. She liked that he was embarrassing us. She liked the idea of everyone seeing that the best-looking boy in the room belonged to her.

I looked her over, perhaps a bit more attentively than I should have. She wore a ribbed turtleneck sweater, dark green, the same color as her eyes. She had a long neck and high cheekbones and a small, narrow nose. Her long brown hair was pulled back from her face and tied behind her with a thin black ribbon, and she was wearing almost no makeup. She reminded me of any number of well-heeled, but unostentatious young women I had gone to college with, girls born and bred and coddled in the expensive suburbs of Massachusetts or Connecticut or northern New Jersey. She was attractive, no doubt; elegant and refined looking, but not too delicate; the kind of young woman who projects intelligence and unaffectedness, but also just a hint of the sensual—if she wanted, she could let down her hair and paint her lips cherry red and look just as alluring and come hither as any other woman in the city. When she smiled, I thought I detected a slight overbite, and even that, I decided, worked in her favor. It made her seem a little less aloof; a little more approachable.

Most guys would have considered themselves very lucky to have scored her.

But Terrence was not most guys. And, for all her finer qualities, there was something about Lisa Turiel that seemed just a little bit beneath him. The J. Crew clothes; the tasteful, medium-sized, silver hoop earrings; the poise with which she sipped from her water glass, just a small sip, so that her mouth was not open for too long (her mother had taught her good table manners from when she was very young). Didn't Terrence deserve someone a little less predetermined? Someone whose style was not borrowed from the pages of *Harper's Bazaar,* but invented all on her own? Someone who wouldn't nag him in public just because he was running a few minutes late? Didn't it bother him—as he trotted her around town to fancy restaurants and film screenings and cocktail parties at famous writers' apartments—that he so obviously outshined her, in every single way?

We ordered our food and a bottle of wine. Terrence told Lisa about meeting Billy Crudup and Cameron Crowe. She told us that while we were off "hobnobbing with the movie people" she had been holed up in the library, doing research on her dissertation. Then Terrence explained to me that Lisa was in her third year of graduate school and that she would be teaching her first class in the fall.

"Maybe Ben has a few teaching tips for you," he said to her.

She seized on the suggestion so quickly that I wondered if the two of them had planned this in advance—the ice-breaker they would use to get our conversation rolling.

"What's it like to stand there in front of them that first time?" she asked me. "I'm scared out of my wits. I'm worried they're going to boo me out of the classroom."

I didn't pause before answering. It was a question that I got from my non-teacher friends all the time. "For a minute or two, you're scared," I told her. "But then you remember that, at some point, kids just get conditioned to have respect for their teachers. Most of them respect the ceremony. Once you realize that it gets much easier."

"Yeah, but it's different for you," Lisa said. "You're a guy. Plus you're tall and handsome. Of course they're going to respect you."

"I don't think that stuff makes a difference," I protested.

"Oh, that's what tall, good-looking guys always say," she came back, giggling a bit, maybe even flirting.

Was she doing this to make Terrence jealous? Was this how she tried to knock him down a few pegs, by flirting with other guys in his presence? Was this the dynamic of their relationship—him obviously outclassing her, her doing whatever she could to feel better about herself?

Our food arrived a few minutes later. As we ate, Lisa asked me to tell her more about my students, and which ones over the years had given me the most trouble. I told them a funny story about Tommy DiGacamo, a senior in the very first class I ever taught, a dim but endearing boy who, whenever he was called on to answer a question, would pause midway through and belch very loudly, sending the room into titters. I told them that I would dispense punishment after punishment unto Tommy, but that I always felt guilty. Secretly I appreciated the belching. It at least added a note of levity to what I knew was a painfully boring class.

"You know, it would probably mean the world to Tommy if you told him that," Terrence said, laughing. "He probably still thinks you hate him. You should track him down. Thank him for being the class burper."

Track him down. I couldn't tell if he was making a private joke about me to Lisa. (Perhaps he had first introduced me to her as some weird guy from high school who was trying to *track him down*). Or maybe it was just an innocent choice of words, the first thing that had popped into his head (though I doubted that). But I decided to brush it aside; that, at least for now, I would have to take whatever ribbing he directed at me. I couldn't risk another two weeks of staring at the telephone, with nothing but silence coming from his end.

"I'm too much the responsible schoolteacher to do that," I said.

"That's boring," Terrence said, holding out the syllables of the word "boring," sounding a little drunk. "When did you get so boring, Ben?" Without waiting for an answer, he stood up and pointed to the bathroom. "I'll be right back. Lisa, try to fig-ure out when Ben got so boring."

As soon as he was out of earshot, Lisa leaned toward me and said, in as soft a voice as the loud music would allow, "It's so nice to meet you, Ben. I wanted to tell you that I really admire you for seeking out Terrence after all these years. I think that took courage."

"It was a loose end that I needed to tie up," I answered.

"I think Terrence is really glad you did it," she said. "I think it's something he wished he had the courage to do himself."

"Courage is a big word," I said. "It was just something I needed to do."

"It's hard for me to think of him as a bully."

"He was."

"He's such a gentle person now," she said, looking down at the table. "That must be hard for you to believe."

"Not at all," I said. "Who's the same person they were in high school?"

"The bully in my high school raped a woman and killed her boyfriend three months after graduation." She put her hand over her mouth and started giggling. "That's not funny, but it's true."

I liked the way she let a hint of unruliness bubble up be-neath her proper surface and then immediately cooled it down. There was a tension inside of her. She was still experi-menting, still fine-tuning her adult voice. I realized I had been a little harsh in my first estimation. She still wasn't good enough for Terrence—but she was better than I had given her credit for. She would make some other guy very happy.

"Well, I never thought Terrence would end up killing any-one," I said, laughing along with her, not entirely certain if I believed what I was saying.

"That's good to hear," she said. "I guess"

"It was more psychological bullying with Terrence."

"I don't think I've even once heard him raise his voice to an-other person," she said. "Maybe it's because he's still trying to compensate for the way he used to be and that's why he's gone so far in the other direction. But honestly he's probably the nicest guy I've ever dated."

I couldn't tell if she was saying this for her own sake, trying to quell the doubts about him that wouldn't go away, trying to reckon with a part of him that she still didn't entirely trust. Or if she was saying it for my sake, pimping him out to me, trying to convince me to become another of his many disciples.

Or maybe—I could hope—she was using me to rehearse the speech she would deliver when she broke up with him. Because he was just *too* nice, a little too perfect, a little too unimpeachable for her to stand next to each day and not feel shamed.

"I believe you," I told her. "And I believe him when he says that he's sorry."

She started to say something else. But suddenly Terrence was standing over us, pouring more wine into our glasses. "Why did things get quiet all of a sudden?" he asked.

"We were talking about you," I said.

Terrence smiled more broadly than I had ever seen him smile before.

"Let's smoke," Lisa said, and started digging through her purse.

"Oh no, here we go," Terrence said.

"Terrence thinks we shouldn't smoke at all," she said, looking to me. "But I think it's OK if we have a few cigarettes when we're out. Three or four cigarettes a week can't do any harm."

Terrence turned to me: "She'll end up smoking two packs."

"That is not true," Lisa said. "Plus, Terrence is a hypocrite. He wants to smoke just as much as I do."

"I think we should smoke," I said, settling the debate.

"I like your friend Benjamin," Lisa said to Terrence.

We stayed at the restaurant for another hour before Terrence asked for the check. He once again waved off my attempts to pay my share. He suggested that we retreat to a small pub a few blocks north and continue our conversation there.

For another two hours we talked: I told them about my favorite part of teaching, when a student you didn't think you were reaching raises his hand and says something precise and intelligent, and you realize that he had been paying close attention all along. Lisa talked about her proposed dissertation topic, on French feminist writers of the 1960s and 1970s. Terrence talked about his impending trip to London in mid-June and about how he had heard so many bad things about Billy Crudup—that he was rude and petulant and a terrible bore as an interview.

And at some point I realized that, for perhaps the very first time, I was bound up in the simple pleasures of being young: hanging out with friends in a bar in the big city; talking; laughing; drinking; smoking. This was what people in their twenties were supposed to do. This was what I had been missing, for too long now, holed up in my apartment in Staten Island. This was the adulthood I had been denying myself for no good reason at all.

It was nearly 3:00 A.M. when Lisa stood up, unsteady from all the wine, and announced that it was time to call it a night.

"Ben, how are you getting home?" she asked me.

Before I could answer Terrence chimed in: "He'll crash at my place."

"No, the ferry runs all night," I said. I certainly didn't want to make the long commute home at this hour. But I didn't think I would be able to fall asleep on Terrence's couch, listening to him and Lisa make drunken love in the next room.

"That's crazy," Terrence said. "You'll end up getting home at six in the morning. You're crashing at my place."

"I don't want to impose on you two," I said.

"There's nothing to impose on," Lisa said. "I'm going home to my apartment. I have an early class I need to get up for."

And so it was settled. Ten years after he had come to my house, I was going to Terrence's apartment. At least for a night, we were going to be roommates.

chapter seven

The Most Wonderful Boy in All of New York City (2000)

Everyone thinks it's a joke. Everyone says you'll get over it. A little good-natured ribbing can't kill you. It's just kids doing what kids do. They horse around. They call each other names.

Everyone says that, once you graduate and head off to college, you'll forget all about it.

But what the fuck do they know?

It's the Wednesday after Labor Day, the first day of sophomore year of high school. I'm back to face their laughter; their torment; their stupid fucking faces. I spent the summer telling myself otherwise: that the school building would burn down; or that my parents would come home one night and announce that we were moving to another town, thousands of miles away, effective immediately.

No such luck.

It's the start of third period. I arrive just before the bell rings. It's a class called "Government and Ethics," required for all sophomores. I look around the room and . . . relief! He's not here. Three periods running, and I still don't have a class with Terrence O'Connell.

Might this be my lucky semester? Might the computer that programs us into our classes have finally taken mercy on me? And might that be all that I need? If only I could make it through one semester outside his scrutiny, without him constantly calling me a gaywad, then maybe they would all forget about me. Maybe that would be enough to make me once again invisible in their eyes.

This is what he's done to me; this is his worst crime of all. He's made me equate anonymity with glory. He's made me think that being a nobody is the greatest triumph of all.

Mrs. Wynne begins assigning us seats. I've never been in one of her classes before, but she's rumored to be very strict—and strictness is something I very much welcome. Strictness makes it that much harder for the other kids to make fun of me. Strictness means she'll cut off any snickering and murmuring before it has the chance to root itself. I begin to relax a bit. I'm safe here. Every day, during third period, this room will be my oasis.

She gets to my name and points to a seat near the back of the room. I walk to the desk and begin to sit down. But Mrs. Wynne stops me and says, "No, Ben, one over." And then she keeps rattling off names and assigning seats. She doesn't pause to explain why she's leaving an open seat next to me.

Panic. A sudden rush of panic.

What if it's his seat? What if it's being saved for Terrence?

But no. It can't be. I remind myself that a lot of teachers leave an empty desk near the back of the room, a spot where they can set up a slide projector, or a seat where they can sit during exams, since it's much easier to determine if someone is cheating from the back of the room than it is from the front. It can't be anything more complicated than that.

Stop worrying so much. Stop being so fucking paranoid. . . .

Except sometimes your paranoia is perfectly justified. Sometimes you're not being paranoid enough.

Because just then Terrence appears inside the doorway, holding out a slip of paper to Mrs. Wynne. He says to her, "Sorry that took so long. There was a line of people to see him."

She smiles warmly at him and takes the note. She points to me and says, "I put you there right next to Ben."

A knot begins to tie in my stomach. What lousy fucking luck! What could I possibly have done to deserve such a punishment?

Mrs. Wynne excuses herself from the room. She says the principal needs to speak with her but that she'll be back in just a minute. We're not supposed to move from our seats. We're not supposed to say a word.

Tell that to Terrence. The next thing I know he is sliding into the seat next to me and whispering into my ear, "Hey, gaywad."

And the moment the door closes behind Mrs. Wynne, he starts up all over again. He doesn't even waste a half-second.

"Did you have a good summer, gaywad? Did you finally take a dick up your ass? Did it hurt real bad? I bet it hurt the first time."

He speaks slowly and deliberately. He starts out whispering, but he just keeps getting louder, so that soon everyone in the seats around us can hear him. The boys all begin laughing. The girls start saying things like "ewwww" and "groooosssss," but they're laughing too. They all think Terrence O'Connell is the funniest fucking person on the planet.

"Did you make him put on a condom before he put his dick in your ass?" he continues. "Or did you just decide to get AIDS now and get it over with?"

I try to ignore him. I concentrate on keeping my face stony and expressionless. I try to pretend as if nothing he says could ever hurt my feelings.

But this cause is a lost one. It was lost years ago.

"What position did he fuck you in? I bet he fucked you like a dog."

By now everyone around us is laughing. And so Terrence decides to direct his next set of comments to the entire room.

"That's what he said to me in June. He said"—and here he adopts a fey and lispy voice that sounds nothing like me, but that the boys in the class find especially uproarious—"'I'm going to get my ass fucked this summer.' Right, gaywad? Isn't that what you said?"

My shoulders are slumped. I'm staring down at my desk. I'm just praying for Mrs. Wynne to return.

This is what you get for thinking that you might get a break from him this semester. This is your punishment for even fantasizing about a forty-minute oasis each morning.

The door opens just then, just as Terrence is gearing up for another soliloquy. The class, which had been rolling with laugher just moments before, immediately gets very still.

Mrs. Wynne barks at us, "What's all this commotion? What's wrong with you people? It's going to be a long semester if this is how you act when I leave you alone for sixty seconds."

And now everyone is starting to look a little sheepish, the way kids always look when a teacher yells at them. I figure that will be the end of it. Maybe now we can just get on with this miserable fucking period, this dreadful first day of school.

But then Terrence—fucking Terrence, will he never shut his fucking mouth today?—*speaks up once again.*

"My fault, Mrs. Wynne," he says. "I made a stupid joke and everyone thought it was funny."

He smirks at her and shrugs his shoulders adorably. I can't believe my eyes. I'm astounded by his audacity. He's openly confessing to her.

And then, just when I assume it can't possibly get any worse, I watch as Mrs. Wynne's anger dissolves right before our eyes. She shakes her head at him and makes a disapproving face. But she's not mad at him. Her frown twists into a half-smile.

Because she likes him; she's a little bit in love with him.

She's the latest in a long line of our female teachers who find Terrence's mischievous streak endearing.

And that's when everything clicks in my head. I realize that he had arrived in class before me, and she had immediately sent him on an errand—probably because they had some shared history together, a class in which he had been her favorite. That's why he hadn't been here to be seated.

Terrence O'Connell is Mrs. Wynne's pet.

And I'm stuck next to him. For all of third period, fall semester.

I'm trapped in prison with the warden's henchman as my cell mate.

But know this much: The humiliation never fades. You don't just get over it.

It burrows inside of you, just beneath the skin, like a scabie, and no manner of scratching or clawing or self-mutilation can make it go away. The funny names; the jokes made at your expense; the taunts that are all in good fun—they come to define your public persona. They become a kind of lens through which everyone sees you. So that your classmates can't think of you without also thinking to themselves: Ben Reilly, he's that faggot, stay far away from him. *So that, after awhile, that's how you start to see yourself, too: as the queer; the homo; the fudge packer; the little pussy boy who will never fight back. And you start to hate yourself so much. Because you weren't doing anything, you weren't trying to stand out, you were just being yourself. Yet everyone hates you for it. They hate your very being.*

And there's no way you can ever make them see you any differently.

*Just a joke? Just a few laughs at your expense? Just get over it? No
way. Not possible. You can't even begin to put such bloodied, muddied
waters under the bridge.*

Fuck you, Terrence. Because *you* did this to me. You're the
reason I can't just be like everyone else.

Fuck you all the way to your grave.

I woke up to the high-pitched screech of a motor grinding, the
sound of the virginal victim in a slasher movie screaming at
highest decibel, just after she's looked into her killer's eyes,
and deep into his soul, and found nothing. My head was hanging off the edge of the pillow. My hair was matted with sweat.
The first sensation I felt was pain—a hot, stabbing pain in the
center of my throat. That was when I remembered where I was.
I had spent the night at Terrence's, sleeping on his pull-out
couch. I had drunk too much wine with him and Lisa, his sweet
but unworthy girlfriend, three bottles between us. I had been
the one who had said we should smoke. Now I was going to be
suffering for it.

"Sorry," I heard Terrence say, his voice coming from somewhere on my right. "I needed some coffee."

I propped myself up against the back of the pull-out couch
and looked around the apartment. He was standing behind a
half-wall that separated the kitchen from the living room, fid-
dling with a coffee grinder. From my vantage point, I could
only make out the upper half of him. He was wearing a T-shirt
that clung tightly to his chest and pulled up on his arms.

"Too much wine," I mumbled. My mouth felt like it was
lined with construction paper. I moved my tongue around inside of it, trying to generate some saliva. But when I swallowed,
the pain in my throat became so intense that I winced. "Too
many cigarettes, too."

"Those goddamned cigarettes," Terrence said. "They make
the hangover fifteen times worse. I've got to get her to stop
buying them."

"Blame me," I said. "I was the one who said we should smoke."

"I *am* blaming you," he said, laughing. I laughed too. And then, before I could answer, Terrence added: "She liked you a lot, by the way."

"I liked *her*." *But not as much as I like you, Terrence.*

"She never seems to like anyone," he said. "She thinks everyone is so dull and pretentious, especially the people I work with at the magazine. But I could tell right away she thought you were great. When you went to the bathroom, she said she thought you were soulful and smart. I think those were the words she used. 'Soulful' and 'smart.'"

"She seems really great," I said. *But not that great, Terrence. You could definitely do better.*

I craned my neck around the room to try to find a clock, before realizing there was one on the wall in front of me. It was just shy of 10:00 A.M. I untangled the sheets from around me and grabbed for my pants on the floor. I stood there awkwardly, trying to remember where the bathroom was, until Terrence saw me and pointed to a hallway off the main room.

His building was located on First Avenue and 88th Street, a post–World War II high-rise with a twenty-four-hour doorman. During the cab ride home from the bar, Terrence had explained that he had been in this apartment for two years, but that now he was looking for a place to buy, because everyone he knew was making a fortune in the real estate market. He said that his first thought was that he would move to the Upper West Side so that he could be closer to Lisa. But now he wasn't so sure.

"Who knows how long we'll even be together?" he had said to me in the cab. "It seems silly to pick a neighborhood just so you'll live closer to your girlfriend, you know?"

I nodded and agreed with him and resisted the urge to tell him that he should dump her.

When I returned from the bathroom, Terrence was walking out of the kitchen with two coffee mugs in his hand. From the waist down he was wearing only a pair of boxer shorts, light blue with black pinstripes. They were loose fitting, probably a

size too big for him. I glanced down at his crotch and then to
the exposed part of his legs—even his leg muscles were defined, like a cyclist's. Then I looked at his feet, a shade paler
than the rest of him, his toes long and skinny—and even his
feet I decided I liked. For the second time in a decade, I let my
gaze linger for a few seconds too long. He couldn't not notice
that I was checking him out.

But this time he chose to ignore it. He simply held out one
of the coffee mugs to me and waited until I took it from him.

"My throat is killing me," I said. "I haven't really smoked
since college."

"I have some orange juice," he said. "And there's cereal. I
never know what you're supposed to do to feed a hangover.
Usually I just suffer."

He walked toward the dining room and took a seat at the
table. I followed and sat down across from him. He began flipping through the previous day's *New York Times,* which had
been resting on the table undisturbed. "Let's be impulsive," he
said, after a few more minutes passed. "I think we should play
hooky today."

"I don't have a job to play hooky from."

"Even better," he said. "We'll make a day of it. Go to a museum. Grab some lunch. Maybe do some shopping. I have to
call and talk to my editor for a minute, but otherwise there's
nothing on my schedule that can't wait until Monday."

*He wants to hang out with me! Still he wants to hang out with me!
Eighteen hours spent in each other's presence, and still he hasn't grown
bored.*

"OK. But only if you let me pay my own way."

"You can pay some of your own way," he said, not looking up
from his newspaper.

"You can't keep paying for everything, Terrence. If we're going to be friends, I can't be your charity case."

If we're going to be friends . . . It was the first time that I had
floated the idea out there, of us being *friends.* I let the words
hang in the air. And I decided they sounded right. Why not?

Why couldn't I become friends with Terrence O'Connell? After all, weren't history books filled with tales of archenemies who finally joined forces and then together conquered the world? Granted, at this particular moment, sitting in Terrence's dining room with an increasingly unbearable sore throat, I couldn't think of a single such example. But surely there had to be one or two. So why not add our names to that illustrious list? Or, even better, why not *create* that illustrious list? Why not go down together in history?

"My family is rich, Ben," he said. "And I make a ton of money. It's not a big deal."

I didn't answer. Instead, I let the silence become awkward, until he finally looked up from the newspaper. I knew he didn't mean anything by it. In fact, I knew exactly what he *did* mean by it, that he simply didn't want money to get in the way of us hanging out together. If anything, I probably should have been *grateful* that he was saying this.

But I thought I needed to take a stand against him. Our relationship would have no chance of working if Terrence didn't view me as his equal.

"And my family *isn't* rich, and I don't make *any* money," I told him, trying my best to sound as if my pride had been wounded.

"I'm sorry," he answered immediately. "I don't mean to rub it in your face. It's just that I've been making a lot of money lately, and I want to be generous with it. I'm not trying to buy your forgiveness, Ben." He paused and then added: "I'm trying to earn it."

"You can't keep paying my way," I repeated.

"Fair enough, you're right," he said. Then he jumped up from the table and went to retrieve the phone from the kitchen. He had capitulated to me so quickly that I was a little bit stunned. Could this possibly be the same Terrence O'Connell I knew in high school?

"Hey, let me call my editor now," he said, back in the dining room. "I'll get it out of the way. Listen, Ben, I'm sorry I made you feel self-conscious. I was being obnoxious." He lowered his

voice and put his hand over the mouthpiece and kept on talking to me: "You know, sometimes I obsess so much about my
motivations that nothing I do ever seems organic, nothing ever
seems—"

He cut himself off. Whatever epiphany he was about to share
with me would have to wait. His editor had picked up on the
other end.

I listened to him for a couple of minutes. He talked about
the movie we had seen the night before; his impending trip to
London; the tack he was thinking of taking for the story he
would write on Billy Crudup. He sounded ebullient, half-
giddy—as if he were writing for *GQ* for the very first time. I
couldn't help but feel envy. This all seemed so unfair; so lack-
ing in karmic justice. Terrence had a job that he loved. Editors
who loved working with him. A bank account that got fatter
every two weeks.

He lived a life that made him want to leap out of bed each
morning and attack the day.

How could one person be so blessed with such good fortune, especially someone who had once been so awful? Would
he ever have his day of reckoning?

Or would the same thing just keep happening?

Would retribution come knocking on his door, only to fall in
love with him, and absolve him of all past sins, within minutes?

What is it like to be out on the town with the best-looking boy
in all of New York City?

In July of 1995, six weeks after graduating from college, I
found myself in a bar in the West Village called Mercy, reading
the newspaper, killing time in the late afternoon before I
headed uptown to meet my old roommate David for our last
dinner before he headed off to Stanford Law School. I was sitting at a table right next to the bar's owners, a couple in their
mid-thirties. They were interviewing prospective job candidates
for the position of bartender.

The first person they interviewed was a young woman, soft-spoken and a bit drab-looking, who said she was pursuing a master's degree in philosophy at NYU. The second person was a man in his forties with a smoker's voice and a distended pot-belly, who told the owners that he used to be an investment banker, until he tired of the money-hungry life and quit his job so that he could concentrate on writing a novel. The third person was a woman in her late twenties, a bottle blonde with fake breasts and a New Jersey accent, who said she had been bar-tending since she was seventeen. The owners asked all three of them the same sets of questions. They nodded and smiled as they listened to the applicants' answers. They told all three of them that they would be making a decision within a couple of days and that the applicants would hear from them one way or the other.

And then in walked candidate number four, and I knew that the other three did not have a fighting chance. This job search was over.

He didn't so much walk in the door as he strutted, languidly rocking his shoulders and his hips back and forth. He had a big, entitled grin on his face, as if someone had just handed him a check for a million dollars and he was on his way to the bank to cash it. He wore a pair of tight blue jeans, so tight that you couldn't not look at his ass. He had jet black hair and a strong, square jaw and bulging biceps and everyone who was sitting in the bar that afternoon—ten or twelve of us, men and women, gay and straight—all of us looked up to note his arrival.

And in that moment I realized something that had never fully occurred to me before. I realized that exceptionally good-looking men get things in this world that the rest of us don't. They get things that even exceptionally beautiful women do not get: attention; respect; adoring scrutiny; the benefit of the doubt. They get all of the world's envy without any of its disdain. They get people telling them how smart and funny they are, even when they are dull and boorish. They get complete strangers to stare at them and fantasize about a life spent in their company.

They get bar owners to offer them jobs right on the spot, after having told all the other applicants that it would take at least three or four days to make a decision.

I remembered all of this as I stood next to Terrence at the ticket counter of the Whitney Museum of Art, as he pleaded with the young woman selling tickets, explaining to her that he was a member of the museum but that he had forgotten his membership card at home—and could she please, *please* give us the members' discount, *please just this once,* he promised he would never forget his membership card again.

He flashed his smile and revealed his dimple and when I looked at the ticket counter girl—who seemed very earnest and very young, barely into her twenties, probably an art history major at Columbia—when I saw her gazing back at him, I thought to myself: *He needn't have even bothered this much. All he needed to do was smile.*

And then I thought to myself: *But perhaps this is what distinguishes Terrence from all the other exceptional-looking men, the passive and aloof ones who don't try very hard at all, because they know the world will give them whatever it is they want.*

Terrence, for whatever reason, still feels the need to try.

Terrence needs to believe that whatever comes to him he has earned.

"I'm not supposed to," the ticket counter girl said, punching buttons on a keyboard, tilting her head to one side, beaming at him.

"Don't tell anyone or I could get in trouble," she said, and she handed him our tickets.

"Sworn to silence," he said, batting his eyelashes at her, smiling just a beat too long, so that she would construe it as flirting.

So that she would spend the rest of the afternoon daydreaming: *What would it be like to have so beautiful-looking a boy on my arm?*

"Have a good time," she called out to us, as we started to walk away.

Terrence twisted his body around and smiled again and waved good-bye. And then off we went. Heads frequently turning in his direction; others' glances lingering upon him, just long enough, so that he couldn't not notice that *everyone* here was checking him out. Everyone we passed wanted Terrence O'Connell as their own.

Off we went. Into the Whitney Museum of Art. Benjamin Reilly and the best looking boy in all of New York City.

The girl behind the ticket counter did not have him. Neither did the museum's other patrons. None of them had a fighting chance.

But I did.

I just kept telling myself that I did.

We wandered through the Whitney's galleries for nearly two hours. At 12:30 P.M. Terrence decided that he was bored and hungry and that he wanted a hot dog, so we cabbed across town to Gray's Papaya, where—for the first time in our reconstituted friendship—he let me pay. (The bill came to $9.) After that, we walked to a Barnes & Noble a few blocks south on Broadway and wandered around for another hour. With each passing minute, I felt more miserable. The pain in my throat was even more intense than before. The muscles in my shoulders and chest were beginning to ache. Even the glands on the right side of my neck felt slightly swollen. I seemed to be coming down with some kind of flu.

"I'm exhausted," I finally told Terrence. "I think I should go home and get some sleep."

"Come with me to Barneys first," he said. "I'm going to Los Angeles on Sunday, and the pool at the hotel where I'm staying is supposed to be amazing. Help me pick out a swimsuit and then I'll let you go."

The mention of Los Angeles took me by surprise. And it stung. We had spent nearly twenty-four hours together, and only just now I was finding about his imminent trip to Los Angeles?

What if he has no long-term use for me? What if I'm just a friend of convenience? What if, after we part ways today, it will be another two weeks before he deigns to return my call?

"I didn't know you were going away," I said, trying to sound as if I didn't care.

"Just for four days," he said. "I'm taking a couple of meetings. My agent here wants to set me up with a film agent out there. I have a couple of screenplay ideas I'm thinking of pitching."

Ugh . . . please make it stop . . . enough! *Now he's a screenwriter. He's adding yet another job title to his already too-long resume. What next for the indefatigable, protean-talented Terrence O'Connell? Brain surgeon? Lawyer? Astronaut? Glassblower?*

"OK," I said. "But then I really have to go." For all my envy, I still couldn't turn him down. No matter how sick I felt, I still didn't want to say good-bye.

In Barneys, we strolled together through the men's department. He held up assorted items of clothing, seeking out my opinion. I nodded or shook my head or shrugged my shoulders. Complete strangers gazing upon us could only have thought one thing: that we were boyfriends here shopping for a weekend trip to Fire Island or the Hamptons; that we lived together and shared everything.

Surely he realized this. He had to understand that when two men go shopping together everyone who looks upon them assumes they are boyfriends. Maybe he didn't care. Or maybe— much more likely—he did care, and he had been very deliberate in asking me to come along with him. Maybe this was his means of overcompensation. This was how he would prove that his name-calling, gaywad-bashing days were far behind him.

Because how could Terrence O'Connell hate gay people if he was willing to let all of New York City think he had a boyfriend? How could he hate *me* if he was willing to let everyone think that I was that boyfriend?

I liked it. Of course I liked it. So silly a fantasy: to have reformed and transformed my oppressor; to have Terrence O'Connell on my arm, for all the world to see.

So silly. And so potent.

So completely and totally addictive.

He settled on a pair of yellow surfer's trunks that I liked the best of all the ones he had tried on. He also bought a windbreaker, sunglasses, and the same polo shirt in three different colors. He didn't wince when the cashier scanned his items and said the total came to $533.

It was nearly 5:00 P.M. by then. I told Terrence I had to go home, that I was positively exhausted. He said that he would walk me to the subway.

"Listen, Ben, this is all new terrain for me," he said, as we stood outside the subway station. "But I'm really glad that we're doing this."

"Me, too."

"I don't have a lot of friends who I feel very close to," he said. "I guess I've been working on trying to open myself up a bit more to other people."

I said nothing. I didn't want to tip my hand. I couldn't let him know how deeply overjoyed I felt about all of this.

Let him think that you have many such friends. Let him think that he needs you in his life more than you need him in yours.

"I'll be back from Los Angeles on Wednesday night," he said. "I'll call you then."

I nodded and said, "Looking forward to it."

I was looking forward to it more than anything in the world.

"Your sister is dying of AIDS and you had to go to Ohio to take care of her? I gotta say, honey, that one is priceless. I wish I had come up with it myself."

It was late the next morning. I had grabbed the phone without checking the caller ID, assuming that it would be Terrence. I figured he wouldn't want to head off to Los Angeles without talking to me one more time.

But it wasn't. It turned out to be Meredith. I hadn't talked to her in over a month, since the morning after Mario shoved Elliot down the stairs.

"Oh, hey, Meredith. I can't talk. I'm expecting another call."

"From who, Marcus Welby, MD?" she said, laughing dryly at her own joke. "Come on, Ben, I can tell when you're lying." She didn't necessarily sound angry with me—only her usual glib and cheerful self, with perhaps a hint of disappointment thrown into the mix.

Oh well, at least she's in good company. Add Meredith McBern to the long list of people I'm presently disappointing.

But I don't care. Terrence is more important than all of them. Terrence is the one I need to make certain I don't disappoint right now.

"What do you want me to tell you, Meredith?" I asked.

"I finally got the whole story from Kate Honig. What kind of crazy nonsense were you making up? Barry Marcus was not amused, I can tell you that."

"Meredith, please, I can't. Another time—"

"The rumors that are flying around about you right now . . ." She made a tsk-tsk-ing noise, but I could tell she was trying to be serious. "Ben, you do realize that everybody knows your sister died when you were a kid, right?"

This took me by surprise. Everybody knew? Had I once told Meredith the story of Mary's death—and then had she gone and told everyone else? I didn't think so, but I couldn't remember. I was about to ask Meredith to explain. But then I caught myself. I couldn't allow myself to be drawn into this conversation.

The old Ben is gone, Meredith. He died when Mario Tropiano pushed Elliot Applebaum down the stairs. And the new Ben can't go on being your friend. The new Ben needs to forget he ever stepped foot inside Tottenville High School.

"Meredith, please, I'm sorry, I have to go," I said, and then started to hang up.

"You shouldn't burn bridges like this, Ben. Not with the people who actually like you and think you have a lot of potential."

"I'm not interested in teaching anymore," I said. "I don't care if I burn those bridges."

"I didn't mean potential as a teacher," she said, very quietly and plainly. "I meant potential as a human being. You know? Life potential."

The sincerity in her voice startled me. I had never realized that sincerity was even a part of Meredith's emotional repertoire. What could I possibly say in response to this? What do you say to someone who meets your bad behavior by taking the high road; someone who cares about you too much to let you self-destruct?

All I could think to do was to repeat the words to an old R.E.M. song, "World Leader Pretend," from *Green*. I used to play that CD over and over again junior year of high school. It was the CD I was trying to get Terrence to listen to just before everything went wrong.

"This is my mistake. Let me make it good." I whispered it just under my breath.

"What?" she asked. "I didn't hear you, Ben."

But I didn't have to elaborate. Just then the call-waiting beeped. My anxiety immediately gave way to sheer jubilation. I was being rescued! By Terrence! I had been right all along. He wanted to make sure he talked to me one last time before leaving for Los Angeles.

Terrence O'Connell: once my bully, now my savior.

"Meredith, that's my call, I gotta take it," and I clicked over without even giving her a chance to say good-bye.

"I'm coming over to pick you up."

Strike two. This time it wasn't Terrence, but Danny, telling me I had no choice in the matter. We were going to lunch to sort things out.

"I'm sick with the flu," I told him.

"This isn't negotiable," he said.

"I can barely move."

"You can sit at the table in the restaurant and barely move there." And before I could protest any further, he hung up the phone.

He arrived exactly one hour later. He drove us, in silence, to the Golden Dove diner. He didn't actually speak to me until after the waitress had taken our orders.

"I want this to stop," he said. "It's stopping today. Whatever is going on with you, it's stopping today, and we're going back to normal."

Did Danny even understand the irony here—that he, too, had once tried to run away? And that, for many years after running away, he kept as far away from us as he possibly could? Shortly after graduating from high school, he moved out of our family's house and into an apartment in Elizabeth, New Jersey. He took a part-time job at a Body Shop in the Menlo Park Mall and began attending community college. His visits home became less and less frequent, until, a year into his studies, he abruptly dropped out of school and moved to Stony Brook, Long Island, with a girl he knew from the mall. He found a job as an assistant manager at The Gap and began keeping his distance from us even more strenuously, showing up only on holidays or very special occasions, rarely calling home.

"What's wrong with him?" I asked my father, after learning that he wouldn't be attending my college commencement.

My father said, "Oh, nothing. He's just very busy. He works a lot of hours."

But then, in the winter of 1996, just as suddenly and unceremoniously as his return from exile the first time around, he reentered our lives. He moved back to Staten Island and reenrolled in school. He started dating Megan, whom he had known since high school, and four months later they were engaged. He began taking on an oldest child's burdens and responsibilities: dutifully appearing every ten days to mow my parents' lawn, even though my parents were perfectly willing to hire a landscaper; or chauffeuring me to Brooklyn College for three consecutive days while he worked on repairing the busted carburetor of my ten-year-old Honda Accord. In the spring of 1998, he graduated from the College of Staten Island with a bachelor's degree in accounting and began working in the billing department of a small law firm in New York City. He and Megan were now talking about having a baby.

He never explained to us his change of heart. I assumed it was all because of Megan—that he liked her so much that he determined to invent and sustain a charade for her; that he wanted to show her that she was marrying into a normal family. But whatever his motivations, the rest of us all played along. I never brought up the subject of his days in exile. I never mentioned the name of our dead sister. My parents didn't either. In his and Megan's presence, we all acted as if nothing had ever gone wrong in any of our lives.

"Are you HIV-positive?" he asked, after I didn't answer his first question. "Is that what this is about? Just tell me. I'm not going to judge you."

"I don't have AIDS," I said. "And I'm not trying to upset anyone. There's just a lot that's been going on. I haven't had time to call."

"So you go around telling people that Mary is still alive?" he said. "That's crazy, Ben. Crazy people say things like that."

"It was something I came up with off the top of my head. I didn't mean anything by it."

He kept on talking as if he hadn't heard me. "You don't have the right to take a sledgehammer to things, Ben. Just because you've felt slighted in the past doesn't give you the right to make people feel bad now." His voice was low and humorless. I had never heard this sort of intensity from him before.

"I'm sorry I made up that story," I told him. "It was stupid. But I'm not trying to destroy anyone's life. I met this person who I used to go to high school with, and we've been seeing each other. I've been busy with that."

He cocked one of his eyebrows and frowned, letting me know that he didn't believe me. "Tonight you and I are going over to mom and dad's for dinner," he said, "and you're going to apologize to them for all of your crap."

I stared at him and said: "How can you take the moral high ground here? You have an entire history of disappearing from their lives."

Danny shook his head at me and said, "You don't know what you're talking about."

"You moved to Stony Brook. You disappeared for years."

"One thing has nothing to do with the other."

"And what happened that week in high school? When you ran away? Where did you go?"

His eyes narrowed and filled with anger. For a moment, I thought he might reach across the table and try to hit me.

"Is that what this is all about?" he said, his voice starting to rise. "You're jealous that I got more attention than you did."

"Just answer the question," I shot back at him.

"What happened then doesn't have anything to do with this, Ben," he said.

"Then tell me."

"No."

"Why is it such a big secret?" I asked him.

"Fuck off, Ben."

We drove back to my apartment in silence. As he pulled onto my street, he told me that he would return at six to take me to dinner at our parents' house. I told him not to bother; that I wouldn't be there; that I would make certain to be anywhere but in my apartment.

I got out of the car and slammed the door shut and stalked off to my front door. I thought he would get out and follow me, restate his intentions more forcefully, tell me, "You damn well better be here or else." I thought he might threaten to make it physical.

But he didn't. He just sat there for a few more seconds and then put the car into gear and slowly drove away.

chapter eight

Myth and Fact
(2000)

What kind of flu are we talking about? What kind of flu lasts exactly five days, the symptoms not getting any worse, but not getting any better? What kind of flu mysteriously appears, pretty much overnight, and then disappears just as suddenly, also overnight? What kind of flu bears all the hallmarks of mononucleosis—it makes your throat feel unimaginably sore, and it makes the glands in your neck too tender to touch, and it saps you of every ounce of strength in your body—but it is not mononucleosis, it is something chronic and terminal, something you can't get *just* from kissing? What kind of flu sets in exactly twenty-eight days after you've had sex without a condom with a stranger in a hotel room in a city you've never visited before?

What kind of flu isn't the flu at all?

For four days, I lay on the couch in my apartment, flipping through the same two dozen television channels over and over again, suffering. By Tuesday night, I determined I would have to see a doctor. Maybe this wasn't a virus; maybe it was a bacterial infection that could only be eradicated pharmacologically. My health insurance had expired the last day of April, and I was beginning to worry about conserving funds. But I pledged to make an appointment the first thing in the morning. Even if I had to pay $200 or $300, it would be worth it to get rid of this miserable, nagging flu.

Except when I woke up on Wednesday, the flu was gone. Well, not entirely gone: My throat was still a little scratchy; the glands on the right side of my neck were still tender. But by that afternoon, even those symptoms had faded away. I suddenly felt the way you feel after you drink a tall glass of orange juice and a strong cup of coffee in the morning, the sugar and the caffeine flooding your bloodstream, making you eager to take on the day. It was the worst flu I could ever remember having, but now it was almost hard to believe that I had ever been sick at all. Now it felt like I had all the energy in the world.

This isn't how you come out of a flu, is it? Doesn't it take at least a week until you feel completely steady on your feet again?

So much energy. Vast reserves of it, begging to be used. I should have gotten out of the house. Gone somewhere. To the movies. Or the grocery store. Even just a walk to the park. *Anywhere,* really. Anything to get me to stop thinking. Always, always thinking. Always thinking the worst. . . .

But what else did I have to do? I had no job. No plans for finding a job. No interest in any of my old hobbies or friends. Nothing to do but wonder how long it would take for Terrence to call me upon his return from Los Angeles. So I stayed inside. I stretched out on the couch. I let my mind wander. I started to think about my symptoms.

What kind of flu nags at you, never becoming completely unbearable, so that you slip into unconsciousness and sleep it off, but never getting any better, either? What kind of flu strikes the same note of insistent misery for five consecutive days and then disappears altogether?

Bored and anxious, tired of counting the hours until Terrence's return, I signed onto the Internet. I figured I would just quickly put my mind at ease.

I typed the words "symptoms" and "sore throat" and "swollen glands" into the search window. I stared at those words for thirty seconds and then I added one more: "HIV."

The search engine returned hundreds of matches. The first six matches on the list all had the same title: "Acute Retroviral Syndrome."

I clicked on the first match. I scrolled down the Web page. My eyes scanned back and forth across the screen, reading and rereading each sentence three or four times. My heart began to pound. The bottom of my stomach dropped out.

Surely I had it all wrong; surely the explanation couldn't be so simple and so awful. Surely I was jumping to hasty conclusions, based on incomplete and highly manipulatable data.

Or maybe the symptoms do not lie.

Acute Retroviral Syndrome is your body's first reaction after you've contracted the Human Immunodeficiency Virus. It occurs anywhere between ten to forty-five days after initial exposure to the disease. It lasts for as few as two days and for as long as two weeks—though on average it lasts five to six days. It produces a series of flu-like symptoms: sore throat; low-grade fever; swollen glands in the neck, armpits, and groin. Sometimes you experience a mild rash on the torso. Mostly, you feel a burdensome, if never quite overwhelming sense of torpor and fatigue—the way people report feeling when they have mononucleosis. For five or six days, you want to lie on the couch and do nothing. And then, finally, the symptoms disappear, as suddenly and as mysteriously as they arrived. And then you feel fine.

Acute Retroviral Syndrome is your body's initial response to the virus entering your bloodstream. Your immune system rises up for a fight; it tries to make the virus go away. But the virus doesn't go away. It seeps inside of you, and incubates, and then reemerges a few years later. At which point it attacks your immune system and leaves you defenseless. It develops into full-blown AIDS. It kills you.

I clicked from one Web page to another. I told myself to take deep breaths and calm down. I tried to convince myself that I had contracted mononucleosis. I had never had it as a teenager, and now it was just that I had kissed the wrong guy, or maybe drank from one of my students' cups in the cafeteria without realizing it. But it was hardly a big deal. It would nag at me for a couple of weeks, a month or two at the most, and then

I would recover. No one in the recorded history of kissing had ever died from mononucleosis.

I found another Web page titled "How To Determine If You Have Mono." It was written for teenage girls. "The first symptom you will likely experience is a sore throat," the Web page said. "It will quickly worsen and feel like the most painful sore throat you have ever had."

I followed the train of logic: My sore throat had been the most painful sore throat I had ever had. Acute retroviral syndrome is often confused for mononucleosis, and vice-versa. Good news, right? Think again. Mono, this Web site noted, does not go away after six days. It just keeps making you feel lousy, and there are no sudden bursts of energy and well-being while you're suffering through it.

I could rule out mono.

But I couldn't rule out the disease that was often confused for mono. There was no ruling out HIV.

I did the math in my head: The first day I experienced symptoms was exactly twenty-eight days after I had sex with Alex in Indiana. After I had fucked him in the ass without a condom.

My mouth went completely dry. My stomach just kept sinking deeper, so deep that I wondered if I would ever have an appetite again. I had had sex once in six years. And it was enough to give me AIDS.

I kept on surfing the Internet for the next four hours, until my eyes started to ache. I read three dozen versions of the exact same information. All of the Web sites listed the same symptoms and the same time frame. They all had a section on the "myths and facts" of HIV transmission. They all presented the same relentless and damning case against me.

Myth: You cannot contract HIV as long as semen or blood is not exchanged.

Fact: I had fucked him in the ass without a condom. All bets are off.

Myth: You cannot contract AIDS if you are the "insertive" partner—the giver; the pitcher; the top; the one who sticks it to the other guy.

Fact: I had fucked him in the ass without a condom. I could have made his ass bleed. The blood could have entered through my urethra or through an imperceptible cut on my shaft.

Myth: You cannot contract AIDS from just one sexual encounter.

Fact: I had fucked him in the ass without a condom. All it takes is one instance of unprotected sex with an infected person to get yourself infected.

Myth: Everyone gets one get-out-of-jail-free card. Everyone is allowed one instance of recklessness. One little slipup can't possibly destroy an entire life.

Fact: Picking up a complete stranger who barely speaks English in a bar in a strange city and then taking him back to your hotel and submitting to his aggression and fucking him in the ass without a condom because you are afraid he will punch you and make a scene and wake up all of the other guests in the hotel and the police will have to be summoned and you will be humiliated and shamed and your name will be printed in the local newspaper—fucking a stranger without a condom out of desperation and fear and loneliness may only be human, but it is still tantamount to a death wish.

Fact: People with death wishes do not have to work very hard to contract HIV.

I felt tears forming in my eyes. There was nothing to feel but shame. There was nothing to think about but every shameful memory that had ever crossed my mind, ever since the day in seventh grade when I discovered the pictures in my father's night table and could no longer pretend otherwise: that I was a boy who wanted to fuck other boys; that I would grow up to be a man who wanted to fuck other men.

I remembered a train ride home from college for Christmas break after my freshman fall at Wesleyan. I remembered opening up a magazine and turning to a four-page article with the headline: "Faces of AIDS." I remembered that it featured three pages of thumbnail portraits, of all the men in the entertainment and fashion industries who had died the previous year

from AIDS. Scores of dancers, designers, choreographers, producers, off-Broadway actors—pictures of fey and effete men,
many of them bald or with buzz cuts, wanly smiling through
their misery, men who had probably known one another and
who had no doubt passed the virus around among their circle,
as casually as a gaggle of suburban housewives might pass
around a recipe for chocolate chip cookies. Because that's
what gay men did. They fucked each other, and then they
fucked each other's friends, and sometimes they all fucked together, in groups of three or four or five or six, because all they
could think about, all day and all night, was fucking. They
fucked themselves to death.

I remembered reading that article and thinking: *I will never,
ever become like these men. I refuse to be that kind of faggot.*

And then another memory, from my childhood, of the Halloween after my sister died. I remembered sitting on the living
room floor after Danny and I had returned from trick-or-treating. We were dividing up our candy, making trades, three
Snickers bars for one pack of Skittles, a dozen Tootsie Rolls for
a single Nestle Crunch. My mother was sitting on the couch
watching the television newscast. The newscast had a live report from the annual Halloween parade in Greenwich Village.
I remembered looking up from my mountainous pile of
candy—we had been out trick-or-treating for hours, we had
started the moment we arrived home from school that day—to
the images on the television, of drag queens prancing through
the streets in their feathered, sequined, and rainbow-hued cos-
tumes, throwing open their mouths, cackling and screaming
and making all sorts of transgressive and hedonistic noises.

And I remembered hearing my mother's voice from the
couch, she was talking to no one in particular: "What a bunch
of sickies."

Shame. A tidal wave of shame, crashing over me, pulling me
under, to a place where I would no longer be able to breathe.
For the rest of my already numbered days, all I would feel was
shame. I had lived up to my own worst stereotype. I had become that which I despised the most. A man who couldn't re-

sist fucking another man in the ass. A victim of his own unman-
ageable impulses. Another soon-to-be-dead gaywad.

I was the sickie now.

Terrence O'Connell had been right about me all along.

He called at four the next afternoon, earlier than I had been
anticipating. "I just walked through the door," he told me.
"God, Los Angeles is the worst."

"Did your meetings not go well?"

"They were fine. Just exhausting. A little depressing. They
want to buy my soul. The minute you have a bit of currency in
the entertainment industry, they want to buy your soul."

"That doesn't sound so bad," I said. "They pay well, right?"

"Hey, would you be up for coming into the city? I need
someone to help me recover. You can bring your stuff and stay
over, so you don't have to schlep all the way back tonight."

I agreed to meet him at his apartment. It took me three
hours to shower and dress and make my way uptown—three
calming and blissful hours. For three hours, I wasn't dying. He
had called me as soon as he had returned to town; he wanted
me to help him recover from the trauma of his trip. Surely,
these were good signs—very good signs—of a friendship in full
bloom. Maybe, too, they were signs of something more inti-
mate on the not-too-distant horizon. Maybe I wasn't *entirely* deluding myself. Maybe there was a glimmer of hope. That I
hadn't fucked *everything* up. That something might still work
out between us.

I couldn't not hope.

When I knocked on his apartment door, he yelled for me to
come in. He was sitting on the couch, staring at the television,
frantically punching the buttons on a video game controller.
On the screen, digitized masses of muscle were kicking, punching, and body slamming one another as pixilated blood splattered in slow motion across the frame.

"I know this qualifies me as a loser," he said, speaking very
slowly, unwilling to shift his attention away from the screen.

"But it's the only thing that mellows me out and gets me to stop obsessing about my future."

He let out a long, low screech, a howl of both outrage and humiliation. I looked to the television, where an "Instant Replay" of his defeat was now unfolding. I watched his Asian surfer character being raised over the shoulders of a hulking, blonde-haired military character and then getting smashed, headfirst, into the pavement. His character's brains splattered into a mess of pink and brown goo. The words "YOU LOSE" flashed across the screen.

"You lost," I said.

"I can't seem to beat this one character. I've been trying for the last hour."

I laughed and said, "Maybe it's time to put in a new game."

He turned to me and asked, "Hey, do you want to play?"

"I'm not very good at video games," I told him.

"I don't know how to play, either, and I've been playing it for two years" he said, moving over on the couch to make space for me. "You just push all the buttons at the same time, really hard and fast, and you try to kill the other guy."

I sat down next to him. He handed me a controller and told me I had to choose a character—apparently there were two dozen to select from, and they each had their own set of individual strengths and weaknesses. I settled on a half-man/half-lion, and Terrence complimented me on this choice (apparently this character could especially do brutal things with his tail). Then he pressed the "Start" button. Terrence's Asian surfer destroyed my man-lion in less than a minute.

"You gotta push the buttons really, really fast, all sorts of different combinations of them," Terrence instructed. He did a quick demonstration for me, and then he pushed the "Start" button again. We fought again. He won again. He pushed the "Start" button again.

And again . . . and again . . . and again . . . for the next hour we sat side by side on his couch, saying very little to one another, playing this same video game, round after round after round. Just *playing*. Like two adolescent boys on a lazy spring afternoon, trying to put off the inevitable hour when they will have to retreat to their separate houses and do their homework

"I think you're lying, I think you've played this before," Terrence said, after I body-slammed his character and then followed it up with a swift kick to his jaw.

"I don't think beating you once every fifteen rounds means I've played before."

We fought again. I sneaked a glance at his face. His eyes were bright and wide and laser focused, like a native under the spell of a missionary preacher. All through our adolescence, he had never once looked as sweet and ingenuous as he did right now. He had never looked quite this adorable.

"We should go eat soon, it's almost nine," he said, his tone perfunctory.

"OK."

But then neither one of us moved. We kept playing, blissfully unconscious of anything but our pleasure in this moment. As if another version of our history together existed, in an alternate universe that we had somehow tapped into; a history in which we had been friends for the past two decades. As if the real history—my sister's death, my brother's exile, Terrence's calling me names and pushing me down the steps, the years of boredom and frustration, the forty-five minutes of fucking without a condom in a hotel room in Indianapolis—had all been imagined. We kept playing until the rounds evened out, one win for him, and one win for me. And then, very abruptly, Terrence stood up and shut the television off. He said it was time to go to dinner.

I giggled and teased him. "The only reason we're stopping is because I was finally winning."

He laughed and nodded at me. "I will not let you beat me at my own video game. You are correct."

We took a cab to a pizza place near Lincoln Center that Terrence said had the best pizza in New York City. Even though it was after 10:00 P.M., there was a waiting list with a half-dozen names in front of ours. When we were finally seated, thirty minutes later, I turned and saw that Woody Allen was sitting three tables away.

I gestured toward him and said, "You know, I don't think I've ever seen a famous person in a restaurant before."

"I was in Beverly Hills for five days, and I didn't see a single famous person," he said.

We had gotten so caught up playing video games that I had forgotten the reason he wanted to meet me tonight. He wanted to tell me about his trip.

I asked him, "So how did it go there?"

"It's weird, you *never* see famous people in L.A.," he said, continuing with his previous thought. "They're all living in these bubbles. These multi-million-dollar plastic bubbles. But then you come here and Woody Allen is eating pizza right next to you. I don't know how people can live out there—it all seems so precious and synthetic to me. The agent I'm probably going to sign with wants me to move there, but I just don't know if I can do it."

Move to Los Angeles? Since when had he been thinking of moving to Los Angeles?

"Is that something you would do?" I tried to sound calm and indifferent, but my voice cracked. I couldn't be indifferent to the thought of him moving away and leaving me behind.

"The agent said he could get me $250,000 for the screenplay I've been working on," he went on. "It's not even finished, but he said that between the novel coming out and having a name at *GQ*, I'd be able to capitalize on the heat on me. That's the phrase he actually used. *The heat on me.* That's how they talk out there."

I started to protest, to tell him that he shouldn't rush to make such an important decision. But he talked right over me.

"The thing that gets me is that I know he's right. It galls me that I have to listen to the advice of these people. They're just used car salesmen in $2,000 suits. But he knows what he's talking about. He reps a bunch of young writers. He's signing them to major deals left and right."

"You would leave your job at the magazine?" I asked, losing

my cool a bit, sounding incredulous and half-outraged, like a parent who has just spent $150,000 on his child's education, only to have the kid announce that he wants to be a circus performer. There was no way I could be indifferent about any of this. Terrence couldn't leave New York. Not when things were just beginning to come to a boil between us.

"I don't know, maybe I would take a leave of absence," he said. "It just seems like there's a real opportunity to set myself up. This whole game, that's what it all boils down to, Ben. It's all about getting yourself set up. Not to sound totally shallow, but I tend to think it's all about making yourself famous. So the novel getting published helps to sell this screenplay, and then maybe the screenplay getting sold might encourage a producer to buy the rights to the novel. And all of that, hopefully, gets people buzzing, wanting to work with me."

He stopped and began shaking his head, a bit embarrassed to be talking about himself in this manner, as nothing but a commodity. But then he started right up again: "I know it all sounds so petty. But I've seen it happen for other people. They get some buzz going on themselves, and then they coax it into something bigger. This guy I worked with at the *Village Voice* is a millionaire now, and all he's ever done is sold a couple of pitches based on two of his articles. But I've also seen how briefly that window stays open for people. How quickly the buzz just moves on to the next guy. That's where I feel like I am right now. And it feels . . . I don't know . . . it all feels so precarious. Like if I make one bad decision, then all of the possibilities are going to collapse on me."

He stopped and again shook his head, this time even more vigorously than before. "Can you tell I've been thinking about all of this?" he said. "I'm sorry to sound so self-involved."

"You're allowed," I told him. "It's your life. It's important." *But does your life have to come at the expense of leaving me behind in New York?*

"I just don't have anyone to talk about this stuff with," he said. "My parents don't quite get it. They couldn't even comprehend why I wanted to write a novel when I already had a great job at *GQ*. And I can't talk to the people at the magazine, because they're all so competitive. And Lisa, I don't know . . . lately I can't seem to talk about anything with her."

"Are you thinking of breaking up?" I asked. I thought I might float the idea out there, perhaps plant the seed in his head. At the very least, I thought it would get us off this topic of him moving away to Los Angeles. He couldn't go. I had to make him stop considering it as a possibility.

"I don't know," he said. "Do you think we're totally wrong for one another?"

"No, I didn't mean that," I said. "You just sound . . . you made it sound like things weren't really great. Last week, in the cab, when you were talking about looking for a new apartment, when you said—"

"I don't know." He shrugged and frowned at me. "I don't want to talk about it. I feel like there's too much on my plate right now to even think about Lisa."

He abruptly pushed away from the table and excused himself to go to the bathroom. He was gone for almost five minutes, so long that I wondered if I had made him angry; if he was sitting in a stall and stewing. But when he came back, he seemed relaxed and happy again. Terrence went back to talking about his trip. He told me more about the three agents he met with in Los Angeles, and he described each of his meetings in very funny detail. He said that the agents all stared at him the same way, the way a hungry man might stare at a loaf of bread in a bakery window, with covetousness and a hint of paranoia, because they were worried someone else might come along and buy the loaf of bread out from under their noses. He told me about the hotel where he stayed; the dinners he had at the Ivy and at L'Orangerie; the drinks he had at Sky Bar; even the movie he saw on his one free night there. He talked so much that, ten minutes after I had stopped eating, he was still only halfway through his share of the pizza.

"I'm sorry to keep blabbing on and on about myself," he said, when he finally finished. "I hate conversation hogs."

"You just had a big trip," I said. "Whenever anyone gets back from a big trip, they want to tell someone about it."

"There are no smart people in Los Angeles," he said. "For five days, I didn't get to talk to a single smart person."

"Well, now you're back in New York."

And you must stay here, Terrence. You must. *I will make you. Even if it means that I have to keep you bound to the radiator in your apartment, I insist that you stay in New York.*

"I think maybe the problem is I don't have enough smart people in my life," he said. "It just seems like there's so few people on my level. On our level. You know what I mean? I always feel like I'm dumbing it down."

I didn't respond. The waiter brought the check. I snatched it off the table before Terrence could and handed over my credit card.

"It's not that I think people are stupid," he said. "Just simple. They'd rather things remain on the surface. There are so few people in my life who I don't have to dumb it down with."

I still didn't say anything. We sat for the next minute in silence. The waiter returned with the credit card slip. Terrence watched me sign it.

"I've felt that way for so long," he said, very softly, almost as if he was talking to himself. "I've probably felt that way since the fourth grade."

Back in his apartment, Terrence opened up two bottles of beer and planted himself next to me on the couch. "So what were you up to while I was gone?" he said. "It occurs to me that I probably should have asked you that about five hours ago."

I laughed and shrugged my shoulders. "I was mostly laid up," I told him. "I had some kind of flu." *Some kind of gay flu.*

"Are you OK?"

"I'm fine now. It disappeared as fast as it came on. I had it for five days and then I didn't." *But now I think that I have AIDS.*

He started to say something, but then hesitated. His brow

furrowed and a hint of disgust seemed to flash in his eyes. For a moment, it almost looked as if he was afraid of me.

"That sucks," he said. "I'm glad you're better."

Before I could answer, he stood up and pointed to the bathroom. "My contacts are killing me," he told me. "I'll be right back."

Did he know? Did he know about Acute Retroviral Syndrome? Did he know that when gay men suffer a flu-like illness that lasts for exactly five days, it usually means that they have contracted HIV? Was that why he left the room so abruptly? Was he afraid that it might be catching? Was he in the bathroom right now, preemptively sterilizing it, in case my blood spilled onto the sink at some point later in the evening?

Was this what I now had to look forward to? A lifetime of people eyeing me suspiciously and then immediately excusing themselves from the room?

He returned a few minutes later. He was wearing black-rimmed, Clark Kent-style glasses that made him look the hero in a screwball comedy—the uptight efficiency expert who is secretly a gorgeous hunk. He had also taken off his button-down shirt and changed into a tank top undershirt, ribbed and white and clinging tightly to his body. When I saw his bare shoulders, which were even broader and more densely built than I had realized, I felt a stirring in my groin.

"I didn't know you wore glasses," I mumbled, trying not to stare at his shoulders.

"Since the summer between seventh and eighth grade," he said, returning to his seat on the couch. "I used to refuse to go out in public unless I had contacts on. I was rabid about it. I don't think I ever showed up once at school wearing my glasses."

"They look good on you," I told him. I was trying to sound encouraging, a bit of the cheerleader—but *not* as if I was flirting.

"I don't know," he laughed. "I think they make me look like a raccoon."

"No, they look really good on you." This time I sounded a little too aggressive. This time I hurtled right past flirting. Now it sounded like I was hitting on him.

His laugh came out as a snort, that same old nervous sound of his.

"I'm sorry," I said. "I didn't mean to—"

"No, it's nothing."

"—to embarrass you. I just meant—"

"I have to learn to take compliments better. I have to learn how to just say 'thank you.'"

"—I just meant you shouldn't be afraid to wear them, you shouldn't—"

"Thank you. Thanks. That was nice of you to say." He wanted it to stop. He wanted us to be talking about something else.

But why stop? Why not nudge it a little bit further? Life is too short—every moment counts—especially when your life expectancy has just been cut in half—especially when you could literally die any day now.

Twenty-seven is far too old to have never told another person that you have a crush on him. Especially if you have had a crush on him since the seventh grade.

"Terrence, I like you," I said, my tone neutral and matter-of-fact. "I have a crush on you. I've had a crush on you for as long as I've known you."

He didn't respond. I tried to make eye contact with him. He was looking at the floor.

"I'm sorry, I thought you realized that," I said, after nearly a minute passed in silence.

"I guess so. I guess I did. I mean, the thought had occurred to me. It's just that—"

"That you don't have a crush on me. That's OK."

"No, it's not that," he said. "Or, I guess it's partly that. I mean, I *don't* have a crush on you. But I guess I'm just surprised by your saying that you've *always* felt that way. I treated you horribly, Ben. I treated *everybody* horribly. At some point, I stopped treating people horribly, because I realized that, if I kept on behaving that way, no would ever find me attractive." He paused again and made another of his snorty laughs. "But was that not correct logic?"

"I don't know."

"Did you have a crush on me *because* I treated you so badly?"

"I don't think so," I told him. "I think it was more how you looked. I found you attractive. But who knows? Maybe you're right."

"Who else did you have a crush on in high school?" he asked.

"Probably everyone who had a penis," I said, laughing nervously.

"Like who?"

I should have told him a few names. I should have just answered his question. I certainly remembered all of their names: Seth Kern, Dave Leferink, Thomas Agnello, Vincent Grasso. I could have easily run down the list of boys I fantasized about in high school. Besides, he had already rejected me; he had already told me he *didn't* have a crush on me.

So why go on inflating his ego? Why go on letting him think that he was the only one?

Because I couldn't help myself. Because I thought it might help my cause.

"I don't remember anyone else, really," I said. "I just remember having a crush on you."

He nodded at this. Then, after a few moments of silence, he said: "That day, junior year, in the locker room. Were you actually checking me out?"

"Yes," I said, my cheeks suddenly burning hot.

"OK."

"I thought you realized that. When we were walking back to my house, you kept saying, 'I know what you were doing.' I kept denying it, but you were so insistent."

"I wasn't really sure," he said. "I've always been a little slow when it comes to stuff like that. I never quite realize when another person likes me."

"Or maybe you just have bad gaydar."

He laughed and said, "Maybe."

"Well, I was checking you out," I told him. "I guess I owe you an apology. What can I say? The hormones were raging. I wish I had a better excuse than that, but I don't."

"Did I look good?" he asked. "When you were checking me out."

At first I didn't respond. Part of me still feared him. Part of me wondered if this all might be a trick, and that if I had told him the truth—that *of course* he looked good, that in fact he looked sublime, divine, exquisite, unforgettable, unimaginably perfect, indescribably *hot*, that the image of him in his underwear was still burned into the deepest recesses of my brain—it would turn ugly. I worried that he would push me down the stairs all over again.

Fool me once, shame on you. Fool me twice . . .

—shame on me. I couldn't help myself. I had to keep trying.

"Of course, you looked good," I said, grinning at him. "You looked great. I'm still here, aren't I?"

He didn't react, other than to stare ahead and slowly nod his head.

A minute or two more passed in silence. Finally, Terrence stood up and said that he was going to bed. He turned and started walking to his bedroom. But then he stopped and turned back around and cocked his head to the side.

"I feel so clueless sometimes, Ben," he said. "I feel like there's so much going on just outside of my periphery. Do you ever feel that way?"

"I guess."

"It's not that I don't think I'm a perceptive person," he said. "But sometimes I wonder if I'm just looking in the wrong direction. And all it would take is for someone to tap me on the shoulder and say, 'Hey, look over here,' and then my understanding of everything would be different. It's like in that movie, *The Vanishing*. Have you ever seen it? This guy goes into a gas station bathroom and when he comes back out his wife is missing. And he goes on this search for her that goes on for years and years, and he goes insane in the process. And then he finally discovers what actually happened. It turns out that all this other stuff had been going on around him, but he just didn't notice it. He was there. Basically he *saw* her kidnapping. But his eyes were focused on the wrong thing. He was looking in the wrong direction. He misunderstood everything."

He paused and shook his head and then added: "Sometimes my life feels like that movie. Do you ever feel that way, Ben?"

I looked at him straight in the eyes and I lied: "I don't think the idea has ever occurred to me."

chapter nine

Offers
(2000)

Two days later, arriving home from an afternoon movie, there were two messages on my answering machine. Two offers.

From Danny: "I thought about what you said, and I decided that maybe you're right. Maybe I owe you an explanation. So I'll make you a deal. If you're willing to put all of this stuff to rest and apologize to mom and dad, then I'd be willing to sit down with you and explain what happened. I think that's a fair exchange. Call me back and let me know what you think."

From Terrence: "I was wondering if you were free next weekend. I'm going to Denver on Tuesday. I've been talking about doing this Columbine story forever, and I just need to finally get myself out there and do some research. Anyway, a friend of mine has a house up in Vail, and he offered me the keys for the weekend. I had bought Lisa a plane ticket, figuring that she could meet me in Denver on Thursday and we could drive up, but it turns out she has some final paper due that she never told me about. Would you be up for taking her place? It's great there in the off-season, if you've never been."

Couple. Couples. Coupling. Couplehood. Boy-plus-girl. The boy has a penis and the girl has a vagina. They go together, one fits into the other, and once connected they have the power to make babies, to advance the human race, to procreate, and leave you behind. You cannot fit in singly. You cannot be gay. The moment you admit to liking other men, they will damn you. They will tell you otherwise. They will drown you in liberal bromides. They will assure you that they support your civil rights. But as soon as you draw too close, they will clam up. They will get defensive. They won't want to talk about it. They will push you down the steps in your house and leave a crescent-shaped scar behind your ear, a permanent mark that you are different from normal, and lesser. They will call you a sickie.

I decided not to call Terrence back right away. Later tonight, certainly. But for now I needed to make him wait. If I had any hope of a long-lasting relationship with him, I couldn't just instantly acquiesce to whatever plan he proposed.

I decided, instead, to go to the mall and do some shopping. If I was going on vacation with Terrence—and, really, there was no question of this, I might make him wait for my answer, but my answer, when I delivered it, would be yes—I might as well treat myself to some new summer clothes. I wandered in and out of the stores. I walked up and down the long, fluorescent-lit corridors. I saw wives helping their husbands choose the right cut of khakis at Banana Republic, pleated front and easy fit, better to disguise the excess weight that had gathered around the men's waists since they had married. I saw college-age couples browsing through the CD racks in the music store, bespectacled and too-skinny young men, trailing behind pimply, slightly overweight young women. I saw handsome seventeen-year-old boys sitting side-by-side, hand-in-hand, with their girlfriends at the tables in the food court—the boys absent-mindedly feeding the girls McDonald's French fries, one at a time, like a trainer feeding carrots to a horse. I saw a gaggle of junior high school girls, moving in lockstep, giggling and play-slapping each other on the backsides—but even they were part of this grotesque display of heterosexuality, on the prowl for junior high school boys, so that they too could pair off and return the next weekend as part of a *couple*. Even the junior high schoolers existed in defiance of me.

But I couldn't tear myself away from it. I couldn't stop look-ing into their faces, hating them and envying them, wondering if they realized how very lucky they were.

They didn't look back at me, of course. They probably didn't even notice me staring. Or, if they did notice, they made a con-scious effort to pay me no heed; to pretend I wasn't there. And who could blame them? Because to acknowledge my presence was to acknowledge something awful; to acknowledge my pres-ence was to contemplate the inner thoughts of a lonely and de-pressed creature, one of those unfortunate souls who, as the years pass, turns fat and smelly and begins mumbling to him-self in public. And, really, who wants to think about a person like *that* . . . a person always alone . . . always puttering about . . . long since celibate (because who wants to have sex with a person like *that*) . . .

Who wants to contemplate: *What went wrong in that guy's life?*

But what if they were forced to think about me? What if I made them take notice?

What if they knew that I liked to have sex with men?

What then?

Then they wouldn't look past me. Then they wouldn't be so polite and accommodating.

Then the girls would be frozen with fear, that I might swoop in and steal their boyfriends away, before they would even have time to register what had happened.

Then the boys would fear something far worse—that I would take everything else away; everything in the world that mat-tered to them. They would fear that, with one heated glance held too long, I would poison them. I would turn them into that which they most despised.

They would see me staring at them. They would register me as a threat. And then they would turn and run away. Because everyone who has ever seen a horror movie knows that the best defense against a vampire is not a necklace of garlic, or a bottle of holy water, or a crucifix held out far in front of you. The best defense against a vampire is to avoid the vampire at all costs.

The best defense against a vampire is to make certain that the two of you are never in the same room just after the sun has set.

Quickly, run, as fast you can, get as far away from him as possible, don't let him turn you into something so vile. Don't let it be so that he can wander around the mall on a Saturday night and not *feel self-conscious. Don't let his threat gain a foothold.*

And if the vampire refuses to leave you alone? If he won't stop looking at you; coveting you; desiring your blood; trying to turn you gay?

Kill him. Drive a stake through his heart. Plead not guilty by reason of self-defense. Tell the judge: I vanquished that faggot in the interest of protecting my God-given way of life, my heterosexual primacy. I destroyed him because I didn't want to become another gaywad.

A jury of your heterosexual peers will choose not to convict.

I wandered into the bookstore determined to find something I could read on the airplane. Since reconnecting with Terrence, I hadn't been able to concentrate long enough to read even a newspaper article, much less a book. I was standing in the fiction section when I heard a familiar voice behind me, a jubilant and slightly awed young voice.

"Mr. Reilly, hey, how are you?"

I spun around. Jamie Ryan, one of my former students, probably the brightest student I had ever taught, was standing in front of me. Jamie had been in three of my classes during my last four semesters of teaching. He was tall and lean, a co-captain of the track team, and he had a wide and generous smile. Now, with track season over, and with a bit more weight on his frame, he reminded me of Terrence in his junior year of high school: another effortlessly seductive boy, so comfortable in his own skin, whose shoulders were expanding by leaps and bounds.

He held out his hand for me to shake. He was standing next

to a plain-looking girl with heavy-lidded eyes and a pageboy haircut whom I had never seen before.

"Jamie, wow, what a surprise." I put my palm into his. He shook my hand so forcefully that it started to ache.

"You remember Laura Grasso," he said. "She was in our AP Language and Literature class last year."

"Hey, Laura," I said, squinting a bit, looking into her face. I was certain I had never seen this girl before.

"I got into Yale, Mr. Reilly," Jamie said. "I found out the same week you left, and I never got a chance to tell you. I wanted to thank you for your recommendation letter. I think it really made the difference."

It took me a few seconds to process this information. He had gotten into . . . Yale. *Yale? That* Yale? Just like Terrence.

What is it about these able-bodied, sandy-haired, blue-eyed, seventeen-year-old boys that proves so irresistible to the admissions officers at Yale?

"That's great, Jamie." I tried to sound encouraging, but instead it came out sounding perfunctory, a little churlish. Even for this sweet-natured, hard-working boy for whom I harbored a dirty old man's crush, I couldn't suppress the envy. I couldn't pretend that I didn't want his perfectly uncomplicated, extraordinarily promising, seventeen-year-old heterosexual life.

"Thank you," he said. "I'm really, really stoked."

"A good friend of mine went to Yale," I said. "You remind me of him actually."

"I still can't believe I got in," he said.

I looked over at Laura, who was looking back at me expectantly. She was waiting for me to ask her what college she had been accepted to. But I didn't care. I couldn't even fake caring. I was certain this girl had never been a student of mine.

"Oh, hey, did you hear about Elliot and Mario?" Jamie asked, after the awkward pause carried on too long. "It turns out it may have been Elliot who instigated the fight. A couple of Elliot's friends came forward, and they said they saw Elliot trying to choke Mario. Apparently when Mario pushed Elliot, he was doing it in self-defense."

I nodded my head slowly at Jamie, not wanting him to stop. This recounting of Tottenville High School's ongoing soap opera enlivened him; it brought out a hint of mischief in his eyes.

"All the charges against Mario have been dropped," Jamie went on. "They lifted his suspension, too, but he's finishing the year at Moore. And still nobody knows what started it. Nobody even realized they knew each other before they got into that fight. Crazy, huh?"

"Not so crazy," I said. *No one knew that Terrence and I knew each other. No one knew that he followed me to my house that afternoon.* "Maybe they were secretly boyfriends."

Both Jamie and the girl were puzzled by this suggestion. A bit of color seemed to drain from their faces. I kept on staring at Jamie, taking in his eyes, his chin, his ears, his nose, all of him so unblemished and unspoiled. So very adorable. Once again, the awkward pause carried on for too long.

"Is everything OK with your family, Mr. Reilly?" Jamie asked finally. "When you left there were all these stories about why, and I heard—"

"My sister passed away," I broke in. "I had to go to Indiana to put her affairs in order." *She died of AIDS. And now I have it too.*

"I'm so sorry," they both said at exactly the same time

"I wish I could have stayed on for the rest of the year." *And I wish I could be there on the day you turn eighteen.* "I may start teaching again in the fall," I continued. "But I'm not sure. I've been thinking of trying something new."

"Well, you were a really good teacher, Mr. Reilly. I hope you don't give it up entirely."

The girlfriend—what was her name?—was shifting awkwardly in place alongside him. Jamie was nodding at me, bouncing his head gently up and down. They were waiting for me to say something.

I had nothing to say. I smirked. Then the smirk quickly turned into a frown. I felt a rush of revulsion come over me. I hated these kids. I hated their youth. Their optimism. Their blank slate. Their boundless promise. Mostly I hated the fact that they were dating.

But then I took another look at Jamie, still smiling back at me, still a little awed to have run into his English teacher in the bookstore in the mall. So charming. So friendly. *So fucking cute.* How could I possibly hate a boy like this? How could I not have a bit of a crush on him?

I took a step closer to him. I slowly looked him up and down, from head to toes and then back again, taking him all in. I leaned in still closer, so that our mouths were only a few inches apart. I looked directly into his eyes, and I kept my voice low. I said it loud enough for the girlfriend to hear, but low enough so that Jamie would know that it was meant only for him.

I said, "When you guys decide to break up, you should give me a call."

Confusion danced across his face. He smiled in the manner of a man trying to pretend that he's in on a joke that has just sailed over his head. He must have thought I made some literary reference—some passage from some book we had dwelled on in class that he was now too embarrassed to admit he couldn't remember.

"I don't . . ." he started to say.

But then, in the very literal blink of an eye, he got it. He understood. His smile curdled into a scowl. He took a hesitant step closer to the girlfriend.

This would get around. I knew this would get around. Just as I knew, that day in the seventh grade, when Terrence first called me gaywad, that it would get around. It would spread through the cafeteria, the gymnasium, the hallways, and the locker rooms, until it wholly obliterated my reputation. Until I could never step foot inside Tottenville High School again.

But I didn't care. Not this time. Not anymore.

Let them talk. Let Jamie and his little cunt tell all of their friends. Let them tell all of the other teachers, and let them all speculate on my erratic behavior. Let them call me barking mad. Let them say I had a nervous breakdown. Let me be known once again as the gaywad. Now

*and forever the gaywad. Gaywad, gaywad, gaywad, GAYWAD! The
gayest gaywad of them all!*

*It doesn't matter. Because I won't be there to face their scorn. I'll
never again have to listen to their shit.*

Because now I have Terrence.

And with Terrence I'll be safe.

It was after ten when I finally returned Terrence's call. I
didn't think he would be home. I figured he would be out on a
date with Lisa or at a party thrown by one of his writer colleagues, doing something fabulous without me. He picked up
on the first ring.

"Where were you all day?" he asked. "I called three times."

"I meant to get back to you sooner," I said. "It was a long day.
I had a run-in with one of my students at the mall."

I told Terrence the story of what happened, except I altered
the ending. I didn't tell him that I had made a pass at Jamie,
and that both Jamie and the girl reacted with terror and disgust. Instead, I told Terrence that, just as we were parting ways
at the bookstore, I said to Jamie, "Try not to break up with her
too soon."

"Oh, that's not so bad," Terrence said. "Teachers say goofy
stuff like that to their students all the time. The kids just think
the teachers are trying to sound young and hip."

"They looked like I had assaulted them." *Perhaps because I
had. I told one of my former students to dump his girlfriend and give
me a call. I told a seventeen-year-old boy that I wanted to go on a date
with him.*

"You know, when they do break up, they'll blame you," Terrence added, laughing.

"I can come to Vail with you," I said, deciding I should
change the subject. "If the offer still stands."

"Of course the offer still stands."

"But only if I can pay my own way."

"It's too late to pay your own way," he said. "The Condé Nast
travel department has already paid for your plane ticket. And

the place isn't costing me anything, so it's not costing you anything, either. You can buy me dinner one night, how about
that?"

We negotiated a deal. He would let me pay for one dinner,
and we had to order an expensive bottle of wine, and the bill
had to come to at least $200. All other expenses we would split
evenly.

"Have you ever been to Colorado?" he asked, after we had
settled on our terms.

I didn't answer him. I had something else I needed to tell
him first; something that I had wanted to get off my chest for
the last three days.

"Terrence, just so you know, I didn't mean to make things
awkward between us the other night. By saying that I have
crush on you."

"You didn't."

"It's just that I thought you knew," I said. "I thought it must
have been obvious."

He took his time answering. I could hear him breathing
through his nose, slowly and patiently, thinking through every
word before he spoke.

"Well," he finally answered, "thoughts go through your head
all the time—"

"—it's just that, I wanted to—"

"—but until someone says something out loud and makes it
concrete . . . well, until then they're just thoughts. Just speculation. And you can't act on speculation. You have to act on facts.
But I don't want you to think you scared me or made me uncomfortable." He paused and then added: "Or that I don't
want to be your friend."

"So you'll forget I brought it up?"

"Is that what you want me to do?" He sounded taken aback,
maybe a little irritated, like a four-star chef after a diner has returned the filet mignon to the kitchen and asked that it be
cooked until well done. He would do as he was told, but he
couldn't mask his disapproval.

"I don't know," I said. "I'm not sure what—"

He cut me off and started speaking very quickly, in short, declarative bursts. "Ben, listen, you told me something that was on your mind. You were honest with me. I respect that. That took courage. That took a lot of courage. And when you tell someone that you have a crush on them, it makes them rethink things. Not in a good way. Not in a bad way. It just makes them think." He waited a few beats and then lowered his voice and added: I'm still thinking."

"Can I ask what you've been thinking about?"

He chuckled and said, "No."

"No?"

"I'm not sure I would even be able to articulate my thoughts to you. I've been thinking about a lot of things. But, I tell you what, I'll let you know when I've drawn some conclusions. How about that?"

"So I should go on crushing on you?"

"I'll leave that up to you," he answered. I could almost hear him grinning on the other end of the line.

My heart started beating faster. I felt my penis getting stiff. What was going on here? His flirting seemed a little too obvious; a little too willful. I started to wonder if this conversation might lead to phone sex. Is that what he was guiding us toward? Would that be the way he slid into a romance with me? By establishing sexual intimacy at a distance, so that I wouldn't be able witness his shame and uncertainty firsthand?

Did he want for the two of us to jerk off together on the phone?

"I can, if you want me to," I said, flirting back.

"Whatever works, Ben," he said, in perhaps too whispery a voice.

Whatever works, Ben. Was that an invitation? It certainly sounded like one. Was he trying to get me to ask him what he was wearing? Was that all it would take to ignite our long-gestating, long-overdue romance? For me to say to him: *Are you naked right now, Terrence? Are you wearing only your underwear?*

For a minute, neither of us spoke. I couldn't bring myself to make the first move.

Another minute passed. Still nothing. He was waiting for me to say something.

But what if I was misreading the signals? What if he didn't want phone sex at all and was fishing for something else entirely? What if I ended up sabotaging all the groundwork that I had already laid?

I couldn't bear to play his fool again.

So I decided, instead, to change the topic altogether.

"What did you do tonight?" I asked him finally.

He sighed softly. Was he disappointed? Was he sighing in frustration? Had he been hoping for a different question entirely? Had he been hoping that I would ask him if he had a hard-on and would he please describe it to me in very precise detail?

"I stayed in and put on my slippers and read magazines," he said. "So much for my fancy Manhattan life."

"That sounds relaxing," I said. *Were you wearing anything other than your slippers?*

"Actually it was kind of boring. I was glad when the phone rang and it was you."

Take off your slippers and whatever other clothing you are wearing and tell me why, Terrence. Why were you so glad that it was me calling? I was silent on my end of the line.

"Honestly, I was sitting here half the evening hoping that you would call," he said.

Why, Terrence? Tell me why. Because you are falling in love with me? Because you want nothing more in this world than to reach out and caress my neck and breathe into my ear and press your mouth against mine? Is that why? Because you love me as much as I love you? Reach beneath the waistband of your underwear, Terrence, do it right now. Press your hand against your balls and squeeze your cock. Describe your cock to me as it gets hard.

"I was at the mall saying mean things to my former students," I told him. "I figured you would be out. Otherwise I would have called sooner." *Please forgive me, I meant nothing by it. Please do not think that my delay in returning your call is a sign of my lack of interest.*

"I think Lisa and I are headed toward a break up."

It took me a few seconds before I could react. I probably should have felt ecstatic. Lisa Turiel and Terrence O'Connell would soon be no more. Her absence would clear the path for me to take her place.

But mostly I felt chagrin. Was this the topic—and not phone sex—that he had been trying to steer us toward?

"Is it something you want to talk about?" I asked.

"Kind of."

And with that my window of opportunity closed. It slammed shut. It crashed right down, right on my genitals, leaving them swollen and blue and still desperate to get off. I would not be having phone sex with Terrence. He would not be telling me all about his throbbing purple cock and his preferred means of stroking it. Not tonight. Probably not ever.

"What's going on?" I asked dutifully.

"I don't want to bore you."

"Go ahead."

And he did, for the next thirty minutes; he talked and talked and talked about his girlfriend. He told me the problems had started months ago, but lately they had gotten worse. He was bored with their conversations. He was beginning to think that he had overestimated her and that at heart she was really quite dull. He had been relieved when she told him that she couldn't go with him to Vail—at least he wouldn't have to fake it through another weekend. He said that he still liked her, maybe he even loved her, but he couldn't seem to make it work. He blamed himself for the collapse of the relationship. He said he had been working too hard, and he hadn't devoted to her the attention that she needed.

"But maybe that's a sign of the larger problem," he told me. "Maybe the reason I work so much is because I want to avoid her. I mean, if I found someone I wanted to be in a relationship with, I would make the time for that person."

Like me, Terrence. Someone like me. You would make time for me.

"This is such stupid, banal, break-up crap," he said. "I'm embarrassed that these words are even coming out of my mouth."

"No, it's OK," I said. *Especially if it makes it so that one day the two of us can be together. If that's the case, you can blather on to me all night.*

"I appreciate you letting me get this off my chest."

"Is there anyone else you've been seeing?" I asked him. "Or that you think you might want to start seeing?" *Please, please, please, please let the answer be me. Please just say the name: Benjamin Reilly.*

He didn't miss a beat. Terrence O'Connell still had the power to knock me off my feet and crush me in an instant.

"There's nobody else." He paused and then said: "I think this is just about me. Maybe I should use that line on her. 'Lisa, it's not you, it's me.' Do you think she's heard that one before?" He chuckled at this and then let out a long sigh. "What can I say, Ben? I'm not as original as I pretend to be."

We finished our conversation a few minutes later. He thanked me again for listening to him. He said that I'd probably have to listen to more of it when we were in Vail. Before I hung up, he took down my address so that he could overnight me the airplane ticket. If we didn't talk before then, he said, he would see me at the airport in Denver on Thursday.

"This should be a lot of fun, Ben. I'm really glad you're coming. Have a good night."

I took a deep breath, and I went for it. I decided I had to throw it all on the line and tell Terrence O'Connell how I truly felt about him. *Finally,* I went for it.

"I'm in love with you Terrence," I said. "And I want to have phone sex with you. Right now. Tell me what you're wearing. Tell me, Terrence. Please tell me."

But he didn't answer. He had already hung up the phone.

You're slipping. You're slipping. You're letting yourself fall. You're turning into the very worst version of yourself you can be.

How do you explain it? You wish you could, but you can't.

You can't even begin to understand what's going on inside of your head.

In the spring of my freshman year of college, nearly two years after I had last seen him, I dreamed of Terrence O'Connell. I dreamed he was a boxer in a championship ring, wearing boxing gloves, and those baby blue underpants with the white waistband, and nothing more. In my dream, I was . . . well, I'm not exactly sure who I was. I may have been one of his opponents; or I may have been the referee; or—most likely—I was a ringside spectator, in silent awe of his every move. The images were brightly colored, but also a little soft and fuzzy—I guess everything was slightly out of focus except for Terrence. My dream had no story, or at least none that I could remember the next morning. Mostly I just watched Terrence floating around the boxing ring, his smooth and muscular seventeen-year-old arms held high above his head in a pose of glory, a look of steely, humorless determination on his face. Time seemed to be passing: The background behind him would periodically alter; the noise from the crowd would vary in texture and pitch. I must have been watching him as he fought a series of bouts. But I never saw Terrence throw a punch or knock out another boxer. In my dream world, he never even broke a sweat. He simply existed in a state of perpetual, effortless victory.

I woke up from this dream that seemed to last all night feeling calm and strangely happy. It took me at least a minute to realize that the excess moisture in my underwear was not sweat or pee, but semen—and quite a bit of it. Terrence O'Connell had brought me to orgasm in my sleep.

And how do you explain *that*? I had spent the previous two years trying to obliterate him from my memory. But now here he was in my dreams, emerging from exile to remind me that he still had his claws in me. To remind me how much I still desired him.

Is there a medical term for what I felt? Is it described and analyzed, complete with illustrative case studies, in some abnormal psychiatry textbook? I wanted the boy who had humiliated me; who had ridiculed me; who had pushed me down the stairs in my house. I wanted him now more than ever before.

How do you explain such foolish and self-destructive behavior?

You can't. There's no explanation. There's no way to make sense of it. Other than say that Terrence O'Connell once poisoned me, and I couldn't get the poison out of my system. The poison was slowly but steadily driving me mad.

And that I only had two options: I could sweat out the situation, hoping and praying that the poison might eventually be flushed out of my bloodstream.

Or I could go out and find the antidote.

And the only one with the antidote was Terrence.

Late into the night, unable to sleep, I dialed my brother's number. It rang four times. I expected the machine to click on. But then I heard the sound of the receiver being knocked off its cradle. And then I heard Danny's voice, groggy and petulant.

"Hello."

I told myself I should just hang up. But I didn't. I waited. I said nothing. I tried to figure out what to say.

"Who is this? Ben, is this you? What are you doing Ben? It's the middle of the night."

I still didn't say anything. I looked at the alarm clock. It was 3:28 A.M. I told myself: *Just hang up and never talk to him again.*

"Ben, please stop this," he said. His voice was getting clearer and louder. I pictured him sitting up in his bed, waking up Megan alongside him. He wouldn't be able to fall back to sleep after this.

"Don't start pranking me in the middle of the night, Ben. That's nuts."

I took a deep breath and then slowly exhaled.

I said, "I'm ready to listen to your story."

part three

chapter ten

Runaways
(1982–1986)

The first time Danny Reilly ran away, he did not get very far, and he did not stay away for very long. It happened on the Wednesday before Thanksgiving in 1982, seven months and two days after his older sister left their house, entered the hospital, and never returned home again. It was, at least until classes ended at 2:30 P.M., and he began making his way to his locker, a perfectly unremarkable day for Danny. He arrived at school on time (since Mary's wake and funeral, for which he had missed three days in April, he hadn't been absent or late even once). He listened carefully in each of his eight classes, copying into his notebook almost every word his teachers spoke. He diligently raised his hand whenever his teachers posed questions to the class. He asked his own carefully reasoned questions, hoping his teachers might expand upon their well-trod lesson plans; and when their answers were too brief or too facile, he asked if they might be able to go into a little more detail; there were still a couple of points he wasn't quite clear on. Throughout the day, he ignored the murmurs and whispers of his classmates: *Shut up already, Reilly.* Or: *No one cares; stop asking your stupid questions.* Or simply: *I hate that fucking kid.* He had been ignoring these murmurs and whispers for weeks now. He had learned to ignore them so effectively that it was almost as if they had never been murmured or whispered at all.

Danny—in his meager defense—had no idea he was behaving oddly. As far as he was concerned, he was simply being himself. In the weeks and months following his sister's death, he cut himself off from all of his friends. He removed himself from his regular lunch table and began sitting alone at another table, tucked away in the farthest corner of the cafeteria. He turned down every invitation he received to play handball after school or to meet at someone's house to play Atari. On weekends, he spent all of his time in his bedroom. Danny wasn't trying to be difficult or rude—or at least he didn't think he was trying to be difficult or rude. It was just that he didn't want to be bothered anymore. He didn't want to talk to his friends; didn't want to be around them. Mostly, he didn't want to have to put on the daily show, the endless posing and jockeying and acting cool that goes into being a junior high schooler. Instead, he began applying himself to his studies with a fervor and dedication he had never applied to anything before. Two months after the funeral, he was scoring 95s and 96s on every one of his exams. Over that summer, he read all twenty novels on the eighth grade summer reading list, even though he was only required to read three. And all through that fall, he would spend hours each night on his homework—sometimes four or five hours, when ninety minutes would have more than sufficed. He even got it in his head that, if he worked hard enough, he could be the valedictorian at his graduation, despite the fact that this was a statistical impossibility.

His classmates weren't the only ones who registered a change in Danny's behavior. His parents, too, noticed that their older boy was acting unusual. But their reaction was much different. They felt immensely, immeasurably grateful. Still shell-shocked by Mary's death, they now spent their days in a laconic fog, unable to communicate with each other, or with either Danny or his younger brother, Ben. They regarded Danny's studiousness as an extraordinary gesture—the noble efforts of a brave and sensitive young man. He was determined *not* to contribute to their already suffocating sadness by lashing out or misbehaving. So they chose to ignore some of Danny's more puzzling actions—the three days in August, for instance, when he refused to leave his room for anything other than trips to the bathroom and the refrigerator, because he said he *had* to finish *Bleak House* by the end of that week or his entire summer would be ruined. They ignored, too, the warnings of Danny's history teacher, Mrs. Dobrin, who—during an open school night session in October—said that Danny seemed very different to her this year and suggested that they consider taking him to an adolescent psychologist. Danny's parents thought Mrs. Dobrin needed to mind her own business. They spent the drive home that night bemoaning the state of the New York City public school system.

"You would think they would want to encourage the kids when their schoolwork is finally interesting them," Danny's mother said to Danny's father.

"They're like efficiency experts," Danny's father answered. "They're trained to find things wrong with the kids, and if they can't, they invent something in order to justify their own jobs."

It might have carried on like this for much longer. Danny might have drifted even farther afield. And—who knows?—perhaps *that* outcome would have been preferable to what did end up happening, the seven runaways. But on that day before Thanksgiving, two hundred and sixteen days after his sister Mary went off to the hospital, never to return home again, a bully entered Danny's life—very briefly, for only a minute or so, but just long enough to alter Danny's perception of things. A bully with the very best of intentions, if not the best means of expressing them. A bully who Danny would later come to regard as a kind of guardian angel—the corporeal proof that some kind of higher power was watching over him and making sure he didn't fall too far. A bully named George Pulaski.

He was a tall, broad-shouldered boy, solid-bodied, but somewhat shapeless. He had been born in Poland in 1967. His parents, who were both journalists for a newspaper in Gdansk, defected to West Germany during the 1972 Munich Olympics.

Two years later, they emigrated to the United States, causing George to fall two full grades behind at school as he struggled to learn English. But none of his classmates ever dared make fun of George, not even of his droning, Eastern European monotone. For one thing, George was much larger than the other kids in his grade. For another, there was something very intimidating about his appearance. He had a high forehead and a smushed-in nose, and when he narrowed his icy blue eyes and wrinkled his brow, he came across as humorless and potentially deadly—a young Russian mobster in training. Most of the other kids, all through elementary school and junior high school, simply thought it best to keep out of his way.

Until that day before Thanksgiving, George Pulaski had never really spoken to Danny Reilly, other than to curtly bark orders at him if the two of them happened to end up on the same volleyball team during gym class. Until that day before Thanksgiving, Danny Reilly wasn't even sure that George Pulaski knew who he was.

But as Danny was walking out of his last class that day, he sensed someone walking very close behind him. Danny hoped he was imagining things. He didn't want to have to turn around and confront the situation, no matter how small or insignificant the situation might be. He just wanted to go home and study.

"Hey, faggot." The voice, which Danny recognized immediately, was coming from only a few inches behind his ear.

At first, he didn't do anything. He just kept walking. *Never let a bully know that he's gotten to you,* Danny told himself, *and he will be forced to let it drop.*

"Hey, faggot," George Pulaski repeated, a little louder this time. "I need to talk to you."

Danny stopped in his tracks. Maybe George had made a mistake. Maybe, from behind, he had simply confused Danny for someone else. He decided it was best to turn around and clear this up quickly.

"You're Dan, right? I'm George."

Danny said nothing. He assumed this had something to do with schoolwork. Maybe George—a middling-bordering-on-terrible student who, no matter how many times Mrs. Piel went over them, couldn't seem to grasp the most basic precepts of algebra, that 2 multiplied by x equals $2x$—was going to try to strong-arm Danny into allowing him to copy Danny's homework assignments. Or maybe George would want Danny to write an English paper for him (George wasn't doing too well in that class either, Danny was pretty sure). He decided, right then, that he would agree to do whatever George asked of him, just to make him go away. Just to get this oversized Eastern European eighth-grader off his back.

"Listen, Dan, I know you don't know me very well," George began, in his flat and honking voice. "But someone needs to tell you this, because it's starting to get out of hand. People think you're a freak. The other kids, they hate you. They talk about you behind your back. They've been saying a lot of crap, about how your parents molest you and that's why you won't talk to anyone. One kid started a rumor that you killed your older sister. I heard a few guys talking at lunch yesterday saying that they were going to beat the shit out of you today. I was surprised it didn't happen. They all hate you, man. Do you understand what I'm saying? They think you need to be taught a lesson. You need to start watching your back. Because I don't think they're fooling around."

Danny stared at George Pulaski, wholly dumbfounded. He began to feel a piercing pain in his eyes and in his temples, almost as if someone had literally torn away a blindfold that had long been wrapped around his head, exposing him to the blistering haze.

They all hate you.

Danny certainly didn't dispute anything George had just told him. He knew that some of the other kids snickered at him when he passed them in the hallways. He knew that people were calling him names behind his back; that some of his classmates weren't even doing it behind his back—they were calling him names right in front of his face. But Danny had no idea how far things had progressed. He had never imagined that things were on the tipping point of violence.

They think you need to be taught a lesson. You need to start watching your back.

Danny knew that his behavior had been a little erratic; that he had been acting a bit moody. But, at least until now, he didn't think of himself as someone who might unnerve and incite others.

I don't think they're fooling around.

Until now, he didn't realize that maybe everyone was right about him, too. He had become a robot in the classroom; a zombie outside of it; a recluse in his own home. For these past seven months, he had gone a little crazy, and there had been no one around to rescue him.

George Pulaski came out of the blue and made Danny Reilly realize all of this.

"Why are you telling me this?" Danny asked, not challenging George, just curious (and perhaps a little touched that George would make such an effort to reach out to him).

George Pulaski looked at Danny as if he had just been asked the dumbest question in the history of dumb questions. He answered: "Because no one else was going to tell you, man."

And with that he shrugged his shoulders and made a face—a winsome and none-too-optimistic look, poised somewhere between a grin and a frown, a look that seemed to be saying, *I've done all I can, hopefully you will use this information wisely, and not get yourself killed.*

Then George Pulaski turned around and walked off in the opposite direction, never to speak to Danny Reilly again.

Danny slowly made his way to his locker. He walked a little unsteadily and haltingly, almost as if he feared his legs might give out on him. He felt tears welling up in his eyes, but he swore to himself that he wouldn't cry until he was out of the school building. He kept that promise, but only barely. Outside of the building, he made his way into the narrow alley that separated the handball court from the baseball field, where high school students would sometimes come on the weekends in order to drink beer and smoke pot. He threw his book bag on the ground, and then sat down on top of the book bag, and then he pulled his knees in close to his chest and buried his head into his lap.

And then he wept. *Finally,* he wept.

It was the first time since his sister's death that he was even able to cry—so perhaps he was simply making up for lost time. At the wake and the funeral, he *wanted* to cry. He thought he should have cried; that he owed his sister at least that much. But every time he thought he might cry, his father—as if operating by some kind of sixth sense—would appear behind him and softly pat him on the back and say to him: "Be strong now. Be strong." In the months following the funeral, Danny still wanted to cry. But by then he found that he couldn't cry. When he thought of his sister, he no longer felt sadness. Instead, he felt a hot and pointed anger, a sense of *indignance*—as if someone had cheated him out of what was rightfully his. He wanted to know why, when she said good-bye to him that morning in the kitchen—the morning their mother made him wake up early, for the express purpose of saying good-bye to his sister— Mary didn't tell him that she loved him.

She needed to say it. Those words needed to have come out of *her* mouth.

Because then he wouldn't have felt too embarrassed at having to say it first. He wouldn't have feared he was making too big a deal of things.

If she had said, "I love you, Danny," then he would have been able to answer her; he would have said it right back, without missing a beat, "I love you, too," before she disappeared from their house, and from his life, forever. And at least then she would have known, and *that* would have been something, maybe not much, but still something that she could have taken with her into the hospital and held in her heart as she waited to die. If only she had said it, and Danny had said it too; well, at least then she would have died knowing that her younger brother loved her, and more than that, that he idolized her and admired her and thought she was brave and funny and fearless and beautiful and just about the coolest older sister in the world; he loved that she protected him; he loved that she looked out for him and defended him against their parents, who never seemed satisfied with anything he did. He loved her so much, *so fucking much*. He was embarrassed to say how much he loved his older sister.

And how much he missed her.

Danny wept for fifteen minutes, maybe a half-hour—after awhile, he lost track of time. He sobbed and heaved, his entire body shaking, tears and mucous streaming down his face, until he felt as if there were no more fluids left inside of him. And then, finally, he started to calm down. He gathered up his things and made his way to the bus stop. He thought again about everything George Pulaski had told him, and he decided he would heed the Eastern European's advice. He was going to try to set things right again. The time had come for him to move on.

But salvation begins at home, and as Danny Reilly rode the S79 bus south on Hylan Boulevard toward his house in the Oakwood section of Staten Island, he realized he didn't want to go home. In fact, home was perhaps the last place on the planet he wanted to be. He couldn't bear the silence in that house any longer. With no one talking. With no one even occupying the same room for more than thirty seconds at a time, someone was always sheepishly scurrying out of someone else's way whenever two people unintentionally came in close contact. He couldn't bear the disdainful looks on his mother's face when she arrived home from work each night, haggard and pissed-off, as if each day was an elaborate con at her expense, a trick she kept falling for. He couldn't bear to look at his father, drinking Michelob after Michelob—he downed the long-neck, brown glass bottles as if they were iced tea, as many as eight of them in a night—getting quieter and more lethargic as the evening crawled along, until finally he fell asleep in the easy chair in his bedroom, three feet in front of the television. He couldn't bear to look at his younger brother, Ben, who alternately seemed very scared and very enraged, almost like a dog who has just been struck by a car.

Danny hated that house so much. He hated it with every fiber of his soul.

He stayed on the bus, past his stop, all the way south on Hylan Boulevard, and then all the way west on Richmond Avenue. When the bus stopped in front of the Staten Island Mall, and the majority of passengers departed, Danny decided to follow them. He had seven dollars in his wallet, which he knew wouldn't last him very long, but—he hoped—might be enough to last him through the night. For two hours, he pretended as if he were shopping. He went from store to store, patiently examining the products on the shelves or the clothes on the racks, making certain not to call too much attention to himself. With two of his dollars, Danny purchased a magazine devoted to computer and video games. With three of his dollars, he purchased two slices of pizza and a root beer. For the next couple of hours after that, he sat in a corner of the food court, reading his magazine, slowly chewing his food and sipping his soda. Then he resumed his browsing, for another hour or so, until it reached the point where he had wandered into and out of virtually every store in the mall. That's when it started to dawn on him that he shouldn't have gotten off the bus when he did. You can't run away to a place patrolled by security guards that closes every night at 9:30 P.M.—not if you don't want to get caught.

He decided he would have to give up for tonight.

But he also knew he would try this again.

It was after 10:00 P.M. when Danny finally walked through the door of his house. His mother was on the couch, dozing in front of the television. Her eyes briefly fluttered open as Danny passed through the living room, but then they closed just as quickly. His father was in his parents' bedroom, in the easy chair in front of the television, drinking a Michelob. His brother Ben was in the room they both shared (their parents had yet to agree to Ben's repeated requests that he be allowed to move into Mary's old room), also watching television. Danny didn't bother to brush his teeth or change into his pajamas. He just took off his shoes and his shirt and climbed into bed. He dreamed, all through that night, of George Pulaski—the conversation they shared being played out over and over again. He woke up the next morning exhausted and despairing. All he wanted to do was crawl underneath his bed and cry. But it was Thanksgiving. The family was expected to be in Brooklyn at his grandparents' house for dinner. He got caught up in the busy activity of the day—getting cleaned up and putting on nice clothes; eating his grandmother's food and then playing touch football with his cousins. It wasn't until much later, during the drive back home, that it finally occurred to him that no one had bothered to ask him where he had been the night before or why he had arrived home so late. They might not have even noticed that he had been gone.

He tried to pull it together. In the subsequent months, he really did. He started engaging with his old friends. He forced himself to sit at the lunch table he had abandoned months earlier. He stopped being such an aggressive brown-noser in class. He got through each day by taking one day at a time.

The trouble was this: His heart was no longer in it. None of it. He couldn't bring himself to care. He spent most of his days just staring off into space, wondering about Mary, wondering if some shred of her spirit might still exist somewhere, in the woods or in the sky or in the ocean or buried deep beneath the earth. He wondered if there was any way he could find it and get to it; if there was any way he might be able to take his place alongside her.

By the time Danny entered high school, in the fall of 1983, he was sullen and tired all of the time. His parents noticed this change, but they did not think much of it. They assumed it was just another phase Danny was passing through, and that eventually he would snap out of it. But Danny couldn't snap out of it. He couldn't stop feeling like there was a disease inside him, just as there had been a disease inside Mary—a disease in his blood that his heart pumped all through his veins. He came to believe that something inside of his family's house was feeding this disease, the way shade and a little water might feed ivy, allowing it to cling to his being and grow uncontrollably, until it grew so dense and so vast that it couldn't be eradicated. Until it strangled all the life out of him.

Stuck. Trapped. Nowhere to go. Nothing to do. Nothing on top of nothing. He felt like he wanted to crawl out of his own skin. He felt like his skin was keeping him trapped inside.

He couldn't think of anything else to do, other than to run away.

The second time Danny ran away, in November 1983, he made only a halfhearted attempt—it was more of an experiment than a runaway. He wanted to see how long it would take before his parents noticed he was gone. He found the phone number of Eddie Donovan, his joined-at-the-hip best friend through sixth grade, until Eddie transferred to Catholic school, and the two boys began seeing each other less frequently. Danny called Eddie and asked if he might be able to stay at Eddie's house for a few days. His parents, Danny told Eddie, were going on vacation, and they didn't want to leave him alone in the house. Eddie thought this an extremely odd request (he hadn't actually seen or spoken to Danny since Mary's funeral). Eddie's parents thought it even odder (why couldn't Danny's grandparents, who were both still alive and still living in the downstairs apartment of the Reilly house, keep an eye on him?). But the Donovans couldn't come up with a good reason to deny Danny. Mrs. Donovan, who brooded that Eddie hadn't made many new friends in his two years at Catholic school, was actually enticed by the idea. She thought that perhaps it might be good for these two lonely boys to reconnect. So, on the second Friday in November, Danny showed up at the Donovans' house after school with a weekend bag stuffed full of his clothes. He quickly fell into his old, easy ways with Eddie, playing board games and watching cartoons that neither of them wanted to admit they had outgrown. And he quickly felt at home among the Donovans. Mrs. Donovan kept the thermostat turned up a couple of degrees too high, making the house seem cozy and warming—a place you might retreat to in order to take a long and recuperative nap. She also made heaping platefuls of delicious and fancy-seeming food: blue cheese mashed potatoes; grilled salmon with dill sauce; chicken cordon bleu. Danny started to think that he wouldn't mind staying at their house much longer. He even began hoping that his parents might forget about him altogether. But they didn't. The call finally came, on Sunday morning, just as Eddie's mom was readying to shuttle them all off to church. Danny's father—having already called the police, the hospitals, the morgues, and a dozen of the teachers and administrators at Danny's school—decided to try the Donovans. Mrs. Donovan was horribly chagrined. She apologized profusely to Danny's father. She said that it had been very foolish of her not to have called Danny's parents to check the veracity of his claims about their going on vacation—it was just that she had never known Danny to make up so elaborate a lie. Mrs. Donovan drove him home immediately. As he stepped out of her car, Danny tried to thank her for her hospitality. He really had appreciated it, more than she could have realized. But Mrs. Donovan scowled at him and drove away, and Danny never saw or spoke to her or Eddie again.

The third time Danny ran away, in late June of 1984, he smoked marijuana for the very first time. Otherwise nothing especially remarkable happened. He spent three days and two nights wandering around South Beach and Midland Beach, shuttling back and forth between the two, which were located a few miles apart on the eastern shore of Staten Island. He made certain to avoid the police officers who patrolled the area and the hypodermic needles that littered the sand. He slept under the rotting and musty boardwalk at South Beach, remaining semiconscious all through the night, convinced that a homeless person was going to sneak up from behind him and poke him with a dirty needle. On his second night on the beach, he met a drug dealer named Spencer, a skinny guy in his early twenties, with a pimply face and stringy black heavy-metal-rocker hair, who claimed to have graduated a few years earlier from Danny's high school. He seemed to materialize out of thin air, asking Danny, "Hey, man, you want to party?" Danny shrugged his shoulders, which Spencer took as a yes, and the two of them shared a joint. Danny, who liked how placid and optimistic the marijuana made him feel, promised Spencer that he would buy more marijuana from him, as soon as he was able to save up enough money (a promise he kept, at least two or three times a month, for the next two years). But the day after he met Spencer—his third day on the beach, after his second sleepless night beneath the boardwalk—Danny decided he was too cold and hungry to stay away any longer. He returned home that evening. His parents shouted at him, separately and together, for two hours. Danny promised them that he wouldn't run away again.

The fourth and fifth times Danny ran away, in April 1985 and then August 1985, he ran away to the same place, farther away than he would have ever thought himself capable of running. He saved up money from his allowance, and he stole more money from his father's wallet and his mother's purse, and then he took a train from Penn Station in New York City to 30th Street Station in Philadelphia. Both times he wandered around the city during the day and slept in the parks at night. He decided he liked Philadelphia a great deal. He found it clean and manageable, but also bustling with people and movement—a place where one could get lost, but not necessarily swallowed up whole. But both times he returned home after three nights, because he was running out of money, and he didn't want to place himself in desperate straits. He didn't want to become one of those runaway kids you hear about, who trade blow jobs for cash, sucking off obese, hirsute men for twenty-dollar bills. Both times his parents greeted his return with fury and vituperation. They spent the weeks following the runaways monitoring his every move. But there was only so much they could do. Danny's mother couldn't afford to leave her job to stay at home with him. And, even if she could, there was no controlling him once he got to school—what was to stop him from leaving the building and running away once again? So they hoped against hope: that the studious and responsible Danny would come back to them; that things wouldn't end too badly.

The sixth time Danny ran away, in December 1985, he was only gone for a night. He took the bus to Wolfe's Pond Park, at the southern end of Hylan Boulevard, and he smoked pot until he passed out near the swing set on the small playground there. He returned home the next afternoon and told his parents that he thought that maybe he needed to see a psychiatrist.

"You need to stop running away is what you need to do," his father shouted at him, making like he was going to smack him across the face, until he caught himself and lowered his hand and galumphed out of the room.

"People in our family don't see psychiatrists," his mother said. Then she sat down on the living room couch and buried her head in her hands and started crying. Through her tears, she muttered to him, "Please stop this, Danny. Please. Your father and I can't take this."

Danny didn't know why he couldn't stop. He didn't even know what he was trying to prove, since he never ran away without the intention of also, at some point, returning home. Was he still grieving for his dead sister? He suspected that might have been part of it (though, to be perfectly honest, he didn't think very much about Mary anymore). Was he just another sulky adolescent acting out against his parents, the way all adolescents do, crying out for their attention? Maybe—though he thought that was too easy an explanation. He suspected the truth ran much deeper, to much more inexplicable places. He suspected he would never fully understand the truth, at least not in this lifetime.

Only the dead can comprehend these mysteries; only Mary could help me understand what's going on inside of me. But she's not telling. She'll never tell.

The seventh time Danny ran away, in April 1986, it wasn't much of a runaway at all. It was an aborted runaway; half a runaway; a coda to his six previous runaways. He boarded the Staten Island Ferry on a Sunday evening. He had the vague plan of heading into Manhattan and seeing how many days he could fend for himself there. But as he sat on the outdoor deck, the freezing cold, early spring wind rising off the water and tearing into his face and body, making him quiver and shake, he realized he didn't want to go to Manhattan. He didn't want to go home. He didn't want to stay on the boat. He didn't want to jump off it. He didn't want to sit still. He didn't want to stand. He didn't want to die. He didn't necessarily want to live. He just *didn't.* He felt a disappointment so piercing and concentrated he feared his heart would simply stop right there. He wondered if you could die from disappointment. There wasn't a single person in the world to whom he could have expressed his feelings. Worst of all was the fact that, even if there were such a person, he didn't think he could even begin to articulate these feelings. He couldn't explain them, other than to speculate that he felt the way ghosts must feel like, floating through haunted houses, trapped between the living world and the dead one, shackled by chains, unable to liberate themselves, doomed never to rest in peace. Doomed to an eternity of anxiety and rootlessness and moans of agony that the living will pretend they do not hear.

Danny rode the ferry to Manhattan, and then he stayed aboard the ferry and rode it back to Staten Island. He made the round-trip a half-dozen times, before departing on the Staten Island side, and waiting for the bus, and then slowly making his way back to his house. Early the next morning, just before sunrise, after a tortured, sleepless three hours spent twisting and turning in his bed, during which he played out in his brain every possible scenario for the next few years of his life and determined that all of them were unbearable, Danny swallowed six Valium, eight pills for high blood pressure, and a half-dozen Bufferin—everything he could find in the bathroom medicine cabinet. His parents discovered him, unconscious in his own sick, two and a half hours later.

"You ran away seven times?" I asked Danny, a little incredulous, not entirely believing him, assuming some of it had to have been made up for effect.

We were sitting, again, in the Golden Dove diner. It was the night before I was scheduled to fly to Denver to meet Terrence. Our waitress was eyeing us irritably from the salad station. We hadn't ordered very much food, and we had taken up her table for much too long—going on two hours now.

"Six and half times," Danny said. "Seven. Depending on how you call that last one."

"How come I don't remember any of this?"

Danny looked out the window and shrugged. "I don't know, Ben. We were all living on different planets then. The four of us. Dad could have gone and shot up a post office and you might not have noticed."

I still wasn't buying this. Something about Danny's story was not quite right. "So they just let you keep running away?"

"They didn't know how to make it stop. There was nothing they could do."

"It sounds like they didn't even try."

"*You* didn't try," he said, not attacking me, only playing the devil's advocate. "You didn't do anything to stop me."

"I didn't know you were running away every three months."

"Yes, you did," Danny came back sharply. "You did, Ben. Maybe you forgot. Maybe you ignored it. Maybe you just weren't paying attention. But you knew. And you didn't do anything, either. Maybe the point is that no one was capable of doing anything. They were so unhappy, Ben. We all were. You can't make other people happy unless you make yourself happy. Isn't that what therapists always say? No one had the wherewithal to make it stop."

I sat there for a minute or two, looking away from him. I didn't know what he wanted from me. I wasn't about to ask.

"Let it go," he said to me finally. "She died. Their daughter died when she was eighteen. You have to cut them at least that much slack."

"I never even understood what happened to her after she left for the hospital."

"She had some kind of tumor in her brain," he said. "There were complications following the surgery. It looked like she was going to be fine and then the next thing they knew she was dying. I don't know. They never really explained it to me, either."

"What happened when you got out of the house?" I asked him. "What happened to you in Stony Brook?"

"Nothing happened."

"Why did you come back so different?"

"Nothing happened, Ben. I grew up. I got older."

"You came back a different person. Something must have happened there."

He shook his head, and then he smiled the saddest smile I have ever seen anyone smile. "Nothing happened," he said. "Nothing changed. Don't you get it, Ben? I hate them. I still hate them. I will hate them until the day they are dead and buried. But it's not their fault. I can't really blame them. They didn't know any better. Mary died, and they were crushed, and we were the collateral damage. That's just the way it worked out."

chapter eleven

To Bully
(2000)

The young man in the airplane seat next to me wore a char-coal-colored business suit, a little tight through the shoulders, but otherwise handsome and expensive looking. He wore black wire-rimmed glasses with thin, round lenses. He had blonde hair, buzzed close to his head around the sides, left just a little bit longer on the top. He was of average height, probably 5 feet 9 inches. He was very thin, but he looked agile, not frail—he looked like someone who might have played tennis in college. He held a bulky black cell phone close to his ear, and he yammered on about "spreadsheets" and "data sets" and "trying to get the numbers to work out," in an engaged but humorless tone of voice. He talked his way through two requests on the public address system asking that all portable electronic devices be turned off and stowed away. A flight attendant finally appeared in our row and told him he had to hang up the phone immediately, he was single-handedly delaying our take-off. He smiled and apologized profusely to her—he said that he hadn't heard the warnings. He turned the cell phone off and leaned back in his seat and closed his eyes. But then, just a few minutes after take-off, before the announcement giving everyone permission was even made, he pulled out a laptop from a briefcase beneath the seat in front of him, powered it up, and started typing away.

For the first ninety minutes of the flight to Denver, I sat quietly in my seat, flipping through a copy of *Time* magazine (I never did get around to buying a book that night I ran into Jamie in the mall), sneaking glances in this man's direction, wondering how people picked up complete strangers on airplanes. It happened all the time, in movies, on television shows, in the pages of *Penthouse Letters*—surely if it happened so often in people's imaginations, I reasoned, then it had to happen at least occasionally in real life. I sat there fantasizing about the two of us striking up a conversation: lively; intellectual; a little flirty. He would like me. I would like him. We'd instantly *click*. And then, early in the third hour of the flight, when everyone else would be napping, before the flight attendants would have made another run down the aisle with the drinks cart, the two of us could sneak off to the lavatory in the back of the plane. . . .

All we would need is a few minutes, ten at the most. Surely it can't be that *difficult to pull off?*

"Can I flip through your magazine, if you're finished with it?" he asked, after suddenly and noisily closing his laptop.

"All yours," I said, handing it over, even though I wasn't even halfway through it.

"I never buy magazines, because I tell myself I'm not going to distract myself from my work," he said. "But then I get bored with my work and I have to go begging for magazines." He grinned at me. I saw that there was a tiny chip at the bottom of his right front tooth. It made him look mischievous, a bit of a rebel—the kind of guy who holds up his middle finger behind his back while his boss is giving a motivational speech at the staff meeting.

"Well, at least you save money that way," I said.

He nodded, but his smiled quickly disappeared. Suddenly he was almost frowning. "I guess so," he mumbled. He turned away from me and began scanning the magazine's table of contents.

What just happened? Did he think I was accusing him of being cheap?

"What kind of work do you do that makes you get bored so quickly?" I asked, trying not to let this window of opportunity close so immediately after it had opened.

This question didn't insult him. This one he seemed to like. "Consulting," he said, the lilt returning to his voice. "I was just working on a PowerPoint presentation for a meeting tomorrow with our clients. They've been paying our fees for six months, and they're getting antsy for some results. The problem is we don't really have any results to give them." He chuckled and shrugged his shoulders, an adorable little gesture that seemed to suggest he didn't take himself very seriously; that, despite the suit and tie, he was still a little boy at heart.

"Some of my friends from college are consultants," I told him.

"All of my friends from college are consultants. Or investment bankers. I think I need to start running with a different crowd." He stopped and laughed again.

This is good. The conversation is starting to flow. He's smart, funny. He's got a sarcastic sense of humor. He's a little short for me— but so what? I could see myself falling for a guy like this. I'd be happy to be his boyfriend.

"Where did you go to school?" I asked.

"Yale," he told me. "I graduated in '99. I've been consulting for a year now, but I'm not really sure I'm cut out for the business world. Sometimes the work just seems a little pointless."

"It's hard to find the right job just out of college," I answered helpfully.

I waited for him to ask me what I did for a living. Or, at the very least, to ask for my advice. Surely he would recognize me as a kindred spirit—smart, East Coast–educated, twentysomething—only a little bit older and wiser. He would want a few suggestions on how he should go about living the rest of his life. But he didn't. He turned away and started flipping through the magazine. He was shutting down the possibility of something blossoming between us.

"My best friend went to Yale," I said, trying to keep this alive.

"What year?" he said, without looking up from the magazine.

"He would have graduated before your time. He was class of 1995."

"It's a great place," he mumbled, and that was all.

Oh well. So much for that. Not going to happen. No fucking in the bathroom on this trip. The flight attendants can rest easy.

I gave up on the handsome young consultant and decided, instead, that I would try to take a nap. For the past eight days, sleep had been increasingly difficult to come by. I would close my eyes and think only of having contracted HIV. My mind would begin racing, contemplating all the tests and doctors visits and mounting bills that would soon be in store for me. I was able to keep the panic down during the day, by keeping busy with newspapers or television shows or just by thinking about Terrence. But at night, in the dark and alone in my bed, the terror welled up, and there was no avoiding it. For many more months and years, probably all the way into the foreseeable future, until AIDS finally killed me, sleep was going to be hard to come by.

Except today I had a bit more luck than usual. The white noise of the engines soothed me. Perhaps the sleeplessness of the last few nights had finally caught up with me. I closed my eyes and, this time, I didn't see images of decay and emaciation, of gay men covered in bleeding and crusty brown sores. This time I drifted off within minutes. I didn't dream of anything.

I don't know how long I slept. But when I opened my eyes, I sensed that the consultant was looking at me. I turned to face him. He quickly turned his head away.

Had he been checking me out? Was it possible that, for as long as I had been napping, he had been sitting there taking me in? Was he the one who had been fantasizing about *me*?

I tried to think of something to say, to suss out the situation.

But, just then, the flight attendant appeared in our row, instructing me to return my chair to the upright position and fasten my seat belt. A minute or two after that, the plane was landing. The moment we hit the ground, the consultant turned his cell phone back on and started another conversation. I realized I had never even gotten his name.

Oh well. No such luck. Not this time. Just another dreamy, handsome, Yale-educated boy who looks at me, and then through me.

I was walking out of the bathroom inside the airport terminal, trying to figure out where I was supposed to meet Terrence, when I felt the tap on my shoulder. I turned around. The consultant was standing in front of me. He was holding out to me a small, folded piece of paper.

"This is for you," he said.

I hesitated to take it. My first thought was that it was some scrap of paper that he thought I had dropped—maybe he was one of those annoying do-gooder types who is always trailing behind people and picking up their litter, not understanding that the littering is intentional. My second thought was that he was some kind of religious nut—that he was passing along information designed to save my soul, directions to a Bible study group or a pithy aphorism about Jesus. I stood there for a few seconds, not knowing how to react. Suddenly I felt him grabbing my hand and pressing the piece of paper inside of it.

"OK" was all I could get out, before he disappeared into the mass of bodies moving toward the baggage claim and out of my life forever.

I waited another minute before opening up the note. I wanted to make sure he was gone; that he wasn't hanging back to see my reaction. For some reason, I was terrified of what it might say. What if the note had somehow been designed to humiliate me? What if it said that he knew I had AIDS, and he was going to tell everyone about me?

Finally I took a deep breath and opened it. The words were neatly printed in black ink on six evenly spaced rows.

I've never done anything like this before, but I just wanted
to tell you that I think you are a very handsome man. I will
be in Denver for the next week. If you are interested in
meeting for a drink, please give me a call. If you are not
"that way" please forgive me and accept this note as the
highest compliment. Kevin. 917-524-0595.

I read the note again and then again. I stood there in the
middle of the airport terminal as dozens of harried travelers
streamed past me. It took me a minute before the full weight of
it sunk in. I had just been handed a note that might have come
straight out of junior high school (but, at least for me, during
my own junior high school years, never did). I had just been hit
on by a complete stranger, probably for the first time in my life.

Surely this was a sign; a harbinger of many more good things
to come. I had just been hit on by a handsome, attractive,
smart, successful young businessman. Someone I would have
slept with in a heartbeat. Someone I would have been de-
lighted to have as my boyfriend. I couldn't remember the last
time I felt so excited and flattered and enlivened all at once.

Most certainly this is a sign.

This is a message sent directly from God.

*This is God letting me know that this weekend with Terrence is des-
tined to go my way.*

"Dude, this is incredible. What a freakin' stud you are."

We were in Terrence's rental car, a silver Jeep Grand Chero-
kee, driving north on the highway past downtown Denver. I
had just handed Terrence the note, telling him he was never
going to believe what had happened to me in the airport. He
held the note out in front of him over the steering wheel and
slowly read it aloud.

He laughed very loudly and then read the note again. "What
kind of gaydar were you sending out to this guy?"

"I barely paid him any attention," I said.

"How did he even know?" he asked me. "Don't take this the wrong way, but you don't exactly come off as the biggest flamer on the planet."

"My good looks and charm must have bowled him over," I said, grinning widely, basking in this small triumph. "I bowl everyone over."

He started to laugh and then stopped. He was silent for the next minute, just long enough so that I started to wonder: *Is he mad that he didn't think of this strategy himself? Is he furious that someone has stolen me away from him before he had the chance to make a move of his own?*

"Well, I gotta say, I'm a little jealous," he finally spoke up. "Stuff like that definitely does not happen to me."

"It doesn't happen to me, either," I said. I had to tread carefully here. I wanted him to be jealous, but not *too* jealous—not so jealous that he would think he couldn't have me for himself. "Maybe I'm just looking especially hot today," I added.

He turned his head and quickly eyed me up and down. "Well, I don't know if you're *especially* hot today," he answered, "but you definitely look good."

"It's the new haircut," I said, even though I hadn't gotten my hair cut in two weeks.

"Are you going to call him? I think you should."

"No, that's crazy."

"Why not? He can't be working all weekend. I'm sure he'd be willing to come up to Vail to meet with you. Or you could take the car and drive down to Denver."

"Well, it's a New York number," I said. "If anything, I'll call him when I get back." *Jealous but not too jealous.*

Fifteen or twenty minutes passed. Terrence put in a CD of old Fleetwood Mac songs, and he relaxed into the driver's seat as we cruised past the farthest suburbs of Denver.

"You can take a nap if you like," he said, after another twenty minutes or so had passed. "I'm not someone who gets mad if the passenger isn't engaging fully with the driver. I went up to

Maine with Lisa last year, and I slept for about an hour of the drive. She pouted the first two days we were there. She thought it was rude of me to take a nap. But that's just the privilege of being the passenger, isn't it? You get to take the nap."

"I slept on the plane," I told him. "Tell me about your research. Tell me how your visit to Columbine went."

He sighed heavily and shook his head. "Not so good," he started. "I couldn't find anyone who would be willing to cooperate with me. I spoke to a few of the kids who were there that day; and the principal agreed to meet with me, after I called him about a dozen times. But they all said the same thing. They don't want to keep dwelling on what happened. They want to put it behind them. That's the phrase they all used. *It's time to put the tragedy behind us.* They all sound like they've been brainwashed."

"I can see where they're coming from," I said. "If I lived there, I'd probably want to put it behind me too."

He sighed again, a loud and grumpy sigh that reminded me of the fact that Terrence O'Connell had never been especially willing to admit defeat.

"It's frustrating, Ben," he said. "Honestly, I just don't get the logic. When something bad happens in my life, I try to step back and learn from it. But these people aren't interested in that. They just want to get things back to normal. They all kept saying, 'If we change the way we live, then we'll be giving the killers exactly what they wanted.' But what kind of backwards logic is that? Human history is all about lives being altered in response to tragedy. Can you imagine people saying, after Jesus' crucifixion, *We have to get things back to normal again?* I don't get it. Maybe it's just the culture. Maybe it's America. I know Oprah Winfrey is really popular, but deep down I think we're a pretty therapy-averse people. We don't want to have to think about the things we might be doing horribly wrong."

He chuckled softly at this observation and then started up again. "I'm not saying that God used those Columbine killers as some kind of dark angels, to send a wake-up call to these people. But don't you think that, if you were one of these parents, or if you went to school there, that that thought would have at least crossed your mind?"

"I think you're being a little unfair," I answered. "They're still grieving."

Terrence ignored this and kept on talking. He had clearly been rehearsing this speech for the last few days, waiting for someone to deliver it to. "The thing is, they still have a ticking time bomb on their hands. Nothing's changed. It's just a matter of time before something like this happens again. It's like a disease, it's like herpes or something—just because you can't see any outward signs or symptoms doesn't mean the virus isn't there, getting itself ready for another outbreak. But you can't just sit there and let it fester. You have to figure out a way to destroy it."

"There's no cure for herpes," I said. "You have to just suffer through the outbreaks."

"You get my point."

"You don't know what it's like to lose a child," I told him. "Or a brother or sister. You don't know what that feels like. How it can just paralyze someone."

"Not to be glib, Ben, but I don't think you can compare the loss of your sister to this situation." This was the Terrence of yore: high on confidence; not about to let anyone stand in the way of his being the beacon of authority. He already had to give up writing his magazine article about Columbine. He wasn't about to give up his righteousness on top of that.

"I don't want to play the game of 'my tragedy is bigger than your tragedy,'" I said. "That's a bad game to play. Someone always has a trump card."

"Ben, no offense, but I just don't see the comparison," he answered, now sounding very glib indeed. "Your sister's death wasn't the result of a systemic social problem."

I made a face and didn't answer right away. I considered what he had just said. He was right, of course. Her body betrayed her. Disease struck her down. She had some kind of tumor in her brain. There had been complications following the surgery.

It was as simple and as pathetic as all that.

But could the same standards apply? What if Mary's death *had* been a part of something larger? What if the tumor that destroyed her had been the metastasization of all the damaged cells in our family? What if her death hadn't been the cause of all the sadness that followed, so much as it was a prelude to that sadness—the overture to our family's twenty-year-long tormented symphony? What if it had been a wake-up call that the rest of us had failed to heed—and now, following Terrence's logic, what if twenty years hence we were sitting on another ticking time bomb? (In that case, which one of us would die next?)

What if?

"I'm just saying that you're being a little mean," I said finally. "You can't understand what these people have been through."

"I don't mean to judge," he said. "It's just frustrating. I'd like to think I could write something that might help. Something illuminating. But they have to be willing to let an outsider in. They have to want to be helped."

I didn't say anything. I was thinking about Mary, standing in our cramped kitchen, trying to soothe my father's nerves in the minutes before he and my mother would take her to the hospital. Did she know, that final morning at home, that she was headed to her death? Did she understand her own destruction as inevitable? And, if she did, what were her final conscious thoughts? Did she lie on a hospital bed, hooked up to machines that couldn't keep her alive, thinking to herself: *Why do I have to be the unlucky one? I didn't cause this systemic problem.*

So why must I be the one who is sacrificed to it?

Terrence must have interpreted my silence as anger. "I'm sorry, Ben," he said, his voice very soft and sincere. "I didn't mean to talk about your sister like that. You're right, I don't know what it's like to lose someone you're close to."

I was about to tell him that it was OK; that maybe I was just being overly sensitive. I was about to let him off the hook once again.

But then I thought better of it.

Why not let Terrence O'Connell twist in the wind? Why not let him stew in his own guilt?

Aren't I owed at least that much in revenge?

And who knows? It might even help my cause. Maybe I can make Terrence O'Connell feel so guilty that he would feel as if he owed it to me to sleep with me.

I closed my eyes and pretended to fall asleep.

We pulled into town a little before seven, just as the sun was beginning to set. I stepped out of the car, and I was surprised by the chill in the air—the temperature was at least twenty degrees lower than it had been in Denver. The house was a modest cottage tucked up on a small hill, about a mile northwest of the town center. At first glance, it looked shabby and unkempt, bordering on derelict. The brown wooden shingles had faded from exposure to the sun and were now colored a hepatic shade of yellow. The overgrown hedges and shrubbery that were planted across the front yard looked as if they hadn't been trimmed in a couple of years. The windows—opaque with dust and dried dirt—looked as if they hadn't been washed in even longer.

"It belongs to my friend James' family," Terrence explained, as he lifted our bags out of the back of the car. "He was my roommate at Yale. We used to come here a lot during college, during spring breaks and over the summer. His father just died, and his family is eager to sell it."

We walked up three wooden plank steps that creaked loudly beneath our feet. Terrence inserted a small copper key into the lock and turned it, but the door wouldn't give. He locked and unlocked it and tried again. Only on his third try, pushing with the full force of his shoulder, did he finally get the door to open.

"That can't be a good sign," he said, walking into the foyer. "The lesson here, Ben, is never make the mistake of telling someone you might be in the market for a vacation property."

A vacation property? This was a new one.

"Are you?" I asked.

"I might be. Finding an apartment in New York is my main priority. But my accountant says I should consider buying a vacation place, too. Otherwise I'm going to be paying through the nose on my taxes over the next couple of years. I mentioned that to James a few months ago, and I swear I literally saw dollar signs flash in his eyes. Ever since then, he's been begging me to come out for a weekend and try it on for size."

I trailed a few paces behind Terrence as he led us inside the house and started wandering around. The decor suggested a sort of disco-era ski lodge: leopard print and bear skin throw rugs; a tweed-upholstered couch; a dining room chandelier composed of a hundred or so small crystals that connected to form a perfectly round globe.

"I don't remember it looking so beat up," Terrence said, leading me onto the large outdoor deck just off the kitchen, which had a built-in hot tub that looked out onto acres of freshly blooming trees. "It used to have more of a love shack quality. A little old school, but still mack daddy, you know?"

"No," I said. "I have no idea what any of those words mean."

He laughed and said, "I don't either. But I remember thinking it would be cool to live here. James' dad was this old Hugh Hefner type. He always had four different girlfriends hanging out in the hot tub with him."

"How much are they asking for it?"

"Eight hundred thousand," he said. "According to James, that's actually the bargain-basement price, because he and his sister just want it off their hands. An $800,000 bargain sounds like a contradiction of terms to me, but what do I know?"

I didn't answer. I was fixated on that number. *Eight hundred thousand dollars.* He was considering purchasing an $800,000 house in Vail *and* an apartment in Manhattan, for who knew how many hundreds of thousands (or millions) more. Would this madness never cease? Was Terrence O'Connell's well of cash bottomless?

"I'm going to jump in the shower," he said. "Do you want to go to dinner around eight?"

I still didn't answer. I was too busy thinking about this $800,000 house, Terrence's potential asset. I was too busy imagining what it would be like if half of it were all mine; if half of everything Terrence owned were all mine.

If half of Terrence's very being could be mine.

The streets and walkways of the town center were almost totally deserted. The stores all had "Who's Still in Vail? Sale" signs in the windows. The cashmere shop advertised 75 percent off the entire stock, and I joked to Terrence that, even with the discount, I still wouldn't be able to afford anything in there. Terrence explained that he preferred coming to Vail in the off-season—when the town felt less like a high school lunchroom where you are constantly being judged, and more like a low-key private club that you could escape to. He said that, if he bought the house, he would probably only use it in the off-season and then rent it to skiers in the winter. He showed me around the town for twenty minutes, before we wound our way to a restaurant called Sweet Basil. Only three of the other tables were occupied. We ordered our food, scallops and beef tenderloin for Terrence, tuna tartare and mushroom risotto for me. Terrence picked the cheapest wine on the menu. When the waiter walked away, he explained to me that he didn't like to drink good wine while he was still adjusting to a higher altitude.

"You have to be up here for two days," he said, "before you can order a decent bottle."

I nodded and marveled: How rarefied an opinion! How precious! Opinions as such do not come cheap. Opinions like those could only be cultivated through years and years of high-priced experience. I thought to myself: *Soon, maybe sooner than either of us realizes, I will be able to talk like that also. Terrence will teach me. I will be a fast study.*

The waiter returned and poured the wine. But before I could even take my first sip, Terrence looked across the table at me and said: "I broke up with Lisa on Monday morning."

I absorbed the information silently, doing my best to maintain a poker face. I had assumed a breakup with Lisa was imminent, but I never expected it to happen so soon. I figured things would drag out for at least a few weeks longer.

I immediately put my wineglass down without drinking from it. There would be no more drinking for me tonight. I couldn't risk dulling my senses. I needed to be careful about the tone I used with him; about every word that came out of my mouth. First and foremost, I couldn't let him know that this was the most encouraging news I had heard in a very long time.

"What happened?" I asked.

"The other night we were talking on the phone, and she pointed out that we hadn't had sex in a month. She wasn't angry or anything. I think she just kind of meant, *Hey, it's been too long; we need to have some sex soon.* But I thought to myself, *Well, that sort of says it all, doesn't it?* I mean, it's not *that* complicated. If you haven't had sex with someone for a month, it usually means you don't want to be with that person. So I slept on it, and then I called her right before I left for the airport, and I told her that I thought we should break up. She didn't put up much resistance. She sounded a little sad, but basically I think she agreed with me. I think we both realized it was time to move on."

"Are you relieved?" I knew, as the words were coming out of my mouth, that I sounded too eager. I knew that these were entirely the wrong words.

"Relieved?"

"Just that she's not hanging over your head anymore." Strike two. It came out sounding all wrong.

"She was never hanging over my head," he said, his irritation increasing with every word. "That makes it sound like she was some kind of albatross."

"I didn't mean it that way, only that—" But I didn't know how I meant it. All I knew was that I felt so happy and relieved. Suddenly, there was one less obstacle in my path.

"She wasn't an albatross," he repeated.

"Well, I'm sorry to hear you broke up." *No, I'm not. Not in the least.* "I hope you're not feeling too miserable about it." *Not so miserable than you won't let me make love to you later tonight in the hot tub.*

"I'm glad I flew out here," he said. "The Columbine business was a good distraction for me, even if it didn't turn out so well."

"I hope I wasn't the cause of any of it."

Once again it was the wrong thing to say—tonight was my night for saying all the wrong things. He wasn't ready for the possibility of the two of us being a couple. Not yet. The wounds of the breakup with Lisa still hadn't scabbed over.

"What does *that* mean?" he asked, scowling at me.

"Nothing."

"Nothing." He parroted it back, mimicking me. And all at once, we were back in seventh grade. He was taunting me for refusing to fight with him.

I couldn't let it stand. No more. If these last few weeks had taught me anything, it was that I could no longer back down from a fight with him. Certainly not if I had any hope of the two of us ever being together.

Because this is what Terrence O'Connell has been missing from his life; this is what he's long been seeking out. He needs a person in his life who isn't afraid to bully him back.

"It means what it means," I told him. "You know what I'm talking about. Don't act like you don't. It doesn't take much to see what's been going on here."

"Did you talk to her? Were you trying to get her to break up with me?"

I laughed at him.

This is what Terrence O'Connell is missing in his life: an antagonist brave enough to laugh in his face.

"Spare me the paranoia, man," I said. "*You* broke up with her, not me."

He sneered at me. "What's your agenda, Ben?"

I smirked back at him. "Same as it ever was, Terrence. Nothing's changed on my end."

He didn't react. He kept staring at me. For a moment, I thought he might get very angry and begin shouting at me. But then, in an instant, his expression softened. "This is stupid, Ben," he said. "I don't want to get into a fight with you. I think I'm just a little raw about the whole subject right now. Why don't we try to talk about something else?"

He wanted to let it rest. But what kind of bully would that make me? A bully can never let it rest. A bully can never back down from the promise of a rumble.

A bully must seize upon his opponent's primary weakness and attack mercilessly, until nothing of his opponent remains.

"I'm not trying to pick a fight," I said, trying to sound conciliatory and predatory all at once. "I'm just saying it's something you might want to think about."

His eyes widened. He twisted his face in dismay. "You want me to think about the possibility that I broke up with her because of *you?* Because, what, I'm in love with you?" Then, when I didn't answer right away, he added: "Ben, my friend, don't flatter yourself."

"The evidence is compelling, admit that much at least," I shot back. "You stopped sleeping with her, what, a few days after we started hanging out? A few hours? Have you slept with her even once since we started hanging out?"

"One thing has nothing to do with—"

I cut him off. I wasn't going to let this drop. Not a chance. *No fucking way.* I was owed at least this much in revenge.

"And instead of going out with her on a Saturday night, you sit home and wait for me to call you. You buy me nice meals.

You take me shopping. You fly me out here to spend the weekend with you. And when her name comes up in conversation, you say, *Oh, please, let's not talk about her; I can't bear to think about my* girl*friend*. Like she's your dirty secret. Or the old ball and chain that you're out cheating on. You don't think any of that might mean something?"

"Why are you baiting me like this?" he asked.

"What are you so afraid of?" I asked, taunting him, refusing to relent.

This is what it must have been like for him, all those years, spewing bile and slander, calling me gaywad, day after day. This is what it means to be a bully: You keep prodding and poking, just because you feel like it; you attack a defenseless victim just because you can.

How petty and how puny.

And how intoxicating! How could I possibly stop now?

"We've had some pretty weird conversations over the last few weeks," I said. "Can you acknowledge that much? Or are you in total denial?"

"Every conversation we've ever had has been weird. Since the day we met."

"You're still the same, Terrence," I said. "Ten years pass, and it's still the same routine. You expect everyone to worship you. But if someone asks you to meet them halfway—if someone expects some kind of reciprocation—you retreat. You're a narcissist. Do you realize that? Everything you do, you do it in order to make people love you. But the notion of giving something back in return is alien to you. Because narcissists are never able to love someone back. They can't stop loving themselves long enough."

"Is that how you view me?" He looked cast adrift, helpless; I had violated him at his core. All of his years of hard work and reformation, all of his time spent trying to become Terrence the Kind—and yet he hadn't once considered this angle. He had never considered the fact that to be a champion bully you must first be a world-class narcissist.

"Yes, that is how I think of you," I said. And then, worried that

I might be carrying all of this a few paces too far, fearful that I might push him away from me for good, I backed off. Ever so slightly, but just enough to put him at ease, just a little bit . . .

This is the fine art of bullying: knowing when to go in for the be-heading, and knowing when to just keep feeding and fattening your turkey.

I said, "I'm not saying that you're a bad person, or that I don't respect the person that you've become since high school. It's just that I don't think you're being totally honest with your-self. Or with the people around you."

He took more than a minute to answer. The waiter brought our food and asked us if we needed anything else. We smiled and pretended we were having a wonderful time.

When he spoke again, the words came out haltingly: "Just because I'm not sure if I want to sleep with you doesn't mean that I'm a narcissist. I'm not meeting you halfway because I'm not sure that I can."

I immediately looked away. I couldn't hold his gaze. His two sentences took away all of my momentum.

Just because I'm not sure if I want to sleep with you . . . which meant . . . which meant . . . he had thought about it . . . the possibility has crossed his mind . . . he had turned the idea over in his head . . .

And knowing this was almost too much for me to bear.

This is the surest means of defusing a bully's power: by nullifying his righteousness; by getting him where he lives. By saying to him: "Yes, you are right, my bully, I may secretly be in love with you, maybe I even broke up with my girlfriend because of you. But what of it? Now what else do you have in your arsenal? Now that I have admitted my pri-mary weakness, what else do you have left to exploit?"

With one simple confession, Terrence had trumped me. He had turned the tables entirely.

How foolish of me to think that I could out-bully the greatest bully of them all?

"I didn't mean to suggest that you dumped her for me," I mumbled.

"Ben, you had things figured out when you were very young," he said. "You realized you were gay when you were, what, ten or eleven? But it doesn't work like that for everyone. You shouldn't judge people who have taken a different route in figuring things out."

I was shifting awkwardly in my seat, looking toward every corner of the restaurant. I inadvertently caught our waiter's eye, and he scurried over to make sure that nothing was wrong with the appetizers, which were resting before us untouched. Terrence assured him that they were fine—it was just that we had gotten so caught up in our conversation we hadn't been able to pause to eat. "We're old friends," he said. "We haven't seen each other in a while."

"We're not old friends, Terrence," I said, after the waiter drifted away. "We're new friends. Or maybe just old enemies."

"It was just something to say to get rid of him."

I was regaining my spirit, rising up again for this fight. I couldn't let his one admission waylay me—even if it was the admission I had been waiting fifteen years to hear. It didn't mean anything. Not until he put his words into actions. Not until push came to shove.

"Perhaps it's wishful thinking on your part," I told him. "That way you never have to reckon with the fact that we *were* enemies and that you treated me horribly. You can pretend it never happened."

"We should eat. It's starting to look weird."

"I'm sorry it didn't work out between you and Lisa," I said. "I'm sorry you two broke up. But it wasn't my fault." I paused for a few beats and then added: "And all I'm saying is that I think you owe everybody a little bit of soul searching. Least of all yourself."

He sighed heavily and angrily, like a put-upon father rapidly losing patience with his tantrum-throwing child. Was this it? Was he about to finally lose his temper and tear into me? Were we finally going to *fight*?

But no. Instead, he capitulated to me entirely. "You're right,

Ben," he said. "I know you're right. Maybe that's why I'm putting up such resistance, because I know how right you are. One of the reasons I think I've had so much professional success is because it's so easy for me to throw myself into my work. It gets my mind away from having to think about personal relationships. You can get a lot done when you're avoiding a sex life. You've probably realized this by now, but I don't have many close friends. And I think that's because, at some point, everyone realizes I'm in a state of arrested development. I think they just kind of give up on me."

He wanted me to put him at ease; to give him a little pep talk and tell him: *I'm not going to give up on you, Terrence, I'll stand behind you until the end.*

But no way. Not a chance. Not now.

Now it was time to go in for the kill.

"Terrence, listen, you're allowed to go at your own pace," I told him. "But your actions do affect the rest of us. You need to keep that in mind."

"I'm sorry if it seems like I'm not being upfront with you," he answered. "I'm just . . . It's just that I'm trying to figure things out. It's not easy for me."

As brusquely and coolly as I could, I said to him: "That's good for you, Terrence. But at some point, my *new* friend, you're going to have to put up or shut up."

> bully (bŏŏl-ē)—n. 1. a blustering, quarrelsome,
> overbearing person who habitually badgers and
> intimidates smaller or weaker people. 2. Archaic. a man
> hired to do violence.—v.t. 3. to intimidate; domineer.—
> v.i. 4. to be loudly arrogant and overbearing.

To bully is to loom so large in another's life that he can no longer see the world around you, or beyond you, or without you.

To bully is to be the first thing your bullied victim thinks about when he wakes up in the morning, the last thing he thinks about when he goes to sleep each night, the only thing he dreams about in between.

And the ultimate mark of the bully, the sign of a bully *par excellence:* to make it so that the bullied person believes you to be justified in sending down so many tortures; to make it so that your bullied can no longer function *unless* he is being bullied.

How simple. After fifteen years, I finally understood.

And how intoxicating! Oh, how intoxicating it is to be a bully!

chapter twelve

Push
(1990)

Bribes. For as long as he could remember, Terrence O'Connell had been on the receiving end of his mother's bribes. Bribes large and (mostly) bribes small. Bribes intended to make the household run a bit more smoothly. Bribes offered up in hopes of compelling Terrence to do exactly what Marta wanted him to do. Bribes like these: *Clean your room and we will go to McDonald's; do not pester your father after he returns home from work and, come the weekend, I will take you to the toy store and you can pick out any toy you like; rank in the top ten of your class each quarter and I will give you a bonus in your allowance; score over 1400 on your SATs and I will write you a check—a dollar amount commensurate with your score.*

And just this morning yet another bribe. A bribe mentioned almost in passing over the breakfast table—as if Marta had *not* spent the last two weeks fine-tuning the details of this particular offer. A bribe, like all of the bribes before it, entirely unsolicited on Terrence's part.

The bribe was this: Do not complain or put up a fuss because we are upending you from your high school just prior to senior year and in exchange we will send you to Europe upon graduation, as many countries as you would like to visit, for as long you want to stay, no dingy student hostels; you can stay at good hotels, and eat at the nice restaurants, especially the ones in France, all expenses paid by your father.

What do you think, Terrence? Do you think that might be something you would enjoy?

He had found out that they were moving only the night before. His father had returned home from a business trip, and the three of them—Jay was away at college now, in his senior year at Yale—went out to an expensive steak house for dinner. Terrence thought it was strange that they would be eating somewhere so fancy on a Monday night, until he realized— midway through the main course—that they were celebrating. Marta explained to Terrence that his father had just been made an extraordinary offer by a company in Indianapolis, earning nearly twice his previous salary. A house-hunting trip was scheduled for Memorial Day weekend. A moving crew would come to their house in Staten Island on the first of July to pack up all of their belongings. They would fly to Indiana that night and stay in a hotel until the movers caught up with them. Terrence's father would start his new job the following Monday, and then Terrence would begin his final year of high school the third week of August, at an excellent public school called Arlington. His parents assured him that the move would not impact his college applications; that in fact the move might actually benefit him. "It's much easier to get into an Ivy apply- ing from a Midwestern state," his father had told him, "than it is applying from New York."

Terrence listened to all of this carefully, but dispassionately. He spent most of the dinner thinking about the bribe that he knew would be forthcoming—the little something his mother would offer to make him acquiesce to this plan. When his fa- ther asked him, "Do you have any questions?" he didn't re- spond. Terrence wasn't stupid. He knew that, the more bothered he seemed about all of this, the more lucrative his mother's eventual offer would be.

And now here it was, right on schedule. And, truth be told, it was better than he had been expecting. He could spend a month in Europe, or six weeks, or even longer. He could visit Paris or Munich or Rome or Barcelona—whatever cities he pleased, really. He didn't have to worry about the cost. His father would soon be earning a small fortune.

"We think it would be a wonderful adventure," Marta said. "What do you think, Terrence? Do you think that might be something you would enjoy?"

Terrence shrugged his shoulders and went on eating his cereal.

"Or would you be more interested in Australia or New Zealand?" Marta asked. "A lot of kids your age visit Queenstown. All the adventure sports are there. And they speak English."

"Our summer is their winter," Terrence said shortly.

And with that, he rose up from his chair and grabbed his backpack and said, "I have to get to school," even though he didn't have to be there for another forty-five minutes. Terrence had learned, very early on, never to accept his mother's first offer. He would wait for this pot to be sweetened, before agreeing to Marta's terms.

Bribes. Oh, how he quietly relished them! The parenting magazines might have argued otherwise, but Terrence never really considered the possibility that the bribes would spoil him or make him feel entitled. Instead, he always understood the bribes as importing to him a valuable lesson: They made him believe in a world where he would be rewarded for doing *exactly* what people wanted him to do. Years later, in the months after graduating from Yale, when he was trying to make a go of freelance writing, he would put that lesson into action. He would incorporate into his second drafts every suggestion his editors made on the first drafts. He would say yes when those editors wanted to change a few words or even whole sentences. He would take whatever assignments were offered him, no matter how inane or beneath him the idea seemed. It paid off, too. The editors would tell him that he was the most responsive writer they had ever dealt with, and then they would keep offering him more work. In those months right after college, Terrence would come to see his mother's bribes as being partly responsible for all of his professional successes.

But even back then, as a teenager, when the stakes were considerably lower, Terrence grasped the wisdom of Marta's approach. He wasn't the type of boy who needed to be pushed toward success—he would have found it on his own, one way or another. But Marta kept bribing him anyway. And the bribes made him understand, from a very young age, that life would always be a bit of a game. They made him realize the value of being a mercenary.

The truth of the matter was this: He didn't care that they were moving to Indiana. If anything, he welcomed the possibilities. Yes, he was a little concerned that changing schools might affect his chances of getting into an Ivy League college. But he knew that, as long as he was diligent about securing letters of recommendation from his teachers at New Dorp, it probably wouldn't matter. Besides, there was a considerable upside: He would finally, *finally* be getting out of Staten Island. His family had moved here from Boston when he was seven, when his father took a job as the chief legal counsel for the Staten Island University Hospital system. But by junior high school, he had come to despise the place. He found most of the people coarse and unambitious. The adults were working-class, barely high-school educated; the older kids he knew—the ones in Jay's high school class, for instance—all went to college nearby and still lived at home with their parents. And his own classmates he could barely stomach. He was friends with maybe a half-dozen of them, but they weren't very smart or interesting. They were strictly friends of convenience—the people you keep close by so you have *someone* to hang out with; so you don't go insane from boredom. He always knew he would leave them behind.

As he rode the bus to school that morning, he considered the opportunity before him. For a whole year, he could work on inventing his new self—the new self he had long been contemplating. He would have a full year to develop this new persona before having to go off to college and make his formal debut as an adult. There were no real drawbacks, either. If his new persona didn't work out—if, in the pursuit of turning himself into a more emotionally engaged and empathetic individual, he ended up becoming Indiana's most notable social pariah—he could just start from scratch a year later. He could go off to college and try out yet another new persona, and no one would be any the wiser.

Even without the promise of a summer in Europe he would have acquiesced. He would have been secretly grateful for this chance at a fresh start.

He stepped off the bus and started making his way to school, keen on sharing his news with his classmates. He was looking forward to rubbing it in their faces . . . *I'm moving on, you'll never see me again. The best you will be able to do is to brag, once I am famous, that you knew me back when.*

But then, as he wandered around the schoolyard that morning waiting for the first bell to ring, staring at the familiar and ugly faces all around him, wishing he could end this chapter of his life right now, another thought occurred to him. A mischievous, mean-spirited, quintessentially Terrence O'Connell-ian thought.

He thought to himself: *Why not play up the part of the wounded victim? Why not act out a little bit?*

Why not cause some trouble?

Nothing too far out there, of course. Nothing that might end up getting reported to a college admissions officer. Just something to ruffle a few feathers. A prank. A scheme. A little something for him to be remembered by. His teachers would shrug off his actions—they would say he was just being a moody adolescent, lashing out upon learning that his life was being sent into flux. His parents would be so chagrined by his bad behavior—they would so quickly rush to blame themselves, because they had just turned his life upside down—that they might double his spending allowance in Europe. They might even offer to buy him a car.

He spotted his friend Joe DeNino across the schoolyard. Terrence hurried over and grabbed the hood of Joe's sweat-shirt, just as the bell rang and Joe was about to enter the building.

Terrence thought that he needed to celebrate his good news; and, also, that maybe he could recruit Joe in his troublemaking efforts. Joe was as utterly unremarkable a teenager as could be imagined—not bright or athletic or remotely funny—no one could ever understand why Terrence put up with him. But Terrence actually minded Joe the least of all of his friends. For one thing, Joe didn't pretend to be any better than he was—he seemed to understand and accept his deeply mediocre place in the world. Much more importantly, Joe always did whatever Terrence asked him to do, usually without Terrence ever having to ask twice.

"Let's cut first period," Terrence said. "Let's get breakfast. I have news to tell you."

They made their way to Go-Go Souvlaki, a Greek diner a few blocks from school. Terrence told Joe to order whatever he wanted—breakfast would be on him. This emboldened Joe, who was only 5 feet 8 inches, but weighed at least 220 pounds, to order two plates of food, steaming scrambled eggs with home fries and a stack of oversized blueberry pancakes that Joe drowned in a quarter-bottle's worth of syrup. They sat there for more than an hour, through all of first period and most of second. Joe blathered on about the professional wrestling telecast he had watched the night before and about the upcoming Yankees game for which his father had box seats. Terrence said very little in response. He stared blankly at Joe, trying to make sense of the gibberish spilling out of his friend's mouth. For a good ten minutes, he couldn't stop staring at a piece of bright yellow egg that clung tenaciously to Joe's chin.

He thought to himself: *This is perhaps my best friend here. This doughy boy with his blowfish features, a fan of wrestling and baseball. He will be lucky to make it through a full year at the College of Staten Island, and then he will be lucky if a plumber is willing to take him on as his apprentice. This is a person with whom I spend a substantial portion of my spare time.*

"Do you want to go bowling on Friday night?" Joe asked him.

Terrence was barely paying attention at this point. He was

thinking about his advanced placement English class the previous semester. The class had been discussing Shakespeare's *Henry IV* plays, when he got into an argument with his teacher. She said that, at the end of part two, Shakespeare wanted the audience's sympathies to rest with Falstaff, the fat old man spurned by his friend Prince Hal, who abandons Falstaff and his ne'er-do-well ways, so that he can go off and become the king of England.

"But if Hal is destined for greatness," Terrence had protested, "then our sympathies should be with him, for recognizing his opportunity and seizing it. That makes him a great hero."

The teacher shook her head vigorously. She said that Terrence was wrong. She said that he was "sabotaging the text" to fit his argument. She said that, if you read the words closely, it was clear that Shakespeare's sympathies rested with Falstaff. She then launched into a ten minute lecture about how, "as students of literature," they must never "sabotage the text." They must never manipulate the meanings of things, she told them, just to fit their own world views.

Except Terrence wasn't wrong. Not then. Not now. He was simply smarter than everyone around him. He was smarter than his classmates; smarter than the people who thought themselves good enough to teach him. And he alone understood what Shakespeare was really getting at: that the world divides between kings and wastrels; legends and also-rans; a couple of lucky winners, and all the other losers.

"What was your news that you were going to tell me?" Joe asked, as Terrence was paying their bill.

By then, Terrence had decided against telling Joe that he was leaving Staten Island. He would tell the principal and his guidance counselor. He would tell the teachers whom he needed to write letters of recommendation. But for everyone else it would be a surprise. They would arrive on the first day of school in September and discover that he had disappeared.

He lied to Joe. He said his big news was that he was getting a car for his seventeenth birthday in August. He promised Joe that he'd drive him to school every day of senior year.

And as they walked back to school, Terrence made another decision: He decided that whatever his insurrection—whatever trouble he chose to cause before leaving Staten Island—he would do it alone. He would not recruit others to aid him. He didn't need their help now. He wouldn't need it ever.

He would conquer the world as a one-man army.

By the time Terrence and Joe returned to school, sneaking in through a back door that was almost never locked, the third period bell had already rung. Mr. Lavner was the one teacher in the school who seemed to hate him, and Terrence knew that his lateness would be greeted with taunts and merciless badgering. In front of the entire class, Lavner would accuse him of being a pretty boy who spent all of his time primping in the locker room. He had less than two minutes to change into his gym clothes. But he couldn't seem to snap himself out of a daze. Already he was imagining his life in Indiana; imagining the person he would become there. He would keep his head down in the hallways, but raise his hand up high in class. He would impress all of his teachers instantly (there wouldn't be a Lavner there to see right through him). But to his fellow students he would remain elusive, stoic—a little too cool for their Midwestern school. He might make a friend or two, just to keep busy on the weekends, but he would never invite them to his house. He would avoid being drawn into cliques, and he would refuse to take sides in schoolwide disputes. He would incite their envy for his ability to hover ever so slightly, ever so indifferently, above them all.

He was standing there in his underwear, staring absently into his locker. He no longer cared that his lateness was now a certainty; that, at some point during his "refereeing," Lavner would punish him by throwing the pink rubber "Lavner Ball" at his chest with such force that it might leave a purple blotch on his torso. Soon, very soon, Mr. Lavner would also be part of Terrence's past, never to be remembered again.

He heard footsteps and then a noise—the soft chirp of sneaker rubber stopping short and screeching against the linoleum floor. He looked up to see Ben Reilly standing across from him, just at the end of Terrence's row of lockers. Their eyes locked for at least ten seconds. Ben didn't move. His stance—legs firmly planted and slightly bowed—suggested an old movie cowboy at high noon, readying to draw his pistols. His eyes looked even stranger, focused and feral, like an animal about to go on the attack.

Terrence felt confused and anxious. He feared that Ben was going to charge at him. Smash him into the lockers. Start pounding on him uncontrollably. He looked *that* unhinged.

Ben Reilly. His long-suffering stooge. For five years now, Terrence had teased him and called him names—slurs shouted loud for everyone to hear in the lunchroom, or whispered softly into Ben's ear (so often, with their last names starting with O and R, and a notable paucity of Ps and Qs in their class, they ended up seated next to one another in class). A new slur for each new day: *Gaywad, faggot, pussy, cocksucker, queer, homo, fudge packer, ass muncher, Rock Hudson's boyfriend.* And sometimes something very simple and pointed: *You're going to die of AIDS, you little faggot.* How easily those names stuck. And how feebly Ben fought back. So that they soon became the names everyone called him. So that soon he was the unfortunate kid—there is one in every school—whom no one wants as his friend.

Sometimes Terrence felt bad for Ben Reilly, a tall and strong-looking boy who acted so fragile and wilting. Terrence couldn't even remember why, in sixth or seventh grade, he had decided to pick on him in the first place. He harbored no real ill-will toward him. If anything, he suspected Ben might actually be a decent and intelligent guy. It was just that Ben had probably been in the wrong place at the wrong time, standing nearby on a day when Terrence had been bored and was looking for someone new to pick on.

Except now Terrence wondered: *Am I the one in the wrong place at the wrong time? Is this kid finally going to snap?*

Terrence was about to say something. But just then Ben broke the stare and slowly looked Terrence up and down, three or four times in a row. Terrence didn't understand what was happening. Was this Ben's idea of a prelude to a fight, like a bull snorting and tossing his head in preparation to charge? Terrence felt embarrassed to be standing there, almost naked. He didn't like the idea of someone paying such close attention to his body—and certainly not in the manner that Ben was looking at him right now. He thought about trying to put Ben in his place, perhaps barking at him, "Stop looking at me, you little faggot." But then he thought better of it. He had to tread delicately here. He didn't want to do anything that might set Ben off.

Ben went on looking at him for a few seconds longer—he must have stared at him for a full minute in total. And then, finally, he moved on, and kept on walking to his locker.

Terrence didn't know what to think. He felt a complex set of emotions suddenly surging inside of him. Something like relief, as if he had just dodged a bullet; and something like fury, like the victim of a crime who is now eager to see his punisher fry in the electric chair.

"What the fuck was that?" he blurted out, and then instantly regretted saying it.

He quickly put on his gym clothes and hurried into the gymnasium. Lavner was running late himself, so Terrence's tardiness was not noted. And as he took his seat on the floor, Terrence felt his anger giving way to more elusive emotions.

He remembered the time when he was eight years old, when his brother Jay dragged him by his ankles through their house, causing rug burns on Terrence's back that would take two months to heal. Their parents were at one of their father's work functions, and Jay had been charged with keeping an eye on his younger brother. Terrence had been driving Jay crazy that evening, refusing to leave him to his schoolbooks. He was the one who had initiated the roughhousing, by sneaking up behind Jay and flicking his ear with his index finger. And even as it was happening, he kept prodding his older brother. "Drag me across the rug, I dare you," he had shouted, until it burned so hot that he couldn't do anything but scream; until Jay was so enraged and worked-up that he couldn't make himself stop.

When their parents returned home a few hours later, Terrence's brother was sternly punished, while Terrence was carefully tended to and fussed over. But the incident left a deep impression on him. In the months and years that followed, Terrence came to believe that, in all violent encounters, there was no such a thing as a truly innocent victim; that the "victim" was almost always asking for some kind of trouble. He rarely spoke these feelings aloud. He knew that others did not agree with him. He knew that others did not even consider these ideas appropriate. But Terrence also knew that he was right. He knew that people didn't like to take responsibility for their own actions. He knew that they would push a situation as far as they possibly could, until the situation turned ugly, and then they would wrap themselves in a cloak of victimhood. That night with Jay, getting dragged across the carpet, Terrence learned this simple truism: It takes two to make misery.

Except this . . . *this* he couldn't quite grasp. He didn't understand what had just happened.

If Ben had started fighting with him—if Ben had shoved him into the locker, or sucker punched him, or knocked him to the ground and started kicking the shit out of him—well, *that* he could have understood. That he probably even deserved. But Ben's staring was an even deeper violation, something penetrating and cold and otherworldly. Ben's staring reminded him of the way Arnold Schwarzenegger stares down his prey in *The Terminator,* the robot getting the specs on a future kill.

Terrence knew he had to strike back. When Ben finally got to his gym seat, and Lavner called him on his lateness, Terrence couldn't stop himself from piping up, "He was too busy in the locker room watching all the guys undress." Everyone around him snickered, but—once again—he instantly regretted saying it. This was precisely the sort of thing that might provoke Ben further. It was the wrong way to go about evening the score.

The day dragged on slowly. Terrence barely paid attention in his classes. He replayed the incident over and over again in his head. He kept coming to the same conclusions: That Ben was crazy like a fox; that with one inscrutable, uninvited stare, he had upended the entire dynamic of their relationship.

Late in the day, he determined he had to talk to him. He didn't want this hanging over his head. He didn't want to have to be on guard during his final five weeks at New Dorp, trying to anticipate Ben's next strike. Terrence waited for Ben after class. Then he waited another forty-five minutes, until Ben emerged from an academic olympics practice. While he was waiting, he decided he would pursue a reconciliation. Terrence certainly didn't like the idea of letting Ben off the hook. But he also knew that sometimes, especially when one's one self-preservation is at stake, it's best to declare a draw.

Just this once, he thought, he could accept *not* being the winner.

Ben was jittery when Terrence finally caught up with him. He wouldn't look Terrence in the eye. Terrence told Ben that he didn't care if he had been checking him out. He told him that he wouldn't tell anyone. He even came very close to offering Ben an apology.

Except Ben didn't react the way Terrence was expecting him to react. He was petulant and combative. He didn't want Terrence walking alongside him, and Terrence had to walk very quickly just to keep a few paces behind. A couple of times during their walk, Ben sounded so irate that, for the second time that day, Terrence worried that things might spill over into violence.

Still, Terrence kept walking alongside him. He wasn't entirely sure why. But there was something about Ben that he found intriguing. He was smart, hard working, sarcastic; it was clear that he, too, was destined to escape all of the dumb people who surrounded them. At some point, it occurred to Terrence that the two of them probably looked upon the world in much the same manner: with a forceful skepticism; and with the keen understanding that others would inevitably fail to live up to their expectations. He realized that they might easily have fallen in with one another and become friends.

What if I carved out an identity that has nothing to do with who I really am? What if I picked all the wrong friends?

This was the real reason he was looking forward to moving: Because he hated to consider the possibility that he had flubbed the first sixteen years of his life; that he had screwed up *everything.* His parents needn't have offered a bribe. He would have done it for free.

He would have bribed *them* for the opportunity.

They made their way to Ben's street. They were standing in front of Ben's house. Ben was inviting him inside.

Terrence knew enough to say no. He knew that this might be a trap. But he wanted to see where this might lead. Terrence said: "OK."

They sat on the couch, side by side, saying nothing. The awkwardness grew palpable almost instantly. *He is smarter than me,* Terrence kept thinking to himself. *He is manipulating this situation to his advantage. This will turn ugly, and Ben will emerge triumphant, and I will only have myself to blame. Once again, I will have been a partner in my own defeat.*

But he didn't want to leave. He wanted to stay. For whatever reason, he wanted to keep talking to Ben.

Ben offered to give him a tour of the house. Terrence said that would be great.

"That's my sister," Ben said, pointing to a large picture of a very pretty girl resting on a shelf in the living room wall unit. "Her name was Mary. She died when I was nine. She had just turned eighteen when she died." And, all over again, Terrence felt unnerved to be in Ben's presence. Ben's voice sounded babyish and half-catatonic, like the little girl in the movie *Polter-*

geist turning away from the television and telling her parents, "They're heeeeeeerrrre." Would Ben show up at school one day speaking Seussian nonsense, a puddle of drool cascading down his chin? Would his name come to be spoken of as urban legend at New Dorp . . . *a few years ago, there was this kid, he got picked on all the time, one day he just lost it, he started banging his head against the lockers, bleeding all over the floor in the locker room . . .*

Or might Ben just show up at school one day and kill them all?

They made their way to Ben's bedroom. Ben excused himself to go to the bathroom. Terrence wasn't sure why his first impulse was to look under the bed. Perhaps it was the mention of Ben's dead sister, combined with the fact that the house seemed so drafty and ghoulish—the kind of house, Terrence thought to himself, where all sorts of creepy things lurk beneath the beds. He wondered if he might even find Ben's sister's body under there, mummified.

He didn't. Instead all he found was a single green and red shoe box from Thom McCann. He thought it might hold a pair of old shoes or maybe some brittle and fading vacation pictures that the family had never gotten around to arranging inside a photo album. He opened it without considering the right or wrong of the matter. For Terrence, this was no different from opening up the medicine cabinet in a stranger's bathroom. You didn't do it out of malice, and you weren't necessarily trying to create mischief. It was just something you did. You did it to prolong your private time or to get a better grasp of unfamiliar surroundings. You did it, maybe, to see how this particular family's secrets stacked up against your own.

But you never expected to find anything worth remarking upon. Most people's bathroom medicine cabinets contained nothing of note. Most people had the good sense to bury their secrets deep inside a closet not accessible to strangers just passing through.

He didn't feel anything at first, other than a sort of non-

plused calm—the feeling that comes when you finally encounter something you had only considered in the abstract, *so
this is what it looks like, it's both better and worse than I imagined it
would be.* The models had blandly handsome faces and well-
developed muscles, but what mostly caught Terrence's attention were their erect penises, centered squarely in the middle
of the frame. Terrence had seen pornography before, but he
had never seen a man reduced to such puny terms, as nothing
but a commodity for another man's base consumption. A *gay*
man's base consumption. The models did not smile in the pictures—they looked lethargic and dazed and a little hopeless.
He wasn't even certain that these models qualified as men. Neither one of them looked much older than sixteen or seventeen. They might very well have been boys the same age as
himself or Ben.

Terrence turned the pages over in his hands and studied
them. He felt as if he were handling contraband—drugs,
weapons, classified FBI documents, something he had no right
to be handling—and that he would be strenuously punished if
anyone found out.

Is this what it means to be gay? he wondered. *Is this what gay men
like? For their gratification to come at the expense of humiliating an innocent teenager? For their fantasies to be cheap and grimy and loaded
with shame?*

Terrence felt a nausea deep in the pit of his stomach. *This is
why the world hates gay people,* he thought to himself. *This is why
people call them faggots.*

And this is why people are justified *in hating them. Because gay
people thrive on corrupting others; because they get off on the humiliation.*

*Because they take all that is pure and promising on this planet and
coat it with a sticky layer of goo.*

Terrence was incensed. He felt as if Ben had violated him yet
again, for the second time today. (Was this Ben's power over
him now? From here on out, would Ben be able to violate him
without even being near him?) And his revulsion was com-

pounded by the fact that he couldn't take his eyes off these pictures; and by the fact that an erection was steadily stirring in his pants.

"You can put some music on if you want, Terrence. The CDs are on the shelf near the closet."

Ben's voice was drawing closer. Terrence didn't have time to react.

"Do you like Depeche Mode? Or R.E.M.? *Green* is a really great CD, if you've never listened—"

Terrence couldn't move. It took considerable effort for him to even lift his eyes up from the pictures and look to the door.

Terrence felt ashamed to have been caught. And then scared. And, finally, deeply indignant. He was the one who had been wronged by Ben, not the other way around. He had to fight back. He had to humiliate this little faggot.

The next five minutes passed in a blur. Ben kept talking, he wouldn't shut up. He kept trying to move closer to Terrence, and Terrence became convinced that Ben was going to strike him. He had to get out of there—out of the bedroom, out of the house, as far away as possible. But he was resistant to even stand up. He was afraid that Ben would see his erection.

He tore the pictures into two. He did it on impulse, but immediately it felt like the right thing to do. He wanted the evidence of what he had seen, and whatever it had stirred up inside of him, to be destroyed. He kept on tearing the pictures, into what seemed like a thousand tiny little pieces, trying to prolong the process for as long as he could, until the pieces became so tiny they fell through his fingers and to the ground.

Finally he felt his erection starting to soften. He stood up. He told Ben to walk in front of him, because he didn't want Ben to see him walking with a still semi-hard penis.

The shove was not premeditated. The idea came upon him just as they were a few inches from the stairs that led down into the dining room. He surprised himself by acting so quickly. He shoved Ben with certainty and with righteousness, with cleanness and with authority. A hand to the back. A knee to the hamstring. Ben went sailing right over the three steps. His head smacked against the wood floor with a thud.

Terrence hesitated only briefly before he walked past Ben, and down the main staircase, and out the front door, which he slammed shut with as much force as he could muster.

He started walking back toward school. He took slow, deep breaths, trying to calm himself down. But he couldn't. His heart was pounding. His cheeks were flush. He was sweating through his clothes.

Had it all been a trap on Ben's part? Had it all been planned, from the encounter in the locker room that morning, to his leaving Terrence alone in the bedroom to find those pictures? Was that how gay people operated? They violated straight people, tricked them, lured them into dark corners under false pretenses—and then pounced?

He tried to stop thinking about it. He had vanquished Ben. He had knocked him off his feet. It was over. In two months, he would leave Staten Island, and this deeply icky memory, behind.

But he couldn't calm himself down. He couldn't stem the rage that was racing through his veins. He clenched his jaw. He ground his teeth so hard he thought he might cause them to chip. Never before had he felt such anger toward another person. He convinced himself that he had not shoved Ben hard enough; that he had to go back and shove him harder.

He made his way to the city bus stop, a few blocks from his school. He stood there waiting for the bus that would take him home, replaying the day's events in his head, trying to understand how things had slipped so far out of his control. He saw his bus idling at the very next traffic light on the horizon. He saw the bus moving toward him, pulling over to the curb to pick him up.

And then this thought occurred to him: *I should kill him. I should go back to school and find a pair of scissors and then go back to his house and stab him in the throat. I should make certain that he never does to someone else what he did to me today.*

The driver opened the door to let Terrence onto the bus. Terrence began to step on. But then he froze. He stood there for ten seconds, staring down at his hands, until the driver finally asked if something was wrong.

"I left something in my locker," he said, and he started to back away.

Why not? Why not kill that little gaywad?

Why not let *this* be his high school swan song, one final, ruthless act of transgression that could be left behind in two months, along with his half-witted, unimaginative teachers; his dense, dim-bulb friends; his parents' cavernous and sterile house; this entire congested community of working class Irish and Italians too witless to figure out for themselves a better place to live? Why not, along with everything else, leave behind Ben Reilly's dead body?

It would be his final act as the ne'er-do-well prince.

Then he would go to Indiana and become king.

The front doors of the school were still open. The security guard knew Terrence and waved him through without asking for identification. A few other kids were still milling through the hallways, finishing up their extracurricular meetings. Terrence walked directly to the yearbook office, to which he had a key (he had recently been appointed the editor of the next year's edition). He found the scissors he knew would be there, in the metal drawer of a large table on which the designers fiddled with page layouts. He put the scissors in the right pocket of his jeans, pushing them down as far as they would go, and then he untucked his shirt to cover the rubber handles that stuck out of the top of his pocket. He turned off the lights and locked the office. He left the building through a back door near the lunchroom, making certain that no one saw him leave.

He quickly worked out a plan in his head. He would return to Ben's house. He would ring the doorbell. Ben would open the door, and Terrence would say that he wanted to apologize. Ben would open the door wider, and then Terrence would push his way in. He would drive the blades of the scissors into Ben's jugular vein. He would pull the scissors out of Ben's neck, and Ben would collapse to the floor and bleed to death, right there in the hallway of the house. Terrence would then go up to Ben's room and change into some of Ben's clothes, just in case any of Ben's blood would have splattered on him. He would find a shopping bag or a knapsack in which to store his own clothes. Then he would walk to the first pay phone he could find and call a car service to drive him home. Then he would shower and throw away Ben's clothes that he would be wearing, and his own clothes that would be bloodied, and the scissors. He would put all of the incriminating evidence into a trash bag, and then place that bag inside of another trash bag (best to double bag it, he didn't want any blood spilling out), and then place *that* bag at the bottom of the outdoor garbage pail. He was pretty certain that the next morning was a trash pickup day. The evidence would be buried deep inside the Fresh Kills landfill within twenty-four hours. As for an alibi, he was not worried. He was fairly certain no one had seen him walking home with Ben that afternoon. There was no reason anyone would connect the two of them at all. And if by some fluke the police did happen to question him, he would just say that he had been at school the whole time, holed up in the yearbook office. The security guard, who never saw him leave the building, would have to corroborate his story.

Momentum. Bad ideas need only momentum to become bad actions, and Terrence generated his momentum the old-fashioned way—by making a run for it. As soon as he got a few blocks away from school, he pulled the scissors out of his pocket. He gripped the closed blades tightly in his hand, like a relay runner in the Olympic 4x100. And then he raced to Ben's house, taking long, liberating strides, steadily increasing his pace with each passing second. For Terrence, this was not just a matter of meting out justice (though, after the events of today, he certainly believed that Ben deserved to be punished; that Ben had brought this punishment on himself). It was more about proving to himself that he could do something ruthless and unalterable, something epic and merciless. The moral logistics of all this—that he was about to take someone's life, and that that was obviously a very bad thing, which could land him in jail for a very long time—didn't interest him. The moral logistics barely seemed worth considering. His momentum carried him right past such prosaic concerns. Righteousness trumps morality any day, and he knew he was right about this. This was exactly what he needed to do.

Momentum. His momentum carried him all the way to Ben's front door, gripping the scissors in his right hand, holding them just behind his waist, like a suitor concealing a bouquet of flowers, pressing the doorbell button with his left index finger, hearing a sharp, clear ding echoing in the distance a moment later, waiting, waiting patiently for Ben to descend the steps and open the front door, so that Terrence could push his way in and kill him.

Momentum brought him right here.

And then . . .

—nothing.

He waited to hear footsteps from within. Nothing. He peered through the frosted glass window on the front door, looking for the shadows inside to change texture and shape, searching for any sign of movement. Still nothing. He stared at the doorknob, expecting it to turn, and for the door to open, and for Ben to be standing before him. But nothing.

He rang the bell again. Nothing. He loudly rapped on the door with his knuckles. Nothing. He tried to open the door, but it was locked.

Terrence rang the bell again. Nothing. Nothing at all.

He stood there. He looked up at the sky, which had turned from bright blue to slate gray in the last two hours. He rang the bell again, but this time without any expectation of Ben answering. He rang the bell mostly just to hear it ring one more time. His momentum, in an instant, had dissipated. Terrence suddenly realized how ridiculous it was to be standing there with a pair of scissors in his hand, poised to murder his classmate. He realized, too, how ridiculous it was to think that he would have gotten away with it. Someone, surely, had seen them leaving school together earlier that afternoon. The police would have brought him in for questioning. And Terrence would have wilted—he wouldn't have even lasted ten minutes under their scrutiny. He would have spent the rest of his life in jail.

Terrence backed away from the house, down the front walkway and to the sidewalk, with its long and deep cracks running through the cement. Terrence looked at those cracks and wished that he could sink straight through them and reemerge in Indiana. He walked to the street corner and stood there for awhile, waiting for a second wind that wasn't coming. All the momentum had abandoned him, and all of the adrenaline, too. He felt too exhausted to even make his way back to school.

A car turned onto the street, a boxy brown Ford that looked to Terrence as if it couldn't go much faster than fifty-five miles per hour. It drove a third of the way down the street and then turned into Ben's driveway. It was Ben's father arriving home from work.

Terrence began giggling. How foolish! How comical! Had he gone through with it, he would have been caught with blood on his hands by Ben's father. He would have been carted off to jail within a matter of minutes.

The truth of the matter was that he liked Ben Reilly. He suspected that they had a great deal in common. And he was intrigued, now that the initial shock of discovering those pictures had worn off, that Ben should know so early in his life that he was gay. It made Terrence want to ask Ben more questions: *When did you know for sure? Have you ever had any doubts? Are you scared?*

But it was too late for that now. It was too late to be friends. He decided, right then, that he would never speak to Ben Reilly again, and he would never speak ill of him to others, either. In fact, in his final five weeks at New Dorp High School, he decided he wouldn't speak very much at all. The time had come for him to cut all of his ties, to begin distancing himself from everyone. Let them interpret his silence how they pleased. Let them think he was being snotty or aloof or just plain weird. It didn't matter to him anymore.

He would be in Indiana soon enough.

"When my mother called me to tell me that you showed up at their house, my first thought was: *He found out. Someone told him that I tried to murder him that day, and now he's coming to get his revenge.*"

We were sitting in a mostly empty bar, just before midnight on Friday night. Terrence had begun his story early that afternoon, while we were out mini-golfing. And he continued it all through the day, in bits and pieces, as we walked around town, as we ate dinner, and now, at this dreary and underlit hole-in-the-wall.

"You don't really think you would have been capable of *killing* me, do you?" I asked.

"I think if you had answered the door that day you wouldn't be sitting here right now."

"I was unconscious on the couch in my living room," I murmured.

He didn't say anything.

"You *really* think you might have killed me?"

"I've thought about that day so much over the years, Ben. And a few years ago something finally dawned on me. I realized that just as every successful life is defined by one or two good decisions, every unsuccessful life is defined by one or two bad decisions. We all have opportunities to do very mean things. And I don't mean the little day-to-day mean things, like cutting ahead of an old lady in line at the grocery store. I mean big, cataclysmic, gruesome things. Look at those Columbine killers. They were messed-up kids. A bad idea popped into their heads, the way bad ideas pop into all of our heads. And

then they had a decision to make. Clearly they chose wrong—
they made the worst choice imaginable. But they're not so different from the rest of us. How can anyone think those two
boys are so different from the rest of us?"

"Not different, necessarily," I said. "Only destined for—" But
then I didn't know what else to say. I didn't know what they
were destined for.

"Have you ever contemplated evil?" Terrence asked me.

"I just can't imagine ever being in a position where I would
choose to do such evil."

"Maybe the moons haven't aligned in your life yet," he said.
"Maybe for you the moment where you will be tempted to do
something really destructive is still on the horizon.

"Maybe," I said.

"What bugs me, what's always bugged me," he said, throwing
a twenty-dollar bill on the bar and getting up from his stool, "is
the idea that I never really made the decision for myself. It was
made for me. It was made by the fact that you didn't answer the
door. At this major flash point in my life, I was a moral cipher."

A deep chill had set into the mountain air—it couldn't have
been much more than forty degrees out—but Terrence asked
me if we could walk for a bit. For the next ten minutes, he
didn't say anything. He had the faraway, palpably anxious air of
a man on the verge of confession—a man running through his
head every possible permutation, and every possible repercus-
sion, of what he is about to say.

"Do you remember it the same way?" he asked finally. "That
day, I mean."

"I don't remember staring at you in the locker room for so
long."

He laughed and said, "You did. Trust me, you did."

"And I guess I remember the actual push differently. I remember you kneeing me in the hamstring and my legs giving
out, but I don't remember you pushing me with your hand."

"I did. It was a concerted effort. I got you airborne. More of a shove than a push."

"Is that the difference between a push and a shove?" I asked.

He shrugged at me and then he said: "It wasn't planned at all. I know that's hard to believe. I thought of it, and then I just did it."

"I believe you," I said. "You probably won't believe me when I tell you those pictures didn't belong to me. It's a moot point. I was in possession of them. But they weren't mine. They were my father's. I found them hidden in his night table when I was in the seventh grade."

Terrence grimaced and asked: "Did he ever do anything to you or your brother?"

"No, nothing like that," I said. "I just found them one day mixed in with all his other porn. Who knows? Is he gay? Did he just like looking at pictures of naked men? I don't want to know. It's one of those mysteries that you have to accept will never be solved."

Terrence didn't say anything. We kept walking. I felt so calm and so happy to be in his presence. I thought to myself: *There is no feeling like this in the world, to be able to confess to another person a secret that you never thought you would be able to confess, and to have that person believe you, and not judge you.*

"You loomed so large in my consciousness," I said to him after awhile. "As you were telling your story, I kept thinking, 'He had no idea.' How every day I would go home and cry. Or how every morning I would dread going to school. It's funny that you thought I was going to try to attack you that day. I was terrified of you. You had no idea."

"I didn't."

"And despite everything I had a crush on you. You had no idea about that, either?"

He laughed softly. "No idea at all," he said. "What sixteen-year-old thinks of himself in terms of another person? Not me. Empathy came very late for me."

I wanted to tell him. Right then and there, I wanted to tell him that I loved him. I felt as if I had all the momentum in the world.

Just tell him and he will have to respond. Maybe he will say that he loves you, too.

But then nothing. I still couldn't. Once the bullied, you are always the bullied. You are always the one waiting for your bully to speak first and dictate the rules.

We walked back to Terrence's car and climbed inside. Terrence turned over the ignition, but then we just sat there idling. Two minutes passed. In my mind, I willed him to act.

Let him lean over and press his lips again mine. Please, God, just let it happen . . .

But then nothing. Another minute passed. Finally, he shook his head and laughed.

"Am I a fraud, Ben? Do you even believe a word of my story? Or does it all come off sounding fake and contrived? That was my ritual when I sat down to write my novel. Every day I would spend two hours writing, and then I would read what I wrote, and I would ask myself: *Is this believable or is this contrived?* If I thought it was believable, I left it alone. But if I thought it sounded even remotely contrived, I would cross it out and rewrite the section again the next day.

"But how could I apply that standard of judgment to a novel, when I can't even apply it to my own life? When every aspect of my own life story feels contrived to me?"

"I think you're maybe being a little hard on yourself," I told him. "Our stories match up. You don't remember things all that differently from the way I do."

"The facts, the details—those match up. But the conclusions I've drawn? Do you really believe that someone can change? That someone who was selfish and cruel—someone who at sixteen nearly murdered his classmate—do you think someone like that can change? Do you think someone can wake up one day and say, 'Now I'm going to lead a humane life?'"

"I don't know," I said.

"I don't either."

chapter thirteen

Shove
(2000)

Disease. Decay. Dying. Death. *AIDS*. This is what starts to happen, this is how your mind goes racing. You close your eyes at the end of each day and think, *I have contracted the virus that is going to kill me, it is presently swimming through my veins.* You open your eyes each morning and think, *I still have it, it didn't go away while I was asleep, it was not just some bad dream.* You spend each day trying to keep distracted, forcing your mind onto other things, inventing mundane tasks and pointless errands to keep yourself busy. But this strategy only works for so long. Soon you are thinking: *Immense, archipelago-shaped sores, in shades of deep purple, brown, and black, will take up residence on my torso. They will cover my body the way spots cover a giraffe. A grayish-white film will coat my tongue. I will be insatiably, impossibly thirsty. Each night I will wake up from a fever dream, and my pillow will be soaked in sweat.*

It no longer mattered if I was wrong; if I didn't really have it; if it had just been a coincidence, and I had merely been suffering from the flu and *not* from Acute Retroviral Syndrome. My future had already been sketched out—this death sentence had in effect been passed down. Because even if I had dodged a bullet this time, there would be the next time, or the time after that. At some point, I would slip up, and *that* slip-up would cost me my life. As with parasite-infested drinking water in Mexico, or malaria-infected mosquitoes in sub-Saharan Africa, vigilance only carries you so far. Sooner or later, the little buggers will get to you.

Before long all of us who are gay will be defeated by it.

This became my only comfort; this was how I got through the day. I would think to myself: *If I have contracted HIV, at least I will have gotten it over with; at least it will no longer be hanging over my head as a possibility.*

And maybe it's better this way.

Because isn't a certain death preferable to the anxiety of a very possible one on the horizon — to knowing that, with the next condom you fail to unwrap, with one thrust of your cock inside a diseased and bloody orifice, you will be destroyed?

Isn't it best to just accept your punishment now, and get on with what's left of your life?

I opened my eyes shortly after 6:00 A.M. on Saturday morning. The same old thoughts instantly flooded my brain: the virus; the poisoned blood cells; the sores and the thrush; the opportunistic infections. My soon and certain death. Every morning for the past two weeks, I had woken up with these same unbearable thoughts.

But this morning another thought occurred to me, so simple and so plainly obvious: *I should go and get tested. Right now, before Terrence wakes up. In this place where I am wholly anonymous, where only Terrence knows my name, I should find a clinic and be tested for AIDS.*

And then it will be over. By lunchtime I will know.

It seemed to me the only way to quell this plaguing terror. It had to be here, because back in New York I would never be able to bring myself to do it. I would be too terrified of running into someone at the clinic who recognized me; terrified of someone seeing me and *knowing*. But here I could give them a false name, and I could make up a story. I could tell them that I came in contact with infected blood, but *not* that it had been sexual, I could tell them that I had been in a terrible car accident, and the person in the passenger seat had bled all over me. I could tell them whatever I pleased, really, and they wouldn't be able to dispute me. Professional obligation would require they take my word for it.

Here, in Vail, Colorado, I could slip out of the house without Terrence knowing and get tested. If I moved quickly enough, I might even be back home before he woke up.

I rose from bed and put on my clothes and marched to the kitchen without even pausing to use the bathroom. If I was going to do this, I could not allow myself second thoughts—I had to let the momentum carry me all the way there. I found the phone and I dialed information, and I whispered as I asked the operator if there was a 24-hour AIDS Helpline in the area. The operator gave me a number with a Denver exchange. I dialed that number, and a cheerful-sounding woman with a molasses-coated Southern accent answered. I told her that I needed to be tested and that it had to be today, preferably this morning. She kept me on hold for nearly ten minutes before giving me the phone number and address of a clinic in Eagle. She told me that I didn't need an appointment; that I could walk in and be tested anonymously. She assured me that it was "gay-friendly."

She said to me, "Don't you worry, honey, you're going to be just fine. The important part is to get yourself tested."

I thanked her and hung up the phone. I took the keys to the rental car and left Terrence a note that said I had to run an errand, but that I would be back before noon. The clinic was called "Eagle Health Associates," a fifteen minute drive from the house. I pulled in to the parking lot just after 7:30 A.M. A small sign on the front door said that the clinic opened at 8:00 A.M. I waited in the car with the ignition turned off, my jacket wrapped tightly around me. It was so cold outside that I could see the vapor when I breathed—my last visible breaths as a man without AIDS. I watched as, just before 8:00 A.M., a young woman with curly red hair unlocked the front door and went inside. A few minutes later, two more women arrived. Four others streamed in after that, two women and two men.

Just go in there. It will be "gay-friendly." They see people just like you every single day. They have diagnosed hundreds, probably thousands of gay men before you, men whose sexual indiscretions are far dirtier and more deserving of punishment than yours. They won't judge you.

But I couldn't do it. Eight o'clock came and went. And then 8:15 A.M., 8:30 A.M., 8:45 A.M. A half-dozen more people streamed into the clinic, as I waited in the car. Finally, I decided to return to the house. This had been a terrible idea, a ridiculous idea. It had only been six weeks since I'd had sex with Alex, and I had read on a Web site that it takes six *months* after a high-risk encounter to be 100 percent certain that you are not HIV-positive. In which case, they would be able to tell me I had it, but they wouldn't be able to tell me—not for certain—that I *didn't* have it. I was just going to have to repeat the same humiliating routine in a few more months anyway.

And besides, did I even want to know? What's so great about learning that you have contracted an illness that is going to kill you? Is ignorance not bliss?

I turned over the ignition and put the car into gear. But then I stopped. I changed my mind back again. I had to do this. And it had to be here in Vail—it was the only place where I would ever allow myself to be tested. I turned the ignition off. And then back on again. And then off, and on, and off, and on, and off—until another twenty minutes had passed—until, finally, it got so cold inside the car that my toes had gone numb. I told myself I had no choice but to get out and move around or risk frostbite. And then, once I was out of the car, I found myself walking to the front door of the clinic, one step at a time . . . *you have to do this, just keep going, the results will be negative, you are HIV-negative, just keep saying it in your head, negative, negative, negative, negative, NEGATIVE. . . .*

When I opened the door, I saw the redhead sitting behind a glass window, about ten feet in front of me. I looked to my right, where there was a small waiting room. Two women, both in their late twenties, were sitting in opposite corners, on shabby-looking chairs upholstered in fraying green fabric.

(Were they here to get tested also? Had their boyfriends cheated on them with other men and now they feared that the infection had been passed along?) The redhead slid open the glass panel in front of her. She half-smiled and looked at me expectantly. I leaned into the counter and said, in as low a voice as I could manage without making it seem like I was whispering, "Hi, I'd like . . . I'd like to get an HIV test."

She looked down at a ledger in front of her and slowly tapped the eraser of her pencil against its pages. "Do you have an appointment?" she asked.

"No . . . um, no. They told me I could just walk in."

"Who is *they*?" Her voice was suddenly supercilious, faintly mocking. Her smile turned into a skeptical frown.

"The help line. The woman I talked to on the help line—" I heard the door open behind me. I turned and saw a blonde-haired woman, probably in her mid-thirties, holding the hand of a red-nosed, bleary-eyed little girl.

I felt my stomach drop. What kind of "gay-friendly" clinic was this? Two women sitting in the waiting room? Another woman and her young daughter next in line? Was this some kind of OB-GYN center? Or—even worse—a pediatrician's office?

I turned back around to face the redhead, and I began stammering. "The woman I talked to . . . she told me . . . I thought this was . . ."

The redhead's voice, so icy just a few moments earlier, now turned chirpy and welcoming. "No, it's not a problem at all, we can do it, you may"—she began shuffling around pieces of paper in front of her—"you may have to wait a few minutes. But we can do it. What kind of insurance do you have?"

"I want it to be anonymous." Now I really was whispering. I didn't want the little girl behind me to hear. I didn't want her to ask her mother, "Mommy, what's an HIV test?" Because she would ask it loudly, so loud that the two women in the waiting room would hear her, and then everyone in the clinic would know. They would all know that I was gay and that I had AIDS and that I had shown up at an OB-GYN clinic to get tested. "I'd like to . . . I'd like to pay for it myself."

The redhead cocked her head to the side and furrowed her brow. "OK," she said. "I need to—" She cut herself off and began looking all around her. But there was no one else in her little glass-enclosed room to help.

"I'll be right back," she said. Then she lifted herself out of her chair and disappeared through a door to her left, glancing back at me one last time. She looked suspicious, maybe even a little scared, almost as if we were in a movie, and I was the serial killer on the run, and she had just seen my picture on the TV news. And now she was scurrying off to call the authorities.

How fucking stupid of me! How could I have thought this would be simple? I was far from New York or San Francisco or Los Angeles. I was in a resort town in Colorado, a place where married people and old people come to ski and eat and get spa treatments. People in this town don't need an AIDS test. Who is this town would have even *heard* of an AIDS test? How could I have thought that Vail, Colorado, would have its own clinic for gay people—open on a Saturday morning, no less, just in case you were up the entire night before at a circuit party, getting fucked in the ass by a half-dozen strangers tripping on Ecstasy?

How could I have thought that walking in here would be anything other than tantamount to a public confession, to standing naked on a pedestal in the town square and shouting, *I am a gay man, and I have had gay sex, and now I think I have AIDS?*

The redhead returned a minute later, holding a clipboard in her hands. She passed it to me and said, "Not a problem at all. You need to fill these forms out. The test is anonymous, but we need to create a patient record for you. And it costs eighty dollars."

I filled out all the forms, using the name "Jay O'Connell" and my real address in New York. I returned them to the receptionist, along with four twenty-dollar bills. Fifteen minutes later, another woman appeared in the waiting room and pointed at me and led me to an examination room. She took my blood pressure and stuck a thermometer in my ear and recorded the results on a chart.

"You're just getting an HIV test, nothing else is wrong?" she asked me, looking up from the chart. "You don't need to see the doctor?"

"Just the test."

She made a few more markings on the chart and said, "I'll have Sam come in and draw the blood. He just finished his first year at medical school in Denver. He's working with us for the summer."

The summer intern! All my eighty dollars earned me was a visit with the summer intern. The real doctor was passing me off.

The real doctor probably doesn't like to dirty his hands with possible AIDS cases . . . the blood might spill . . . the infection might spread . . .

Sam entered the room less than a minute later.

And the litany of humiliations continued.

He was good-looking, spectacularly good-looking, almost aggressively good-looking—the kind of guy who rubs his good looks in your face, with his mop of thick, curly black hair and dark brown eyes, with his broad shoulders and pumped-up chest, with his bright pink lips and unshaven face. The kind of guy who doesn't even have to try to look perfect; he could just stumble out of bed and still everyone would want to sleep with him. He was wearing bright green scrubs that fit his body tightly. A gold chain with a small crucifix hung from his neck. And on the third finger of his left hand—*surprise, surprise*—was a thin silver wedding band.

How fitting all of this was! How predictable! That the most spectacularly gay-*unfriendly* clinic in Colorado should have in its employ this most perfect heterosexual specimen: handsome; square-jawed; muscular; Christian; married; twenty-three years old; a medical student with a vastly promising life in front of him; *most certainly HIV-negative.* This was the man who would draw my blood and tell me if I was going to die because I had unprotected gay sex. Sam from Denver. The summer fucking intern.

His voice was stoic and cheerless. He said only a few words of brusque instruction—"Turn your arm this way, this will sting for just a second"—as he prepped the needle and inserted it into my vein and drew the sample.

"That about does it," he said, once the test tube filled with my brownish, gummy-looking blood. My HIV-infected blood.

"Do you feel light-headed?" he asked. "Are you OK to walk around?"

"I'm fine," I told him. "Should I wait outside for the results?"

He looked at me confusedly. "Um, if you want to wait out there for five days," he said.

"Five days?"

"Yes."

"It takes that long?" I asked, my voice cracking.

"It takes that long."

"Is there any way—"

"We can't give you the results over the phone, either. Make an appointment to come in on Thursday morning."

"I can't. I don't live here. I live in New York."

"You live . . ." His voice trailed off. He contorted his left eyebrow into a question mark.

"I live in New York. I'm just here visiting. On vacation—"

"And you came here because . . ."

"Well, a friend invited me out here for—"

He cut me off. "No. What did you *do,* man? Why are you getting tested?"

"I had unsafe sex."

"With a guy?"

"Yes."

"Did he ejaculate inside of you?" So formal. So brusque. In asking these obscenely personal questions. Was the concept of a "good bedside manner" not discussed at the University of Colorado Medical School?

"No . . . I was . . . I was the . . . insertive partner?"

"How many times?" So cool and clinical. Is this how all married, Christian men treated the gay heathens among them?

"Twice. With the same guy. It was just one night, I didn't—"

"Anything else? Any other instances of unprotected sex?"

"No, I hadn't really been having sex. I hadn't—"

"You don't have it—" he hesitated and looked down at my chart to find my name—"Jay, you don't have it. You have something else going on inside of you right now, something inside your head. When you figure out what that is, you'll see that you don't have HIV."

"But I had all the symptoms of Acute Retroviral Syndrome," I told him. "Four weeks after the encounter. For exactly five days. I seroconverted."

"We'll mail you the results, Jay." He backed away from the examining table and opened the door. "But no, you don't have it. If that's all you did, you don't have it."

It was after eleven by the time I got back to the house. Terrence was standing in the center of the living room, wearing only the yellow swimming trunks that I had helped him pick out at Barneys. A heavy white bath towel was draped over his shoulder. He was puttering around in a circle, taking small steps, shuffling left and right. His face was scrunched up in intense concentration, searching for something.

"There was a book I was reading yesterday," he said, after I came inside the house. "Did you see where I put it?"

I shook my head. He continued baby-stepping his way around the room, looking for his book. I waited for him to ask me where I had been, but he didn't.

"I was just about to try the hot tub," he said. "Come join me."

When I returned from changing into my swimsuit, Terrence was already submerged to his neck beneath the foamy water. His eyes were closed. His head was resting against the porcelain rim of the hot tub. I climbed in and slid down directly across from him. The hot tub was large, probably twelve feet in diameter—large enough so that our bodies had almost no chance of touching. The water bubbled and fizzed all around me. It felt soothing, but hardly relaxing—it's hard to relax when you are in a hot tub, very close to being naked, with the boy you want more than any other boy in the world. Had Terrence planned it this way? Was this his means of bringing us to sexual congress? *First I will confess to you; I will purge myself of the sins of that day in high school when I seriously contemplated your murder? Then I will invite you into my hot tub, where the only thing for us to do will be . . .*

Will be *what?* We sat in silence for nearly five minutes. Nothing was happening. His eyes were closed. I couldn't be certain if he was even awake.

I tried to figure out what to say, to steer us onto the right course. A few more minutes passed. Until, finally, I came up with this: "Terrence, can I ask you something? About something you said last night?"

He slowly opened his eyes and raised his head upright. He smiled at me—his insouciant, inviting, little-boy-Terrence grin. The wistfulness and disappointment he had expressed to me the night before were gone. Instead, I was looking at a different Terrence entirely: the Terrence who had charmed his way into the Whitney Museum of Art without his membership card; the Terrence I had played video games with; the Terrence who had flirted with me on the telephone and told me that I should go on crushing on him.

This was the Terrence I loved the best.

"You said that you were intrigued—or impressed, I can't remember the word you used—that I knew so early on. That I knew I was gay. What did you mean by that?"

"Well, how old were you?" he asked. "When you realized?"

"I don't know. Seven or eight."

He paused to take in this information. Then he said: "When I saw those pictures, Ben, I was disgusted. Or at least I thought I was *supposed* to be disgusted. Teenage boys are supposed to be revolted by homosexuality, aren't they? But then when I stepped back and thought about it, I don't know, I guess I felt envious. I kept thinking to myself: *He's lucky. He has the most difficult thing in the world all figured out.*"

"It's hardly enviable," I said.

"That's where you're wrong," he said.

"Terrence, are you . . . ?" I didn't want to say the word. I didn't want to scare him off with the certainty and the finality of the word. I wanted him to think that he could kiss me and make love to me—and yet still have some wiggle room; that having sex with me wouldn't necessarily mean he was *gay*.

He shook his head at me. He sunk down a little further in the hot tub. From below the water, he shrugged his shoulders. And then he sighed, a long, exaggerated, preposterous sigh that seemed to last a minute long.

"Well, Ben," he said finally, "you might be onto something there."

It's happening. This is real. I'm not deluding myself.

He's trying to come out of the closet to me.

He's giving me an opening. I just have to seize the opportunity, before he snatches it back, before he loses his nerve. . . .

"Terrence, there's only one difference between our stories," I said. "In my version, I come to the conclusion that the reason you followed me home was because you wanted to hook up with me. And in your version, well, I guess you never really determined why you followed me home. You leave that question open to interpretation."

He smiled at me. He took none of this as provocation. If anything, he was enjoying it. "Well, your version certainly sounds more plausible," he said.

"In a *Penthouse* letters sort of way."

He laughed at my joke. I stared into his eyes. He stared right back.

Is this it? Now? Is it time to launch myself forward and throw myself upon him?

I waited to hear the words: *Yes, Ben.* Or: *Go ahead, Ben.* Or perhaps just: *OK.* I knew those words were on the very tip of his tongue.

But then, instead, he said, "I think we should go mountain biking. I called up the bike rental place this morning. There are three trails open, and they said two of them are suitable for beginners. Then maybe we can head over to Beaver Creek for a late lunch."

"You're changing the topic, Terrence."

"Yes, I'm changing the topic."

"Why?"

"Because the topic makes me uncomfortable," he said.

No. Not acceptable. That answer will just not do.

"Is this what you're going to keep doing?" I said. "You hint that something might happen. And then you change the topic? Is that how you're going to go through life? By changing the topic?"

He sat there frozen in place, staring at some fixed point above my shoulder. Another minute passed in silence until he said: "Do you feel like I'm stringing you along?"

Yes. Of course. NO FUCKING DUH. For fifteen years it has felt as if you are stringing me along, using the Guinness Book of World Records *ball of string. And it has to stop, right here and right now, you have to stop stringing me along and let me kiss you. You* must. *I'm not giving you a choice in the matter.*

"I don't think you've been stringing me along," I said. "But—"

"I don't mean to. I don't like people—"

"—what if I said—"

"—who string other people along—"

"—you can't change the topic—"

"—I wouldn't do that to a friend, string him—"

"—what if I said that, Terrence? That you can't change the topic. That you have to come up with some kind of answer right now. That we can't go mountain biking until you come up with an answer."

He lifted his hands to the surface of the water and began analyzing them, holding each wrinkled finger out of front of him for study. He had a crooked and rueful grin on his face, a grin that was also a gentle plea, *let this drop, please, just let it drop for now, and we can come back to the topic later.*

"What exactly is the question?" he asked quietly.

How slow! How prolonged!

My seduction of Terrence, fifteen years long and counting, and he still didn't know what the question was. Still we were at square one. Still I was waiting for the spark to ignite. How many times can you bang your head against the same wall, before you have bashed your own brains in?

Well . . . maybe just one more time.

Surely one more try was in order.

I couldn't not try.

"Can I kiss you, Terrence?"

For a couple of seconds, he didn't do anything. Then he rose up in the water slightly, so that half of his chest was exposed to me. He looked toward me and stared into my eyes. For ten seconds? Thirty seconds? A minute? Maybe ten? Who knows how long he stared at me? In anticipation of that first kiss, time becomes elastic and stretches on forever. It cannot happen soon enough.

I was the one who broke the stare. To look down at his chest, and then at his knees just below the surface of the water. Was that a buckle of his right knee that I saw? A gentle shifting of his weight? Was he getting ready to move toward me, to bridge the distance between us and take me in his arms and kiss me? Were his eyes trying to implore *me* to make that move?

I lifted myself up and leaned forward. My feet found the bottom of the hot tub. I looked into his face. His expression still had not changed.

I stood up and then bent my knees, crouching down a bit, so that the lower half of my body was still submerged in the water, so that my erection would remain concealed beneath the bubbling surface. I took an unsteady step toward him. There were five or six feet between us. I took another step. I searched his face. His expression gave nothing away.

And then, a moment later, I thought I detected a nod. His head moving up and down, very slowly. He was nodding his consent and approval. *Now. Finally. Yes!* It was as if he we had been embroiled in a five-hour tennis match, an epic slugfest for the Wimbledon championship, but now, at long last, we were at match point. It had looked as if might never end, but now I was on the brink of victory. And it was sublime! Intoxicating! The tension and the excitement and the exhaustion and the determination were all commingling to create magic. To create *history*—a classic moment that would be celebrated and analyzed and parsed out for many decades to come.

I took two more steps closer. I paused. I took one more step closer. I leaned into him.

Finally, finally, finally, *finally* . . . fifteen years after I had fallen in love with him, I was finally kissing Terrence O'Connell. My lips were pressing against his . . .

Or maybe not.

I felt his hands on my shoulders, gently but firmly holding me at a distance.

"No, Ben," he said. His mouth was no more than six inches away from mine.

"No," I repeated back to him.

"No, I can't kiss you," he said. And then he abruptly turned his body around and climbed out of the hot tub and grabbed his towel and wrapped it around his waist. He started moving toward the glass doors that led into the kitchen. He moved so quickly that I barely had time to register the weight of his actions—namely, that it was over; that I had made a clear and forceful pass, and he had turned me down.

"I'd like to kiss you," he said, stopping just before the door and turning around to face me. "I've thought a lot about what it might feel like to kiss another guy. But I can't."

"Why not?"

"I just think it would do more harm than good."

I didn't say anything. I certainly wasn't about to concede defeat. When you are gay—when unrequited desire is your stock in trade—you learn not to relent so quickly. You learn to give the other person every opportunity to change his mind.

"What would happen after we kissed, Ben?" he asked.

"Would we just go mountain biking and get on with the weekend? Would we have sex? Because I really don't think I'm ready for sex. And even if I were, it seems wrong that it should be with you. It would be too weird."

"So we can't kiss just because we once hated each other?" I said. "Just because you once pushed me down the stairs?"

Just because. *Just* because. As if it had been no big deal at all. As if I never really minded. As if I would let him push me down the stairs any old time he pleased. I thought of the scar behind my ear, and how I had just betrayed it, all for the possibility of getting a boy into bed. If there were a hacksaw available, and if it would strengthen my chances of getting to sleep with Terrence, would I be willing to cut off that ear entirely?

Was any part of my body sacred to me, other than my cock?

"We're friends now, Ben," he said. "Friendships never survive these situations. I don't want you to be the guy who helped me come out of the closet. The guy who I sleep with once and then never talk to again."

"It doesn't have to be like that," I protested.

"I just don't see how it's possible for us to make the transition into being boyfriends. I don't think our friendship would survive that."

"And I disagree."

He turned around again. He opened the glass door. He took a step into the kitchen.

Desperate, flailing, time running out. I tried another tack: "Were you hard before, Terrence? In the hot tub—talking to me—did you have a hard-on?"

He turned back to face me. "Yes. So what, Ben? It doesn't change anything."

"You can't deny your nature," I told him. "You can't keep doing that. You can't just make decisions about who you are, and then abide by them, like some robot. You can't program yourself to act a certain way. If you were hard, it means something."

"I'd rather that we be friends."

My voice was rising, it was turning too shrill. But I didn't care. I had to do whatever I could to keep the possibility of kissing him alive.

"In college, I had a friend named Jonah," I said. "We're still friends. I visit him in Boston every summer. But sophomore year I fell in love with him. I thought about him all the time. I couldn't eat. All these ridiculous, clichéd symptoms of love sickness—I had them. I finally worked up the courage to tell him. He took it in stride. He told me that if he was gay, he would sleep with me in a heartbeat. But he said that he was straight, and I accepted that. And we ended up becoming very good friends.

"But, you know what, Terrence? I would have traded that entire friendship—the eight years I've known him—to have had sex with him just once. I know that must sound so puerile. But it's true. It's just the way we're constructed. Or the way I'm constructed. As a sexual being. As a gay person."

"Is that how you feel about me?" Terrence asked.

I shrugged my shoulders. *Yes. No. Maybe. At this point, who knows?*

"I'm sorry that I'm disappointing you, Ben," he said. "I'm sorry this isn't working out the way you wanted. It's funny. I think if we had encountered each other a few years ago, I would have said yes so much more readily. I wouldn't have wanted to disappoint you. But I need to stop doing that. I can't go through life doggedly trying to please everyone. Ironically, I think that's something I've learned from you. I admire that you resist people's expectations of you. You're never worried about whether or not people like you. That's probably the reason I started picking on you in the first place. I resented your confidence."

Except . . . wait a minute . . . hold on here . . . I *did* worry . . . every day. Every day of seventh grade, every day of eighth grade, every day of ninth, tenth, and eleventh grades, every day until God finally answered my prayers and made Terrence O'Connell disappear, I worried. Terrence O'Connell had drawn all the wrong conclusions, based on incomplete data, based on a misreading of the facts. He had sabotaged the text of my life. He didn't understand. My inaction—my willingness to stand there day after day and take his taunting—had not been an act of resistance, but of capitulation. I didn't fight back because I didn't have a leg to stand on. I believed every epithet he ever threw at me to be the truth.

I worried. Believe you me, Terrence, I worried. I worried about living an entire life in which people would call me a gaywad, every single day.

I still worry.

"So it's my fault that you won't sleep with me?" I said, resigned now to my defeat. "My character is too noble?"

He laughed, even though I hadn't been trying to make a joke. "Something like that," he said.

"I may never stop pining for you," I said.

"I think we should go mountain biking."

Terrence wore a pair of snug-fitting, military-green cargo shorts that flattered his butt, making it look rounder and higher than I had ever noticed it being. He wore a faded blue T-shirt with the word YALE printed in white block letters across the chest. His exposed arms and legs had darkened after just two days in the sun, and his hair had lightened a bit—so that it almost looked blonde again, the way it had in junior high school. And as he took his mountain bike from the manager of the rental kiosk, and as he lifted the bicycle up over his head and carried it to the spot where we would have our mandatory safety briefing, and as his back arched and his biceps flexed, and as his T-shirt pulled up on his torso, exposing the flesh between his belly button and his waist and the trail of sparse brown hair that grew there, and as the sun baked down on him, and as the bulky, boxy bicycle became a feather in his hands, a child's toy, Terrence looked to me like a Greek God; like a man who could do anything. There was no other way to describe him in that moment, other than to say that I would carry this new image of him with me for many years to come; it would be placed in the photo album in my brain that was already overstuffed with hundreds of other images of Terrence.

There was no way to describe Terrence O'Connell in that moment other than to say I would never stop pining for him.

The bike rental manager—a skinny, curly-haired sixteen-year-old who spoke in the slow-motion patois of the permanently pot-addled—took his place in front of us, next to a portable television just outside the kiosk. There were eight of us renting bikes this afternoon. He asked if anyone was planning to ride their bikes *up* the trail, and two thin, ropy men in their thirties, blonde and sunburned, raised their hands. The rest of us would ride the gondola to the top of the mountain and bike our way back down. Two of the three open trails were suitable for beginners. The ride down would take approximately forty-five minutes.

"But even the beginner trails get a little steep," the teenager said. "And the gravel can be very slippery. The snow melted late this year, so the ground is still moist."

He turned on a video which illustrated how to stop the bicycle using the hand brakes and which stressed the importance of staying close to your biking partner. After the video ended, the manager explained that there were emergency phones at a couple of points along the trail and that we could call down from them if we needed assistance. Then he wandered back to his seat behind the cash register, failing to notice that two of the women in our group had raised their hands to ask him questions.

"I think I would sooner take my chances than call that guy for help," Terrence said.

We wheeled our bikes to the base of the gondola. The operator took them from us and sent them up the mountain on the back of an empty lift chair. He then pointed to the spot where we should stand and wait for the next chair to scoop us up. I had never been skiing before, so I was surprised by the low-tech inelegance of it all: the creaky, splintered-wood chair that slowly pulls up from behind and taps you on the hamstrings, requiring you to jump a little off the ground and fall backwards into it; the rubbery, sagging cable wires, from which the chairs dangled uneasily, like heavy ornaments pulling down on the branches of a Christmas tree; the utility poles and the rusted turbines, compelling everything forward, but just barely.

"I've never been on a gondola before," I told Terrence, as we began our ascent.

"Really?"

"We didn't go on many vacations when I was growing up. When we did, it was usually to amusement parks. We weren't a skiing family."

"You should learn," he said. "I'll teach you. It's fun."

Promises, promises. So much to look forward to, in a lifetime spent as Terrence's friend.

Just not sex.

He'll do everything with you but fuck.

I looked up ahead of us. The gondola seemed to stretch on forever. There was nothing but utility poles and empty lift chairs in front of us. There was nothing but half-bloomed trees dotting the steep, craggy mountainside all around us.

"I guess I never realized how high these go," I said to Terrence. "In the movies, the gondola ride seems to last about five seconds."

He laughed softly, mostly to be polite. We hadn't said very much to each other in the car ride here. Now he was mostly just enduring the conversation, giving me one or two sentence answers. He was probably regretting ever inviting me along for this weekend in the first place.

"I think this one goes on for about ten minutes," he said. "James and I used to ski these trails all the time, but it's been awhile."

Ten minutes. Ten minutes alone on a gondola with Terrence. Ten minutes to resolve everything that was unresolved between us.

It was hardly enough time. It had taken ten *years* for the two of us just to get this far. What could I possibly hope to accomplish in just ten minutes?

But I had to do something. I couldn't let it keep carrying on like this, hoping and waiting, praying that he might one day get horny enough to submit to me.

I had ten minutes to give it one last try.

"I didn't mean to pick a fight with you this morning," I said.

"I know that."

"You don't realize the sway you hold over me."

"I think you're right," he said. "I'm sorry."

"Please don't apologize. Not for that."

He didn't answer.

"The thing you don't get, Terrence, is how hard it is for me to hear that you *might* be interested. That you've *thought* about kissing a guy. It would be one thing if you said you were straight. That I could deal with. Even if you told me that you *are* gay, but that I'm not your type—I could deal with that, too. I'd probably consult a plastic surgeon to try to transform myself into your type. But eventually I'd get over it.

"But this middle ground. This maybe-maybe not stuff. It's exhausting for me. Because it makes me think that if I just say the right thing, I can have you. If I can just crack your code or figure out your secret password."

He didn't speak for nearly a minute. The gondola raised us higher. Still there was no end in sight.

Then, very quietly, almost underneath his breath, Terrence said: "I've kissed a guy before."

"What?" I said sharply. I couldn't have possibly heard him correctly.

"Well, you were talking about how I've *thought* about kissing another guy," he answered. "But I've done more than think about it."

"What? When?" *Please let him say that it was back in college, please let him say that this had been a very long time ago, when he was young and drunk and disoriented, please do not let this have been recently, please not that, anything but that. I just don't think that's an admission I can handle.*

"The Monday before last," he said. "When I was in Los Angeles. I met this guy in the gym at my hotel. One thing led to another. We ended up back in my room. We did more than kiss. I gave him a blow job."

I felt my cheeks get hot. My temples began to throb, as I pictured him down between the legs of some nameless gym rat. This could not be so.

"Why would you do that?" I asked. *Why would you do that to me? Why would you fly off to Los Angeles and cheat on me?*

"I don't know," he said. "He was attractive. I was curious. I just got caught up in the heat of the moment."

"What did he look like?" I asked.

"Dark hair, tall."

"What was his name?"

"His name was Ryan. He told me he was an environmental engineer."

"Was he a good kisser?"

"I think so. He's the only guy I've ever kissed, so it's hard for me to compare."

"Did he have a big dick?"

"Ben, come on—"

"Tell me if he had a big cock. Was he uncircumcised? Did you suck his big, uncut cock?"

"I'm not going to talk to you if you act like this."

"Did he come in your mouth?"

"Stop it, Ben."

"Did you swallow his load?"

"Why are you acting like this?"

"Because this is a betrayal."

This is a betrayal of the very highest order. This places you on the level of Judas Iscariot, Benedict Arnold, Alger Hiss. This makes it so that you will be remembered as one of history's greatest charlatans. You led me on with your tantalizing display of innocence. You led me on with the promise that, if I hung around long enough, I would be your first. You made me fall in love with you and absolve you of all your crimes. You made me hang on your every word, daydream about your every phone call. You made me pray when I had never prayed before, I prayed that you would call me, I prayed that you would want to spend more time with me; and when you did call, I believed that my prayers had been answered. For the first time since I was a wide-eyed little boy, I believed unequivocally in God; I believed he was watching over me. You made me believe, Terrence. You made me think that I had a chance.

You lied to me; you deceived me; you misled me; you cheated me; you manipulated me; you obscured the facts. There are a million terms for what you have done here, Terrence O'Connell, call it what you will. But this is a betrayal of everything that we shared.

There is no worse betrayal.

He didn't answer. A couple of minutes passed. The end of the lift finally came into sight.

"I was dating Lisa at the time," he said finally. "If anything, I betrayed her. But not you. *You* I would think would be happy for me, that I'm finally starting to figure things out."

"Fuck you, Terrence," I shouted, just as we came upon firm ground, just as a pimply-faced college kid raised our safety bar to let us off the lift chair.

The operator pointed at our bikes, which were resting against a wall ten feet away. "You need any other help?" he mumbled, looking down to the ground, making it clear to us that he didn't want to get in the middle of our little spat. Our little gay spat.

"We're fine," Terrence said curtly.

We picked up the bikes and started walking them up a gravel-covered path, toward the start of the trail, about fifty yards away. "That wasn't a very nice thing to say, Ben," Terrence said sourly.

"You deserved it, Terrence," I said. "You deserve worse."

"Why?" he asked, his voice starting to rise. "What is the great crime here?"

"You buried the lead, Terrence. For the last ten days, you left out a very critical detail about what was going on. You let me go on thinking that you were still figuring things out. And then you finally decide to tell me about what happened, but only *after* I've completely humiliated myself and hit on you. That's just ruthless. You're a total fucking narcissist, Terrence. You lie to me and lead me on, and yet now I'm supposed to be happy for you—because, what, you've finally figured out you like sucking dick? It's undiluted narcissism. Don't you realize that? It's a sickness. It's epidemic with you."

I was looking at the ground, kicking up dust and tiny gray pebbles as I marched along with my bicycle. I couldn't bear to look up at him. But I assumed he would be contrite; that I once again would have bullied him into an apology.

I was wrong.

Terrence O'Connell, finally, was ready for another fight.

"If I'm such a narcissist, then why do you want to fuck me so much?" His voice was a hiss, the sound of a drop of water spilled onto a scalding hot grill.

"I just do, Terrence," I barked at him. "Sometimes you get things stuck in your head and you can never get them out. You just hope other people will be sensitive to that and not try to take advantage of you."

"Fuck you, Ben," he said. "I've never taken advantage of you."

"Then why did you wait so long to tell me about your little boyfriend in California?"

"You idiot. You arrogant fucking idiot." He was nearly shouting now. "Because I was embarrassed. Because I was confused. Are those not legitimate reasons for not wanting to confess something like that to you?"

Maybe. Maybe not. It didn't matter anymore. I couldn't back down. Never again could I back down from a fight with Terrence O'Connell.

"What did this guy have over me?" I asked.

He sighed and shook his head at me. "How many times am I going to keep answering the same question, Ben?"

"One more time. Answer it one more time."

"No," he said. "There's something really masochistic about this, Ben. You just want me to keep rejecting you over and over again. Why can't you just let it rest?"

"Because I can't. It's not in my nature to let stuff like this rest."

"Can you let it rest long enough so that we can bike down this mountain?" he asked, exasperated, perhaps on the verge of taking a swing at me. "Then maybe we can go home and pretend this day never happened."

He got on his bike and began peddling, intent on putting some distance between the two of us. I watched him drift away, ten yards, then twenty, then around the first turn, out of my sight line. I stood there waiting, not certain what to do next. A couple of minutes passed. The early morning clouds had disappeared and the sun now burned hotly, casting everything in a glimmering, whitish haze—the color of milk just about to spoil. I finally climbed onto my bike and started peddling, very slowly at first. I concentrated on the winding path and the moist gravel ahead of me. I took the first turn carefully, never fully loosening my grip on the hand brake. The borders of the trails were lined with trees and bushes in some places. But in other places there was nothing—just space and air, or deadened twigs and branches, and then a dangerously steep drop-off. One could easily go tipping right over the edge of the mountain.

A minute or two more passed. I started to feel more confident on the bike. I picked up my pace and began peddling faster. I rapidly gained momentum. The downhill grade of the mountain was steeper than I first realized, and much steeper than our instructor had let on. For a moment, as I took an especially sharp turn a couple of miles per hour too fast, I feared that the bike might speed out of my control and that I would go hurtling into a tree. But then I found the hand brake, and I pumped it gently. The bike slowed down, and I regained my balance. And then I started peddling again. The cool mountain air rushed against my face. It seemed to be encouraging me forward. I redoubled my efforts to catch up with Terrence.

I had decided that I needed to ask him one last question.

A few more minutes passed. I kept on peddling with increasing force and determination. But then it occurred to me that Terrence, too, would be peddling quickly. He was probably flying down this mountain. He would be trying to put as much distance between us as possible.

So I started peddling harder. And then harder. I decided I needed to peddle twice as fast as he was peddling. Whatever it would take to catch up with him.

And then—just when I had decided that I would put my safety on the line, that I would take every turn at record pace— I saw him, about twenty yards ahead, straddling his bike, his feet planted on the ground. He was stopped at the farthest edge of a very wide turn where there was a break in the trees. He was looking out onto the horizon, a limitless view of ash-colored mountains in front of him, and a tiny, miniature-scaled view of the town laid out far below.

He heard me coming and turned around. I pressed on the brake and came to a stop. I was on higher ground. The slope between us looked to be seven or eight degrees. We were separated by about ten yards.

"Is everything OK?" I asked.

"I was waiting for you," he said, his voice emotionless. "I didn't want to get too far ahead. They said that we're supposed to stay together." He started to lift his right foot onto the right peddle and adjust himself back onto his bicycle seat.

"Do you need a minute to catch your breath?" he asked me.

"Terrence, just one more question," I said. "Just answer me one more thing."

He sighed and said, "This has to stop, Ben. Enough of this."

"Was it something I did? Are there things about me that you just despise?"

"Enough." His voice was rising. In a few more seconds, he would be shouting again.

"Just answer that question," I said. "Please."

He shook his head vigorously at me and raised his voice still louder. "No. Stop this." Then he caught himself. He seemed to calm down, just a bit. He said, "I'm not going to start telling you all the things I don't like about you."

"Why not?"

"Because that's crazy. Because it would be cruel and pointless."

"But I want you to tell me. I'm asking you to tell me."

"Stop it," his voice much lower now, a little grave-sounding, like a cop talking a jumper off the ledge. "Stop this. Right now."

"Just tell me."

I thought he was going to start peddling away. I thought he was going to peddle away from me for good. But he didn't. He put his feet back on the ground. He looked at me and shook his head in dismay. And then he said to me: "You know what turns me off, Ben? *This.* This relentless, weird crap. This obsessive, faggoty behavior of yours. It's creepy. It's bizarre. You make things up. You lie. You make up some crazy story about a guy hitting on you on the airplane out here. Who knows why? But it's weird. It makes me not want to be with you."

"I didn't make that up."

"You did, Ben," he shot back at me. "I know you did. I've seen what your handwriting looks like and that note was written in the same handwriting."

"I didn't write that note, Terrence," I said. My face was flush. My heart was pounding. I hated him more than I had ever hated him before.

And yet still, even after all of this, if he would just let me, I would make love to him, I would drop to my knees and give him a blow job in a heartbeat, right here on the mountain. If only he would just say: OK.

"You're still telling lies about where you got those naked pictures that were under your bed. You expect me to be totally open and honest with you, but half of what you tell me sounds made up."

"I'm not lying, Terrence," I shouted at him.

"Whatever, Ben. Whatever you say. I just think we need to get to the bottom of the mountain, and get through the rest of the weekend, and then take a break from each other."

"So now you're breaking up with me?" I said. "You're breaking up with me without ever having had sex with me?"

He frowned at me and said: "I was never going to have sex with you."

My eyes started to be burn. I felt my stomach lurch. I could taste bile in the back of my throat. He was *never* going to have sex with me. He never would have let it happen.

Anything else I could have handled. Any other accusation I could have taken in stride.

A bit of a loose cannon? Sure, probably, fair enough.

Willing to write a note in your own hand and pass it off as a message from a secret admirer? Perhaps.

Gaywad, faggot, queer, cocksucker, a man who will die a protracted and ugly death from AIDS? All of those labels I could accept and wear proudly.

But this confession was too much to bear. This could not be brushed off.

I was never going to have sex with you.

I saw what had to be done, and I did not hesitate. Revenge fifteen years hence is a long time coming, but it is still revenge, and it is still sweet.

I started peddling toward him. I aimed the front wheel of my bike at the center of his bike's chassis. I knew that if I let the momentum carry me downhill, and if I got my bike to strike his at just the precise spot, I would send him hurtling backwards, right off the trail, right over the edge of the mountain. I would send him tumbling to his deserved death.

I didn't peddle very hard. I had to make certain my bike didn't gain *too* much momentum—I didn't want to send myself over the mountain along with him. I visualized it in my head. I saw my front wheel smashing into his bike. I saw his bike and his body lifting off the ground, falling backward. I would tell the authorities that it had been a terrible accident. I would tell them that Terrence had been unable to deal with his homosexuality; that he had tried for so long to suppress it, but he couldn't stop himself from acting on his worst impulses, and he hated himself so much because of it. And so he rode his bike over the edge of the mountain in despair.

"What are you doing?" he said, as he saw me coming toward him. But then he understood. He realized that I had every intention of crashing into him.

He scrambled to get his feet back on the pedals. But he slipped. The kiosk manager had been right: the gravel was moist and crumbly. Terrence's right foot never got off the ground. Instead, it started to slide away from his body, and away from the bike. For a moment, it looked as if Terrence and the bike were going to topple over and fall to the ground in one big, tangled mass; for that same moment, I worried that I was going to end up peddling right over his body and over the edge of the trail myself.

But Terrence managed to steady himself. His foot found earth. He steadied the bike. He got his butt up on the seat and his feet onto the pedals.

Such is the doomed fate of the overachieving perfectionist: He doesn't realize that sometimes you need to underperform; he fails to grasp that sometimes screwing up is precisely the thing that saves your life.

He looked up at me to see how much more time he had left before I hurtled into him. But by then it was too late. My front wheel was smashing into his left leg. His body started to fall.

I heard a cracking sound. Then Terrence let out a scream.

I had done it. I had vanquished him. I had killed him. I had sent him sailing over . . .

Or maybe not. After connecting with his leg, my front wheel became entangled with the spokes of his back wheel. We both crashed to the ground, him on top of his bike, me on top of him, my bike on top of me.

"What the fuck are you doing?" Terrence screamed. "Get the fuck off me."

I managed to throw my bike off me and quickly scramble to my feet. What *was* I doing? What the hell had just come over me?

"Did it break?" I asked him. "Is your leg broken?"

"I don't know." There was a gash just above his knee that was bleeding. There were scrapes up and down his legs and arms.

"Oh, God, I'm sorry," I said. "That was dumb."

"You're going to have to help me up," he said. "I have to see if I can walk on it."

I moved both of the bicycles out of the way, steering them about five yards away and resting them against a tree. Then I walked back to Terrence. I lowered myself down next to him and placed my arm around his back and my hand beneath his right arm. I lifted him upright. He clung so tightly to me that I could tell right away that he wasn't going to be able to put any pressure on his left leg; that almost certainly it had been broken in the fall.

"Why the fuck would you do that?" he asked.

"I'm sorry, Terrence," I said. "I don't know what I was thinking."

He gently pushed me away and said, "Let me see if I can stand up on my own." He stood on one leg, and placed his arms at his sides to balance himself. There was a look of intense concentration and anxiety on his face—for a few seconds, he looked like a little boy embroiled in an especially competitive round of Simon Says. But when he tried to bring his left foot down to the ground, he cried out in pain and started to lose his balance. I had to grab hold of his torso in order to stop him from collapsing.

"You're going to have to find one of those emergency phones and call down," he said.

"OK," I said.

But then I just stood there, holding onto him, considering his broken form. A line of sweat ran down the center of his T-shirt. His hair was drenched and pasted to his head. His hands were covered with gravel. His faced was scrunched up in agony—so much agony that I wondered if he might be on the verge of tears. But even here—dirty and hobbled and burning under the springtime Colorado sun—he looked gorgeous. He looked rough and tumbled and rugged and manly. Despite it all, my crush on him would never go away. I would always see him as someone too beautiful for me; someone whose beauty would always paralyze me and prevent me from fighting back. He would never meet me halfway, either. My desire would never be requited. I would forever be stuck between the rock of my love for him and the hard place of his bullying, unyielding, unchanging ways.

The idea came upon me in an instant.

I thought of Terrence standing outside of my house, holding a pair of scissors in his hands, ringing my doorbell, over and over again, but no one coming to the door to answer, his window of awful opportunity slowly closing shut.

But my window was still open, open just a sliver, just enough for me to slide through, just barely. Just enough to cause some trouble.

"Ben, come on, please go call for help," he said, whimpering and exhausted. "My leg really hurts."

I stood there for a few more seconds, lamenting. I lamented our first kiss; the whirlwind romance; the epic conversations; the sumptuous meals; the exotic vacations; the great sex; the shared experiences; the life together; all the people who would have said, "Ben has really landed himself quite the catch. How did Ben ever find himself such a wonderful boy?"

I lamented all of it that never was.

And then with both hands to his chest, I shoved him as hard as I could, right into the air, and straight over the side of the mountain.

chapter fourteen

Even-Steven
(2000)

The moment I saw Terrence's body fall away from me, I did not feel regret and I did not feel guilt. I felt the opposite, the calming sense of having done something cruel but nonetheless essential to your own survival, like laying out poison for the rats that have infested your basement. I felt, too, a sense of accomplishment—the distinct satisfaction that comes with knowing you will get away with something awful. I guess I felt the way you do after any petty triumph.

Had I succeeded in killing him, I probably would have felt much differently. I would have felt regret and guilt and shame; I probably would have collapsed to my knees right there and started weeping for all the mistakes I had committed unto him. But I knew right away that I did not kill him. I heard his body land on the ground. Then I heard him bellowing and moaning, and the sounds were too strong to be coming from a nearly dead person. I scooched up to the edge of the trail, and I peered over the side. Terrence had tumbled down the mountainside and landed on small clearing, about twenty feet wide, cluttered with bushes and broken tree branches. He hadn't fallen very far, no more than fifteen feet, maybe the length of a stairwell. He probably had never even been airborne—his fall would have been more of a slide.

It took a total of sixteen people to rescue him. Two men had to be dropped down onto the clearing, and they had to stabilize him onto a stretcher. The first stretcher they used turned out to be broken—it wouldn't expand long enough for Terrence to fit on it—so another stretcher had to be located, and then Terrence had to be stabilized once again, and then *that* stretcher had to be hoisted up onto firm ground, using two sets of ropes and eight men pulling on those ropes. Then Terrence had to be carried down the mountain to a spot where a helicopter could safely land, and then the stretcher had to be loaded onto a helicopter. The entire mission took nearly two hours.

It turned out to be worse than I expected. His leg was broken in two different places. One of his ribs was cracked. His head had landed against a rock, and while the bleeding wasn't heavy the EMTs couldn't manage to keep him awake. They tried to keep him talking, by peppering him with questions about his job and his family and his friends. During their most successful stretch, they got Terrence talking for fifteen minutes about the girlfriend with whom he had just broken up and how guilt stricken he felt about leaving her. But during the short helicopter ride to the hospital, with the EMTs running out of questions for him, Terrence closed his eyes and this time couldn't be wakened. He had slipped into a coma.

For three hours, I sat in the waiting area of the hospital, flipping through magazines, including a two-year-old *Rolling Stone* featuring a profile of James Van Der Beek that Terrence had written. Shortly after 6:00 P.M., the emergency room doctor—a tall, slim man in his early thirties with a Clark Gable mustache and prematurely graying hair—finally came through a set of swinging doors. He started talking in a rush, shooting me questions and then not waiting for my answers: "Are there parents or a significant other we need to call? He lives in New York City, right? Do you live with him? How did he fall?"

"His parents live in Indiana," I told him. "There's no significant other."

"How did it happen?"

What started it?

"I'm not . . ." I got out, before my voice trailed off. How could I even begin to answer that question?

"Did you push him?" the doctor asked.

"No . . . of course not . . . he fell . . . he slipped . . ."

"He'll be OK, but he's going to need to sleep it off. That may take a day or two. Do you want to call his parents?"

"I don't know them very well," I said.

He looked at me skeptically. For a long moment, I feared that he had seen right through me; that he was about to say, *I know you're lying, and I'm going to tell the police.* But instead he said, "Well, maybe you can help the nurse figure out if his parents' number is listed. She can call them." And then he wandered back through the swinging doors out of which he had emerged, and I never saw him again.

A detective named Jerry Stableford—a beer-bellied, aging frat boy with bloodshot eyes and a scraggly mustache—showed up about forty-five minutes later. He took me to the hospital cafeteria and watched me eat a broiled hamburger, slathered with liquidy, orange cheese. I recounted to him the story I had been practicing all afternoon: Terrence had taken a turn too fast on his bike and crashed to the ground, breaking his leg in the fall. While I was trying to help him off the ground, he accidentally slipped out of my grasp and fell backward, over the edge of the trail. The gravel was still moist from all the recently melted snow. He had simply lost his footing.

Stableford wrote down every word I said, not seeming at all suspicious. After he finished questioning me, he told me I needed to stay in town until Terrence woke up from his coma. Stableford apologized, but he said he would need to interview Terrence before he could formally put his investigation to bed. He made air quotes around the word "investigation," making me think he wasn't taking the possibility of foul play very seriously.

For the next two and a half days, I holed up in the house. I slept and watched television and waited for Stableford to call. I replayed the events of the day in my head, wondering if I should have done anything differently. Over and over, I came to the same conclusion, that I had done the very best I could. Terrence had dealt me a lousy hand, but I had held my own against him. We had played to a draw.

And he was my bully no longer.

The phone finally rang early Tuesday morning, just as I was stepping out of the shower. "He woke up yesterday," Stableford told me. "He corroborated what you said happened, of course. I'm sorry that we had to keep you trapped here—it's procedure. I hope you didn't have to get back to work in New York."

I felt no relief as Stableford told me this, only the satisfaction of expectations realized. I knew Terrence would not press charges. I knew, too, his version of the story would not waver much from mine. If nothing else, he wouldn't have wanted to deal with the embarrassment of having to explain what we were doing together in the first place, and why we were having a loud and bickering argument on the mountain.

"Is he going to be OK?" I asked.

"He's got a few broken bones, but he'll be fine," Stableford said cheerfully. "I'll tell you something, though. He probably has a good lawsuit on his hands. There were two accidents on that same trail in the last two weeks. It's like a water slide up there, the gravel is so wet. They should never be renting bikes to people this time of year."

"Are the doctors allowing visitors?"

"Yes, but . . ." He hesitated for a few moments, as if he were embarrassed to tell me something. But then he blurted it all out at once. "Well, his parents are here, and the mother doesn't seem very fond of you. She's convinced you tried to kill him." Stableford chuckled at this last bit of information.

"They don't like me," I told him. "They've never really liked me for some reason."

"The mother won't give up on it," Stableford said. "She just keeps telling me that I need to interrogate you again. That was the word she kept using. 'Interrogate.' She thinks she's in a detective movie." Stableford's chuckle turned into a full-blown bellow. He was relishing all of this overheated family melo-drama. It was a nice break from his routine of drunk driving ar-rests and raccoons trapped in attics.

"They don't like people like me, they don't like my relation-ship with Terrence," I said, deciding to play things up for his benefit, letting him think that Terrence was my boyfriend and that his parents were trying to drive a wedge between us. I fig-ured he deserved at least that much entertainment, consider-ing he had just exonerated me on all charges.

"Well, you're certainly allowed to see him. Just be ready to deal with mom."

I packed up my stuff and loaded it into the rental car. I made a few phone calls and sketched out a plan. I would drive to the hospital and try to visit with Terrence. The airport shuttle would then pick me up at the hospital at 2:30 P.M., which would place me at the Denver airport by 5:30 P.M., which was enough time to go standby on the last flight back to New York. I didn't know if Terrence would agree to see me, but I couldn't not try to end this properly.

I pulled into the hospital parking lot at 1:45 P.M. I stopped in the hotel gift shop. I wasn't sure what the appropriate get-well gift was for a person you've just attempted to murder, so I settled on a couple of impersonal items, chocolates and a pa-perback detective novel. I bought a postcard, too, from a tall metal rack that stood next to the cash register, a picture of the Vail mountains covered in powdery snow. Back in the main lobby, I asked a receptionist if I could borrow a pen. I ad-dressed the postcard to my brother.

Dear Danny, It's over now. I've found out about everything I needed to find out about. I'm sorry I was such a pain in the ass. Ben.

I read it over. I thought it struck the right tone. But I also thought that I owed my brother a little more. So I added this postscript: *I'm going to start putting my life back in order.*

I stepped into the elevator and pushed the button for the

fourth floor. When I stepped off, Marta O'Connell was no more than fifteen feet away, standing in front of the nurse's station, talking to a male orderly. The moment I started walking in that direction, she turned and saw me. Whatever color was left in her already exhausted face instantly drained away.

I watched as she whispered something to the orderly and then disappeared around a corner. The orderly remained in place, his arms folded across his chest. I walked up to him and told him that I wanted to see Terrence.

"Mr. O'Connell's mother has asked that you leave the building."

"Has anyone asked Mr. O'Connell his opinion on the subject?"

"Do I need to call security?" he said, glaring hard at me, not moving an inch.

"Go ahead," I said.

I never thought he would actually do it. But without missing a beat, he spun around on his heels, leaned over the station countertop, picked up the receiver, and then calmly told whoever answered that there was a problem on the fourth floor and that "a troublemaker" was going to have to be escorted out of the building.

I was incredulous. Weren't these sorts of things supposed to play out a little longer? Wasn't there supposed to be some yelling and shouting? I weighed my options. I could make a run for it and try to get to Terrence's room before the orderly, or the security guards, or Marta (who was probably the toughest of them all) could stop me; and once there I could plead my case directly to Terrence, to cast off the goons and let me speak with him one last time. Or I could turn around, get back on the elevator, and go wait in the parking lot for my shuttle— and just let it all be over and done with.

I bartered with myself: Yes, I had just pledged on a postcard to my brother to put my life back in order; and, yes, I had every intention of keeping that promise. But did that necessarily mean starting *just this second*? Couldn't I risk getting myself thrown into jail one last time? (After all, I hadn't yet *mailed* the postcard.)

I decided to make a run for it.

I shifted my weight backwards, readying myself to leap into a sprint. But just then I saw Thomas O'Connell, rounding the same corner around which Marta had disappeared less than a minute earlier.

"Ben," he called out to me. "How have you been?" He drew closer and reached out his hand for me to shake.

"I've already called security, sir," the orderly broke in. "They're on their way up."

And just as he said it, the elevator doors opened, and out stepped two beefy linebacker types, barely out of their teens, dressed in black security uniforms.

"No security, no, no, no, no, we don't need security here," Mr. O'Connell said, in his booming captain-of-industry voice. "My wife was overreacting. As usual."

The security men stopped in their tracks. The orderly asked him if he was certain. Mr. O'Connell ignored him. Instead, he put his hand on my shoulder and led me to the small seating area a few feet away.

"It was an accident, Mr. O'Connell," I said. "I'm so sorry for what happened."

"I know, Ben," he said. "But my wife doesn't believe you. Or me. Or Terrence, for that matter. She's got this cockamamie idea in her head that you set out to kill him. She's been suspicious of you ever since you showed up at our house that night."

"I didn't—"

"I know. You don't have to convince me. But when my wife decides she's right about something, there's no changing her mind."

"She was so kind to me that night," I said. "I thought *you* were the one who was suspicious of me."

Mr. O'Connell smiled broadly at me and slowly nodded his approval, as if he was a math teacher and I was his student who had just worked out a proof that had long seemed unsolvable.

He said, "I apologize if I seemed distant with you that night. I was a little distracted. We had just gotten off the phone with Terrence."

"Had something bad happened?"

"He had called to tell us that he was thinking of breaking up with his girlfriend Lisa," he continued, settling back into his chair. "Did you ever get the chance to meet her? A really lovely girl. I liked her quite a bit. Anyway, I think she's the fifth girl he's dated since Yale. Maybe the sixth, I've lost track. All lovely girls. But Terrence decided to break up with her. The instant a girl decides she wants to get more serious with him, that's when he breaks it off."

He stopped suddenly and began shifting anxiously in his seat, looking all around the waiting area. The silence between us carried on for so long that I stared to worry he was just going to get up and leave me sitting there.

"I still don't think that I understand," I ventured finally.

"Ben, please don't take this the wrong way," he said. "But, well, my wife decided, pretty much from the instant she laid eyes on you, that you were gay. And, to be perfectly honest with you, we've had our suspicions about Terrence for a while now. You can only break up with so many girlfriends before your parents start to wonder." He stopped and let out a nervous burst of laughter. "Anyway, Marta met you and liked you, and I think she got it in her head that maybe she could orchestrate some kind of love connection between you and Terrence. It's batty, I know. That's my wife. She can be very impulsive like that, especially after she's had a couple of glasses of wine. But she just wants Terrence to be happy. We both do." He paused and then added: "Of course, the second you left the house, she decided she had made a horrible mistake. She somehow became convinced that you were going to kill him."

I didn't know what to say in response. Had my fervor for Terrence been so obvious that his mother had sensed it the moment she met me? Had I done or said something that made her realize, after the buzz of the wine wore off and she replayed the meeting in her head, that as much as I wanted to make Terrence fall in love with me, a part of me also wanted to see him destroyed?

I looked at Mr. O'Connell blankly, fearful that I was blushing, afraid that my face was suddenly giving everything away.

"Ben, please don't tell Terrence I told you this," he went on. "I think I understand what's going on with you guys. And I'm pleased. I truly am. But I don't want to rush him. He can tell us whatever he needs to tell us in his own time."

I smiled and nodded in agreement, secretly amused that even Terrence's father thought we might have made a good couple. Part of me wanted to tell him the truth. He had been so forthcoming with me, and so sincere and gentle in his manner, that it made me want to confess to him in return. But I also knew that it was probably best to let all of this rest. This was Terrence's secret to share with them, not mine.

"I'd like to see him," I said instead. "If that's OK. I only have thirty minutes, then I'm headed back home."

"He wants to see you," Mr. O'Connell said. "But first let me get rid of Marta." He patted me on the shoulder as he lifted himself up from his seat.

He paused and stood in front of me for a few more seconds. Just when I thought he was about to walk away, he started up again.

"I think you've been a good friend for him, Ben," he said. "He's always been so singular in his motivations, to the point where he locks out everyone else. But since you've known him—since he's started mentioning you to me when we talk on the phone—he's seemed so much more at ease. So much less self-possessed. I think you've gotten him out of his own head."

The room was painted in nursery school colors, shades of Ernie and Bert orange and yellow. It was large enough for three patients, but Terrence was the only one there. His third of the suite was already overrun with clutter: floral arrangements lining the window sill; a stack of magazines on the night table next to him; a cluster of get-well balloons that had lost their weights and risen up to the ceiling. He smiled when he saw me standing at the door. He nodded to gesture me in.

"My dad says you're headed back to New York."

"The shuttle bus is picking me up in twenty minutes," I told him. "I left the rental car in the parking lot."

A thick, dense-looking white cast extended from just above his left ankle to the top of his thigh, and his right arm was in a sling, resting against his chest. But otherwise he looked surprisingly healthy. He was propped up by pillows. He didn't seem to be in any pain. For as many bruises and broken bones as he had sustained, his face remained unscratched and unblemished. *More than a few of the nurses here,* I thought to myself, *would be willing to sleep with him in a heartbeat.*

"You got me out of having to interview Billy Crudup," he said. "I was starting to dread it. Everyone kept telling me he's an asshole."

"I'm sorry," I said. "For whatever that's worth. It was so stupid of me."

"After going through many experiences in their lives, oftentimes students have regrets of past actions," he said.

"I don't think I know that one."

"It's something I came across recently, when I was doing research for a story."

"I don't really regret what I did," I told him. "That's the thing. I don't know if that mitigates my apology—I don't know if you can apologize for something you don't regret doing. But I can't pretend to be regretful. It's more like—"

"You had no other choice," he said.

I waited a few seconds, and then I said, "I think that's a good way of putting it."

He nodded at me, just as his father had done a few minutes earlier, as if I was the pupil finally grasping his most complex lesson. He said, "That day in high school, me pushing you, nearly killing you, I never felt any regret, either. I always felt like I *should* have felt regret. But I didn't. I eventually decided that, when you're smart and self-confident, regret can't really be in your repertoire. You have to believe in yourself even if you're dead wrong."

"Thank you for not turning me in, Terrence," I said. "You could have. Very easily."

"No. That wouldn't have been fair play."

"So now we're even-steven?"

"Now we're even-steven," he said, slowly repeating the words back to me, nodding and grinning.

I walked over to the window and placed my presents on the sill, in between two bouquets of flowers. I wasn't sure what else to tell Terrence. I had expected him to be angrier with me. I thought we might have to hash a few things out.

"How long will it take before you're healed?" I asked him finally, after two or three minutes passed in silence.

"The cast needs to stay on for eight weeks," he said. "And then probably six months or so of physical therapy. For the first part, I'm going to go back to Indianapolis. My mom can tend to me, and I can work on my screenplay and collect disability checks from *GQ*."

"I'm so sorry, Terrence."

"Stop. None of that. No regrets. No apologies. That's all settled now."

"OK."

"Just understand that we can't be friends anymore. We both need to move on."

"I understand," I answered. "Even-steven."

He was surprised, I think, that I wasn't putting up more of a defense—he, too, had been expecting this to play out a little longer. "I'm glad we reconnected," he said. "In spite of everything, I really am glad. It was good to be your friend. But sometimes people burn through each other really quickly. I think that's what happened with us."

"You're breaking up with me," I said, smiling at him. "I think I'm breaking up with you, too."

I stood at the window a little while longer, before I decided I had run out of things to say.

"I should go now, Terrence. I'm glad we cleared all of this up."

"One other thing, Ben," he said.

I don't know why, but I thought he was going to tell me that he loved me; that, even if we couldn't be together, he wanted me to know that he loved me.

"Yes," I said, sounding way too hopeful.

"I lied to you, about that guy in Los Angeles. There was no guy. Or there was a guy, but nothing happened. I saw him leaving the gym as I was on my way in. Everything else I made up. Everything else was my fantasy." He shook his head and let out an embarrassed giggle.

"I feel like a fool," I said. "For reacting the way I did."

"I did it to get a rise out of you," Terrence answered.

"I fell right into your trap."

"Did you make up that note? From the guy on the airplane?"

I didn't hesitate in answering him. No more hesitating with Terrence. No more stories. "Yes," I told him.

"I wasn't sure. I was jealous when you read it to me."

"I wrote it because I wanted to make you jealous."

"It worked."

"I was going a little crazy," I said. "I was telling people that my sister was still alive, but dying of AIDS. I was convinced that *I* had AIDS." *You go a little batty,* I wanted to tell him, *when you fall in love with someone who will not have you.*

"Even-steven," he said. "We both wanted to make the other person jealous."

"Even-steven," I repeated to him. And I think that, for the most part, I meant it.

I looked at my watch. It was 2:25 P.M. I had only a few minutes left. Just enough time to clear up one last item between us.

I said to him: "I found those pictures in the middle of a stack of magazines in my father's night table. I would sneak them into my room and jack off to them and then sneak them back.

But, at some point, I just took ownership of them. They weren't mine. They were my father's. I didn't make that up."

He nodded and said, "I believe you."

"I don't know why my father had them," I said. "I don't know what it means that he had them. I never will."

"Even-steven, Ben," Terrence said. "That means it doesn't matter whose pictures they were. Or how they ended up under your bed. Or why I looked under your bed and pulled them out of that box."

I heard a noise behind me. I turned around. Mr. O'Connell was standing in the doorway. He apologized for interrupting, but said the airport shuttle was in the parking lot waiting for me.

"Dad, can you do us a favor," Terrence said. "Can you go and stall them for a bit? Ben, are your bags in the rental car? Dad, take Ben's bags and load them into the shuttle."

I handed Mr. O'Connell the keys to the car. He nodded and quickly disappeared.

"This is terrific," Terrence said. "They do everything I ask. Had I only known, I would have slipped into a coma years ago."

I laughed at this, and then I told him, "I hope you get well soon."

"What will you do next?" he asked.

"I'll go back home. I'll see if there are one or two bridges I haven't burned. Maybe there's some substitute teaching work I can get. Beyond that, I don't know. I've been thinking it might be time that I moved away from New York. Maybe I'll give Los Angeles a try."

"I hear the guys who cruise the hotel gyms there are really hot," he said, smiling at me.

"I've heard that, too," I said.

He nodded at me. He was dismissing me now.

"Do you believe in God, Terrence?" I asked.

"Your shuttle is waiting, Ben," he said. "You don't want to miss your plane."

"My last question to badger you with. Just answer me that last one."

"Sometimes I do, sometimes I don't," he said.

I answered, "When you stood outside my door with the scissors and rang the bell, nothing happened. The decision was made for you. When I pushed you the other day, well, obviously *something* happened there. But you didn't end up dead. You'll eventually be good as new. So it's like the decision was made for me, too. There were no grave consequences for either one of us."

"Is that God?" he asked. "Is that what you're suggesting?" He paused for a few seconds and then added: "I don't know. What makes it so that God was watching over the two of us, and not watching over those two Columbine boys, preventing *them* from killing people?"

"I don't know," I said. "But if it's just a matter of choice—if you *choose* to do evil—then what makes the consequences of some people's bad actions so much worse than the consequences of others'?"

He laughed. "Ben, are you asking me why aren't I dead?"

I laughed, too. "I guess that is what I'm asking." And then I thought to myself: *How easy it is for us to talk; how readily we get one another; how quickly we fall into the habit of age-old, lifelong friends.*

"I don't know," he said. "Maybe you didn't push me hard enough."

"And maybe you should have just looked in the mailbox when you came to my house that day," I said. "We kept a spare key there."

He didn't answer. He closed his eyes. We were finished. My shuttle bus was waiting."Good-bye, Terrence," I said. "For good, I guess."

I started to back out of the room. I paused and looked at him one last time. His leg in a cast. His arm in a sling. His ribs all taped up. His body immobile, incapable of resistance. I wondered what he would do if I simply took off my shoes and crawled in bed alongside him, and snuggled up close to him, and breathed into his ear, and kissed him all over his face, and held him tightly. I wondered if he might finally acquiesce.

But no. No more wondering.

When I got to the parking lot, I found that Mr. O'Connell had already transferred my bags and paid for my shuttle. When I protested, he waved me off and said: "Nonsense, it's not your fault that Terrence can't drive you back to the airport." He shook my hand vigorously and told me to keep in touch.

At the airport, I checked myself in and found a post office, where I bought a stamp and mailed the postcard to Danny. Then I found a restaurant and ordered a hamburger. Later, when the waitress brought me my check, she asked me if I had been visiting Denver.

"I was up in Vail, actually," I said. "I was on vacation with an old friend. I pushed him over the side of a mountain and he slipped into a coma. But he woke up and we squared everything away. There are no hard feelings."

She nodded slowly and made a funny face and then wandered off without saying another word. I left her a twenty-dollar bill for a $9 check. For being my confessor—the first and last person I would ever tell this story to—I thought she deserved at least that much.

I wandered over to the departure gate. At 6:30 P.M., they called my name. I exchanged my standby ticket for a boarding pass. The agent told me that I had another fifteen minutes before boarding.

I found a pay phone. I punched the buttons and waited through a long silence, before a voice told me that my credit card had been accepted. My mother picked up on the other end.

"I'm in Denver now," I told her. "But I'm on my way home."

"OK," she said.

"When I'm back tomorrow, I would like to come over," I

said. "I would like you to tell me the story of Mary's death. I need to understand how she died."

For a minute, my mother said nothing. The only sounds I heard were the faint murmurings of the television in the background.

Finally, very softly, so softly that it was a whisper, she said: "I would like that. I would like to do that very much."

And then she began crying. And through her tears she told me that, all this time, going on twenty years now, she had wanted to talk about it; all this time she felt as if she had never given my sister a proper eulogy.

But that she had never known how to bring it up; that she was still afraid to bring it up; that, after all this time, she still didn't know where to begin.

Commitment
(1982–2004)

At approximately 7:15 A.M., on Thursday, April 22, 1982, my sister Mary hugged my grandparents one last time and climbed into the back seat of my father's brown, four-door Ford Taurus, wearing her yellow linen-and-cotton $115 dress from Macy's that my mother had purchased for her a week earlier, because she wanted Mary to look beautiful on the day she went into the hospital. Traffic was especially heavy on this morning. The car crawled across the Verrazano Bridge, and then made its way, even more slowly, across the Brooklyn-Queens Expressway, through the Brooklyn Battery Tunnel, and then up the FDR drive. My mother asked my father if there were any side streets they could take that might get them there faster. This was what she always asked my father when the two of them were stuck in traffic, and normally this question would have sent my father into a rage. But not on this morning. On this morning, my father shook his head and whispered to her, "We'll get there as soon as I can get us there."

The headaches had started four months earlier. My sister, attempting a recipe that she had clipped out of one of the women's magazines that my mother subscribed to, stumbled back from the stove, fell into a kitchen chair and remained there, doubled over, clutching the right side of her head and dry-heaving from the pain, until my parents arrived home forty minutes later. There was some discussion of taking her to the emergency room. But then the pain relented some, and my mother gave my sister two Tylenol and told her to sleep it off. My mother assumed that it was just a fluke. She suspected, too, that my sister may have been exaggerating things a bit, so that she wouldn't have to go to school the next morning.

But the headaches returned. Every four or five days, and then every two or three days, each one more sustained and more crippling than the last. My mother made an appointment for Mary with our general practitioner. He recommended that Mary see a neurologist immediately. The neurologist ordered a CT scan. The CT scan revealed a walnut-sized tumor attached to Mary's pituitary gland, just near the base of the gland. The doctors were at a loss to explain *why* it was there: There was certainly no history of cancer in our family; and there were no reports of similar instances of tumors in the brains of young women in our community. But the doctors insisted that the news wasn't so dreadful. They had caught the tumor very early, before it had become malignant and began metastasizing throughout her brain. They were confident that it could be completely excised with surgery. They placed Mary's chances of full recovery at 85 percent, maybe even higher—though they warned that, because the tumor was attached to her pituitary gland, there was the strong likelihood that she might never be able to conceive a child.

That first morning at the hospital Mary went through a series of routine preoperative tests. That afternoon she met with the two surgeons who would be operating on her. At 5:30 P.M., a nurse brought in my sister's dinner—as it turned out, her last meal—a broiled chicken breast, steamed carrots, and applesauce. My sister took two bites and pushed the tray away. She told my parents that she wasn't feeling very hungry.

My parents left her at 8:30 P.M. They took a cab to the Stanhope Hotel. My father's boss, in addition to overlooking many missed hours while he was accompanying Mary to her many doctors' appointments, was footing the bill for the hotel, which my parents never could have afforded themselves. My sister's surgery was scheduled for 8:00 A.M. the next morning. My parents arrived back at the hospital an hour before that. They saw her one last time. They told her not to worry. They insisted to her that everything would be fine.

Mary laughed at them. She said that they were more worried than she was. She said, "I *know* I'm going to be fine."

The surgery lasted for seven hours—an hour longer than planned. The doctors, using sewing needle-sized instruments, traveled through my sister's nostrils, and then used laser beams to slowly eradicate the cancer cells in her brain. For six hours, my parents sat in the waiting room, afraid to move, afraid to talk to one another, afraid to eat. When the surgery went over schedule, they were afraid to even ask a nurse what was happening. They were afraid to speak aloud the possibility that something had gone wrong.

Shortly before 3:00 P.M., the chief surgeon found them in the waiting room. He said that the operation had been a complete success. He told them that my sister was in the recovery room. She would be awake soon, the doctor said, and my parents would be allowed to see her within the hour. My parents hugged. My father went off to the hospital cafeteria to buy them both sandwiches. My mother stayed in the waiting room and wept. For ten minutes, she quietly sobbed and thanked God for listening to her prayers. Then she found a pay phone and called my aunt, to share with her the good news. My aunt found me and Danny playing wiffle ball in the street outside our house, and she wept also, as she hugged us and told us that our sister had pulled through the operation just fine.

Except that the operation had not been a complete success. Mary had not pulled through just fine. Everything was not going to be as it had once been.

At 4:00 P.M., the chief surgeon returned to the waiting room, accompanied by Mary's other surgeon and the anesthesiologist. There had been an unforeseen complication. During the operation, my sister had suffered a very mild stroke—so mild that neither the anesthesiologist nor the attending nurses had registered anything out of the ordinary. The doctors were uncertain how severe the damage had been. They needed to run more tests and monitor her more closely. She still had not woken up from the surgery.

Three hours later, as my parents sat in opposite corners of the waiting room, helpless and terrified, my sister suffered another stroke. The doctors could not understand why this was happening. Perhaps there had been some unintended trauma to the brain during the surgery. When they finally spoke to my parents later that evening, they said that it would be some time before they would know how much damage the strokes had caused. My sister still had not woken up from the surgery.

Over the course of the next thirty-six hours, Mary suffered three more strokes, each one more severe than the previous one. At 3:00 P.M. on Sunday afternoon, the doctors told my parents that their daughter was brain dead. At 8:00 P.M. that evening, my parents—who had not left the hospital, or even slept, since Thursday night—wobbly signed their names to three sets of legal papers. Forty minutes later, my sister was removed from life support, as my parents wailed with grief at her bedside, confronting a sadness so penetrating and all-consuming that they did not even think it humanly possible. The human body, my mother thought to herself, is not equipped for such pain.

In the days that followed, they told me none of this. They told me that there had been complications after the surgery. They said that it had been an accident. When I told them I didn't understand, they shook their heads and looked away. They retreated to separate rooms and cried themselves to sleep, for many more years to come.

At the time, I was only nine years old. What parent, paralyzed and muted by grief, would choose to explain the mechanics of post-surgical complications, the cruel vagaries of modern medicine, to a nine-year-old boy? What parent wants to tell their youngest child this inexplicable truth: That the Lord giveth and, sometimes, in the very next breath, taketh right back?

But I was bright, precocious, sensitive; I thought of myself as much older—when you are the youngest child, you always think of yourself as much older, at least as old as your next oldest sibling. I could have understood. I wouldn't have needed every last detail explained to me. Only enough details for a picture. I needed to repeat my questions until they were answered. I didn't. I waited too long. I let it drop. I decided it was information not worth knowing.

To my dead sister, I apologize.

On Monday morning, April 14, 1986, my father lifted my brother into his arms and loaded his cold, limp body into the back seat of the car. My mother sat next to Danny, stroking his fine brown hair, trying to discern a pulse in his neck. My father raced through five red lights and a half-dozen stop signs. They made it to the hospital in eight minutes. It was decided that Danny's stomach would be pumped immediately. Ninety minutes later, the doctor returned to the waiting room and told my parents that Danny would pull through just fine. My father, his shirt still moist and soiled from Danny's vomit, looked to my mother. She stared back at him, frozen in place, willing herself not to cry. She told herself that this time the doctor was not lying; this time there would be no complications. My father was thinking the very same thoughts, and also this: *He will never be safe. I can never stop him from trying to do this to himself again.*

My mother told me that she had screamed when she saw Danny in his bed unconscious. I did not hear her. My mother said that I must have woken up to an empty house; that I must have wandered through the house searching for my father, who usually drove me to school each morning; that I must have had to walk to school and I probably would have been late. But that's not how I remember it. I remember waking up. I remember Danny not being there, but only because Danny was usually out of the house when I woke up, because school started for him an hour earlier than it started for me. I remember seeing my mother still asleep in her bed, just as she usually was when I woke up each morning, because her workday did not begin until 10:00 A.M. I remember my father sitting at the kitchen table, sipping black coffee, flipping through the *New York Post*. I remember him driving me to school. I remember sitting in the lunchroom and hearing Terrence O'Connell call me a gaywad for the very first time.

My brother spent four days in the hospital. He was evaluated by three different psychiatrists. He told them that he had woken up early Monday morning and felt an overwhelming sense of despair and hopelessness and that he had seen no other choice but to kill himself. The psychiatrists agreed that he could go home, but they prescribed for him antidepressants and, as a condition of his release, required that he see a therapist once a week. The psychiatrists instructed my parents to be vigilant but not suffocating. They said that kids go through phases like this all the time and that my parents shouldn't blame themselves.

My brother saw his therapist once a week, for the next sixty-seven weeks, until two weeks before his eighteenth birthday, when the therapist told my parents that Danny did not need to keep seeing her if he didn't want to. A few months after that, Danny moved out of our house and began his second exile.

I knew none of this at the time. I wouldn't have even known to ask.

A few years later, he would come back to us, as if all had been forgotten, as if nothing had ever gone wrong in the first place.

On July 10, 2000, a few days before my twenty-eighth birthday, I found in my mailbox a thin white envelope, addressed to "Jay O'Connell." The return address was "Eagle Health Associates" in Eagle, Colorado. The letter inside read: "Dear Mr. O'Connell. The results of your HIV test on May 27, 2000, were negative. Please contact us at the above telephone number if you have any further questions."

At the bottom of the letter was a handwritten note, in red ink. It read: "I told you so! Now play safe." Below that there was a smiley face and the signature "Sam."

On August 1, 2000, I received a telephone call from my erst-while colleague Meredith McBern. She said that she had been out to a gay club in Manhattan the previous weekend with two of her female friends—they liked to go to gay clubs to dance—and she swore that she saw Mario Tropiano, dancing without his shirt on, in the middle of a throng of dozens of other sweaty and well-built gay men. She claimed that this was incontrovert-ible proof that her original theory—that Elliot and Mario had been boyfriends and that Elliot was threatening to expose Mario's secret—had been accurate.

"Are you sure it was Mario?" I asked.

She said she was "mostly positive," but she admitted that she couldn't get close enough to be certain, and that it had been very dark, and maybe her fantasies were playing tricks on her. Then she cackled so loudly and for so long that I began to won-der if she was drunk.

We chatted a bit longer. She said that we should get together at some point for dinner. She didn't want to lose touch. I promised that I would give her a call. I never did.

In December 2000, I read a review of Terrence's first novel in *The New York Times Book Review.* The reviewer was not especially kind. He called the book "illogical" and "emotionally dishon-est." He said that the writing was "often flat-footed." I read the review twice, feeling neither pity for Terrence nor schaden-freude. I told myself that I still wanted to read the book and de-cide for myself. But I never did get around to buying a copy.

The following April I was once again accepted to the Ph.D. program in English literature at the University of Wisconsin-

Madison. I moved there in July of 2001. In Madison, I spent my mornings in class, my afternoons reading novels and my evenings watching movies. I made a handful of new friends. In the spring of 2002, I started dating someone, a lanky and handsome history graduate student named Chad, originally from Chicago. The relationship started off slowly, heated up to a fever pitch, and then cooled back down—a three-act romance, with each act lasting approximately six weeks. It ended by mutual decree. I decided I liked the banality of the entire process, this thing that boys and girls start doing in high school—trying one another out, liking each other but not enough, letting things run their course, and then going on the hunt for someone new. It had taken me more than a decade, but finally I had caught up.

The next year passed quickly and enjoyably. But during the spring of my second year, I grew disenchanted with academia: the abstruse papers that no one in the real world was ever going to read; the stuffy, arcane debates about subjects I didn't really care about. I realized I missed the hustle of teaching high school kids. I missed wrestling for their attention, trying to penetrate their indifference, occasionally making a connection with one or two of them. Maybe I missed, too, the secret crushes I harbored on the especially cute boys.

A conversation with a professor led to an interview at a private high school in Milwaukee. The principal there was impressed by my resume, and he offered me a position on the spot. In Milwaukee, I settled into a happy and satisfying routine: work; books; movies; occasionally a date. Once a week, I spoke to my brother and to my parents on the telephone. Many weeks would pass, and I would not think at all about Terrence.

And then, on June 20, 2004, I found in my mailbox a heavy, square-shaped envelope, with my name and address written in a calligrapher's hand. It was an invitation. I tore it open with curiosity. I was pretty certain I didn't know anyone who had been planning to marry.

"Terrence Ryan O'Connell and Barrett James Hogan request the pleasure of your company at a reception to celebrate their recent nuptials, on August 21, 2004, at 7:00 P.M., at the Plaza Hotel in New York City." Enclosed was a photocopied press clipping from the *New York Post*'s Page Six gossip column. It explained that "much-acclaimed novelist and *GQ* columnist T. R. O'Connell" had traveled with his "Boston-born life partner, investment banker Barrett Hogan" to Massachusetts, a week after that state had legalized gay marriage, and that the two of them had "gotten hitched."

I returned the RSVP card the next day. I booked a flight and a room at the Plaza. While looking for a gift online, I typed Terrence's name into Google and learned that, the year before, he had published a second novel, and that this one, while only a modest seller, had been greeted with raves.

The main banquet room of the Plaza Hotel was beautifully appointed for the reception, with everything decorated in shades of buttermilk and baby blue. The party was swarming with gay men: writers; lawyers; bankers; television and stage actors. I was surprised by how much at ease I felt there, even though I didn't know anyone. I smiled when complete strangers made eye contact. A few times these strangers came up to me and struck up conversations. They asked me which of the grooms' sides I was on. I told them that I had gone to junior high school and high school with Terrence, and that we had once been very close friends, though more recently we had fallen out of touch. They all wanted to know what he was like when he was younger. They said that, for whatever reason, he was one of those people you just couldn't quite imagine as a teenager.

"It's hard for me to notice any difference," I said. "When I look at him, I still see the same Terrence."

At 8:30 P.M., Thomas O'Connell came up from behind me and grabbed my shoulder. When I turned around, he seemed elated to see me. We talked for twenty minutes—in this sea of gay men, I was clearly his buoy. He told me that he was sorry things hadn't worked out between Terrence and me; in all honesty, he said, he liked me much better than he did Barrett. He told me that Marta had long since gotten over her suspicions of me. He said that he would tell her that I was here; that she would want to come over and apologize. She never did.

At 9:00 P.M., there were speeches—from Mr. O'Connell and Mr. Hogan and from Terrence's literary agent. At 9:30 P.M., I sat down to dinner, next to a thirty-two-year-old linguistics professor at Columbia. We traded academic war stories. He seemed envious that I had broken free and was now teaching high school. He asked me if I would meet him for brunch the next morning, before I returned home to Wisconsin. I told him I thought that would be nice.

And, finally, at 10:00 P.M., Terrence found me, while I was sipping champagne and watching people on the dance floor. He was wearing a black tuxedo, with a pale pink shirt that complemented his bright blue eyes. He looked as handsome and as effortless as ever, as if not a day had passed since our first dinner at Patria. Barrett was standing next to him, in a matching tuxedo, except that his shirt was pale orange. Barrett was darker than Terrence and a bit more broadly built. But otherwise they were two of a kind: tall; magnetic; the best-looking boys in the room.

"Thank you for coming, Ben," Terrence said to me. "I saw you before, but it took me a while to get over here. We have four hundred guests. I didn't realize I knew four hundred people, but I guess I do."

Terrence introduced me to Barrett. I congratulated him. I said that he had landed himself quite the catch. He thanked me and said that he would leave the two of us to talk.

"Does he know what happened between us?" I asked Terrence, after Barrett had wandered out of earshot.

"No one does," Terrence said.

I stood there nodding at him, not knowing what to say. He flashed me a sheepish, boy-caught-with-his-hand-in-the-cookie-jar grin. In a previous life, I would have thought that he was flirting with me.

"You weren't this gay the last time I saw you," I said, gesturing around the room.

"No, I wasn't," he said.

"It seems to suit you well."

He smiled and nodded slowly and said nothing.

There was a long pause. Finally he said to me, a little nervously: "This is weird. I didn't mean for it to be. I just wanted—"

"—to see how I was doing," I offered.

"Yeah, and . . . I guess . . . I guess I wanted to tell you that I'm sorry."

"I don't—"

"—for treating you the way I did. That weekend in Vail."

I smiled at him and shook my head. "Terrence, I nearly killed you. You're not the one who should be apologizing."

He ignored this and went on talking. "I wish I could take it all back, Ben. Everything. All the way back to the seventh grade. I just wish I could erase it all and start over."

"The last thing I want to do is go back to the seventh grade," I said, laughing a bit, trying to keep this exchange light.

Terrence looked toward me, forlorn and uncertain. He had rehearsed these words in his head many times; he had thought over and over about what he might say to me if we ever met up again. But now it wasn't going so well. For once in his storied and successful life, the words simply weren't coming to him.

How strange, after all these years, that Benjamin Reilly should be the one who made Terrence O'Connell nervous, and not the other way around.

"I'll be in Chicago the first week of October," he ventured. "Maybe I could drive up to Milwaukee. Maybe we could reconnect."

I felt a knot immediately tighten in my stomach and then a stirring in my groin. I looked away from him, afraid that if I held his gaze much longer, I would begin to blush. Eighteen years later, Terrence still had the power to send butterflies fluttering through my stomach, just by hinting that we might get together. He still had the power to give me a hard-on.

And this would always be his power over me. This was the thing I would always have to live with.

"I'm not sure that's such a good idea, Terrence," I mumbled.

"No, you're probably right," he said.

"Sometimes I think it's just better to leave things be."

"I should go," he said abruptly. "I need to say hello to more people."

"It was nice to see you again," I said. "I'm glad to know you're doing well."

He started to move away, but then he stopped. He smiled again—a crooked, rueful, faintly churlish smile that seemed to encapsulate my two decades of knowing him.

He said to me, "Do you think it could have ever worked between us, Ben? If we had somehow figured out a way to put water under the bridge, do you think we might have been boyfriends? Would that have even been possible?"

Yes. No. Maybe. Who knows?

How could I ever possibly answer such a question?

"Do *you* think we could have been boyfriends?" I asked.

"Probably not," he said. "But that doesn't stop me from thinking about it. Honestly, it's something I think about all the time."

He shrugged his shoulders adorably and stared enticingly into my eyes—one last flirty gesture from the flirtiest boy in the world. Then he walked away, this time for good, directly into the arms of another set of guests, whom he greeted with a big smile and a spirited bear hug, exclaiming that he was so glad to see them and so grateful that they could come.

I never saw or heard from Terrence O'Connell again.

acknowledgments

Tara Callahan read the earliest draft of *A Push and a Shove*, and immediately understood what worked and what didn't; ditto for Sarah Johnston, my second reader. Had I only paid more careful attention to their considerable insights, I probably would have finished much sooner. A number of others read the manuscript, in whole or part, and offered invaluable suggestions: Suzanne Leonard, Patricia Rodriguez, Robert Wilonsky, Juan Nuñez-Martínez, and Christopher McCabe. Thanks also to Jan Miller, Shields-Collins Bray, Evan Smith, Howard Karren, and Michael Ellenberg, whose aid and encouragement enabled this book to see the light of day. I couldn't have been luckier to cross paths with my agent, Eric Myers, or my editor, Joe Pittman, both of whom have made the process of getting a first novel published seem like the easiest task in the world. Finally, a special note of thanks to Julie Heaberlin. In 2000, Julie hired me to be the film critic at the *Fort Worth Star-Telegram*, despite the fact that I was grossly underqualified for the position, and she's remained my most vocal champion and most selfless mentor ever since. She patiently read draft after draft of this novel, usually grasping what I was trying to do long before I even understood it myself. *A Push and a Shove* would not exist without her.